GREEN CARNATIONS

BY

A C TURNER

GREEN CARNATIONS

"The love that dare not speak its name."

A woman's reputation is very precious, but the county set of Somerset like to gossip about the Countess of Tawford and her friend, Claude.

She's the toast of the county, but she carries a painful, burdensome secret.

Is she a woman without morals or integrity - or is this a tale of innocence and experience?

Why should the arrest of a public figure affect her - and how can a flower hold the key to unlock the door to her lonely prison?

***

A C Turner was born in North London. She studied Literature at the Universities of Hertfordshire, England and Wisconsin, USA.

I should like to dedicate this book to my son, Ellis. His constant kindness, practical support and understanding have been very important to me through many years of difficulties in my life. I doubt whether I should have been able to write this book without him.

I should also like to thank all the people who have been supportive to me with their encouragement to complete this project, and who helped to proof read and edit this book.

PROLOGUE

30TH NOVEMBER 1916
METHUEN PARK, SOMERSET

Water washes over the rim of a brass urn and splashes onto a patch of moss beneath, as elegant, bejewelled fingers turn off the verdigris-encrusted tap. Small droplets of water run down a once fashionable, but now loosely fitting oyster-coloured satin gown and onto the permanently shaded path circling the ancient building in the woods.

Some distance away, beneath a diminishing canopy, a solitary uniformed figure is limping towards the chapel. The fading rays of the autumn sun, together with a soft breeze produce a dappled effect of constantly alternating light and shade on the limping man.

She turns and walks away slowly - each precarious step measured on the damp, uneven stones covered with algae and sodden leaves.

His boots crunch as he steps on the growing carpet of crisp horse-chestnut leaves which remind him of his own slightly gnarled hands threaded with swollen veins.

She mounts the steps to the chapel with its air of well-tended neglect. Tightly laced boots echo on the cold stone floor and emphasise the lonely silence within. Although she is surrounded by generations of deceased ancestors, familiarity with this house of death renders her immune to the musty smell of decay. The late afternoon sun shines through a stained glass window depicting St Sebastian dying in a hail of arrows. Its soft, warm fingers trace a myriad of rich, yet soft, glowing tones onto the pale coloured gown, and the dust that her rustling skirt has disturbed, dances around her in the autumnal light.

He treads carefully to avoid the abundant fruit of the Horse-Chestnut trees. Their russet sheen reminds him of glowing auburn tresses.

On a table in an alcove lies a cardboard box containing two dozen flowers and a pair of silver scissors. She places the urn next to them and methodically cuts the stems and begins to arrange the blooms as she has done many times before. When she is satisfied with the finished effect, she places them in a small niche below two imposing marble plaques.

The inscription on the larger plaque reads:

SEBASTIAN PHILIP HENRY RAEMOND
NINTH EARL OF TAWFORD
BORN 16TH OCTOBER 1854
DIED 30TH NOVEMBER 1900

Dominus illuminatio mea, et salus mea, quem timebo?

Psalm 26, v. 1. Cf Book of Common Prayer 125:24

The plaque next to it reads:

CLAUDE EUGENE JACQUES TANQUEREL
LE COMTE DE LA MORCIERE
BORN 27TH JUNE 1863
DIED 1ST JULY 1916

De profundis clamavi ad te, Domini; Domini, exaudi vocem meam.

Psalm 129, v 1 Cf. Book of Common Prayer 1 34:11

On the altar, is a wooden cross, flanked by a pair of brass candlesticks. Their contents are tall and she has to stretch to light them. The sun is setting rapidly now and the chapel is full of eerie shadows and the creeping cold causes her to shiver as she draws her shawl around her shoulders.

She kneels down at the prie-dieu; her lowered head causes her long hair, still beautiful, though not so vibrant now, to tumble forward. As the shadows move in on her and the gloom descends, it creates an illusion of a Pre-Raphealite painting.

Silently, she mouths her prayers. Her tired eyes, now framed with small lines and dark circles, stray to the names on the plaques - the husband and the lover; her love for them both inexplicable and her grief unbearable. She reflects on how desperation, youthful naiveté and lack of judgement caused her to make an unwise decision that led her into this strange love triangle – and ultimately to a life of loneliness. Now she wonders how long it will be before her own plaque joins the two that are already there.

Outside, in the parkland of the estate, the shadows are lengthening and disappearing into the darkness of another long night, and all the while, the solitary figure draws ever nearer to the chapel.

Rivers of despair run down her face as a slight sound distracts her. She looks across to the flowers. She attempts to lean over and save a single bloom making its escape, but she is not quick enough and it falls towards the ground.

                It is a green carnation!

"Here is the most recent letter Ma'am," the housekeeper said with spiteful relish as she handed it to her mistress. The envelope had been steamed open. Although Miss Salathial pretended that she had not read the contents, Caroline Grenville knew that she had, but did not acknowledge this. She carefully withdrew the letter and began to read.

Warrington Grange
Watheford
Somerset

29th May 1885

My Dearest Claude,

I am in serious trouble. I have, for some time, suspected that I am with child. I am now certain of it and very frightened. When my mistress learns of this, she will surely dismiss me. Oh how easily those few foolish moments of passion has led to a situation that will affect the rest of my life. You cannot begin to know how much I value your feelings for me. Only one other has ever shown me such tenderness and love. Oh Claude, I know that we have only known each other a short time, but our intimacy and the secrets that we have shared together go beyond what many people share in a lifetime and I know that I can rely upon you to help me in this desperate situation.

Perhaps it would be wise to reveal my situation to that personage of nobility – for having a title, position and wealth, he could solve my problems, but obviously, my situation must remain secret for the present. I fear that my indiscretion would affect his opinion of me. Unintentionally, I am guilty of ruining the life of another.

If your financial situation were better, perhaps we could marry, but what would Sebastian have to say on the matter! But this is no time for jesting. Oh God, What am I going to do? Only you can save me. I await your reply in earnest.

With love and affection,
Aphra

Caroline folded the letter. She showed no emotion as she stood up and walked over to her bureau and unlocked it. She pushed the letter into one of the pigeonholes and turned the key.

"You may go now and continue with your duties," she said firmly. "Say nothing about this for the present."

As the housekeeper quietly closed the door behind her, the mask of control slipped and Caroline, with jaws and fists clenched, sat and silently fumed.

PART ONE - A WOMAN OF IMPORTANCE

25TH AUGUST 1884

It was as well that Aphra did not possess the gift of clairvoyance, for had she done so, she might not have been feeling quite so pleased with herself. Her journey to this point in her life, both literally and metaphorically, had already been strewn with numerous heartaches and difficulties - the quantity of which were in direct contrast to the small amount of years that she had lived so far. So it was as well that she was ignorant of what the future held in store for her.

However, for the present she had every reason to believe that her problems were behind her and was content to stretch out her aching limbs and luxuriate in the comfort of the vast bed in which she lay. It had been a very long time since she had known such comfort and ease. She lay there and began to take notice of her bedroom for the first time since she had arrived yesterday afternoon.

Although the sun had moved around completely now, leaving the room in shadow, she could still make out the main features of a large chamber. A comfortable looking chintz armchair was placed close to the hearth, and although the temperature rendered a fire superfluous, the grate was filled with kindling in preparation for a change in the weather. On the mantelpiece stood a brass carriage clock, two matching candlesticks and a couple of Chinese figures. The hypnotic ticking of the clock, together with the occasional crowing of rooks from the adjacent woods and the bleating of some sheep, was all that disturbed the silence of the room.

Several watercolours, and a sepia photograph of the household staff were displayed against the backdrop of a modern dark green and purple William Morris wallpaper above the wainscot, and a patterned carpet almost covered the highly polished floorboards. To the side of a heavily draped window was a jardinière with a well-tended Aspidistra in it. She noticed how spotlessly clean everything was and reflected on how hard the staff must have to work. She wondered how arduous her own duties would be.

On the small bedside table, she saw an unappealing cup of cold tea. She smiled to herself. Emily must have placed it there. She could picture her tiptoeing in and silently closing the door behind her. That must have been hours ago. She closed her eyes and pondered upon what the time could be and what the other servants would make of her prolonged absence. She was concerned that they would think of her as lazy and taking advantage by sleeping like this in the afternoon.

"This won't do my girl," she said to herself. "Rouse yourself and get up."

But for a few more minutes she was happy to concentrate her thoughts on the change in her fortunes in the last twenty-four hours. She giggled to herself. This time yesterday, she was destitute, dishevelled and desperate. Now, here she was resting in this lovely big bed. She was no longer starving. She had bathed, her wounds were beginning to heal, and she had fresh clean clothes to wear. Moreover, it would seem that she may have amiable colleagues with whom to work - especially Emily, who, she firmly believed, would prove to be a kind and thoughtful friend. She was beginning to recover from her dreadful ordeal and felt so contented that her usual optimism about life had returned. Reluctantly, she forced herself to sit up and leant against the soft pillows as she caressed the nap of the white, lace-edged linen sheets that smelled of lavender.

In the cool solitude, she resumed her perusal of the room. In an alcove, stood a small chest of drawers with a small posy of roses neatly arranged in a pretty vase. Next to this, on a small wooden chair, lay her discarded clothes and an old carpetbag containing her meagre collection of possessions.

The events leading up to her arrival yesterday had been so distressing that she had been in no state to take much interest in her surroundings. Now, somewhat recovered and rested, she could take stock and try to recollect the place to which she had come and the last village through which she had passed. She remembered Watheford as a picturesque little place where two yokels sat outside the inn sipping ale and enjoying a simple ploughman's lunch in the drowsy heat. She had asked them for directions to Warrington Grange and they had kindly informed her of a short cut through the woods. Now she recalled their surprise when she spoke. No doubt, her appearance had led them to the mistaken impression that she was a tramp. She had cupped her hand to drink as she had feebly attempted to operate the ancient water pump and had made a passable attempt at washing off some of the accumulated dust from her face and hands. As she picked up her frayed and dirty carpetbag and began the final leg of her arduous journey, one of the men offered her a piece of bread and some cheese. Gratefully, she accepted this, knowing that she would benefit from some fuel to help her reach her destination.

The walk that took her from the village to the point where she rang the bell outside the kitchen door at Warrington Grange was a trek of nearly an hour and a half. In the months to follow, Aphra would make this journey on numerous occasions and would do it in a quarter of the time. However, her physical condition was such that every step was agony. The rubbing of her badly worn and fraying boots against the now seriously blistered feet meant that the blisters had burst and her feet were bleeding heavily. She limped down a lane past a few outlying thatched cottages and then through a wooded area, which gave her some temporary respite from the searing heat of the sun. After a while, she came to a clearing which led on to the main driveway. She squinted and put her hands up to protect her eyes as the sun reflected off the profuse number of windows of the vast, three storey manor house with its numerous chimneys and imposing entrance.

The grandeur of the place neither surprised nor filled her with awe. She was beyond that. The only thing that she could focus her mind upon was whether or not she would be successful in obtaining the position of employment that she was seeking. If she did not, then she did not know what she was going to do. That generous gift from the kind farm labourer outside the inn was the first morsel of food that she had eaten for days, and the best shelter that she had found had been in an old deserted barn. Mostly, sleep had been on benches in churchyards or under hedgerows or trees. At least there had been no rain, and the nights had been mild. Now, that she was so close, she kept saying to herself that she must be offered the post. The alternative was either death or the workhouse - the former being the more likely outcome, as she had no money for the fare to reach the latter. She made her way around to the side of the house, passing the immaculately tended gardens and the terrace with its intricately laid out parterre, together with its statues and fountain. In the kitchen garden, a couple of young servants who were flirting with each other, stopped briefly to look at this dishevelled stranger making her way towards the back door, then continued with their youthful teasing banter.

***

Grace Talbot, red-faced and perspiring, wiped her floury hands on her apron and tutted to herself as she approached the open back door. It had been one of those days and she just could not seem to get things done. She had sent Maud out into the kitchen garden to pick the last of the gooseberries, some carrots and some rosemary for the lamb.

"I bet she's larking about with that lad."

"Alright, I'm coming," she shouted in a strong west-country dialect. "Do I have to do everything myself? I'll never finish rolling out that pastry," she muttered under her breath.

There was so much to do and being a rather corpulent woman, she felt quite irritable and sticky with the discomfort of the combined heat of this exceptional weather and the recently installed range. Grace tutted again as she passed the mountainous pile of dishes and pans that needed cleaning. She would box Maud's ears if she did not mend her ways!

The sight that met the cook at the back door shocked her. So her first instinct was to tell this scruffy individual leaning against the doorjamb with her grubby hand on the bell pull to clear off. However, when Aphra spoke, the older woman quickly realised that she was facing a genteel, young woman - no older than sixteen or seventeen. Grace looked at the sunburnt complexion and dull, green eyes with drooping lids, that told of days spent on the open road and nights spent sleeping rough.

"I have an appointment with Miss Grenville regarding the position of lady's maid. Please forgive my appearance, but I have had a most arduous and distressing journey," whispered Aphra.

"Well. You'd better come in then. Make it sharp now. I haven't got all day," said Grace irritably, as she stood back for the girl, who almost fell through the door with exhaustion. Aphra followed the stout, middle-aged woman as she waddled into what seemed at first to be a dark kitchen. She blinked repeatedly as she waited for her eyes to adjust to the change from the bright sunlight.

The cook's expansive girth suggested that she ate a large proportion of what she cooked. It gave her a friendly, motherly appearance, in spite of the brusqueness of her initial greeting, and the newcomer slowly warmed to her.

Aphra asked if there was somewhere that she could go to have a wash to freshen her appearance as she had a few minutes to spare. Grace opened a door to the side of the kitchen. It opened on to a small scullery. There was a butler sink and drainer with a dish containing a much-used cake of soap. The cook went and fetched a kettle of hot water from the range and poured it into a large, chipped basin. Then she reached up to a shelf and grabbed an old towel, which she handed to the girl.

"What's yer name?"

"Aphra Chamberlain."

"Aphra. That's an odd name. Never 'eard that one before! My name's Mrs Talbot, and as you can see, I'm the cook. Today, I feel like a bloody dogsbody and seem to be doing everything myself. Don't suppose you saw a girl out there?" She asked as she bustled about. The question appeared to be rhetorical, so Aphra made no attempt to answer.

"She's a dead loss at times."

Grace began to feel a bit sorry for the new arrival and for her initial unfriendliness. The girl looked half dead and close to tears.

"Anyway, everyone calls me Gracie. You can do the same. Mind you, I wouldn't give much for your chances of getting the job looking like that. So you may not be here long enough to call me anything! You look as though you haven't eaten for days. Are you hungry?"

"Yes, very - and this heat has made me very thirsty too!"

"Right, while you make yourself look a little more presentable. I'll find something for you in the pantry. Come straight through when you're ready." Saying this, she closed the door.

Aphra flopped heavily onto an old chair and laid her bag on a small table. She leant back and rested her head on the wall. She could so easily have fallen asleep, but she roused herself to make one last effort to get this position. From the bag, she took out a brush and comb, a clean, but much used blouse and a pair of over-darned stockings. She flinched as she removed the old dusty boots and quickly stripped to her underwear. She ran the cold-water tap and washed as best she could, wincing at the pain as she dabbed at the bleeding blisters on her heels and the sunburn on her face. She scrubbed her dirty, broken nails and sent up a prayer of gratitude for the gift of expensive kid gloves from her previous employer, and her own wisdom at keeping them unworn for this occasion. She then dressed, combed her hair and tied it up with a ribbon and some hairpins. Next, she put on a pair of polished shoes that had seen better days.

She undid the clasp of something concealed in her petticoat. It was her dearest possession - a small gold brooch – encrusted with tiny seed pearls. It was very valuable and Aphra knew that she could have sold it, but she would have preferred to die than part with it. It was all that was left to link her with her mother. She pinned it to her blouse. She noticed a clothes brush hanging on a hook and used this to remove as much of the dust off her skirt as she could. Above the sink, there was a mirror and she checked her appearance. She was shocked at the dark rings around the eyes and the unhealthy pallor of her complexion evident in spite of her badly peeling skin. How dishevelled she still looked - although it was an improvement on how she must have appeared a few minutes earlier.

She limped back into the kitchen. The shoes pinched her swollen feet and pressed upon the blisters. She saw that there was a tray upon which Gracie had placed a glass of milk and a slice of fruitcake.

"I trust that'll suit you. You haven't a lot of time and she's a real stickler for punctuality, that one. You'd better leave that scruffy bag down here. You don't want to take it upstairs, as it won't do much for your chances. She's a fussy one and she'll turn her nose up good and proper."

"Thank you very much," Aphra said – so faintly, that the cook hardly heard her. Never in her entire life had a meal been so welcome. As she was gulping down the last drop of milk, a young woman wearing a black dress with a white apron and cap, walked into the room.

"This is Emily Frances," said Gracie.

"Hello," said the housemaid. "It's nice to meet you. Are you here for the interview with the mistress?"

"Yes," Aphra replied.

Emily was about to say something else, when the grandfather clock in the hall struck the quarter hour and Aphra knew that the time had come for her interview. Emily walked towards the door.

"C'mon. I'll take you up. Just follow me." Emily smiled kindly at the new girl who looked terrified.

Aphra's hand trembled as she removed an envelope from her bag. The expensive brooch and elegant gloves, incongruous with the rest of her appearance, did little to instil confidence in her. With a growing sense of dread, she followed Emily upstairs to the drawing room, where her fate awaited her.

***

Caroline Grenville, sipping Earl Grey tea from a fine bone china cup, looked up at the gold Ormolu clock on the mantelpiece. She felt irritated. Interviewing staff was so tedious. She had already seen three women. Of course, none of them suited her. The first one had obviously no experience or relevant skills, and she was convinced that the references were forgeries. The second was insolent, and the third had had the audacity to ask for a salary that was completely out of the question. She had no doubt that the person expected today was bound to be just as unsuitable. All the doors and windows were open and she had heard no carriage outside, so Caroline suspected that the woman was not coming.

***

As the two young women made their way to the drawing room, they heard the impatient ringing of a bell.

"That'll be her sending for you now," Emily said in a kindly voice with a strong local accent. "I don't envy you. Your clothes aren't the smartest I've seen. If we had time, I'd find you something of mine."

Aphra thanked her for her consideration, but a cursory glance at Emily's shorter and plumper figure, informed her that they would never be able to share their clothes. It crossed Aphra's mind briefly that she would have liked to have had a sister with whom she could share things. However, her attention at this moment needed to be on the interview that was about to take place.

Emily knocked at the drawing room door and at the same time, whispered "good luck."

At her mistress's beckoning, she opened the door.

"Miss Chamberlain, Ma'am."

As Emily stepped aside to enable Aphra to enter the room, the latter made a swift appraisal of the woman seated in the armchair before her. Caroline Grenville appeared to be about four or five years Aphra's senior and was certainly no more than three and twenty years.

Her flawless, porcelain complexion was in stark contrast to the face that had peered back at the younger woman from the mirror a few minutes earlier. Two, bright but icy grey eyes with heavy dark lashes looked her up and down. They sparkled with life and energy and yet were completely devoid of any warmth. Aphra knew that the opinion that was being formed of her was not good. Her mind immediately darted to the idea of where she was going to sleep tonight, where her next meal would be, and the dreadful prospect of hobbling away from this house with the chafing blisters bleeding even more.

"Please, come in Miss Chamberlain." The voice was beautifully modulated, but again, there was no warmth in it. The mistress of the house gestured to her to take a seat opposite.

The shine of Caroline Grenville's ebony curls competed with the purple satin of the fashionable gown with the tight bodice that fitted her slim and shapely figure. The perfectly manicured nails of her right hand tapped impatiently on the small mahogany table next to her.

"May I see your references?" She held out her hand and took the documents, as Aphra, trying to appear confident, sat down on a small wing chair that had been strategically placed so that the sun shone directly into her eyes. This put her at a disadvantage as she was constantly putting her hand up to her eyes and squinting.

While Caroline read the reference from a Mrs Brookes, together with a report card from her school, Aphra turned her gaze to the parts of the room in shadow. It was more comfortable on her eyes.

The room was spacious and airy. The focal point was a grand, marble fireplace and mantel, which supported the clock. Above the cluttered mantel, was a large ornate, gilt mirror that was nearly as tall and wide as the chimney-breast.

Aphra could tolerate the sun in her eyes no longer and slightly adjusted the angle of her chair. The other woman noticed this, but did not acknowledge it.

"These are excellent references, Miss Chamberlain," said Caroline beginning to read the school report card.

"Thank you Ma'am."

The discomfort of the blinding light removed, Aphra continued to take stock of her surroundings. A walnut pianoforte, complete with candelabra, stood on a large Persian rug. There was a variety of items of furniture, including a chaise longue, two sofas, a number of small tables and cabinets. Every surface was covered with an excess of costly bric-a-brac. A number of oil paintings depicting rural scenes, together with some watercolours, adorned the walls.

A huge portrait of a pompous and self-righteous looking man, garbed and ready to ride with the hounds dominated one side the room. Aphra recognised a family resemblance and guessed correctly that this was Caroline's deceased father, Sir Clifford Grenville, who had made his fortune in industry. On the table next to where Caroline sat, was a small, badly-worked, piece of embroidery and a large pile of correspondence.

"Your previous employer speaks well of you. She says that you are very reliable and mature beyond your years and that the standard of your work is very high indeed."

The lady of the house stood up and walked towards the open French windows. Aphra could see the flower filled terrace beyond, which overlooked the parterre. Caroline could never resist the opportunity to show off her exquisite figure. "I'm curious as to why someone with such first rate references, should arrive at an interview attired in such a fashion. Perhaps you can enlighten me."

"Please accept my sincere apologies. I realise that this must appear very insulting to you, but I have been most unfortunate in my experiences of late."

"Yes, yes! Get on with it!" Caroline snapped. "I haven't got all day."

"I'm sorry Ma'am," stammered Aphra nervously.

"Mrs Brookes, the lady who wrote the reference for me, died some time ago. She was very ill and knew that she was going to die and so gave this to me for when I would become unemployed. She left me a small legacy and a few possessions. When I moved out of her home after her family had settled her affairs, I foolishly assumed that I would obtain another position immediately."

Aphra continued relating a tale of disasters that had befallen her until her arrival at Warrington Grange.

"I have been travelling for many days. I used the last of my money trying to get to Westbridge on the coach. It only took me as far as the other side of the town. I have walked for six days without food or shelter."

The advantages to Caroline of Aphra's youthful naiveté and the desperate situation that she now found herself in were not wasted on her. She quickly realised that such an intelligent, well-educated person who possessed such fierce determination would be an asset. As she was young and inexperienced, she could be moulded to suit Caroline perfectly. Furthermore, she could exploit her present circumstances and inexperience to obtain her services at the lowest possible rate of pay.

"It is commendable that you have striven so hard to obtain this position. I'm impressed. Tell me something of your childhood and your education."

"My father established and owned a small number of emporia in Wiltshire. My mother, the only child of a clergyman, taught me at home until I was twelve, when she died. I was sent to school in Bath. As my school report shows, I did well at most subjects. I can sew and write well and think that these skills would be useful if you decided to employ me."

"Your report card from your school shows that you were an extremely good pupil and did exceptionally well at most subjects. Why did you leave at so young an age? Surely, you had another two or three years left to complete your education?"

"Yes, I had hoped to remain at school until I was eighteen. However, my father died nearly two years ago and left no money to pay for my school fees and I was forced to leave before my education was completed. I had considered trying for a position as a Governess. However, I felt that having no experience of teaching or children, I would not be suitable for such a position. Please do not think me too young and inexperienced to be of service to you. Once I am recovered from my journey, I will prove to you that I am a very hard worker. You would not regret the decision to employ me." She realised that she was sounding desperate, but her pride was almost non-existent.

Caroline stood for another minute or so by the window and then returned to her seat. She did not speak straight away, but weighed her words carefully. This young woman was going to be ideal.

"I'll be quite honest with you. You have not presented yourself in the best possible light. However, I admire your determination and endurance. You speak very nicely, and in spite of your youth and inexperience, your references suggest that you will suit me very well. I will give you a month's trial. However, I expect to see a significant improvement in your appearance within the week. You can spend tomorrow recovering from your journey. You will commence your duties the following day, so you will need to be fit for work. I insist that members of my staff are energetic and presentable. You may use the bathroom that I have had installed for the use of servants. I insist on a high standard of cleanliness. Ask Emily about clothes. I think that your predecessor left a few items."

She rang the bell again.

"If I'm satisfied with your progress, then I'll arrange for a new wardrobe for you at the end of the probationary period of one month. You'll be paid an income of eighteen pounds per annum and will be provided with your keep. At the end of six months, if your work is satisfactory, then I will review your salary. You will work six or seven days a week and will be available as and when I need you. You will get an afternoon off once a month. I will keep these references for the time being. Do you have any questions?"

Aphra said that the terms were satisfactory and expressed her gratitude to Miss Grenville for allowing her a day to recuperate. Emily returned and was told to show Aphra to her room.

After the two girls had left the room, Caroline sat and considered her new member of staff. She thought that she had found herself a bargain. She was young, bright and cheap and not too attractive either. Although she had good bone structure and was tall and slim, though somewhat stooped in her deportment, her complexion was rough, flaky and sunburnt and her hair was dull and tangled. She was a bit concerned that perhaps she was not too healthy and would not be able to work hard. She had noticed that her eyes lacked brilliance and there were dark circles under them.

However, what struck her more than anything else was the tasteful and expensive brooch that the girl was wearing. If it had been stolen, then she would have sold it by now to pay for food and lodging. She rightly surmised that it must have had sentimental value. The girl had depth and strength of character. This realisation filled her with a mixture of admiration for a trait that she herself did not possess and a sneering contempt for what she saw as emotional weakness.

***

A few minutes later, the two girls were in Aphra's room. She was pleasantly surprised to discover that it was not in the servants' quarters, but adjacent to Miss Grenville's boudoir. However, her joy was short-lived when Emily pointed out the disadvantage of being next door.

"You'll find that she'll be in and out of here at all hours of the day and night."

Emily opened the wardrobe door and indicated the clothes that had been left by the previous occupant of the room. She then opened one of the drawers and produced a few items of clothing that Aphra would find useful – some stockings, a couple of petticoats, a nightdress and an apron. They were all clean and she was in no position to be too proud to accept someone else's cast-offs. She enquired about the previous owner of the clothes and Emily told her briefly about the French maid, who had left, like so many before her, because she found her mistress's changeable, critical nature and exacting standards too much to tolerate. Aphra suddenly felt overwhelmingly exhausted and Emily, thoughtful and sensitive girl that she was, noticed this straight away.

"I'll leave you for a short while to get settled in," she said.

When Emily had left the room, Aphra lay down on the soft bed. As her head touched the coverlet, she was asleep. The next thing that she was aware of was Emily standing by the bed holding a cup of tea.

"Good morning," she said as she proffered the steaming hot beverage.

Aphra sat up and leant against the pillows and accepted the tea. "Goodness! What's the time? I don't remember a thing after you left the room. I was so exhausted."

"I could see that and so I told Gracie not to bother with any food for you last night. I thought sleep was what you needed most of all. Bet you're hungry now, though, aren't you?"

"Gosh, yes. I'm famished."

"Well, you're in luck. We have porridge and bacon and eggs. One of the good things about working for her highness is the grub. She expects us to work like the horses over at the farm and therefore feeds us well. Also, Gracie is a wonderful cook. So up you get. Splash a bit of water on your face and brush your hair and I'll take you down to the servants' hall for breakfast."

Aphra got up from the bed and limped over to the washstand. Emily walked over and looked out of the window.

Leaning on the sill with her arms folded she said "after we've eaten and I've seen to the mistress, I'll show you where the bathroom is and you can have a nice soak. It'll do you good."

Aphra quickly washed her face and hands and while she was brushing her hair, she looked through the mirror at Emily. The housemaid was of medium height and had light brown, almost mousy hair. Although the colour of her hair was rather nondescript, the mass of unruly, bouncing curls was not. She had the kind of figure that would probably run to fat as she aged and she could never be called beautiful, but her bubbly and friendly manner meant that people always found her most attractive. Aphra decided there and then that she liked her very much.

On entering the servants' hall, Aphra saw that there were six people already eating breakfast. Gracie immediately gestured to a girl who was about the same age as Aphra. She got up from the table and went into the kitchen and picked up a ladle and two cereal bowls. She ladled some porridge into the bowls and placed them in front of Emily and Aphra as they sat down.

"I'm Maud, the kitchen maid," she said with a rather nasal sounding voice. She sniffed twice as she said this.
"You're the scullery maid," said Gracie. "So don't go getting ideas above your station – and stop sniffing. Use a handkerchief."

Everyone laughed at this, including Maud. Aphra was pleased to see what a good natured bunch they were. Emily made the introductions, of which, Aphra absorbed very little. She was still very tired. A white-haired, man with very brown wrinkled skin, called Joseph, was the elderly gardener. Sitting next to him, was Albert, recently employed to assist him. Aphra detected a look of mischief in his eye and decided that she needed to be wary of him. Across from him was a shy looking girl called Ivy, who was the under house-maid. The last person to be introduced was a thin, spotty youth, who could not have been aged more than thirteen or fourteen. This was Mickey, the stable lad, who stopped shovelling porridge into his mouth just long enough to mutter an indecipherable greeting.

Aphra suddenly felt quite shy and awkward as Emily said "this is Aphra

Chamberlain, the new lady's maid."

"Good morning. I'm very pleased to meet you all."

There were two empty places. One of these was at the head of the table. Aphra assumed correctly that this was where the butler sat. Emily told Aphra that Mr Isaacs often took breakfast in his own room and this morning was no exception.

"He needs a bit of peace and quiet from this lot," said Gracie.

"He's a very nice, kindly man. You'll really like him," said Emily and everyone nodded in agreement.

"Well, I must say, you're certainly a jolly bunch," Aphra said as she tucked into her breakfast.

"We won't be so jolly at the end of the week when Ol' Misery guts is back," said Albert.

"Now young'un. That's enough of that kind of talk," said Joseph. "You shouldn't speak of your betters in that way."

"She isn't my better," said Maud. "I think she's a frosty old hag."

"Maud! Mind your language," chastised Gracie.

Aphra's curiosity was now aroused. They were obviously talking about the person who usually occupied the other empty chair at the opposite end of the table.

"Miss Mildred Salathial's the housekeeper. She's visiting a relative and is due back in a few days," replied Emily. "And you'd better watch out. Joking aside, she can be a real tartar."

"Also, she's as thick as thieves with that one up there. So don't go crossing her," added Gracie with an upward jerk of her head. Aphra was determined that she would keep on the right side of the housekeeper when she returned.

Before Aphra had finished her breakfast, Emily rushed off to serve Miss Grenville her breakfast and prepare her bath. The mistress liked to bathe the old fashioned way – in her hipbath in front of the fire in her bedroom.

This was a source of great annoyance to the servants, as the mistress had a modern bathroom, so it was extremely vexing to have to lug buckets of water along to her room, when she could so easily walk the few yards down the corridor. Also, it meant having to light a fire in summer and then afterwards, extinguish it because it made the room too hot for her. Then the bath had to be emptied, cleaned and stored away. Aphra was to learn that this was just one of the many strange and paradoxical things about her new employer.

Later, Emily showed Aphra the bathroom that was on the same floor as her room. This aspect of the mistress's character was one of the bonuses of working at Warrington Grange. Caroline was going to be out most of the day visiting some friends and, as she had told Aphra, was not expecting her to commence her duties until the following day. So, here she was, lying back and soaking in a hot bath, to which Emily had added some ingredient or other that smelt wonderful. Gracie supplied a jar of ointment that she had made up using some of the garden herbs and when Aphra had dried herself, she applied the ointment to her face, hands and feet. She immediately felt a numbing of the stinging sensation and her face felt cooler and smoother to the touch.

When Aphra had completed her toilet, Emily took her on a tour of the house. It was much larger than the house in which Aphra had lived as a child. The main part of the house had been built in the late eighteenth century, and one or two sections had been added in more recent times. The house had been updated with all the modern conveniences expected in a house owned by a wealthy Victorian lady. Aphra noticed a plethora of radiators as they walked up and down long passages and there was at least one water closet on each floor.

"The mistress can't abide the cold," Emily informed her. "It's a good thing, as we all benefit from the house being nice and warm during the winter. It's made me a bit soft, I can tell you. When I think of what I used to put up with at home when I was little."

They climbed up to the top storey where the female servants slept. It was with pride that Emily opened the door to her little sanctuary. Aphra was very impressed with it all, but her favourite feature of Emily's tiny room was the panoramic view from the roof where Emily often climbed out - especially on hot summer nights, when she slept out there.

The room itself was sparsely furnished - in fact a typical servant's room. However, Emily had made it quite homely in the years that she had lived and worked at Warrington Grange. She had made a patchwork quilt and some cushions for the bed and a matching one for the small wing chair. She had embroidered a cloth for the small table in the alcove that sported a pretty vase with a posy of flowers in it. She had attempted a couple of watercolours that were on the mantelpiece. In front of the fireplace was a colourful rag mat and on a shelf near the window were some colourful geraniums grown from cuttings that Joseph had given to her. Beside the bed, on the top of a small wooden cabinet, was a much-used pewter candlestick covered in candle grease. On a shelf above the cabinet, lay a bible and prayer book. Aphra noted their pristine condition.

"You've made this into a real little home for yourself. It's lovely," said Aphra.

"Well, a girl needs to be doing something on the long, dark, winter evenings," Emily replied.

They climbed out onto the roof and looked out over the rolling hills of the Somerset countryside. The bleating of the hundreds of sheep was a comforting sound to Aphra and she suddenly felt at home here. Emily told her that all the land surrounding the property belonged to the mistress.

"She is a very wealthy woman. We get most of our food from the farm – lamb, beef, pork, poultry, wheat, barley, corn, honey, and there's a dairy too – just over there near the cider orchard, and the kitchen garden is always full of vegetables and herbs and lots of soft fruits in the summer." Emily told Aphra that she would show her around outside in a few days' time when she was feeling better.

"I can see that you're not taking all this in and will have forgotten in a day or two. I don't want you getting lost." At this, both girls laughed, but Aphra was very grateful for the consideration and understanding that the other girl showed to her.

The tour had taken almost an hour and after they had made their descent to the lower floors, Emily said "I need to get back to my duties. There always seems to be so much that needs doing. Even though two girls from the village come in three days a week to do the heavy work, we never seem to get on top of it all."

Aphra needed a little more rest. Emily accompanied her back to her room and as she was leaving, reminded Aphra that any items left by the previous occupier of the room were now hers. Apparently, she had left after a particularly acrimonious argument with her employer. She had packed her bags swiftly and had told Emily that she would be returning to France immediately.

"Mon Dieu!" She had said tearfully to Emily, as she stuffed all that she could carry into a small valise. "The next victim is welcome to everything that I leave behind me."

Aphra decided that she would have a look through everything later on, but for now, she really needed to sleep again. She laid her old clothes on the back of a chair, took the nightgown from the drawer and pulled it over her head. Then she slipped between the sheets and was fast asleep again.

Now, she was wide-awake and ready to step into her new life. From the time on the mantel clock, she knew that three hours had passed. She got up and padded across the room in bare feet. They still hurt, but the pain had lessened somewhat. Now that she was familiar with the room, she went through all the drawers and the wardrobe. She also discovered a built-in cupboard in an alcove that she had not been able to see from the bed. On opening the door, she was surprised to see that the shelves had not been cleared of the possessions of her predecessor. Then she remembered what Emily had said about this and made a mental note to check through the cupboard at her next opportunity. For now, her priority was to sort through the clothes that had been left behind to ascertain if any needed altering. She decided to take advantage of her revived energy to inspect the clothes and tackle any adjustments that were necessary. In the wardrobe she found two plain dresses – one grey and one black, a maroon skirt, three blouses and a cape.

The grey dress was the least worn. Her eye for detail told her that there was very little difference in size between her and her predecessor. When she tried on the garment, she was proved correct. She was soon absorbed in her work and thirty minutes of skilful needlework and the dress was ready to wear.

A knock at the door broke her concentration. "Come in," she said and was not surprised to see that it was Emily.

"You've missed another meal. You're going to starve to death."

"I'm sorry. I do hope that Gracie isn't put out. I fell asleep again. Oh, thank you for the tea. I'm afraid it got cold. Please forgive me. I just slept and slept."

"That's alright. We understand. You were in such a state when you arrived yesterday. You looked close to death. You certainly look much better now. Would you like me to go and fetch something for you to eat up here? I can see that you're busy."

"Yes, I'd really appreciate it. It'll give me a chance to deal with these things. It'll be wonderful to be properly dressed again."

"I'll see what I can find. I shan't be long."

"Thank you. I'm really grateful to you – and please tell Gracie that I won't be making a habit of this. I've almost recovered."

Aphra continued to work through the clothes, repairing a hem here and taking in a seam or two there. The discreet addition of a couple of strategically placed darts could improve a rather shapeless garment. A while later, Emily returned bearing a tray with some soup, fresh crusty bread, a slice of apple pie, custard and a jug of homemade lemonade.

"This should see you through the night and hopefully by tomorrow morning, you'll be rested and prepared. You've a tiring day ahead."

"I know," said Aphra. "I'm quite apprehensive about it, but I expect that I'll get used to it in time. Anyway, I definitely feel much better now and can cope with anything. After the nightmare of the last few months and especially the last few days, working hard for the mistress sounds quite appealing," she said with a twinkle in her eye.

Emily said goodnight to her and told her that she would wake her up the next morning.

As the maid was walking towards the door, Aphra said "thank you for all you've done for me Emily. You've no idea what it means to be treated with kindness and respect after what I've been through. Perhaps one day, I'll be able to repay you."

Emily told her that it had been a pleasure and that it was going to be nice having her as a friend.

***

It was the warm fingers of the sun caressing Aphra's cheek that awoke her.

It was a few moments before she realised where she was and that it was the next morning. It was still very early. She got out of bed and went to look out of the window. The view was spectacular and the day promised to be grand. She picked up the few items necessary for her toilet and swiftly made her way along the passage to the bathroom. For the second time, she lowered herself into the warm, rejuvenating water and leaned back and rested for a few minutes. A short while later, she was out of the bath and applying some more of the soothing ointment to her feet. She was relieved to see how much they had improved. She returned to her room and quickly finished dressing.

Today she would commence her duties and was in no doubt that she would be worked very hard. When Emily entered her room at six thirty, she was amazed at the transformation. Gone was the unhealthy and dishevelled tramp of two days earlier and in her place stood a tall, elegant young woman. Her hair, no longer dull and matted, was dressed neatly in a bun. The skin on her face was already less angry looking and there was now a light dusting of freckles across her nose. Although she was still not fully recovered, her appearance was vastly improved.

"You look a lot better," exclaimed Emily. "Madam may not be too happy now that you've scrubbed up so well. She don't like competition."

"Thank you," Aphra replied with a smile. "I feel quite recuperated."

"C'mon. Let's get some breakfast before she rings for you. She'll have you at it all day."

As the two girls entered the servants' hall, Aphra saw that there was a serious looking, white-haired gentleman wearing pince-nez, seated at the head of the table. His demeanour and attire told her that this was Jacob Isaacs, the Butler. Gracie introduced Aphra to him and as she said good morning to him, he nodded his head towards her in polite recognition. She was to learn that Mr Isaacs was a man of few words – unless absolutely necessary.

Porridge was on the menu again this morning, but today kippers replaced the bacon and eggs of the previous day. There was plenty of toast, and some of Gracie's delicious homemade jams - all washed down with cups of hot tea. It felt like a feast.

Much to Maud's annoyance, Albert kept staring at Aphra's changed appearance. He had been about to make some cheeky remark, but when she had walked into the room, it had stunned him into silence for once. He had hardly noticed her yesterday, but today, he had to admit to himself that "she was quite a looker". He was tempted to whistle, but he knew that he would get it in the neck from Maud if he did so.

"Well, you look a better sight this morning," said Gracie as she drained her cup. "A couple of good night's sleep and some of my 'ealthy grub and you look as good as new."

As Aphra ate, she soaked up the friendly atmosphere and quietly observed her new colleagues and the room in which they sat. It was adjacent to the kitchen, and the two rooms were divided by a wooden partition that was full of small windowpanes giving a good view of the kitchen from the table.

The servants' hall was large and allowed room for the long dining table placed in the centre of the room. A plain white cloth covered it and lay beneath cutlery and crockery that were of good utilitarian quality. A large brown teapot stood on a trivet in front of Gracie's plate. She poured out a cup each for Aphra and Emily. Aphra noticed that she replenished her own cup a number of times between reaching out for another slice of toast from the rack and buttering it.

She was constantly telling Maud to fetch things from the kitchen and the girl, who was rather scraggy and not overly intelligent, was continually grumbling and answering her superior back. However, much of this was good-natured banter and seemed to amuse the other members of staff seated around the table.

One by one, they left the table to commence their duties.

"You can start clearing away now Maud," Gracie said as she poured herself a final cup of the now lukewarm tea. "Make sure that you soak that porridge pan," she added.

She turned to the two girls still seated at the table. "She never fails to let the porridge catch. Don't matter how many times I tell 'er."

As Aphra was wiping off a few crumbs from her lip with a napkin, she was brought out of her reverie by the shrill sound of a bell ringing on the wall behind her and she jumped.

"You'd better get used to that ringing my girl. You're on duty now," chuckled Gracie as she gestured with her head and eyes at the impatient bell.

"C'mon," said Emily. "I'll show you the ropes. We'll do things together today and then tomorrow you'll be on your own. I'll need to be catching up with my own duties," she added.

"Good morning Ma'am," said Aphra as she drew open the curtains. "I hope that you slept well." She carried the breakfast tray over to the young woman who was leaning back against the numerous pillows.
"Plump these up for me," the mistress demanded irritably. Mornings were not her best time of the day. Emily had warned Aphra about this as well as instructing her on the basic procedures as they had swiftly mounted the stairs.

The morning sunlight revealed a beautiful, spacious chamber with a large, square bay window that faced the wooded hills. The furnishings were colourful and sumptuous. The room shouted comfort and luxury at every turn. Aphra wondered how someone could awake in such a perfect setting and be so grumpy. However, this was not the time to reflect on such philosophical questions. Whilst her mistress ate her breakfast - mouthfuls interspersed with complaints about the food - Emily instructed Aphra about the mistress's bath – where it was kept and so on. The two girls spent the best part of an hour carrying containers full of hot water from the bathroom to fill the hipbath placed in front of the fire that they had just lit. Aphra could not believe that a fire was required in the middle of August, so when they were out of earshot of Miss Grenville, the two of them moaned about the stupid and selfish whims of the mistress of the house.

"She doesn't usually have the fire lit at this time of the year – especially in this heat. She's just testing you," said Emily.

By ten thirty, Aphra and Emily had finished helping their mistress with her breakfast, toilette and bath. They then spent almost another hour emptying and cleaning the bath and putting it away and extinguishing the fire. Caroline Grenville told Aphra, who was now finishing off these tasks on her own, that when these duties had been completed, she could take a short break for a few minutes and was then to join her in the morning room. Aphra went down to the kitchen and asked Gracie if she could have something to drink.

"Help yourself," said the cook stirring a sauce in a large copper pan.

"There's a brew in the pot. I can't leave this or it'll catch."

Aphra sat on a stool and got her breath back. "She certainly likes her money's worth. What a morning – but it beats tramping round the countryside starving." The two women chatted for a few minutes, and Aphra felt as though she could have just continued to sit there and enjoy the company of the older woman, whom she was beginning to get to know, but she did not dare linger.

"I'd better get back. I'll see you at lunch time," she said, hoping that she would be able to find the morning room without getting lost.

When Aphra entered it, Caroline gestured to her to sit down and for this, Aphra was grateful. For the next thirty minutes, the lady of the house went through the daily routine and duties.

"I'm pleased to see that you have made a reasonable attempt to smarten yourself up," Caroline commented. What she did not say was that she was none too happy at how attractive her maid now looked. It was not what she had expected two days earlier. However, she decided that she would make the best of it – especially as the girl did seem to be tackling her duties well – although it would not do to say this to her.

At twelve thirty, she stood up and told Aphra that she was now going to the dining room for her lunch.

"You may go and take yours now. I'll ring for you when I've finished. You will then come to my bedroom and help me decide what I'm going to wear tonight and tomorrow evening."

The following evening, Caroline would be attending a dinner party at Peacock Hall with the Stapletons. They were neighbours of hers and lived some five miles distance. Caroline was still undecided at this stage what she would be wearing. She told Aphra that she would be trying on some gowns and jewellery and would like Aphra to be on hand to assist if necessary. So after a break of forty five minutes from the relentless work and Caroline's voice continually droning and nagging, Aphra entered her mistress's room to begin the afternoon's duties.

Caroline was already at her wardrobe, removing item after item from the rail and inspecting each garment in turn and usually rejecting it because of some fault or other with it. "I don't want you wasting time, so you can sit at that table and answer that pile of correspondence while I'm busy doing this. It shouldn't take you long and then if I need you to help me, you can stop for a moment and then go back to it."

Aphra began to read through the correspondence with increasing apprehension at how she was expected to reply. She was on probation and knew that any mistake, however minor, could result in her dismissal. However, there was nothing for it but to set to and tackle the chore. For two hours, she sat at the desk, composing ideas on scraps of paper and then discarding them. For most of this time, her concentration was continually interrupted by Caroline's enquiries regarding her gowns. A number of times, she had to stop altogether to assist with fastening a gown that she was trying on. Then she would have to unfasten it again. Her opinion on whether or not something matched was sought and then rebuffed – even ridiculed.

Finally, Caroline decided on a yellow satin gown and diamond earrings and necklace. Aphra thought to herself that she could have chosen an outfit and suitable jewellery in a couple of minutes. However, she suspected that much of the purpose behind this activity had been to show off to Aphra the vast array of expensive clothes, accessories and jewellery that she possessed.

Caroline looked at the clock. It was time for tea. She ordered Aphra to go and collect it. As soon as Aphra had absented the room, Caroline inspected Aphra's writing. She was impressed with what she saw. The girl had done well. Except for a couple of minor adjustments, it was far better than she could have accomplished herself. The girl was most certainly bright and was going to prove to be a treasure. Of course, she was not going to let on to her that she was pleased. She needed to keep her on her toes.

When Aphra returned with the tray, Caroline pointed out the minor adjustments in a manner that suggested Aphra was being criticised. As the mistress drank her tea, Aphra finished the secretarial work. When Caroline was satisfied that the work had been carried out to her exacting standards, she told Aphra to take the letters and place them down in the main hall ready for posting the following day.
"While you are downstairs, you may take a few minutes to have some tea. You are looking tired again. I don't want you fainting on the job. A sick employee is no good to me. Don't forget the tray. I've finished with it. Save your legs and take it back down there with the letters. When you come back up, I need you to help me select a dress for dinner tonight. So don't be long. My cousin, Gregory Herbert is coming, so it needn't take us

long. I don't intend making a real effort for him."

Aphra smiled to herself as she walked into the kitchen. The Mistress could almost sound human, until one realised that her apparent concern for one's welfare was actually more to do with how it affected her. When she returned to the bedroom after her tea, she found that the mistress was getting impatient. Aphra had not even sat down to drink her tea, but apparently had taken far too long.

"Gregory is such a bore, but one must do these things," Caroline complained. A business man like her late father, he was her only living relative and had connections with powerful and important people which Caroline thought might be useful to her one day and this was the only reason that she maintained contact with him.

It was nearly an hour and a half later that Caroline finally informed Aphra that she was satisfied with her appearance. Actually, she was absolutely thrilled with the way that Aphra had dressed her hair. It had never looked this good. It was a shame that there was no-one more interesting than Gregory coming this evening. She needed someone exciting and handsome like Sebastian to admire her, not a boring old fuddy duddy like Gregory.

As Caroline flounced out of the room, she told Aphra to go and get her own dinner.

"I won't need you again until bed-time. Enjoy your evening," she said dismissively. She was very light on her feet and almost floated down the main staircase and the only sound was the rustling of the fabric of the deep blue gown.

Aphra arrived in the Servants' Hall just in time for the evening meal. She was quite exhausted, but pleased that she had survived so far.

Emily enquired how she had managed. Aphra told her about the tasks that she had undertaken and thought that overall, she had done quite well.

Once the meal was finished, Aphra went to her room. Emily was assisting Mr Isaacs with serving the mistress and her guest with their food, but joined her as soon as she was off duty.

As she entered the room, Aphra said "I've been thinking about what you said and wondered if you could help me sort through this cupboard."

It took a few minutes to empty the shelves. Emily expressed an interest in two or three items. There were a few things that would prove useful, including a bottle of cologne, some fragments of material and some ribbons and an outdated, but wearable bonnet.

"I could re-trim this," Aphra said as she tried it on and held a piece of ribbon up to it.

But best of all, there was a pile of books – mostly in French. Aphra was delighted. Now she would have something to read in her spare time – assuming that the mistress allowed her some. Also, it would mean that she could work at improving her French skills, as she had become very rusty since she had left school. When Emily, whose own literacy skills were almost non-existent, realised that Aphra could read French, she was full of admiration, as well as a little bit of envy at the other girl's obvious social and educational advantages.

"Can you really speak and read French? It won't be much use here." Then she added, "I can hardly read and write in my own language."

When Aphra heard this, she said to Emily "I could teach you, if you wished. Improving one's mind can open doors to a better life."

"I'll think about it," Emily answered slightly grudgingly. "It might be a good idea."

What she didn't say was that she didn't think that Aphra's fancy education had done her much good.

Emily left to put her new possessions upstairs in her room and Aphra continued sorting through and replacing things on the shelves. She selected a book on French history and placed it on her bedside table. She put her few possessions from her bag in the top drawer of the tallboy. Her brooch, she had already pinned to her petticoat. She had learned that she must always keep it on her person.

Sitting in the armchair, she looked around at her lovely, comfortable room. The soft light cast by the oil lamp and candles gave the room a warm glow. Although she was very tired, she felt at peace. She reflected on how things were turning out. She was eating well, her feet were not quite so painful, her face was healing and she would soon be asleep in the big, inviting bed. She had enough clothes and possessions to cover her immediate needs and she had congenial colleagues and a very good friendship developing. She gave thanks for the change in her fortunes. She was just drifting off to sleep when she was startled by the sound of a bell ringing. For a moment, she wondered what it was, but the angry repetition of it, informed her that her mistress was back in her bedroom requiring her attention.

Aphra went briskly to attend to her mistress, who was not in a good mood. "I've had the most tedious evening of my life," she complained.

Aphra's earlier feeling of contentment began to evaporate as she listened to the whining and complaining of her mistress. She took the pins out of her hair and brushed it. Then she helped her out of her dress and into her nightgown and then placed the jewellery back in its box.

"That clumsy idiot spilled soup on my gown. See that it's thoroughly cleaned. Don't do it now. You look exhausted. Get a good night's sleep and do it first thing. You've done reasonably well for a first day I suppose, but there is much for you to do tomorrow. I've a great deal of urgent mending that's piling up."

"Goodnight ma'am."

***

Aphra awoke with a jolt. She jumped out of bed and rushed to look at the clock. She was relieved to see that she had not overslept. She bathed, dressed and went downstairs to clean the soiled gown. Whilst doing this, her thoughts travelled back to last year, when she had worked for Mrs Brookes. She had been kept quite busy throughout the day, but it was nothing compared with what Caroline required from her staff.

Mrs Brookes had been elderly and needed help with dressing and answering her correspondence because she had painful joints in her arthritic hands. Failing eyesight meant that the old lady was grateful for Aphra to read to her from her favourite books and to keep her up to date with what was going on in the world, by reading the newspaper to her. The old lady had no family living close by and was therefore lonely, so she enjoyed the bright and lively company of Aphra who sat sewing whilst they chatted about this and that. Often, especially on long winter evenings Aphra would play the pianoforte and sing to her. All of this gave the old lady much pleasure in the closing months of her life. Also, Mrs Brookes had a sweet, good-humoured temperament and was easy to please. Aphra missed her and felt sad that the gentle laughter and warmth that they had shared had come to an end. Mrs Brookes was everything that Caroline was not.

When she was satisfied that the gown was clean enough to pass inspection, Aphra hung it up and went to eat her breakfast. The day passed in much the same way as the previous one and by the time she went to bed, she was fast asleep the minute the covers were over her shoulders.

Although her duties and tasks varied somewhat, each day followed much the same pattern, but on Saturday there was a change in circumstances. The housekeeper returned.

Aphra's first encounter with Miss Salathial confirmed the derogatory comments that had been made by the younger members of staff. Aphra and Emily had been enjoying a few minutes respite from their duties and taking a short stroll in the kitchen garden. Emily had been showing Aphra around the exterior of Warrington Grange, and Aphra, who was now almost fully recovered, was absorbing the details much better than a few days earlier.

They were beginning to become really good friends and getting to know each other quite well and had reached the stage of friendship where they could tease and banter in a good humoured way. They were giggling so much as they pushed and shoved each other that they did not hear the housekeeper as she approached them from behind.

"What's going on here? Who is this person with whom you are misbehaving Emily Frances?"

"Oh, Miss Salathial. I'm sorry. I didn't see you there," exclaimed Emily nervously. Aphra noticed how her whole demeanour had undergone a complete change in the presence of this intimidating woman.
"Evidently!"

"This is the new lady's maid," Emily stammered.

Glaring at Aphra, the intimidating housekeeper asked her if she thought that this was the correct way for a lady's maid to conduct herself.

"I apologise. We did not mean any harm. We just got carried away. We were having such a nice time," Aphra responded politely, in the hope that the housekeeper would mellow towards them and be a little less harsh.

"You're not here to have a nice time. You're here to work and earn the money that the mistress pays you. Now, I'm sure that you both have unfinished duties, so go and get on with them immediately!"

As the housekeeper walked away, Aphra knew that she had made an enemy for life and she would have to work very hard at keeping out of trouble with this woman.

The days turned into weeks and Aphra learned her duties very fast. As she became more familiar with the tasks involved, where everything was and where everything went, so she got more efficient and learned short cuts. She knew her way around the house and grounds of Warrington Grange and no longer found herself wandering up and down long corridors getting lost. Now she learned to become a first class servant and anticipate her mistress's needs before she was even aware of them herself.

Although there were moments when she enjoyed her work, and occasionally, her mistress and she actually shared a joke, she soon discovered how difficult and mercurial Caroline's nature could be. She learned to read the signs and to sidestep trouble if possible. To some extent, their relationship became a battle of wills, which Caroline thought she was winning, whereas in reality, it was Aphra who always kept a step or two ahead.

Aphra had been working at Warrington Grange for well over a month when she decided that it was time to remind her employer about the agreement that was originally made about working conditions and suitable clothes to wear. She had altered all the articles of clothing left by her predecessor and had even made a very adequate job of reworking one or two of the items that she had arrived in and wore these for carrying out duties where her clothes might get spoilt and kept the better items for when it was important to look her best. However, she realised that it would not be long before these garments wore out completely, and she had been told that her wardrobe would be replenished. She picked her moment carefully. That morning, the mistress had received a flattering letter from the Earl of Tawford and was in a particularly amiable mood. Aphra took a deep breath and asked permission to speak to her. She pointed out the condition of her clothes and diplomatically reminded her mistress of her words at the interview. She also mentioned that she had not yet taken her afternoon off. She was pleasantly surprised at Caroline's easy compliance and could not believe the response.

"Yes, I suppose that you have worked reasonably well in some respects. You do seem to learn quite quickly, although there is much room for improvement. Besides, those things are looking quite shabby and I don't want to be embarrassed by a servant who is not suitably attired.

Very well, next Thursday, when you've carried out your early morning duties and assisted me to dress, you may take the rest of the day off and go into Westbridge to make the necessary purchases. The stable boy can take you in the old carriage. I will give you a letter for Mr Carter of Egbert and Carter, the outfitters. Their clothes are plain, but of good quality and quite suitable for a woman in your position. They will need to last a long time, as I cannot afford to keep spending money on clothes for you, so I trust that you will take good care of them. While you're in town, you can do a small amount of shopping for me."

What Caroline did not tell Aphra, but would write in the letter to the proprietor of the store, was that the clothes were to be as plain as possible. The last thing that Caroline wanted was Aphra looking any more attractive than she already did. Over the weeks that she had been at Warrington Grange, her appearance had changed dramatically. Long gone was the sick looking waif who was propped up against the back door. In her place was a very vibrant and beautiful young woman with glowing soft cream skin and glossy hair, who walked tall and proud and whose large, green eyes sparkled with intelligence and energy.

However, it was important to keep up standards, for only the other day, one of her visitors, whom Caroline had been trying to impress, had commented upon the worn appearance of Aphra's clothes. Caroline felt torn between her need of approval from those whose society she craved, and her desire to maintain her position as the county's beauty.

"Speak to Miss Salathial about money. You're entitled to one month's salary. I hope that you will spend it wisely. I do not approve of extravagance. Considering the dreadful state that you were in when you arrived here, you need to be careful that you don't get into that financial position again. I trust that you will put some of it away for emergencies.

Now, is that gown ready for this evening? You can go and fetch it and then get on with that mending."

Aphra thanked her mistress for her generosity and advice and left the room. Her feelings were a confused mixture of surprise, amusement and rage, all of which jostled for superiority. Ultimately, it was the rage that won. Although Aphra was pleasantly surprised at the ease with which her requests were acceded to, she had to laugh to herself at her mistress's statement that she disapproved of extravagance, when it was almost impossible to shut the doors of her bulging closets. However, it was the spiteful way that Caroline had referred to the distressed state that she was in a few weeks earlier that annoyed and upset her. She seemed to be suggesting that the predicament was of her own making. Aphra found it very hard to concentrate on her duties for the next few hours as she was so angry and it was only when she had let off steam to a sympathetic Emily that she was finally able to calm down.

So it was, that on the following Thursday, after a hectic few hours, that Aphra breathed a sigh of relief and sat back in the carriage as Mickey shouted down remarks to her. She leant out of the window to reply to him a couple of times, but as conversation was difficult, they soon abandoned this activity. She settled back in her seat and was determined that she was going to enjoy her day out.

Mickey drove the carriage down the driveway near the woods and Aphra remembered that day back in August when she had been so grateful to those friendly giants for sheltering her from the heat of the sun as she limped beneath them. Silently she thanked them for their protection and helping her towards a better life and prospects. It all looked quite different now. The leaves were turning to gold and she took a quiet pleasure in just sitting there and looking at the beauty of nature. She tried not to be dissatisfied with her lot and counted her blessings daily, but she would have liked more spare time to walk and enjoy the woods and the fields. However, she decided to make the best of the treat that she was having today and quietly absorbed the tranquil beauty.

The fields were now bare and would lie fallow until early next year when they would be planted up again. The last of the crops had recently been harvested and a few crows circled and swooped down to pick up some tasty morsels that had been left behind. It was a lonely, almost desolate emptiness that had a charm of its own.

It took almost an hour to reach the outskirts of the small market town. The contrasting change from the quiet of the countryside surrounding Warrington Grange to the hustle and bustle of the town seemed overwhelming at first to Aphra. There were many carriages going up and down the main street. She had forgotten how noisy life could be in town. Mickey pulled at the reins and the horses stopped. He jumped down and assisted her as she dismounted. She thought that this was completely unnecessary as she was perfectly able to do it on her own. However, Mickey did not need much of an excuse to hold Aphra's hand. He thought to himself that she was becoming more beautiful every day.

The wind was getting up and she shivered. "What are you going to do until it's time to return?"

"I know a spot just outside of town near the river, where the horse can have a drink and a feed and I can put my feet up. Gracie has packed me up with some lunch, so I'll be alright. I might even have a nap," he said with a wink and a smile for her. "Tell you what. I'll meet you outside Egbert and Carters at – shall we say about four?"

"That will be excellent Mickey. Thank you. I hope you enjoy your rest."

With this parting remark, she set off with a spring in her step. She soon acclimatised herself to the noise of the bustling high street and the traffic. Once or twice, she had to jump out of the way of enthusiastic coachmen who had little regard for pedestrians. She stopped here and there to look in the windows of the various shops, planning to explore inside them after she had been to the outfitters.

A bell rang as she entered the shop and it reminded her of one of her father's shops that she had visited a couple of times. She shuddered at this unwelcome memory although the first visit had been quite nice. Her father had shown Mama and her around the store and introduced them to the staff – many of whom had made a great fuss of Aphra. She had been about five or six at the time. However, the second visit had been different altogether. Aphra had been ten years old and she remembered every detail of the incident. Her mother had thought that they would surprise her father as it was his birthday, but when they had opened the door of his office, they found him with that woman. Aphra did not like to think about it. It caused her a lot of pain. She could not bear now to remember the state that her mother was in on the journey back home. Their lives changed from that day. That morning had been the last time that Aphra had seen her mother happy.

"Good day. Can I help you?" A softly spoken man greeted Aphra, who responded with a smile and produced the sealed letter from her mistress. He read the letter and looked up at her.

"I think that we can suit you, young lady. We have all the items that have been requested by Miss Grenville. If you would be so kind as to step into one of our cubicles, I will fetch one of our assistants to measure you."

The dowdy middle-aged assistant was swift and efficient in her task of measuring Aphra. This being completed, a number of items were produced for Aphra to inspect. It was soon very apparent that the clothes were being selected for their plainness. Not a piece of lace or bow in sight. While the assistant went to fetch a dress in a different size, Aphra quickly leaned over the counter and read the letter, even though it was upside down. Yes, as she had thought, her mistress had stipulated that the clothes were to be as utilitarian as possible. The outmoded style was more suited to a dowager than to a pretty young woman. However, Aphra was grateful to be getting the clothes, so accepted the situation.

Later, when she left the shop, the chill of the wind seemed to go right through her. She was now very hungry, and decided to find somewhere to eat. Across the road, she saw a small teashop and made her way there. The wind was biting cold and she was glad to find a welcoming fire burning in the grate. A white haired lady wearing a floral print dress and white apron approached her and greeted her with a warm smile.

"Good day to you, Miss. What can I get you?"

"Good day," Aphra replied. "What can you recommend that's warm and nourishing? That wind has gone right through me. Even my bones are cold."

"May I suggest some nice vegetable broth and freshly baked bread? It should help to keep the cold out for a while. My sister makes everything herself and she's an excellent cook."

"Very well. I shall try some of that," said Aphra. "It sounds very tempting."

It only took a couple of minutes for the arrival of the steaming, aromatic soup. Aphra sat by a window overlooking the street and leisurely watched the noisy bustle of the town. Carriages passed up and down the busy street as brave shoppers darted in between them to get to the other side of the road. A harassed mother, laden with bags of vegetables and groceries, was dragging two fractious children past the shop window. The sight of the young woman, prematurely aged, trying unsuccessfully to cope with the difficulties of everyday life returned her thoughts to her mother. The memories were painful and she did not want to think about it.

She directed her thoughts to the purchases that she had just made and to her mistress. What a strange mixture she was. On the one hand, she was determined that Aphra was not going to attract any favourable attention in regard to her appearance, and yet the cost of this morning's shopping must have been considerable. In her mind, she went over the list of items purchased: - Two day dresses and another, smarter one for Sunday best. There were three sets of underwear and petticoats and two pairs of boots and a pair of smart shoes. A navy blue cape and matching bonnet and gloves, and two nightgowns completed the purchase. Although the items were plain and utilitarian, they were of good quality and Aphra reflected that her mistress must have laid out quite a substantial sum on a maid. She wondered why this could be, for she did not think that she liked her particularly. Perhaps it was because she was pleased with her work and wanted to retain her services. Aphra then thought about the low salary and the difficult nature of the young woman who employed her. She knew that she could possibly get a higher wage elsewhere, but then again, she may not necessarily be in such a beautiful setting. In many respects, her conditions were quite good. She thought about the accommodation, good food and being able to take a bath regularly. Then she thought about Emily and her tendency to mother her. She smiled at this recollection, but at the same time, the sadness returned. She pushed the thoughts away as she finished her meal.

She was now refreshed and ready to explore the town and make her own purchases. She had another hour before she needed to return to the outfitters to collect the items that would be ready to take back with her. The dresses required some alteration and would be delivered to Warrington Grange the following week. Her first call was to the bank where she opened a savings account and deposited a few shillings.

Then she went into a small bookshop and spent some time selecting a suitable reader for Emily together with a book for her to write in. Aphra was determined to repay Emily for her kindness by helping her to read and write. After collecting the few items that her mistress wanted and purchasing a small bottle of cologne for Gracie, she returned to the outfitters. As she approached the store, she saw that Mickey was waiting outside with the carriage. Together they packed the items on the seat inside.

It was getting dark and the chill in the air had increased. There was a travel rug in the carriage and she pulled this over her lap. The movement of the carriage rocked her to sleep for a while. Her dreams were worrying and disturbing. A sudden halting of the carriage woke her up. She could hear Mickey shouting at someone or something. It was nothing, but she was now wide-awake. In the dark silence of the carriage, her thoughts turned towards her mother and her childhood. She had been pushing these thoughts away all afternoon ever since she had entered the shop. Now, she could no longer keep these thoughts at bay.

She had been born in the village of Bishops Langley in Wiltshire. Her mother, Ellen, was the only child of the village parson, the Rev. William Taverner. He was the youngest son of the local squire. His wife, India, was the daughter of a Viscount, who had disapproved of the marriage, considering a parson beneath her station. When she eloped with him, she was disinherited and there had been no further contact with the family.

Aphra's father, Patrick Chamberlain, was a difficult man to understand, even for a warm and affectionate woman such as Ellen. Her intelligence and education had not enlightened her as to his real motives for courting her and it took many years of marriage before she fully realised that he did not love her. He had been young and handsome and the naive Ellen had fallen in love with him. Her mother, India, had had doubts about the union, but had died before she had a chance to warn her daughter. In truth, he was a very cold and ambitious man of dubious background. His easy charm and lies had not only fooled Ellen, but her kindly, naïve father too. Although William was a humble parson, he had inherited some money from his family, so he was quite comfortable in his situation. Patrick had made it his business to win the confidence of Ellen's father in persuading him to buy the newlyweds a large house and to invest in his commercial ventures.

The day that Aphra and her mother had come upon her father kissing another woman was etched on the little girl's mind. She remembered how her mother went very quiet. On the carriage journey, they did not speak. When they arrived home, her mother asked Miss Petworth, the housekeeper to look after Aphra for the rest of the afternoon – telling her that she had a headache. As her mother rushed to the bathroom, Aphra heard her being sick. The melancholy never left her mother after that. Within a few months her mother was very ill and within two years she had lost the will to live and died of a tumour. Aphra did not fully understand what a tumour was, but what she did know was that her mother had died of a broken heart.

The carriage slowed as Mickey steered it into the drive of Warrington Grange. Aphra's attention returned to the present. As they approached the house, she noticed how pretty it looked with all the windows glowing with light. The horses slowed to a trot as Mickey guided them around to the side of the house. He brought them to a halt and jumped down to assist Aphra as she dismounted the carriage. He helped her carry her parcels to the side door and rang the bell.

As Emily opened the door, he drove on towards the stables behind the house. Albert came out carrying a lantern and calling to Mickey. Aphra and Emily could hear the two lads cheeking one another and smiled at the good humour of it all.

"Here, let me help you with these. My goodness, you've got some parcels. Is there anything left in the shop?"

The aroma of a rich beef stew and dumplings made Aphra realise how hungry she was and the warmth of the room was a welcome contrast to the biting cold of the wind howling outside. The other members of the staff were already seated at the table and Gracie had just started ladling out the large chunks of meat and gravy on to a plate for Mr Isaacs. The girls joined the other servants at the table. When Gracie and Maud had finished passing around the plates and everyone had helped themselves to vegetables from the large white glazed tureens, Mr Isaacs said grace and they all tucked in heartily. Aphra faced quite a few questions regarding her sojourn into town and tried her best to make it sound interesting and uplifting. This was quite difficult for her, as the intrusive memories had lowered her mood considerably despite the comforting feeling of returning home. It hadn't helped that Miss Salathial had commented on how fortunate Aphra was to have had so much money spent on her and how she hoped that she would show her gratitude by working harder. However, Mr Isaacs said that he was sure Miss Chamberlain was most appreciative and worked very hard indeed all the time.

After dinner, Emily helped her carry her packages up to her room and sat on the bed as Aphra unpacked things and showed them to her. She felt a little bit envious of all the smart new things, but was also pleased for Aphra. This generosity of spirit was rewarded by the gift of the two books that Aphra had bought for her. The next gift would be the reading and writing lessons.

"You seem very quiet. Is something wrong? Has something happened? I mean apart from the ol' hag having a go at you.

"Oh, it's nothing. I expect that I'm just tired," Aphra replied.

"I'd have thought that you'd have been cock a hoop at a few hours away from this place and coming back with all these lovely things. Instead you have come back looking so sad."

"Perhaps I have a headache coming on."

"Don't lie to me, Aphra. I thought we were friends," Emily persisted. "I've seen you tired beyond belief. This is different. Please tell me. Maybe I can help."

"My trip into town stirred up old memories that I've tried to forget."

Emily was just about to respond when the door opened and Miss Salathial stood in the doorway.

"The mistress requires your assistance now Miss Chamberlain. I believe that your afternoon off has now ended. Please be so good as to bring the packages that you've purchased on her behalf. It doesn't do to keep her waiting."

"Yes, Miss Salathial," Aphra replied. "I will attend to her right away."

The housekeeper left and closed the door.

Emily got up off the bed. "Actually, I've a few chores to finish off. We'll talk later. I'll bring up some cocoa and biscuits." She patted Aphra on the arm as the two girls parted to attend to their particular duties.

It must have been three hours later that they made themselves comfortable by the fire in Aphra's room. She sipped her hot cocoa and blew on it to cool it down. Emily did the same.

"Come on, now. Tell me all about it," she said.

Aphra began by recalling her idyllic early childhood with her mother and her grandfather. She described the beautiful house in which she lived with her parents and the comfortable, welcoming home of her grandfather. The small Wiltshire village sounded delightful and Emily felt that it seemed to come alive, so well did Aphra describe it. She saw tears in Aphra's eyes as she spoke of how walking into the shop earlier that day reminded her of the day that her mother and she walked into the office above one of her father's many emporia and found him with that woman.

"I shall never forget that moment and the expression on my mother's face as I looked up at her. I didn't know that such pain could exist in a person's countenance. When I turned and looked at the woman – her name was Agnes – she just gloated. I hated her and I hate her still. I'm convinced that it was because of her that mama died," she said tearfully.

"I'm so sorry," Emily said, trying to comfort her. She put her arm around Aphra as she leant her head on the older girl's shoulder and continued to cry. After a few minutes, she blew her nose and continued.

"Everything became so difficult after that. Mama became very ill and sad – and even though she loved me very much and tried to be happy for me, she just seemed to fade away. They said that it was a tumour that killed her, but I do wonder if she would still be alive if my father had not treated her so badly. Sometimes, he would be home and behave as though nothing was wrong and at other times he was hardly ever there. He seemed to blow hot and cold and neither of us knew where we were with him. His temper was terrifying at times." She took another sip of her drink.

"Before she died, she told me something that I've never repeated. I'd like to share it with you. I know that I can trust you not to tell anyone."

"Of course you can. Remember, anything you tell me I promise to keep to myself. You have my word on it."

"Thank you Emily. I've needed to share this with someone. For obvious reasons – that is, my present circumstances, this revelation could cause a great deal of embarrassment and trouble. In fact, I'm sure that the mistress would dismiss me if she knew." Aphra shifted her position slightly to get more comfortable.

"My grandmother, Lady India Kingston, who died many years ago, was the daughter of the Viscount of Westbridge."

At this point, Emily took a sharp intake of breath and uttered an expletive that quite shocked Aphra.

"Emily! I didn't expect a young lady to know, let alone use words like that." Aphra drank some more of her cocoa, which was cooling rapidly now.

"Sorry, but I've never been on friendly terms with toffs before," Emily joked. "Besides, I'm no lady – not like you." She turned around and altered the position of the cushion behind her. "You're right, though. The mistress would go mad if she knew. But why don't you contact your family? Surely, it would be better than being a skivvy to her," and she gestured with her head towards the room next door.

"I'm not sure. I need to think about it. You see, the Viscount had forbidden my grandmother to marry my grandfather. He considered that a clergyman, even one from a well-respected family, was beneath her. They eloped and she was cut off from the rest of her family and she never saw any of them again. My great-grandfather would be dead by now. Presumably the present Viscount and the rest of the family know nothing of my existence." Aphra looked down at her nails and picked at one of them. "I wonder what the present one is like. He would be my second or third cousin I suppose."

Emily sat and thought about it for a short while and then said as though thinking aloud. "I still think that you should contact them. They might help you out. I would if it was me."

Aphra shook her head. "No. It's a tempting proposition and, believe me, I've considered it, but I couldn't go begging cap in hand. I think that my mother told me about my connections, so that I'd know that I had some other relatives, but I think that she would prefer me to try and fend for myself. Perhaps I may write to the current Viscount if and when my circumstances improve. I'm not sure."

"It must have been a very sad time for you." Emily tipped her cup back and finished the last of her cocoa.

Aphra continued. "My grandfather had a heart attack shortly after discovering what was going on between my father and Agnes. He had been very shocked at my father's betrayal. He had believed him to be an honourable man and had given him a lot of money. There was a dreadful scene between them and Grandpa collapsed and died the following day.

When I was twelve, mama died. Father sold the house and I was sent to a boarding school for young ladies in Bath. Actually, it wasn't too bad. At first, I didn't fit in and was very lonely, but then I made one or two friends

"Did you like being at school – you know, learning things?"

"Yes, very much. Actually, I was quite a good scholar and the teachers were very kind and encouraging towards me. As time passed, I began to settle in and enjoyed my time with my new friends. I saw very little of my father or Agnes, who was now married to him. She and I had only one thing in common – our mutual dislike of each other. At first, I went home during the school holidays, but felt very unwelcome. Eventually I stopped going, for it was preferable to stay at school. One or two of the other girls did so for various reasons and we found pleasant ways to pass the time and amuse ourselves. In the winter we read or played parlour games or cards. We helped each other with our needlework and painted. In the warmer weather, we would take trips into the city. There were so many interesting places to see – like the roman baths, the Abbey and the pump house.

Agnes encouraged my father to open more shops and he borrowed heavily from the bank. I'm surprised that they lent him so much money. I can see now that he must have got carried along with her outlandish plans. She also spent money like water. My mother certainly never had a wardrobe like hers.

When I was fourteen, I was called into the headmistress's study. Miss Kensal was very kind as she asked me to sit down. She told me how well I had done at the school and how proud of me she was. She was obviously trying to break the news to me gently. She coughed and cleared her throat and then she told me.

'Aphra, I'm very sorry to have to tell you that your dear father has passed away. I understand that it was very peaceful' she said kindly, trying to spare me any additional grief. I was very shocked – not at his death, but at my complete indifference at the news. Until that moment, I had not realised how much I had come to hate him. I felt ashamed of my feelings and tried to hide them.

'I see' I said quietly. 'When did this happen?'

'I understand that it was about four weeks ago. We have only just received this letter from your father's solicitor.'

So Agnes could not even be bothered to inform me of my father's death. She obviously had not wanted me to attend the funeral."

Aphra heard Emily mutter "spiteful bitch" under her breath and although she felt that the term was fitting, she only acknowledged this with a weak smile.

"I felt a mixture of annoyance at this, together with indifference about attending a service where I should have felt a hypocrite.

Miss Kensal continued. 'This is very difficult and embarrassing for me to have to tell you Aphra, but apparently there's no money to pay your school fees. It would appear that your father has not left you anything. I'm afraid that you'll have to leave at the end of this term. I wish that there was something that I could do to help you.' She got up from her chair and walked around the desk and put her hand on my shoulder. 'Perhaps we can assist you to find some employment. We'll give you an excellent reference and report of your time here. Although you are young, you have been a model pupil – bright and hard-working and should do well.'

I left her study and walked down the stone steps to the grounds and wandered around for some time. I saw her watching me out of the window and she probably thought that I was grieving, but I was fuming – fuming that he had left me nothing. He had spent or lost it all, or had left it to her – and to think that it was my grandfather who had invested large sums of money in his business and had also loaned him extra funds on the understanding that my mother and I would be provided for should anything happen to him.

I thought how grandfather must have been turning in his grave. Father had also used vast sums of money of my mother's. I had heard numerous arguments as he had bullied her for months. Looking back now, I'm convinced that he only married her to improve his financial and social status. She left a small legacy to me, but there was very little left as I had needed it for clothes and my personal needs. Father just paid my school fees and did not provide for me outside of that.

I could not grieve for him. My grieving for him – for the love that he never showed us – had ended years before.

I had no idea what I was going to do. I was young and had no experience to gain a position as a governess or lady's maid. I thought that perhaps I could work in a shop of some kind. If only he had lived three or four years longer, then I'd have finished my education and have been in a better position to obtain a good post. I walked around the small terrace to the side of the house becoming more and more angry. I found a bench in a quiet spot where I knew that I was not observed and had a good cry. This helped me to come to a decision and I was soon resolved to set about finding work. I knew that Miss Kensal would do her best to help me and decided that it was no good feeling sorry for myself."

"I think you've been very brave. It must've been very frightening to feel so alone in the world. I'd have been terrified," Emily declared as she leaned forward and put another small log on the fire which was beginning to burn low.

"Thank you. Yes, it was very frightening not knowing what was going to become of me," said Aphra. "It was towards the end of term that I was called once again to Miss Kensal's room. She informed me that she was trying to obtain a position for me with a Mrs Brookes, an elderly woman who lived in Bath."

Suddenly the bell rang and brought both girls back to the present with a jolt.

"Looks like you're back on duty," remarked Emily as she stood up not bothering to suppress a yawn. "I'm off to bed, so I'll leave you to it. You can tell me the rest tomorrow."

Aphra quickly checked her appearance in the mirror. "Oh I've talked enough tonight. It's your turn tomorrow. You can tell me more about your naughty brother's antics at the village school and how he got out of that scrape with the schoolmaster. I think that we need a more light-hearted topic of conversation."

As the weary maid opened the door to leave, Aphra added "thank you for listening to me Emily. It means so much to have someone to talk to. Goodnight. Sleep well."

As the door closed, Emily's retreating footsteps were accompanied by the words "God bless." As the footsteps disappeared, the ringing began again and Aphra hastily made her way to her mistress's room.

An hour later, Aphra was trying to settle down and get some sleep. In a few hours, her mistress would be demanding her attention and she needed to be fit. However, sleep eluded her for the time being. She lay in the dark and her thoughts returned to her mother and she saw her on her deathbed.

She had been so sad and had cried so much. Aphra supposed that she just faded away. When Ellen was dying, the little girl had lain on the bed beside her. She held out her bony hand to her and the child grasped it. It felt very cold. She said that she had something important that she wanted to tell her and started to speak in a very faint voice. Aphra could only just make out what she was saying

"Be careful of men. I made a terrible mistake in believing your father. Yet, if I had not married him, then I would not have you. You have been the biggest and most rewarding joy of my life. I cannot bear to think that you would ever know the pain that your father caused me. I didn't know that a person could experience such emotional agony. So please my dear girl, make sure that the man you choose as your life partner is honest and has integrity. Never lower your own standards or compromise your own principles and choose someone who holds the same values. If someone does not have integrity in one area of his or her character, then it is likely that it is missing in every aspect of that person's life. You probably do not understand what I'm saying, for you are still very young, but when you are a woman, please remember this advice."

The little girl didn't understand, but she memorised every word. The young woman that she was now becoming was still unsure of the full significance of these words, but the time would come many years later, at the most exquisite, yet excruciatingly painful moment of her life when she would fully understand them.

***

In the weeks that followed, Aphra and Emily had little time to themselves and therefore there was no chance for Aphra to continue telling her friend about her early years. Caroline seemed to become even more demanding and the staff were working even harder to keep her satisfied. The nights were drawing in rapidly and lamps were lit and curtains were being drawn at three thirty in the afternoon. Many a morning saw a light dusting of snow across the hills and when it fell deeply, there was an eerie silence out in the fields.

The leisure time that they did have was spent with Aphra giving Emily reading and writing lessons. At first, the progress was slow, but recently there had been a small improvement and Emily was becoming very keen and gaining in confidence. These lessons were either snatched between chores during those few minutes respite from the continual nagging demands from the mistress, or late at night when Aphra could catch up with some of the mending.

There were times, when their morale got quite low. However, it was the thought of the eagerly awaited Christmas festivities that kept everyone's spirits up. To add to this excitement, Mr Isaacs was informed that the mistress would be away spending the Christmas and New Year holiday with friends. Everyone was delighted when he broke the news to them.

Although, they would all keep up their duties of running the household, it meant that life would be much easier and they would be given the opportunity to have some relaxation, and better still, some fun.

At the beginning of December, Aphra and Emily had managed to get an afternoon in Westbridge together. This was because the mistress wanted Aphra to go into town and order the Christmas presents that she wanted to take with her. Both Aphra and Emily also wished to purchase presents of their own. As Aphra was doing shopping for Caroline, it was agreed that Mickey could take her in the old carriage and obviously Emily could go too. It was a real treat for the girls and they were giggling and chatting as they climbed up into the carriage at twelve thirty. There was a lot of banter with Mickey, who was still smitten with Aphra. He dropped them near to the centre of the town and agreed to be waiting there for them at four.

First, they went to the jeweller's in Wood Street. It was a well-respected family firm that had been making silverware and jewellery for nearly a hundred years. Aphra purchased a tasteful, silver hip flask for the Earl. Aphra knew that the Earl had recently paid a number of visits to Caroline and she knew that she was not adverse to the idea of marriage. It would certainly be a large leap socially for the daughter of a man knighted for his services to industry to Countess of Tawford. Aphra had never seen him. He always seemed to visit when she was on an errand – one that took her far away from the rooms where he would be entertained.

The proprietor asked Aphra if she wished to have the item delivered and gift wrapped.

"Yes. Please could it be delivered to the Earl of Tawford at his country residence – Methuen Park? I expect you know the address."

"Of course, Miss," he replied. "Thank you for your custom. It will be delivered next week."

A few other purchases were made and then the girls left the shop. The bell made a tinkling noise as they walked out into the alley. "I've never been in a shop like that before. I could have spent a fortune," said Emily as she pressed her nose against the window.

"C'mon. Back to reality," Aphra said. "I think that Egbert and Carters is our next stop. Shall we separate for a while to save time?"

"Sounds like a good idea to me," Emily didn't ask why. There was no need to do so. Both girls knew the reason. They wanted to buy each other a gift. They went into the store together and then both went in different directions.

There was not much time before they would be meeting up, so she had to move swiftly. She bought presents for all the other members of the household staff.
As she made her way to the entrance, Emily joined her carrying a selection of packages. "Do you think we've time for some tea?"

They made their way to the teashop across the road and were soon enjoying a pot of steaming hot tea and a selection of fancy cakes. Although they were well fed back at the Grange, it was a real treat to be out together enjoying each other's company and being away from the scrutiny of their mistress and the housekeeper.

"Isn't this fun? "I can't remember when I last enjoyed myself so much" said Emily.

"It's wonderful," said Aphra.

"Just think how lovely it will be when she's away. I hope that the Battle-axe goes to stay with her sister. She usually does at Christmas. If she's gone for a week, then we can have a whole seven days without their nastiness. Mr Isaacs is a treasure. He doesn't mind if we enjoy ourselves. Although he's rather quiet and keeps himself to himself, he does join in a bit at Christmas. He leads us in the carol singing. He has a lovely voice."

"Yes, I've heard him at church on a Sunday. It's a lovely tenor and with old Joseph's baritone, they harmonise together well. Oh, Emily. I can't wait. It's been so long since I had a really happy Christmas. I'd been expecting to spend Christmas with Mrs Brookes." She fell silent for a few moments as she remembered the kind old lady, whom she had grown to love dearly. "We're going to have a wonderful time, aren't we?"

After settling their bill, the two girls walked back to where Mickey was waiting for them. He was giving the horse a bit of sugar and talking to it. When he looked up and saw the two girls approaching him, he gave the horse a final pat on the neck and opened the door for them.

"Had a nice time girls? I hope you didn't spend too much on my present."

"No more than you've spent on ours," laughed Emily.

They were quiet for some time and getting a bit sleepy with the movement of the carriage. Then Emily, who had been lost in thought for a while, said "so you got the position with that lady? Was it very different working for her?"

"Yes - to both questions. Mrs Brookes was a treasure. I'd have been happy to work for her for years."

"What was she like?"

"She was rather motherly - which was something I really needed at the time. I was still upset about the whole business with my father. I felt no grief for him whatsoever, but I still mourned the death of my mother."

"I can't imagine what it must be like. My family's very large and there isn't much money. We all fight like mad, but we love each other and so far, everyone is hale and hearty. I really feel for you, Aphra. You must feel so alone in the world."

"Yes, I've felt alone for a long time, but it is much better now - especially since I met you. It's like having a big sister."

"Tell me about life with Mrs Brookes."

"I usually got up early and lit all the fires. It was quite a small house, but so lovely and homely, that I used to feel quite content. It was full of photographs and souvenirs from her long and interesting life. It meant a fair bit of dusting, but I didn't mind, as they were all such lovely things and so interesting to look at. Often, when I was dusting, she would tell me about the people in the photographs and the places from where the mementos had come. She was very interesting and she had an excellent memory. I feel so sad that she has gone from my life, but at least she is not suffering any more.

I would cook her breakfast and take it up to her on a tray. Then I would help her to get out of bed. This always took a long time and was very difficult for her. I could see that she was in great pain and felt so sad that I couldn't relieve it, but she never complained. She found joy in everything around her and it was an honour to be working for her. Her rheumatics were so bad, that she could do little for herself. On particularly bad days, she would remain in her room, and sit in the small chair by the fire and take catnaps.

Sometimes, when she was in less pain, she would come downstairs. On those days, we even managed to have some fun. I'm afraid that routine rather went out of the window and I would just follow her lead. If she wanted me to play the piano for the rest of the morning and lunch was not until three in the afternoon, what did it matter? She gained pleasure from the music and we would sing, and I hope that for a while, she forget her pain.

It was sometimes very disorderly. So, on the occasions when she went to bed early – sometimes before six o clock, I would catch up with anything that needed doing. So I could be washing clothes or preparing vegetables at midnight.

She found it difficult to hold a book or a newspaper, so I would read to her. It was no hardship for me, as I loved the books. One or two, I had read at school, but there were others that I had not had the opportunity to read before, so it was a great treat for me and we shared the excitement of the stories together. She was an avid admirer of Mr Dickens. When you make a little more progress, I shall introduce you to him."

"Does he live nearby?"

At this, Aphra burst out laughing. "You silly goose, Emily. Charles Dickens was a great writer who died before we were born. He wrote the most wonderful imaginative stories about all kinds of people who had hard lives and amazing adventures. I'm sure you'd love to read them. When you read a tale like some of those that he wrote, you get lost in the story and it is as though you are there too."

"I can't wait to read one of those books. I'm certainly going to work even harder at my lessons."

"I'm certain of it." Aphra smiled to herself as she remembered the present she had bought for Emily.

They had been so engrossed in their conversation, that the time had gone quickly and they were now approaching Watheford.

"Not long now," said Emily. "Tell me a bit more, before we get back."

"I got great pleasure myself from reading the books to her and I also learned much from reading the newspaper. She always had *The Times*. I learned all about what happened in the Houses of Parliament, the Stock Exchange and all manner of things that were happening around the country and abroad. I read about countries that I had not heard of before and some of them had the most unpronounceable names you ever heard. Honestly Emily, you should have heard her laugh at my dreadful attempts to pronounce what I was reading. It was very funny."

The carriage halted and they collected up their parcels, Aphra made Emily laugh at a rendition of some of her most spectacular faux pas. As they made their way inside, they were still laughing heartily. Unfortunately, a withering look from the Housekeeper immediately lowered the mood.

They went to their respective bedrooms to put away all their gifts. Aphra then went swiftly to the drawing room to report to her mistress on her purchases. She felt a sense of trepidation, after the scolding from Miss Salathial. However, her fears were unfounded, as Caroline was in a good mood and seemed pleased with what Aphra had done

She told Aphra that the following week she would be going to spend Christmas with her friends, the Davidson's. The wife was an old school friend of hers. For one moment, Aphra had a terrible feeling that she was going to say that she required Aphra to accompany her. However, she went on to say that her friend's maid was happy to attend on her too. Aphra tried to display a look of disappointment. Caroline told her that she would be away for about three weeks and would return in the New Year. This meant that there would be a great deal of work for Aphra over the next few days making preparations for the forthcoming trip. However, Aphra did not mind this at all, for it meant that she would have three whole weeks without the whining and complaining.

"Have your meal now and then continue with that pile of mending. You'd best make it an early night, for I want you up bright and early to get started on my preparations. I don't want to have to do everything myself."

Aphra could hardly contain a snort of contempt. The woman never lifted a finger. She sat around all day, eating chocolates. It was a wonder that she wasn't fat. In fact, it was a downright injustice. Aphra maintained a pleasant smile on her face, as though she were pleased with what her mistress was saying, but in reality, she was imagining her as an ugly, squat lump with festering pustules all over her face and lank, greasy hair hanging in strips around her dumpy face.

She joined her colleagues, who were already seated at the dining table. Maud was serving the soup. As usual, it smelled delicious. There was much conversation already in progress. Emily was relating the details of their trip into town. Maud wanted to know what they had bought and was trying to find out if she would be getting any Christmas presents, and Emily took great delight in teasing her.

However, as soon as the housekeeper entered the room, a hush descended and the meal was eaten in total silence apart from requests to pass this or that. The depressive ambiance of the room was almost tangible. Aphra thought that she could almost taste it. "Talk about the spectre at the feast," she thought. However, everyone's spirits were lifted when Miss Salathial announced that she would be going to her sister's for an extended holiday seeing as she was owed some holiday from the previous year that she had not taken. She then droned on about how she had had to give up her own time to facilitate the smooth running of the house at a time of staff shortages. "What a martyr," thought Aphra in irritation. Then she dismissed these feelings of annoyance and replaced them with the thought that the horrid woman would be away from Warrington Grange for over a fortnight. It was as much as Emily and Aphra could do, not to jump up and down with glee.

However, it was Mr Isaacs who wisely said "we hope that you enjoy a well-earned rest, Miss Salathial and that you return in the New Year much refreshed."

All the staff muttered in muted agreement. Then everyone left the table to remove themselves from the housekeeper as soon as possible. Emily and Aphra had very serious expressions on their faces as they raced up the stairs to Aphra's room. They had decided earlier that they would try and get another reading lesson in if possible, while Aphra sewed. As Aphra closed her bedroom door, Emily fell on the bed and both of them spluttered with trying to hold in their laughter. She put her finger to her lips and reminded Emily of the proximity of the mistress's room and they were quiet again.

Quickly, they settled down. In the wardrobe were a couple of her mistress's gowns that needed to be repaired. As she selected the first one to mend, she wondered how it was that Caroline managed to rip her clothes so much, considering that she hardly ever seemed to move off the couch. Perhaps she was putting weight on after all, she thought with amusement.

Emily opened her book and found the page where she had left off before finishing last time.

"Right, here we are," she said looking up at Aphra, who was threading a needle. "Next stop, Mr Dinkins."

"Dickens," laughed Aphra. "Go on."

Slowly Emily began to read. She hesitated over an unfamiliar word. "Oh, this is stupid. It's so hard to understand and remember. Last week, you tried to teach me about rough and cough. Why are there all these daft rules?" Emily complained

"Don't ask me. I didn't make them up. Believe me, you'll remember. Everyone does eventually."

"Alright." Emily puffed and then carried on. After about twenty minutes, she was getting tired and finding it hard to concentrate.

"I think you've had enough for today. Don't lose heart, Emily. You're making great progress. Think how difficult you found it a few weeks ago. You hardly knew your alphabet and now you manage the small easy words with no problem at all. It's really important that you keep at it. It will get easier, you'll get faster and it will become fun. I promise."

"I know, but it's so boring. I get fed up as nothing interesting happens. It's just learning rules. I can't understand how folks like reading books."

"You will."

Aphra was also very tired and both girls decided to turn in for the night.

When Aphra blew out the candle on the bedside table, she was asleep instantly. The next thing she knew was her mistress was ringing the bell. She jumped out of bed in a panic, thinking that she had overslept. However, when she looked at the clock, she saw that it was not yet six.

"What can she want now?" Aphra thought. She quickly threw a shawl around herself and dashed next door expecting some kind of emergency.

"What kept you?" Caroline said irritably. "I've hardly slept a wink. I've worried all night that I wouldn't get everything done in time. Go and fetch me some hot milk and then we can make a start on planning what's to be done."

As Aphra rushed down to the kitchen, she thought to herself "what is wrong with that woman?" Surely nothing less than attempted murder combined with burglary and the house on fire would produce such a reaction in a person. She heated up some milk in a pan. Fortunately, the range was still fairly hot. As she poured the milk into a cup, she thought that she would like to add a drop of cyanide to it. Trudging back upstairs, she felt quite irritable, but faked a pleasing demeanour as she entered the mistress's room.

"This should help to settle you Ma'am," she said with a soothing voice.

"It's alright for you being so calm and patronising. You've no idea what I've been through. I'll be fit for nothing today and you can't be trusted to see to things on your own." She sipped at the milk. "This isn't hot enough."

"Would you like me to take it back downstairs?" Aphra asked.

"No, I'll make do," she said with a voice full of woeful resignation. "You'd best go and get yourself dressed. There's much to do."

Aphra did as instructed. Within fifteen minutes, she was dressed and returned to Caroline's room. She knocked gently on the door, but there was no answer.

"That's odd," she thought. When she looked inside, her mistress was fast asleep again. She quietly left the room and continued with her day as if nothing had happened. Two hours later, Caroline was ringing the bell again and when Aphra answered the call, she was chided for not returning earlier. Aphra waited for the tirade to finish and politely pointed out that as proof of her obeying her command, the cup had been removed for washing, at which Caroline grudgingly accepted that she had indeed been asleep when Aphra had returned. However, there was no apology and she quickly began giving orders for her forthcoming trip.

The following week passed in a whirlwind of activity. Her mood changed from hour to hour, so that there were times when Aphra did not know what jobs to tackle first. At one point, a day or two before her departure, Caroline was in an extremely irritable mood, when there was a knock at the door. Miss Salathial was standing there with the post, which had just arrived. There was a letter and a parcel – obviously from the Earl. Caroline almost snatched it from the hand of the housekeeper.

She tore at the parcel. There was a box, which she opened and extracted a very expensive gold bracelet encrusted with sapphires and diamonds. She could not hide her delight. Aphra was so pleased and relieved at the change in the atmosphere, that she shared the joy for her mistress.

"The Earl must hold you in very high regard to send such a beautiful and valuable gift," she said.

At this comment, Caroline was thrilled. "Yes, you're right. Aren't I lucky? It must be a sure sign of his intentions towards me." For the rest of the day, she was like a lamb and Aphra enjoyed her best day for a long time.

***

As Aphra watched her mistress's carriage depart down the drive, she could hardly contain her happiness. The following day, the housekeeper left and the rest of the staff decided that they would plan a special celebration that evening. Mr Isaacs opened a bottle of port, which they all enjoyed and then he made a toast to a brief respite. Aphra noticed that he had a twinkle in his eye.

The days leading up to Christmas were busy, but filled with happiness. The staff all kept up their normal duties, but what a difference there was in the atmosphere of the house. Even Mr Isaacs had a spring in his step. One morning, as Aphra was on her way to breakfast, she nearly bumped into him in the corridor.

"Oh, I'm so sorry, Mr Isaacs," she said. "I was carried away with my thoughts and walking too fast."

"That's alright my dear," he said benignly. "It's good to see you so happy. I know how hard you work. I've seen you when you think that no one is watching and I see the sadness in your eyes. I want you to really enjoy Christmas this year. I'm sure that we all will. Sometimes, a little bit of putting one's feet up ultimately produces more work and of a higher standard, so I certainly intend to relax a little bit too."

Aphra thanked him for his kindness. She'd had no idea that he had been keeping an eye on her. It gave her a warm glow to think that he cared enough to pay attention to her feelings. He reminded her of her Grandfather. He too had been kind and thoughtful.

A few days before Christmas Eve, Aphra realised that she had caught up with all her work with the exception of one item. She had been surprised that Caroline had not given her a list of things to do. She suspected that this was because she really had no idea how much work Aphra did. Now all the mending was done, save the one item that she was keeping to be seen attending to when Miss Salathial arrived home a few days before the mistress. She had taken a good look through the closets and satisfied herself that everything else was in order.

As far as correspondence was concerned, Caroline had given her instructions that anything from the Earl was to be forwarded to her, together with anything that may be of a confidential or sensitive nature. Aphra was so familiar with those correspondents that wrote regularly, that she knew, without opening the letters, which things to save and which to forward.

Aphra now had some spare time on her hands, so she had stepped up the reading lessons in the evenings. Emily was beginning to gain more confidence. Aphra could not wait to see her face when she opened her present.

Everyone joined in the decorating of the tree. Gracie had been preparing for months. She had made a plum pudding and a Christmas cake. Aphra spent hours seated at the table with the others making decorations and as much time again in her room making cards and wrapping presents for her new friends.

On Christmas Day, she woke early. She tiptoed along to the bathroom. She stripped off and stepped into the hot water. She lay back and shut her eyes. Her mind wondered back to the first time she had laid in this bath.

It was exactly four months ago that she had arrived at Warrington Grange. What a sorry figure she had cut. She smiled to herself when she thought about Gracie's face when she encountered this scruffy stranger. She had been about to shoo her away, when she heard Aphra speak and knew that she was not a tramp. She was so grateful to her. She wondered how long it would have taken her to die out there in the woods.

And now here she lay in this lovely warm scented water. She stirred the water around with her long shapely legs. Four months of healthy food and fresh country air meant that she had put on a little weight. This was not to say that she was corpulent – quite the reverse was true, for the months of hard work had toned her body. In fact, she had grown a little taller and her waist was smaller, but her breasts had filled out and her hips were more rounded. Of late, she had become rather uncomfortable at the way Albert kept leering at her. She felt embarrassed and didn't know what to do about it. Perhaps Emily would know, for she was more worldly.

Once she was back in her room, she took extra care with her appearance. She had treated herself to a cream coloured lace collar that she could tuck into her plain black dress. Once her hair was dry and finger curled, she brushed it vigorously and tied it back in a green ribbon that contrasted with her auburn hair and brought out the colour of her green eyes. Then she pinned her brooch to her bodice. Daringly, she added just a hint of rouge to her cheeks and a little cologne behind each ear. She looked in the full-length mirror and was quite pleased at her reflection. Her skin was clear and her eyes were bright and although she had auburn hair, the texture was not coarse or frizzy, but soft and glossy. No longer was she a slip of a girl, but a woman and she thought that she looked very nice.

Satisfied with her appearance, she made her way down to breakfast. She was so excited that she found herself running down the stairs. When she reached the bottom, she forced herself to slow down, as she did not want to bump into the butler again. She told herself, that she needed to be more dignified. She entered the dining room. She could see Gracie and Maud in the kitchen preparing the food. They looked up and saw her.

"Merry Christmas, Aphra."

"And a very Merry Christmas to you both," she replied. "I'm so excited. I can't believe that it is actually here at last."

"This one's been all worked up this morning. Can't keep her mind on her work or her hands on the dishes. She's dropped two bowls and broken them. Good thing the dragon's away or there'd be trouble. Ah, there's the gang coming in now. Go and join them and we'll serve up."

Emily was the last one to arrive. She looked a bit flustered and it was fairly obvious to everyone that she had overslept. She gave Aphra a hug. "A really Merry Christmas to you, my dear friend."

Gracie bustled in. "C'mon you lot. Get this porridge down you. It's just this and toast this morning. I've got too much to be getting on with to spend time cooking bacon and eggs. Besides, you don't want to spoil your appetites for the goose. And watch you don't break another bowl young lady," added Gracie. "If you break the sugar bowl, you'll have to pay for it. We can't hide that from you know who."

Aphra asked when the presents were to be opened and learned that it was usually after the lunch dishes had been cleared away. She was soon quite busy helping Emily and Ivy lay the table for lunch. They decorated it with holly, candles and napkins. They used the best tablecloth and cutlery that the mistress allowed for the staff. Gracie told Maud to stay away from the crockery and the glassware, as she was a menace this morning. Maud just shrugged and made her way to the scullery. She sang to herself as her rough, red hands with their bitten nails moved swiftly around the potatoes and carrots.

In the servants' parlour, everything was ready. The tree looked magnificent with its cheerful trimming and beneath it, all the presents. The mantelpiece was covered in decorations and the fire was ready to be lit. There were three oil lamps and two candelabras. One was placed on an old pianoforte that the mistress had given the servants when she had bought a new and better one for upstairs. It was a rare gesture of generosity from her and one that had given much pleasure at previous Christmases. Mr Isaacs played a little bit – usually he accompanied the carol singing. Old Joseph had an old fiddle and was rather good at it. Emily had told Aphra that he knew some merry tunes for dancing to.

Everyone except Gracie began donning their outer wear in preparation for the walk to the village church. She declared that she was doing the Lord's work in the kitchen and had read her prayer book before she put the meat in the oven. She did not say that she thought it would need all the help the Good Lord could give to get lunch on the table without Maud causing some calamity beforehand! Besides, she thought that she might help herself to a drop of sherry before the others got back from church. After all, she deserved it. So, while she bustled about her domain enjoying peace and quiet and a chance to get her thoughts in order, the rest of the staff walked the short distance to the small church in Watheford.

It was a bright and crisp morning – perfect for Christmas Day. As they entered the village, the party from the Grange met up with the locals in their best outfits. The bells were ringing and as they walked through the churchyard, the choir could be heard warming up with *O Come All Ye Faithful* and the congregation, as it filled up the little church, joined in.

There were some familiar faces from the local community. Aphra now recognised the Post-Mistress, Miss Gaffney, Mr Mason, who owned the general store and a couple of the local girls who worked at The Grange three days a week. Albert met a few of his old pals with whom he'd gone to school and who occasionally joined him for a drink at *The Plough*. There was a great deal of "Merry Christmas" and "Seasons greetings," together with hand shaking and backslapping. Mr Isaacs allowed them a minute or two of this and then reminded them that it was time to take their seats and they all filed into the small Norman church. They sat down in the pews that were allotted for their use. The church was now quietening down, except for a few coughs here and there.

Suddenly, everyone stood up as six altar boys entered carrying candles, followed by the vicar. The whole ceremony had a great theatrical atmosphere and a sense of occasion. The vicar entered the pulpit and everyone sat down again. The Reverend Ivan Roberts coughed and cleared his throat nervously. He kept his sermons short, for which his parishioners were extremely grateful. His predecessor was notorious for droning on for over an hour and it was not unusual for snoring to be heard from more than one pew!

The sermon was all about giving – not only at Christmas, but throughout the year. He reminded his flock that they needed to show gratitude to the Lord for all their blessings. A number of people nodded in agreement. One or two others privately thought that it was all right for him, in his warm, comfortable vicarage, with an annual stipend to cover all his needs. However, the majority of the congregation were in a good mood today and were looking forward to enjoying a hearty meal and a few tankards of ale.

Reverend Roberts led them in another carol and then uttered his closing words – wishing them a merry Christmas and reminding them that this was a religious feast and not to over indulge in food and drink. This was said with a suggestion of tongue in cheek and there would be very few who would be taking heed at this – certainly not most of the party from The Grange. As he dismounted the steps, the choir and congregation stood up and began singing *Hark the Herald Angels Sing*. This was Aphra's favourite carol and she sang out with all her heart. The vicar led the exodus from the church and waited outside to greet his flock as they left. The party from the Grange followed Mr Isaacs down the aisle. He stopped and had a brief word with Reverend Roberts.

Once outside, the noise increased and people greeted each other. Mr Isaacs knew that most of his young charges had families in the village and so did not rush them to return immediately. Quietly, he made his way over to the churchyard and spent ten minutes in quiet reflection at one of the graves. Emily introduced Aphra to her large, boisterous family. There were so many and all were talking at once, so that the only names she remembered were Mr and Mrs Frances. As they made their way down the path towards the lych-gate, there was quite a bit of shouting and raucous laughter quite inappropriate for the vicinity of a church.

Mr Isaacs suggested that it was time to get back. Everyone followed him through the woods to the Grange. Maud and Albert spent five minutes canoodling behind a hedge, thinking that no one could see them. However, Mr Isaacs swiftly brought this activity to an end.

Aphra and Emily decided to take a walk in the woods.

"I feel so happy that you're here," said Emily.

"Believe me. I'm happy to be here," Aphra replied. "I can't remember when I last felt so happy. This morning when I lay in the bath, I thought about the day that I arrived. It was exactly four months ago today. If Gracie had turned me away, I would have died out here. I hope that I'm never in that predicament again. I've been putting away some money in savings and I intend to stay here for many years. Hopefully, the mistress will keep me on. She said that she would review my salary after six months, so perhaps in February, there will be a little bit extra. I think that my work has been more than satisfactory."

"Don't depend on her keeping her word. She says that to everyone, but rarely keeps her part of the bargain," Emily warned her.

"I was hoping for a few extra shillings to save. Never mind. I'm not going to let it get me down – certainly not on this special day."

They walked a little further on and Emily told Aphra more stories about her family and village life. Then she asked Aphra to continue telling her about life with Mrs Brookes.

"There isn't much more to tell really. Her health began to deteriorate further and it was very sad to see her in so much pain. Eventually, she ate nothing. She had no appetite. In the end, I knew that she just wanted to go to sleep. One day, she went to sleep and did not wake up. I sat by her bed and was with her at the end. Before she went to sleep, she told me that she loved me and thanked me for making her final days as happy and comfortable as possible. I felt very sad and yet honoured.

She had no children, but there was a nephew called James. He was her only relative. I knew him a little bit, as he had called a few of times towards the end. He was quite pleasant and I know that he was fond of his aunt.

James, Mr Greaves, the solicitor, and I were the only mourners at her funeral. Afterwards, Mr Greaves came back to the house to read the will. The bulk of her estate she had left to James, but it turned out that she had left me fifty pounds. I was quite shocked. I had not expected anything at all. I was very grateful and thought that it would set me up nicely and that I would not have to worry about money. It was a great relief to know that I would be alright, for I have to admit that a few days after she died, I did start to worry what was going to happen to me. When I left the house, James handed me an envelope. It contained a letter thanking me for my services to his aunt, and sixty pounds. He had added ten pounds of his own money. I had been saving my wages and had another five pounds of my own."

"That was not that long ago. If you had all that money, how come you ended up in such a terrible mess by this summer?" Emily enquired.

"Although I was sad about her death and I missed Mrs Brookes very much, I felt very optimistic about the future. I was so naive." She shook her head in disbelief at her own stupidity.

"What happened?" Emily asked.

"After I left Mrs Brooke's house, I took a room in an establishment where the rent was very low. I thought that this was the best course of action, for I didn't want to waste a lot of money on rent whilst looking for work. I had a reference, some experience and thought that my future looked bright and so it would have been, if I'd had the foresight to put my money in a bank."

"Do you mean that you were robbed?" Emily looked at her friend with compassion. "Oh Aphra how horrid for you."

"Mother and Grandfather were always honest and we were taught that at school. None of my friends ever stole. I know now that I was very foolish, but I had never known anyone to steal. I should not have left the money in my room. I had gone out to purchase a newspaper to see if there were any situations. When I returned, I found that the lock was broken and everything of value was gone, including most of my clothes and a few pieces of jewellery. I had some nice things that Mrs Brookes had bought for me and some trinkets that she had given me, including a pair of gloves. Fortunately, I was wearing my brooch that mama gave to me before she died. I had about three pounds left in my bag, together with my reference. There was no one to help me. I spoke to the landlord, but he just made a lewd suggestion, so I knew that I needed to find somewhere else to stay – and soon."

Emily's eyes widened at the prospect of the landlord making unwanted advances towards Aphra. She fully appreciated the peril that Aphra had been in. "You must have been very frightened."

"I was, although I have no idea what he intended to do to me and I didn't want to find out either. I'll admit that I'm quite ignorant in the ways of the world. I pushed the tallboy in front of the door in case anyone else tried to get into my room. I'd paid my rent to the end of the week, but the next morning, as soon as it got light, I put everything that was left in my bag and crept down the stairs and out of the door. I was so scared that I held my breath until I was out in the street."

"That was a sensible move," said Emily, who was much more knowledgeable of the subject having come from a large family and growing up in a house with thin walls. "You were in great danger. Thank goodness you got away. What happened then?"

"I stayed for some time in a better class of establishment, but I was unable to find any work similar to the work I had been doing for Mrs Brookes. I ended up spending a few weeks doing various menial jobs which paid very little money. However, it did help to supplement the small amount that I had remaining in my purse. However, eventually the money ran out and I had to leave. I spent a few nights sleeping in an old church and even had to beg for food. It was so humiliating." Aphra suddenly went very quiet.

"What is it?" Emily asked.

"I feel very ashamed to talk about this. One night, I could not find shelter and slept on a park bench." She hesitated and then continued. "I was awoken in the middle of the night by a dirty, smelly drunkard kneeling on the ground and putting his filthy hands under my dress and feeling inside my thighs. At the same time, he was licking my face. The smell of his breath was disgusting." She shuddered. "Ugh! It was horrible. I pushed him off me and jumped up kicking him so hard that he fell back and hit his head on the ground. I think that I may have killed him, but I just grabbed my bag and ran as fast and as far as I could."

"Oh how terrible! You've really been through it, haven't you? You've no need to feel ashamed. He was just a dirty ol' bugger and if he died – well good riddance to him," Emily said.

"After that, I managed to get work as a maid in a small house in a rundown district of the city. It was not a very nice house. It was filthy and damp and in a dreadful state of repair. The people were awful, and they put upon me all the time. Eventually, it turned out that they were only renting the property and they were in arrears with the rent. It was not long before they were evicted and there was no money to pay me. I had not been paid since I had started there, so they owed me quite a bit. There had been very little food and I was often hungry.

Once again, I found myself homeless, jobless and penniless. I ended up washing dishes in a hotel, but the pay was very low – hardly enough to keep body and soul together. The work was hard and relentless. I slept in the basement on sacking. My clothes were becoming shabbier. I was desperate. One day, I found a copy of *The Bath Evening Gazette*. It was a recent one and when I went for my break, I took it to read. It was there that I saw the situation of Lady's Maid at Warrington Grange advertised. I helped myself to a sheet of writing paper from the hotel and an envelope. I did not feel that this was morally wrong. I was almost destitute and I had been working all hours for months and for a pittance – they owed it to me."

"Quite right too," Emily agreed.

"I wrote to Miss Grenville in such a way that she would think that I was a guest at the hotel. I didn't lie. I was just careful how I worded it. When the reply arrived, it was marked private and confidential. The Manager was curious when he handed it to me, but I gave no inkling as to what it was about. I was relieved to see that I had a date for an interview. I had no idea how I was going to make the journey. I had a small amount left in my purse – which, I might add, never left my side. I told the Proprietor that I would be leaving and he was surprisingly reasonable and handed me the money that I was owed. It was not much, but I hoped that it would get me to Warrington Grange. However, there wasn't even enough for the fare to Westbridge. The coachman put me off the coach on the other side of the town. I had to walk the rest of the way. I had to sleep rough and had no food other than some bread and cheese given to me by a kind man.

It took me six days and that was why I was in such a state when I arrived. Looking back, I wonder how I could have been so naïve, but I had no experience of life."

"Aphra, I had no idea that you had been through so much. You've been very unlucky, but also very brave too."

"Well, I must say I'm glad it's all behind me now. I've had my share of hard times and things can only get better. Speaking of things getting better, that goose should be cooked by now and I'm famished."

When they entered the dining room, delicious aromas emanating from the steamed up kitchen assailed their nostrils and the usual jocularity coupled with grumbling assaulted their ears.

They all took their seats and laughed at what had basically become normal everyday background noise from the kitchen. Everyone could tell from the increasing volume of the noise, together with a few expletives, that the serving of the meal was imminent. Mr Isaacs tutted to himself at the language as he opened a bottle of Gracie's homemade Elderberry wine and began pouring it out.

Within ten minutes, the noise had subsided substantially as everyone tucked into what was a wonderful feast. Mr Isaacs congratulated Gracie and Maud for an excellent meal and also thanked Joseph and Albert for their contributions from the garden. Maud managed to drop a greasy parsnip on the tablecloth, for which Gracie chided her yet again. Maud was about to go into a sulk, when Mr Isaacs stood up and made a toast.

"I should like to wish all of you and your families a very merry Christmas and a happy new year. Also, may there be peace and prosperity for all."

At this, everyone cheered and said "Here here!" He walked around the table refilling glasses as Gracie and Maud cleared away the plates.

"I should like to say something." Everyone looked at Aphra. "It's just that I wanted to say thank you to everyone for such a lovely day so far, but especially to Gracie – not just for a wonderful dinner – that goes without saying – but - well, if it hadn't been for your kindness to me Gracie, I wouldn't be here today. In fact, I don't know if I'd be alive."

"Oh get on with ya' girl. Don't go getting all soft," Gracie said all embarrassed. "Let's get this clearing up done, then we can open our presents."

She told Maud to start clearing away the dishes. Everyone was feeling rather lethargic due to the numerous glasses of elderberry wine. Maud was no different from any of the others and did not feel like doing anything. She started to whine about always being the one to have to do everything and how unfair it was, when Mr Isaacs pointed out that the sooner the clearing up was done, the sooner they could all open their presents. Maud saw the wisdom of this and reluctantly made her way into the scullery. The pile of greasy pans seemed much higher than she remembered it from before the meal. Slowly, she began working her way through it. It was not long before the other women joined her and they got through it much quicker than they had expected. Once order had been restored, Gracie made a large pot of tea, which the girls carried into the parlour together with milk, sugar and the cups and saucers.

When they entered the room, they found that Albert had already lit the oil lamps and the candles and Ivy had got the fire going, so that there was a really homely feel about the room. Mr Isaacs suggested that Aphra, being the newest member of staff, might like to be in charge of handing out the gifts.

"Oh, Mr Isaacs, I'd love to." She was thrilled to be asked. For the next hour she was kept busy trying to decipher names and handing out the gifts to her friends. As expected, the writing led to one or two episodes of muddle, but on the whole, she handled it excellently and enjoyed every minute of it. A few cheeky remarks were made and there were lots of cries of "Just what I wanted!" Everyone seemed very pleased with his or her particular gift and they all especially liked the items that Aphra had either bought or made. Aphra could not wait to see Emily's face as she unwrapped the present that she had bought her. She was not disappointed. Emily was delighted to have her first proper book. Aphra had written inside it. *To my special friend. May you enjoy this and many more wonderful stories in the years to come.*

"C'mon now young lady," said Gracie. "I didn't go to all that trouble to have that present remain in its wrapping."

"Yes, my dear. You've done very well," added Mr Isaacs fondly. "Now it's your turn to see what surprises await you."

Aphra looked at the large pile of gifts and cards awaiting her. "Goodness me. What a huge pile."

"Shall I help with these wrappings?" Emily asked.

"Oh, please do, Emily. Otherwise I'm going to be all night and I'm sure that everybody else would like to get on with something else. I'm feeling rather self-conscious all of a sudden."

Together with Emily's help, she worked her way through the gifts. By the time, she had unwrapped the last gift, she was overcome with emotion. "I'm sorry about this. I know I'm making a spectacle of myself, but you have no idea what today has meant to me. I shall treasure these gifts and the memory of your generosity for the rest of my life – not only for these gifts, but for your friendship too."

Then Joseph spoke. "It's time you dried your tears Miss. I think we need some music."

"Oh, goodie," said Maud. "Are we going to sing and dance?"

Joseph was giving a final tuning to his fiddle as he said. "Oh yes."

He started playing a local tune and Albert and Maud were the first ones up and doing a jig. Mickey and Ivy soon followed. Aphra was not familiar with it nor the next two or three.

When he'd finished, Joseph declared that he needed a rest, so Mr Isaacs was induced to play some carols on the pianoforte. He must have played for almost an hour and they sang every carol that they knew. Gracie suggested more tea, but Albert remarked that he was very thirsty from singing and dancing and something stronger would be far more welcome. This attracted a raucous bout of laughter from everyone and Mr Isaacs asked Maud and Albert to fetch the ale in. He then turned to the cook and asked her if she still preferred tea. The answer was somewhat uncouth – to which he started to tut to himself as was his way.

The ale was distributed and thirsts quenched. Emily mentioned that Aphra knew how to play the pianoforte. She had never told anyone else apart from Emily and her mistress and was embarrassed.

"Emily, I haven't played for a very long time. I'll be dreadful."

"No you won't. Just get on with it." She pushed Aphra off the couch and the rest of the party began clapping, so that she had no option, but to give in and play."

Nervously, she sat down at the keyboard and flexed her fingers. Looking down at the keys and biting her lower lip, she started to play. First, she tried out Beethoven's *Fur Elise*. The change in tempo was just what was needed. Everyone listened spellbound. When she finished, her confidence was restored, not only by the applause, but by the fact that she had produced a faultless performance. She could see that they were all impressed and she went on to play a Chopin prelude and then some Schumann. She finished off with a piece by Liszt. She knew that she was showing off, but she just couldn't resist it. It had been so long since she had played. She stood up, took a bow and started to giggle. Everyone clapped and cheered loudly. After this, she sat back at the keyboard and played the accompaniment for them all to sing some well-known favourites. Joseph played his fiddle and Albert joined in too on his penny whistle.

It was now dark outside and snow had begun to fall. Gracie waddled off to the kitchen to make some sandwiches and cut some cake. Maud followed her. Aphra felt quite warm with all the excitement and decided to step outside for five minutes to get some air. She thought that she would just walk around by the kitchen garden towards the parterre. There was just enough light from the house to see where she was going. She stepped carefully, as snow was beginning to settle and it was a bit slippery. Suddenly, she sensed that someone was behind her.

"Who's there?"
She turned and was grabbed and pushed up against the garden wall.

"Stop it. Leave me al…" she started to shout, but a hand went over her mouth for a moment.

"Shush. We don't want anyone to hear or see us." It was Albert and he reeked of ale.
"C'mon, give us a kiss" he slurred "I know you want me. I've seen you looking at me."

"I've done no such thing, Albert. You're drunk and making a fool of yourself. Now leave me alone," she said.

He put his hand under her cape and started to grope at her as he kissed and licked her neck.

"Please stop it," she pleaded. "Think of Maud. She's your girl. You're being disloyal." He started to pull at her collar, which came away in his hand. He began to unbutton his trousers. She knew that if she didn't act quickly, he was going to tear her clothes off and she was terrified of what was going to happen after that. She fought him with both hands, but he was too strong for her. Although she had led a very sheltered life and knew little of male anatomy, she had learned one thing and it came into her mind just in time. She raised her knee with such speed and force that he doubled up. As he started to straighten up and move towards her again, she removed her glove and struck him across the face so hard that the mark was still there hours later.

"How dare you insult me in this way and how dare you cheat on Maud. Men like you disgust me. You'd better not try this again. Do you hear me?" She realised that she was shouting so loudly at him that in a few seconds, Mickey and Emily came running from the house with Maud bringing up the rear. At first, they couldn't understand what was happening. Emily picked up the lace collar from the snow. The ribbon had also fallen out of Aphra's hair which was now very dishevelled.

Albert dashed past them and into the house. As he pushed past Mr Isaacs, who had come out to see what all the fuss was about, the butler saw the angry red mark of a hand on his cheek. "Go to my parlour," he demanded. When Albert hesitated, he added "Now!" in a voice so unexpectedly loud that it shocked everyone.

Gracie came to the kitchen door. "What's going on?" By this time, both Aphra and Maud were in tears.

Joseph turned to Mickey. "I think the party's over lad. I'd turn in if I were you."

Mickey nodded and said goodnight to everyone and made his way to his room above the stable.

As Gracie and Emily tried to comfort the two weeping girls, Joseph made his way to the butler's parlour and knocked on the door. He'd heard enough to realise what had happened.

"Come in," called Mr Isaacs. He was standing over Albert who was slouched on a chair. "Well lad. I'm waiting for an answer," he demanded. "Did you touch her?"

"What if I did? It's Christmas, isn't it. We were just having a bit of grown up fun."

"It didn't look to me as if Miss Chamberlain was having fun. She looked very distraught indeed." Joseph had never seen the butler looking angry before. He was certainly displaying his authority.

"I suggest that you go to your room and sleep it off. We'll discuss this in the morning when you're sober, but you'll be looking for employment before the day is out. In fact, you could go to prison for this. However, I'm sure that the mistress would not want this incident to become public knowledge, so think yourself lucky."

Albert staggered out of the room and banged the door behind him muttering under his breath at the same time.

"It looks as though he molested the girl from what I heard them saying out there," said Joseph. "I've been watching him leering at her for weeks. It's my fault. I should have said something, but I never thought it'd come to this."

"Don't blame yourself man. How could you have known that he'd behave in such a manner? I'll have to dismiss him, but I'll need to speak to Miss Chamberlain in the morning first. There's no point making things worse for her by questioning her tonight." He looked at his pocket watch. It was nearly eight o clock.

"Let's wind things up for the day. I expect that Mrs Talbot has made that tea" he said in the gentle voice that everyone was used to. "I'll be out in a while."

As Joseph closed the door behind him, the butler flopped into his chair by the fire. He suddenly felt very old.

Gracie already had the kettle boiling. The sandwiches were already made and she had cut a few slabs from the cake. She carried everything to the dining room. After a few minutes, Mr Isaacs joined them. It was a sombre gathering and the sound of spoons stirring cups could be heard above the silence. Aphra had lost her appetite, but Mr Isaacs quietly told everyone that it would be a shame if this unpleasant incident was to spoil their day. They all appreciated the wisdom of these words and tried to cheer up and eat a little of what Gracie had prepared.

Later that night in bed, Emily went over in her mind what had happened out in the garden. She was in no doubt that Albert had attempted to rape Aphra. Strangely, it wasn't this that had shocked her most of all. It was Aphra's reaction. She appeared to be more upset that he was cheating on Maud than the attack itself. When Emily had grabbed hold of her, she was so angry that Emily had difficulty in getting through to her. Where was the serene and accomplished girl playing that beautiful music on the pianoforte a short while earlier?

She had started babbling about her father and saying he was a cheat who killed her mother. As Emily had comforted her, she broke down and sobbed all the way back to the house. At this point, Maud realised what Albert had done and began to cry too. They had gone into the kitchen and when Aphra had calmed down, she turned and looked at Maud.

"I'm so sorry Maud. You didn't deserve this." She put her hand out to the other girl who grabbed it. Maud sat down next to her and put her head in her hands and wept as Aphra put her arms around her.

"I thought he loved me," she wailed. "I don't understand why he did that tonight. I thought we were going to get married. He's a rotter."

Aphra did not know what to say to comfort her. "I know," she said soothingly. Eventually, Maud blew her nose and wiped her eyes.

"You'll feel better in the morning dearie," said Gracie.

"It's going to take a lot more than a night to get over being betrayed by the person she loves most in the world," Aphra said so forcefully that Gracie was taken aback.

At this point, Mr Isaacs intervened and suggested that it had been a long and eventful day and that perhaps they would all benefit from an early night. They all agreed that this was a good idea and within a few minutes each person headed towards his or her respective bedroom. Emily took Maud upstairs after satisfying herself that Aphra was calmer.

"I'll be alright. I'm very tired and will sleep well," she told her, but although she did sleep deeply, it was a sleep filled with nightmares about her mother and herself barefoot and dressed in ragged nightgowns. They were standing in the snow looking through a window crying. Inside, her father and Agnes were laughing uncontrollably at their grief. When she awoke in the early hours, she was trembling and drenched in sweat. She felt so angry that another Christmas had been spoilt by a philandering cheat. She curled herself up into a ball, hugged her pillow and talked silently to her mother as she had often done before. It was the only way that she knew how to comfort herself.

The following morning, Mr Isaacs questioned her about the incident. Naturally, he would have to inform the mistress of the reason for Albert's dismissal. However, once he was satisfied that Aphra had not suffered any physical harm, he told her that there would be no more discussion on the subject. An hour later, she looked out of an upstairs window and saw Albert trudging down the drive in a defeated manner carrying his things in a sack over his shoulder. They neither saw nor heard of him again. It was a long time before Maud stopped crying herself to sleep.

PART TWO - THE UNSELFISH GIANT

It was in January that the mistress informed Aphra that they would be going to stay at Methuen Park, the seat of the Earl of Tawford for two weeks in February. He was hosting a house party for a number of guests, including Caroline. It was common knowledge below stairs that she had set her cap at the Earl and everyone expected that this house party was being given so that the Earl would have an opportunity of getting to know her better and making a marriage proposal.

Although he had visited Caroline a number of times since Aphra had been at Warrington Grange, she had only seen him once briefly. She had been upstairs and glimpsed through the banisters, a very tall and imposing man dressed in expensive clothes that did not seem to fit properly.

"Good afternoon, Milord," said Mr Isaacs. "Miss Grenville is expecting you."

Although Aphra was to learn later that his disposition was kindly and benign, the way in which he carried himself suggested a kind of imperial arrogance, such was the masterful swagger he employed in the way that he strode across the entrance hall.

"Don't worry Isaacs," he said with a dismissive wave of the hand. "I know the way."

Aphra was surprised to hear a soft, lilting, slightly Irish brogue, as he easily mounted the stairs, three at a time. She stepped back into the shadow of a side corridor so that he did not see her as he passed. He must have been the tallest man that she had ever seen, being about six foot five. Here was a man who would visibly dominate any group of people with whom he had contact. From what she could see, she liked his face. It was not what one would call conventionally handsome, for his features were not regular, but it was attractive because it radiated warmth and humour.

Aphra had been kept out of the way, for her mistress feared that her beauty, intelligence and quiet, assured disposition was a threat to her own social superiority, and although it was inconceivable that a man in his social position would be interested in a lowly servant, Caroline was not prepared to risk any possible competition from her attractive maid.

However, Caroline needed Aphra's assistance on this trip and had decided to let her accompany her, for when she had visited her friends at

Christmas, sharing a maid had not proved successful. Besides, she could not arrive at Methuen Park without a personal maid.

The Earl sent one of his best carriages and two liveried coachmen to escort the two ladies to his home. Caroline saw this as proof of his intentions and this boosted her confidence about the proposal even more. After much exhausting preparation on Aphra's part, they set off for Methuen Park, which was located over twenty miles distant from Warrington Grange. During the journey, Caroline talked continuously about the Earl. She stressed the importance of this trip and that she suspected he was going to ask her a very important question, leaving Aphra in no doubt as to her aspirations of marriage.

Although, Caroline seemed excited, Aphra did not feel that there was any real affection for the Earl himself. Admittedly, Caroline found him physically attractive. However, it was the title, the grand house and the estates in both England and Ireland that would earn her respect, not only within the county, but also in aristocratic circles throughout the country. That was the real attraction. It was not so much the money, as the status, for Caroline was very wealthy in her own right. Her father had made a fortune, but his Knighthood had only been granted in recognition of his industrial success. There were some, in the higher echelons of county society, who looked down on Caroline's origins in trade. Caroline desperately craved an improved social position and to become the Countess of Tawford would fulfil a lifetime of social climbing.

In the weeks preceding the visit, she had given Aphra the task of researching the life and background of the Earl. Caroline was very lazy and could not be bothered to attend to this herself, so she told her to take the carriage to Taunton to buy numerous books on the history of his family, social etiquette of the aristocracy and anything pertaining to him or his interests. This included wading through large tomes on politics, farming, art, history, geography and music. Aphra was to do all the hard work and pick out any salient points and note them down for her mistress. Caroline wanted to impress the Earl with her seemingly extensive knowledge of anything that was important to him. Although the task had been demanding and robbed Aphra of much sleep, she had not minded this at all, for she enjoyed learning and was always eager to improve her mind and expand her horizons.

However, there were times when the mistress was being particularly difficult or nasty that she was tempted to feed her the wrong information. However, she resisted the temptation, for she thought such behaviour was beneath her. Besides, it might backfire and lead to her dismissal.

She even recruited Emily to help her find certain items in the books and it was this experience that really opened the housemaid's eyes to the value of reading. Although much of what they looked at went over her head, Emily could see how one's knowledge and understanding of the world could increase. For this alone, Aphra was extremely pleased. On more than one occasion, she noticed her friend absorbed in a new and fascinating subject. She inwardly reflected with amusement, how her mistress would be horrified to know that her housemaid was getting an education and that she herself had supplied the books!

Aphra seemed to be the busiest she had ever been in her life and she often went to bed exhausted from running up and down the stairs all day and then studying well into the night. However, all the preparations finally came to an end, and after a mountain of trunks and cases were loaded onto the back and the roof of the carriage, they set off early on the Monday of the second week in February. It was a cold, crisp morning. The sun was trying to break through the clouds and Caroline was full of optimism about the visit. The journey was uneventful and soon she fell asleep for about an hour, leaving Aphra free to enjoy the scenery of the beautiful countryside that they passed. She had not been to this part of the county before and immediately fell in love with the gentle rolling hills with their patchwork of fields. Here and there were dotted little copses and spinneys. Most of the trees were still bare and the hedgerows were still awaiting the buds to appear. Aphra wondered if they would be showing when they returned home.

The carriage went down a winding road and then slowed down as it turned to the left. They travelled about two hundred yards before the coachman halted at a lodge. Caroline awoke.

"Are we here?"

"I think so," Aphra replied. She leant out of the carriage. "We seem to have stopped at a lodge with some large gates."

"Oh, good. This will be it." Caroline was suddenly wide awake and very animated. "Do I look alright? Get my mirror," she demanded. "I want to check my hair."

The lodge-keeper came out of the small house and opened the gates. The coachman spoke briefly to him and then the carriage continued up a curved tree-lined avenue.   As the driveway straightened out, the imposing front of Methuen Park came into view. Caroline gasped in awe.

"It's truly beautiful," she exclaimed.

"It most certainly is," added Aphra. For a few minutes, both women were silent as they absorbed the size and grandeur of the edifice. They both had their own private thoughts. Aphra was thinking to herself how much work and expense such a place demanded. Caroline was thinking "soon all this will be mine."

It took quite some time to reach the house as the driveway was very long. When the coach stopped, two liveried footmen were waiting to assist Caroline. Aphra was about to follow her, when her mistress said "you can go around to the servants' entrance." Looking up at the nearest coachman, she added "Perhaps you can direct my maidservant to the appropriate entrance, my good man."

Addressing Aphra again, she told her to make sure that the luggage was sent to the correct room.

"Yes Ma'am," she replied. As the carriage pulled away, Aphra watched her mistress mount the steep flight of steps to the grand portico in the centre of the building. She told herself that she was glad to be alone at last, but in truth, she felt a bit peeved at the callous way her mistress had dismissed her after all the work that she had done. Then she chided herself for being foolish.

The coach pulled up outside a door to the side of the house.

"This is where you can go in Miss. Don't worry about the luggage. We'll see that it gets to the correct destination."

"Are you sure? I'm quite happy to help out," she said as she stepped down on to the gravel. "I would prefer to do so. I'm worried about something going astray."

"Things don't go astray here. You go and get yourself some refreshment. The housekeeper will help you out. Just ask for Mrs Williams. She'll make sure that everything goes like clockwork."

Aphra thanked him and made her way towards the servants' entrance. As she closed the door behind her, a cheerful looking woman in her fifties approached her.

"And who might you be, young lady?" She had a soft voice and warm smiling brown eyes.

"I'm Miss Grenville's maid. My name's Miss Chamberlain," she replied, trying to instil some confidence into her voice.

"Well, I'm very pleased to meet you, my dear. I'm Mrs Williams, the housekeeper. I expect that you could do with some refreshment. C'mon. Follow me. The dining hall is just along here."

Any fears or nervousness that Aphra had a few moments earlier were dispelled at the woman's friendliness.

"Don't worry just yet about your mistress. She'll be with his Lordship for a while. Just you sit down there. Elsie, move up and let Miss Chamberlain sit next to you. There you are my dear," she said as she lightly placed a hand on Aphra's shoulder. Aphra squeezed in next to the young woman called Elsie. The meal was tasty and very welcome and Aphra found that the staff were all very friendly and cheerful.

After the meal was finished, Aphra followed one of the footmen along the corridor, glancing into the rooms that they passed. The bedrooms were certainly very grand, with four poster beds and rich brocade hangings and deep, patterned carpets. The walls were covered in oil paintings with ornate gilt frames.

The corridor was long and carpeted with a crimson runner. Again, the walls were covered in numerous oil paintings - some of which she recognised from her weeks of studying for Caroline.

Eventually, the footman stopped in front of a door and knocked.

"Enter!" Came the imperious command.

The footman opened the door and Aphra went in.

"Ah Aphra. I wondered where you'd got to," she said irritably. "What have you been doing all this while? I need you to unpack as soon as possible.

"My apologies, ma'am, but the housekeeper said tha ..."

"Yes, all right, don't witter on. There's plenty of work to be done." She wasn't going to let Aphra know that she had only just returned to her room. She was feeling decidedly peeved that the room she had been given was not as grand as some that she had passed on her way here.
In the grate, a welcoming fire was roaring away, making the chamber warm and cosy.

"This is such a beautiful room, ma'am," Aphra said, recognising the growing vexation and the reason behind it, trying to placate her. "Look at this lovely green brocade above the bed. The stitching on the matching coverlet is very fine, and the bed looks so comfortable. I do hope that you'll sleep really well." As she said this, she began to unpack the two largest trunks.

As she placed various items in the drawers, she said "this is an exceptionally good quality walnut - such a deep shine. The maids must work so hard."

"Well, it's what they're paid for," Caroline snapped. "Besides, what would you know about the quality of furniture?

Hurry up with that gown for this evening. It's very creased. Dinner's at eight, so you'll need to get on with it. I'm quite fatigued after that long journey, so I'm going to rest now. Undo these hooks, so that I can slip into my nightgown.

Go and press the gown. I don't want you to disturb me. You can finish the packing while I'm at dinner."

Aphra left the room and carried the gown down to the servants' quarters. One of the other maids showed her to the laundry room. It was quite a good sized room with two large sinks and a flat table for ironing and folding clothes. In the far end of the room was a large copper for heating the water and washing the clothes. In the corner was a zinc dolly tub.

Aphra spent more than an hour ironing the dress, for she took great care to get the temperature just right. One mistake and her life would not be worth living. When she had finished, she was very pleased with the result and took the gown up to her own room. One of the maids showed her the way.

The staircases leading up to the maids' rooms were quite a contrast to the ones on the other side of the dividing doors. They were plain and utilitarian. The maid was called Daisy and, like everyone else that Aphra had met that day, was very friendly and good humoured.

When Aphra got to her room on the top floor, Daisy left saying that if she needed anything to just ask any of the staff.

Once inside, Aphra hung up the gown and began to unpack her own clothes. The room was nowhere near as comfortable as her room at Warrington Grange. There was a small bed with an iron bedstead. However, there seemed to be plenty of warm blankets and an eiderdown. Once she had put away her few possessions, she thought that she would take advantage of Caroline's afternoon rest and took a short one herself. As she lay beneath the eiderdown, she observed her small retreat. She noticed that warm lined curtains had been hung at the small window and a large deep pile rug lay on the floor next to the bed. It struck her that someone had tried to make this room more comfortable for its occupant. There was no fireplace, so she was extremely grateful to the thoughtful person who had made it feel warmer. She fell asleep briefly for twenty minutes and then arose to go back down to her mistress. After hanging the gown up, and noticing that her mistress was sound sleep, she went down to the kitchen to fetch tea for her.

As Aphra carried the tray into the bedroom, Caroline awoke and began to complain. Aphra took a deep breath and placed the tray on a small table.

"My goodness girl, you've taken such a time. I could have died of thirst. Bring that cup over here."

She almost snatched the cup out of Aphra's hand. "You'd better run me a bath - quick now. I don't want to keep his Grace waiting."

Aphra did as she was ordered - adding some perfume to the running water. The newly installed bathroom had both hot and cold running water. Silently, she gave thanks that she did not have to face the drudgery of lugging buckets of water along the corridor as she did at Warrington Grange.

She noticed that when Caroline was lying in the bath, she was obviously enjoying being able to stretch out and relax in the hot scented water. What really annoyed Aphra was that she was constantly being asked to top up the water when it cooled a little, for she was just too lazy to turn the tap herself. Also, Aphra thought to herself that she could easily use the bathroom at home. She just got Aphra to do all that work out of sheer belligerence.

While Caroline was bathing, Aphra tidied the bed and sorted out the lingerie for the evening. Caroline kept shouting out instructions from the tub, including which items of jewellery she wanted. An hour later, Caroline swept out of the room in a fashionable, gold gown, and her hair and throat dressed in diamonds and pearls.

With a sigh of relief, Aphra made her way down to the kitchen to eat her own evening meal. The friendliness of the other servants made a welcome change from the incessant complaints and demands of her mistress.

She had a few hours before her mistress was in need of her services again, so went up to her room and read for a bit and had a short rest. When Caroline returned to her room, Aphra was turning her bed down and preparing her nightclothes.

"Have you had an enjoyable evening?" She enquired, trying to appear bright and interested.

"Oh, yes," replied Caroline. "Sebastian is such wonderful company and so attentive to me. I think that he's quite smitten. Things are definitely moving in the right direction." Aphra noticed that she was admiring her left finger as she said this. She continued. "However, I can't say that I'm too keen on his mother. What a dragon! Once we're married, I shall suggest to Sebastian that she lives elsewhere. There must be a dowager house on the estate."

As Aphra removed pins from Caroline's hair and brushed it out, Caroline gave a long account of her fellow guests. It was a mixture of sycophantic praise for some and a sneering contempt for others. At one point, Aphra was tempted to stick one of the pins in her scalp, but of course she didn't, and maintained an air of interest and subservience.

After attending to her mistress's toilette, Aphra went down to fetch a cup of hot milk for her and then said goodnight and made her way to her own room.

***

The following day, as Aphra was looking at the paintings in the corridor, she did not see the Earl walking in her direction.

"Good morning young lady! We've not seen your pretty face around here before," he remarked in a jovial and flirtatious manner. She felt a bit flustered and was unable to speak for a minute. It was strange, for even though she felt that there was definitely no physical attraction between them, they somehow seemed drawn to one another in an inexplicable way.

"Oh, Good morning, Milord," she replied and curtsied. "I'm sorry. I was far away and did not see you. Please forgive my lack of manners. My name is Aphra Chamberlain and I am lady's maid to Miss Grenville."

"Ah! Well, I'm very pleased to meet you." He offered his hand to her and she shook it, somewhat perplexed at this unusual gesture. "You did have a faraway look about you. I see that you're admiring my pictures."

"Yes sir. This is a very good Vermeer and I really like the Holbein just down the corridor."

"Ah! So you know your art. I'm impressed. Please feel free to study any of the pictures around the house. Some of them are of my ancestors - an ugly bunch of blighters, if you ask me," he laughed. "Not as handsome as myself!"

Aphra found herself smiling at this.

He started to wander off down the corridor and then stopped and turned towards her again. "There's no need to curtsey. We don't stand on ceremony here."

As they stood there for a few more moments, Aphra was able to make a closer inspection of the most eligible bachelor in the county – if not the whole country. Although his clothes were of the highest quality and extremely expensive, she thought, as she had done when she saw him previously, that he somehow looked unkempt. His hair was slightly lank and kept falling over his forehead. She was conscious of a slight stooping of the shoulders and supposed that this was due to his immense height. He obviously had a fine figure, and she was shocked at herself for thinking that he probably looked better with his clothes off! She demurely complimented him on his beautiful home and gardens.

"I am extremely lucky to live in such a lovely place and count my blessings daily. I am also very grateful for the hard work of the knowledgeable gardeners and the other members of my staff who make my life so pleasant. They all do a first rate job and I shall pass on your kind remarks to them." He laughed as he sauntered off up the corridor "I hope you enjoy your stay with us." Aphra thought him a most surprising and unusual aristocrat in his treatment of staff and his casual manner towards her, a lowly servant.

Over the days that followed, Aphra was to see numerous examples of his kind and friendly manner. She was impressed at how relaxed and happy the household was. Unfortunately, with so much hustle and bustle due to the number of guests staying, the household staff had omitted to tell her something of paramount importance. How this came to happen, who can say? Perhaps, those concerned had thought that someone else had told her. Whatever the reason, Aphra was unaware that the Earl had two strict rules. In this, he was adamant that flouting of this rule would result in that person's immediate dismissal.

The first rule stipulated that the Earl's private rooms were out of bounds to all staff, with the exception of the Earl's private secretary, whose own room was adjacent to his own, and the limited access of the butler. Any cleaning was done to a strict timetable.

The second rule was that a large part of the woodland area down towards the lake was also off limits – except for prior arrangements with the groundsmen. The large numbers of staff were all familiar with this strange set of rules and they put it down to the eccentricities of the upper classes and had long ago stopped questioning the reasoning behind it. However, of these prohibitions Aphra was completely ignorant and this would lead her into a situation that would have consequences that would affect the rest of her life.

The next two days were some of the best that Aphra had experienced for a long time. Her mistress was actually being very pleasant to her. At first, Aphra had wondered why this was. She soon realised that there were two reasons for this. Firstly, Caroline was feeling very happy, secure in the assurance of Sebastian's imminent proposal. Secondly, and by far the greater reason, Caroline wanted to create a good impression at Methuen Park. She did not approve of Sebastian's relaxed manner towards his servants, as she did not like the familiarity that this bred in the lower orders and she would be making some drastic changes when she became Countess. However, for the present, she needed Sebastian to see her in a good light. The result of this was that she had been allowing Aphra quite a bit of free time for herself, which she had used to rest and read. The Earl had told Aphra that she was free to borrow books from his vast and extensive library, which she eagerly did.

***

It was on the afternoon of the fifth day of the visit that she decided to take a stroll. Caroline had told her that as she wished to take a nap, the afternoon was her own to do with as she pleased. Aphra felt relaxed yet energised. The afternoon was cold and crisp, but the sun was shining. She felt that spring was waiting in the wings and she was eager to do some exploration of the grounds. She descended the servants' stairs at the back of the house and quietly slipped out of a side door. Her feet made a crunching noise on the gravel as she quickly passed by the grand terraces with their marble statues, and the flowerbeds of the parterre, now denuded of their colours and awaiting replanting. She briskly descended the stone steps and walked across the lawn towards the trees in the distance.

She wanted to get away from people and buildings and to be close to nature. For some time she walked, passing some of the houseguests taking a stroll. Some ignored her shy smile and others nodded a polite acknowledgement. Thirty minutes brisk walk took her quite a distance from the house into a heavily wooded part of the estate. There was no one around and she enjoyed the isolation and sense of freedom that it gave her. Occasionally, she heard the sounds of the creatures that lived there. For a while, her mind drifted back to the idyllic days of her early childhood and she was lost in thoughts of her mother and grandfather and the happiness that they had shared walking in the woods near her home. She remembered collecting leaves, feathers and stones to take back for her growing collection in the nursery and her mother teaching her all about them.

These reminiscences were interrupted by the sound of horses neighing close by. As she stopped beside a thicket, she could see two horses tethered to a bush. Approaching, she saw two figures embracing one another. She could not see who they were, but she felt embarrassed, for she was in no doubt that this was a romantic and clandestine encounter. They were obviously a pair of courting lovers and she was just about to turn around and walk back the way that she had come, when the taller of the two held his head up. With a start, she recognised the broad shoulders and terrific height. It was the Earl. For a minute, she was confused. She had seen her mistress only a short time ago in her room and she had said that she wished to rest. As she quickly tried to conceal herself behind a tree, her foot broke a twig. The Earl turned around and saw the hem of her gown as she darted out of his vision.

"It's no good hiding, damn you. I know you're there. Come out and make yourself visible. Stop sneaking around or I'll have you flogged!" He had the kind of powerful voice that did not brook challenge. She stepped out from behind the tree. The confusion of emotions that crossed his face alarmed her. She saw anger – even rage, but it was the fear in his eyes that was most disturbing. As the Earl strode angrily towards her, his companion came into view. She didn't understand. It was a young man, but she hardly took in his appearance, for the Earl was shouting so loudly at her. "What the hell do you think you're doing? You know that this part of the estate is out of bounds. Why can't you damned people obey the rules, instead of sneaking around prying?"

"Sebastian, stop it," called the young man in a foreign accent. Aphra recognised it as French. She turned towards him and appealed to him in his native tongue to help her. As the Earl continued his tirade, she could feel tears trickling down her cheeks. By now, he had realised who she was and he knew that he needed to calm down in case she went back and reported the incident to her mistress.

The young man put his hand gently yet firmly on Sebastian's arm. "She did not know that she should not be here. No one has told her of this. She cannot be blamed. Please calm down."

Sebastian took a deep breath and then said "Go to your room immediately and speak to no one – especially your mistress. Go on, go," he repeated.

As she made her way back to the house, she tried to calm herself down. She realised that she was shaking. She felt angry with him for being so horrid and spoiling her afternoon, but she was also angry with herself for breaking down and crying. She dabbed at her cheeks with her handkerchief.

Fortunately, she passed no one as she re-entered the house and made her way to her room. Once there, she threw herself on the bed and wept silently into the pillow. She didn't understand any of it. Why was he kissing another man? Why didn't someone tell her about that part of the estate? She would never have disobeyed if she had been informed first. How dare he speak to her like that! He swore at her – used the words damn and hell. He was supposed to be a gentleman and said words like that. She had thought of him as kind and gentle and good to his staff. He had been so relaxed and gentle when he had spoken to her a few days ago.

She had really warmed to him, but he was really bad-tempered and rude. She never expected such abuse from him. If her mistress was going to marry him, then Aphra was going to look for another position – and soon. She was not going to tolerate anyone speaking to her like that and she didn't give a "damn" if he was an Earl! Her distress turned to indignation and finally to anger. As she got up and went to cool down her face with some water in a china jug, there was a knock at the door.

"Just a minute," she called out.

One of the housemaids was outside. "I've got a letter for you from his Lordship. Shall I slip it under the door?"

"Oh, yes please. I'm not properly dressed," she answered. The letter was pushed under the door. "Thank you very much."

She heard the maid's footsteps disappear down the stairs. She finished drying her face with the towel and then picked up the envelope. It was addressed to Miss Chamberlain. So he remembered who she was. She sat down on the bed and tore open the envelope. She realised that she was absolutely fuming as she read the contents.

***

Miss Chamberlain,

Please come at once to my study. I wish to speak to you in private.

Yours sincerely,

Sebastian Raemond

***

Well, she thought, that's brief and to the point. As she tidied her hair, she wondered why he had sent for her. She assumed that she was going to be dismissed or at the very least, he was going to continue berating her about the incident. She made her mind up then and there that she was not going to be bullied. She walked very quickly and purposefully down the stairs, taking little notice of the opulence all around her. She did not know where his study was, so had to ask one of the liveried footmen.

Her heart was pounding as she knocked at the door. She was so irate, that she did not wait for a command to enter, but just went straight in. He was seated behind his desk and looked up. She could tell that he was surprised at her entering the room without being given permission first.

"Ah, Miss Chamberlain. I would say come in, but you've already done so."

"You wished to speak to me?" She hoped that her voice did not betray how nervous she felt.

"Please, take a seat over here," he gestured, getting up and walking over to some comfortable armchairs near the fire. "It's more comfortable, and certainly warmer."

"I'll stand, if you don't mind. I'd prefer to get this over as soon as possible," she said – perhaps a little bit too aggressively. "I've things to do. My mistress will be ringing for me."

"Don't you want some tea?" He rang the bell on the wall by the fireplace. "Oh, for God's sake, bloody sit down woman and stop being so touchy. All right, so you want an apology. I'm trying – can't you see?"

She moved towards the armchair that was nearest and sat down gingerly. This was not what she had expected. She had come in here expecting a fight and he had completely disarmed her. She didn't know what to say.

He sat in the chair opposite her and his voice took on a softer tone. "Miss Chamberlain, I'm very sorry for my outburst earlier. My behaviour was completely unacceptable. Claude, he's my private secretary, pointed out that you had not been informed of the rules about the grounds, so it wasn't your fault. I was very wrong to have spoken to you in the way that I did. Can you find it in your heart to forgive me?"

She looked up at him and saw that he was genuinely full of remorse. Her anger was abating. Now, she just felt a bit silly for over-reacting. "Of course. I suppose it's understandable that you'd be annoyed if someone had disobeyed you – especially now I know the reason why – although I don't understand. Anyway, it's none of my business."

There was a knock at the door, and one of the maids entered carrying a tray with the tea things upon it. She placed it on a small low table between them. "Shall I pour, Milord?"

"No, Kitty. I'll attend to it. Thank you." As the maid left the room, he began to arrange the cups and asked her how she liked her tea. As he did so, she looked around the study. Although it was plush and grand, it also had a warm, lived in feeling. The walls were lined with books and there was a strong masculine ambience to the room.

When he had finished pouring out her tea, he handed it to her. "Help yourself to the cake." Aphra was still struggling with her emotions. At first, she was going to say no just out of petulance, but then she thought better of it. After all, the rich fruitcake looked very tempting and she was quite hungry after her long walk. She leant over and placed a slice on a small plate.

"I see that you are admiring my bookshelves. Are you enjoying the books that you've borrowed?"

"Yes, thank you," she replied.

"I suppose you're very shocked by what you saw this afternoon – perhaps confused too."

"As I said, Sir, it's none of my business. Don't worry, I shan't say anything to anyone. I give you my word. I don't go in for tittle-tattle." She took a bite of the cake.

"This is rather good, isn't it? The staff in my kitchens are to be commended, are they not?"

She realised that he was actually very nervous and was making idle chatter because of this. "I think that the recipe is one of Mrs Pearson's own." They sat in silence for a few minutes. Aphra was beginning to feel a bit sorry for him. She replaced her plate on the tray and took another sip of her tea. He smiled at her, and reluctantly, she smiled back. She realised that she was not angry any more. Suddenly, she started to giggle.

"What is it? Did I do something funny?"

"No," she replied. "I'm sorry. That was very rude of me, but I was just thinking that when I marched through that door, I came in looking for a fight. I expected to be told to go and pack my bags or something like that – and here I am taking tea with you."

"Well, I must confess that I did not expect to be taking tea with the maid of one of my houseguests. I don't think that she'd be too pleased, would she?"

"Lord, no," she giggled again. "She'd be furious. I suppose that she's wondering where I am, although I'm not really due back on duty for a while. Who's the young man?"

"Claude is a French aristocrat. We've been together for four years. I care very much for him and I know that my feelings are reciprocated. I suppose you could say that the feelings we share for one another are those of a happily married couple.

I know that I have to find a wife to produce an heir. However, this situation could be very hard on the woman that I choose. I am considering marrying your mistress. She is an utterly selfish, cold, spiteful and self-absorbed person and I do not like her one bit. If I did marry her, once an heir was born, I would spend as little time as possible with her. This probably sounds as though I am being unfair to her, but I don't think for one moment that she's in love with me. I think that it is my title and position that is really the main attraction. This makes me feel less guilty about it. I would not want to treat a good woman in such a way."

"But why don't you just find a nice affectionate lady and love her?" Aphra asked. "Why don't you be with her and not with Claude?"

"Because I am not attracted to women. I have no desire to make love with women. I feel like that about Claude."

Well, I just don't understand. It seems odd to me – although I've no reason for thinking that. Come to think of it, why shouldn't anyone love anyone they want if they're not doing any harm?" She sat and quietly thought about it for a while.

After a few moments, Sebastian spoke. "You have a good mind, Miss Chamberlain. Most people are closed to new ideas, but I can see that you are not. It is quite refreshing. I have some books on the subject, if you care to borrow them. Would you like to? They are not anything racy or shocking – just some intellectual arguments looking at this subject from different points of view." He got up and walked over to one of the bookcases. He took down two books and handed them to her.

"Thank you," she said as she looked at the titles. "I'm always interested to learn new things."

"I think that I had better let you get back to your duties. I do not wish you to get into trouble with your mistress. Please do not let anyone else see the books. It could cause problems. My relationship with Claude is illegal and we could both go to prison, so I do not want anything to draw attention to that."

"I understand. You can rely on my discretion completely," she replied.

He had a twinkle in his eye and held out his hand to her. He thought to himself that the maid was a vast improvement on the mistress. She would certainly be preferable as a wife. "Do you know? I think that I can. Are we friends now and am I forgiven?"

"Completely. It's all forgotten," she said, taking his hand.

Later that evening, before she went to sleep, Aphra sat and wrote a letter to Emily.

***

Methuen Park
Somerset

My dearest friend,

I do hope that this letter finds you in good health and that perhaps your duties are lessened at the present time – although, I expect that you are keeping very busy. I know that I am – although I have had some free moments to myself.

Our journey here was swift, uneventful and most comfortable. The mistress slept for about an hour. From the luxury of the Earl's carriage, I quietly enjoyed the spectacular view of the passing countryside. It is so beautiful, even at this time of the year and so varied too. We passed through some woods, which must be glorious in the autumn. Oh that I may have the chance to come here again and experience the different seasons. What a beautiful part of the world in which to live. I should be so happy to spend the rest of my life in this part of the world and I think that I should be content and need nothing else but this beauty to survey on a daily basis.

I have so much to tell you about Methuen Park. You cannot imagine how magnificent the house is. I have never seen a place that is so grand. The entrance hall is quite overwhelming. The stairs spiral around the hall in a very grand fashion and there is a huge chandelier - the upkeep of which must be such a lot of work for the servants. There are so many oil paintings. Do you remember the books on art that we studied together? Well, I have already identified a Vermeer, a Holbein, a Rembrandt and a Titian! Also there is quite a bit of Ming Dynasty and Sevres porcelain dotted about the place. I feel quite pleased with myself that I have learnt all of this.

Of course, it was all in aid of assisting the mistress, but I found that she was not really interested in the subject. Between you and me, she is convinced that he is going to propose, but I suspect that it is not going to happen. She will be like a bear with a sore head when she discovers this!

My bedroom is very simple but clean and comfortable. I suspect that the Earl wants to ensure that all members of staff have at least the minimum level of warmth and comfort. I sleep like a log.

Madam's room is lovely, but not as grand as some of the others and it has certainly put her nose out of joint. She was very tetchy at first. However, since then, she has convinced herself that a proposal is imminent.

The grounds are huge and must cover quite a few square miles. I am hoping to do *some exploration of them in my free time – well, that is when I get some. The whole place makes Warrington Grange seem like a tiny cottage. I have no idea how many rooms there are, but they must be numerous indeed. The decoration and the furnishings are most lavish and it takes an army of servants to keep it all in order, but none of them complain and they sing and whistle as they go about their duties.*

I do hope that you are enjoying the book. I'm sure that you are. It's a wonderful story, isn't it? Mr "Dinkins" has such a way of relating a tale that you feel as though you are there yourself in the middle of the story, don't you? If you have enjoyed reading it, then we will get you some more books. Perhaps you can try one of mine when I return.

His Lordship has been most generous and has let me borrow any book I wish from his extensive library. He must possess thousands – many of them very beautifully bound and decorated in gold leaf. They must be worth a fortune - so I feel a bit nervous handling them. The Earl must be extremely wealthy and yet, you know, in spite of his wealth, title and social position, he is a very down to earth man. He has been most friendly towards me. I understand that he is a very good master and every member of the staff seems to adore him. It is such a happy household.

I do hope that everyone is keeping well. Please give them all my best wishes. I'm missing you all a great deal.

I do hope that you are enjoying this, your first letter. I look forward to seeing you all again in a few weeks.

With fondest wishes from your friend and "sister".

Aphra

***

Sebastian leant back in the armchair and swilled his brandy around in the glass as Claude took a taper from the fire and lit a cigar.

"You'll be making me jealous, Seb," he laughed.

They were enjoying their first opportunity to be alone since the incident in the woods.

"Ah well, you have to admit that she's a great beauty. Quite the most striking woman that I've ever seen. I'm very surprised that Caroline hired her. She does not brook competition - of that I'm quite certain. Now, if I were like most men, I would be quite smitten with her."

Claude nodded in agreement. "Her looks must have led to the green eyed monster rearing its head at Warrington Grange."

Sebastian became pensive and silent, leading Claude to ask him what was wrong.

"I don't know. I suppose it's the thought of marrying Caroline. I've realised that life with her would be very difficult. I'm not sure that I can go ahead with the proposal. I think that I need a distraction."

"Can I be of help?"

Sebastian held out his hand to him. "You always are," he said with affection.

***

In the days that followed, Aphra was kept very busy. The Earl was planning a grand ball. Caroline thought that it was in her honour and was full of it. Her whole conversation was about which dress she was to wear and which jewellery matched it, the effect that she would have on the other guests and so on. It became a bit wearing and Aphra was grateful for the few short moments that she got to herself. She managed to take two or three brief walks in the grounds. However, she never ventured far from the terrace or the grassed area and she certainly avoided the woods. Late at night, in the quiet of her room, she read the two books that the Earl had loaned her. Curled up in bed, by the light of the oil lamp, she was quite absorbed by the contents. She learned a lot and by the time she had finished the second book, she felt that she understood the relationship between the Earl and his French lover. Who was she to judge how other people lived their lives and whom they loved – as long as they were hurting no one else.

The morning after she had finished reading the books, she got up early and went down to the study to return them to the shelf from which they came – so as to ensure that they were not discovered by anyone. She saw some blank sheets of paper on his desk, so wrote a discreet note to say that the books were returned with thanks and just signed it A.

Later that morning, when the Earl sat down at his desk, he read the note and smiled. Since the encounter with the maid, he had been giving her some considerable thought. He had an idea, which he put to Claude, who was in full agreement. After lunch, the Earl made a point of seeking out Aphra. He thought correctly that she might be taking her walk in the garden. He found her near the terrace.

"Good afternoon Miss Chamberlain. I see that you are taking the air."

"Good afternoon, Milord. Yes, it's a fine day, although there is a chill in the air."

"Is your mistress resting? Does she not like to walk?"

"She prefers to rest rather than walk."

He offered her his arm. "Come take a walk with me. I have a suggestion to put to you." After her initial surprise at this gesture, she put her arm through the crook in his and they made their way down the steps and across the lawn towards the woods.

"Do you think that we should be going in this direction? We don't want to get into trouble."

"Oh I think that we'll be quite safe today," he replied with a grin.

"What is this suggestion that you have in mind? I'm intrigued."

"As you know, the ball is on Saturday and I was wondering if you would like to attend," he ventured.

"Me! She'll have a fit. She won't allow it." She felt quite shaken at the idea.

"Oh, I think that I can get her to play ball – if you'll excuse the pun."

Aphra looked very doubtful.

"Claude needs a partner, so I thought that he could escort you," he added.

She went to say something, but he interrupted her. "And before you say that you have nothing appropriate to wear, that problem can be overcome. As you are probably aware, my sister died last year."

Aphra nodded and made an acknowledgement of his loss. "That must have been dreadful for your family. I am truly sorry."

"Thank you. I have mentioned this situation to my mother and both of us are quite happy for you to wear one of her dresses. It's about time that we came to terms with her death and sorted out her things. You are about the same size, I should imagine, and, funnily enough, her hair was similar in colouring."

"I don't know what to say."

"Say yes."

"Perhaps if you speak to my mistress first, she may agree to it."

"She'll have to agree to it, if I insist. She knows that to please me and get me to propose to her, she'll have to do what I ask," he added with assurance.

Aphra agreed that she would go if her mistress allowed it.

"I'll speak to her later, but in the meantime, Claude will speak to you."

"I think that I should be getting back, Sir."

He agreed and they climbed up the stone steps leading to the terrace. Unknown to them, they were being watched from the house. Caroline had just awoken from her nap and had gone to look out of the window at the view. It was not the view that she had expected to see and she was not pleased.

A few minutes later, Aphra was knocking at her door. Caroline decided that the best way to handle this was to say nothing for the time being. "Come in," she called out. She had returned to bed, so that Aphra would not guess that she had been looking out of the window. They had a brief exchange of words and Aphra got on with her duties as normal. Later that evening, she thought to herself that her mistress's manner seemed unusual. She could not exactly work out what it was. She seemed tense and yet was not difficult or unpleasant.

She pushed the idea out of her mind as she had enough to think about with this suggestion of the Earl's. What a strange man he was. Fancy paying such attention to a servant. He really was quite down to earth. She found herself liking him. He had lots of charm and she felt that she was falling under his spell. She smiled to herself. It would not do to start falling in love with him. Now that would be just a waste of time. Oh, she thought, if only Caroline knew the truth. She would be horrified. It amused her greatly when she thought about her mistress' plans to be Countess.

The following afternoon, when she was taking her walk in the grounds, she heard footsteps behind her. "Excuse moi, Mademoiselle Chamberlain."

She turned around and smiled at Claude. "Bonjour, Monsieur." He seemed so pleased to have someone speak to him in his own tongue, that he immediately began talking rapidly. She put her hand up and requested that he spoke much more slowly. "I have not spoken any French since I left school and my vocabulary is very limited."

He laughed and apologised. "I promise to speak more slowly and if I forget, you will just have to remind me." He suggested that they take a walk together and gestured that they enter the woods. She was about to protest and say that the Earl did not allow it. Claude laughed and said, "I think that you know the reason for that rule. There is hardly any point in stopping you from entering the woods now."

He offered her his arm and they walked along the path, making polite conversation about generalities. It was a bit difficult at first, for they both had their weak areas regarding language. However, after a number of misunderstandings and an equal amount of laughing, they became more comfortable and confident with each other. Claude brought up the subject of the Ball. Aphra told him that it would all depend upon the reaction of her mistress. He replied that he did not think there would be a problem. "Leave it to Sebastian. He will ask her in such a way that she will not be able to refuse. When he suggests that I have designs upon you, I think that she will be relieved that you are not going to be in competition for him."

Aphra was shocked at this remark. "Where would she get that idea from?"

"I gather that she saw you both out on the terrace yesterday. I understand that she saw Sebastian kiss your hand. She is very threatened by you. Did you not know that?"

Aphra did not know how to reply to this, so said nothing at first. She had suspected that Caroline kept her in the background if she could. Aphra did not like to be conceited, but she knew that her looks were such that men admired her.

"Anyway," said Claude. "Sebastian has spoken to his mother, the Countess, and she has agreed that you can wear one of the dresses of his deceased sister. You are very similar in build and colouring, so I am sure that you will find something suitable. This is going to be most enjoyable. I will be pleased to escort such a beautiful and charming young woman, who is intelligent and can speak to me in my own language."

Aphra thought that the whole project sounded rather daunting and told him that she was very nervous. "I don't feel very confident about this. I have had no experience of such occasions and I'm scared that I may make a *faux pas*."

"Oh, you'll do very well and I won't let you slip up. Just lean on me," he replied in a mixture of English and French.

"Very well." She agreed that she would let him take the responsibility if anything went wrong.

"We can go now and take a look at the clothes, if you like."

"Very well, but I can't be long. My mistress will soon need me to attend to her."

"Do not worry about her. Sebastian will keep her occupied for a while."

Aphra was surprised that he led her through the main entrance to the house. When she seemed reluctant, he waived her doubts aside. They mounted the stairs and went along a corridor. Claude opened the door to a large, airy, bedchamber. It was a beautiful, feminine room with the four poster bed reaching almost to the very high ceiling. The hangings were of a rich crimson colour and all the upholstery on the furniture was in a matching fabric. There was an ebony dressing table which supported a silver framed mirror and matching silver and glass accoutrements.

Seated on a high back chair of gold damask, next to the marble fireplace, was a rather grand, but formidable looking elderly lady with a tartan rug over her knees. Remembering what Caroline had said about the Dowager Countess being a dragon, Aphra felt very nervous and unsure how to behave. Should she curtsy?

Then, suddenly, the lady spoke. "Come over here child where it's nice and cosy." She beckoned to Aphra. The voice was gentle and benign. She smiled and Aphra realised, with relief, that she was not formidable or intimidating at all. "Let me look at you? Ah yes, you'll do very well. You are more or less the same height as my poor girl and your hair is almost the same shade." She looked sad as she said this. Aphra did not know what to say for a minute. Then she made a slight curtsy and offered her condolences at the loss of the Countess's daughter.

"That is very kind of you. Yes, it was a great loss, but one has to come to terms with these things. This is why I want you to use one of her gowns. She would be pleased. She was a very kind and generous girl."

"I will try to do her justice and honour her memory, ma'am," Aphra said gently. They spoke for a few more moments. While they were talking, Claude walked over to one of the wardrobes and took out a few gowns and laid them on the bed.

"I still keep her gowns. I have them in here near me. I know it's silly, but I can't seem to let them go. Let's go and have a look at them."

The Countess stood up. It was obvious that this was very difficult for her and Aphra offered her arm for the old lady to lean on. The Countess gladly accepted the offer. They walked over to the bed where Claude had laid the dresses. It was then that Aphra noticed the woman standing in the shadows. "This is my personal maid, Dorothy. She'll help you."

The Countess inspected the dresses. One she rejected, because it was marked, another one because it was unsuitable and another one, because, she said it would not suit Aphra. This left two gowns. "Would you like to try them on?"
Claude then made an excuse to leave the room. Aphra went behind a screen and tried on the first dress – a pale green silk one. When she came out from behind the screen, the Countess told her that she looked very nice and that the fit was extremely good. Then she went and put on the other gown. It was ivory satin and it complimented her skin and hair colouring perfectly.

"Now, that's the one! My dear girl always loved that gown and looked wonderful in it. Do you like it?"

"Oh, yes," replied Aphra. "It was my first choice as soon as I saw it. Are you sure that you feel comfortable with my wearing this – especially as your daughter was so fond of it?"

"Of course, my dear. I've taken a shine to you and I can't think of anyone I would prefer to wear it – certainly not that social climbing madam downstairs. I suspect that she's a nasty piece of work. I can't abide her. I do hope that my son is not foolish enough to marry her. It'll be the biggest mistake of his life. I'm sorry. I'm being indiscreet and she is your employer. But I warrant she's a tartar to work for. Am I right?"

Aphra smiled, but diplomatically said nothing.

"I like that. You know how to be discreet," continued the Countess. "That's very wise.

So we're agreed that this is the gown? Dorothy, see what you can find to go with it – shoes, stockings and petticoats. I'll take a look for some ornamentation. You'll need a pretty comb to put in your hair. I'll see what I can find. On Saturday evening, come here when you have finished seeing to your mistress and Dorothy will assist you to dress and will do your hair."

Aphra helped the Countess back to her chair.

"That is my lovely girl, Cecilia," she said pointing to the painting above the fireplace. Aphra looked up at the large picture of a beautiful, auburn haired young woman. She was dressed in a summer gown of white muslin and holding a parasol.

"She's lovely. She has a kind smile and eyes that laugh," said Aphra. "Oh, you must miss her so much."

"I do, but my son is a wonderful comfort to me. I just want to see him happily settled with the right woman."

At this remark, Aphra felt a bit uncomfortable, knowing the Earl's secret

Dorothy showed Aphra some shoes and other items of attire. When they had selected them, Aphra thanked her for her assistance.

"Until Saturday, my dear," said the Countess.

Aphra curtsied and left the room.

The old lady watched her leave the bedchamber. "She'd make a far better wife for my son than that harpy he seems to be dallying with at the moment."

Outside in the corridor, Claude was waiting. "Did you find something that is - eh tres jolie?" He kissed his fingers in a typical Gallic gesture.

Aphra told him that she was very happy with the choice that they had made. He took her arm again and led her towards the staircase leading to her mistress's room.

"I feel so fortunate, yet apprehensive, about wearing Cecilia's beautiful gowns. I hope that I won't let the Countess down," Aphra said.

"You'll do very well. You'll be the belle of the ball," he said as he took his leave of her, kissing her hand. "Now do stop worrying."

Caroline was coming up the stairs. She just caught a glimpse of them parting. She was really most vexed at this turn of events. Sebastian had just forced her to agree to Aphra attending the Ball as partner to this damned Frenchie. She'd had no option but to agree and appear not to mind. She was going to look a fool with her maid at the Ball. She'd be the laughing stock of the county. She'd pretended that she'd thought it was a marvellous idea. She had to, if she wanted Sebastian to propose to her, she had to keep him sweet.

Aphra was already busy attending to her work when Caroline walked into the room.

"Have you had a nice afternoon Aphra?" She asked through a fixed smile. Aphra found it very hard to keep her expression bland, so shocked was she at being asked this question for the first time. Her mistress had never before bothered to enquire about how she felt or what she had been doing.

"Yes Ma'am. Very pleasant. Thank you. Did you enjoy your tea with his Lordship?" She tried to keep her voice from shaking. It made her nervous if Caroline was being nice.

"Yes, Aphra. Thank you for asking. It was most pleasant. The Earl is such good company, but then you know that. I understand that you took a walk with him yesterday afternoon."

Aphra went to explain that the Earl had sought her out, but Caroline silenced her with a gesture of her hand. "Oh, there is no need to explain. Sebastian told me all about it. He is such a kind man and is concerned that his Secretary, who is some kind of companion to him, should not feel left out on Saturday night. He said that as you were quite presentable and spoke French passably well, that you would be a good partner for him. Isn't that just typical of him? What a dear man he is. Of course, I told him that I was in whole-hearted agreement and that I was only too pleased that my maid could be of service to the Earl.

All this was not exactly true. What Sebastian had actually said was that it would be nice for Claude to get to know her maid. By implication, suggesting that if Caroline and he were to get engaged, then having their personal attendants being on good terms would be an excellent idea. He wished that he could have taken a photograph of the expression on her face. She was horrified and for a few seconds, this was written all over it. Then, she quickly pretended that she was all for the idea. Shortly after this, he turned his back on her and caught a glimpse of her face in the mirror. She was seething with anger. He quickly turned around and just caught her attempt to hide it. Later, he had a twinge of guilt at getting so much enjoyment out of the situation, but it did not last long.

"You can run my bath now, Aphra and while I am bathing, you can sort through those items that I mentioned to you earlier. I wish to relax for a few minutes."

Aphra went and did as she was told. She knew that her mistress was lying in the bath and fuming with anger. She needed to keep out of her way, as it would not take much to tip her over the edge into a full-blown rage. As she helped her dress for dinner, she was extra careful not to do anything that might anger her. However, she made an exceptionally good job of her hair and general toilette. "You look lovely, Ma'am," she said truthfully. She did look lovely. It was just that she wasn't lovely!

"Well, thank you Aphra. You've done well. I'm very pleased. I love my hair like this," she said as she picked up her fan from the dressing table and made her way towards the door.

"I hope that you can do just as good a job on Saturday night, Aphra. I'll expect you to take extra care as I want to look my best for such a special occasion. Get yourself some rest now. We don't want you looking half dead on Saturday night."

"Yes, thank you ma'am," replied Aphra. "No, you'd like me completely dead," she muttered under her breath as Caroline left the room.

***

Aphra rose early on Saturday morning, bathed and washed her hair. She had already checked that everything was ready for the evening. She had been particularly clever in that she had given Caroline the idea that there was still some mending to do. She did not lie. She had left one small item outstanding, so that when asked, she could reply that she was not yet finished. She worked exceptionally quickly, but always left something unfinished. That way, she always had a little bit of time in hand. It was especially important that she had time to spare tonight. As expected, Caroline waited until she was nearly ready to spring on Aphra one or two unexpected tasks. Aphra thought that this might happen. However, they were small duties that she could complete very easily and swiftly. Then Caroline enquired if she had finished the mending.

"No, Ma'am."

"Well, I shall expect it to be finished by first thing tomorrow morning."
"Yes. Ma'am. I'll do my best," she replied with just the right amount of deference and anxiety in her voice.

"See that you do. Just because his Lordship has been kind enough to ask you to help out at the Ball, does not mean that you can shirk your duties. Remember who pays your salary," she continued.

"Yes, Ma'am. I'm sure that everything will be finished by tomorrow morning. Thank you Ma'am," she added with a suitable touch of subservience to her voice.

Caroline was enjoying this. She wanted to make Aphra nervous and spoil her evening. Hopefully, she would be in such a rush and late, that she would arrive at the Ball looking flustered and awkward.

She surveyed her reflection in the mirror. She looked marvellous in red satin and matching rubies. They contrasted with her alabaster skin and ebony hair and brought out the bright grey in her eyes. The tight fitting bodice showed off every advantage of her elegant form. "You look really beautiful," said Aphra. "That gown becomes you so much."

Caroline looked at her maid who looked a bit hot and flushed. She pretended to smile benignly. "Thank you, dear. Now I'll leave you to get on with all those little jobs that are outstanding. Don't forget to clear up the bathroom – oh, and those other bits over there. Then you'd better hurry and go and tidy yourself up. Will you be wearing that grey dress?

You always look very presentable in that." The question was rhetorical and she opened the door and whispered. "Well, I mustn't keep the Earl waiting. Tonight is going to be a very special occasion."

Aphra sat on the bed and rested for a few minutes, and then dashed around and completed her chores in no time. She ran up to her room and put the last few stitches in the unfinished item. She quickly made her way to the Countess's room. As she passed the windows overlooking the gravel drive and turning circle, she saw the lights of a line of carriages outside. She felt very churned up inside to think that she was going to be a part of it all. Arriving at the Countess's room, she tapped lightly on the door.

"Come in, my dear girl," called out the elderly lady, who was taking a rest on her bed? "I expect that you're very excited."

"Actually, Ma'am, I'm terrified. I think that I would rather not go, but I do not want to disappoint the Earl or Monsieur le Comte."

"Oh, hush child. You'll be fine. Dorothy's in the bathroom and waiting for you," said the Countess.

Aphra discovered that Dorothy had run her another bath. "Goodness. I shall wash myself away. This is my second bath today."

"The mistress thought that you'd be rushed off your feet and said that a few minutes soak would refresh you before you go down to the ball."
Forty five minutes later, Aphra was dressed and seated in front of the dressing table, with Dorothy putting the last touches to her hair.

The Countess said to Dorothy. "Don't forget the emeralds. They'll look perfect with her colouring."

"Oh, milady, I couldn't. They're so valuable," protested Aphra. "It wouldn't be right."

"Nonsense, my dear. Cecilia would be delighted to know that her favourite jewels were going out dancing wrapped around such a beautiful throat," said the old lady with a twinkle in her eye.

Both women complimented Aphra on her appearance. Dorothy went to find Claude, who was waiting in the corridor below. Aphra looked in the mirror and was stunned by her own reflection. No longer did she look like the subservient maid. She was an elegant lady. This opinion that she had formed of herself was borne out by the look on Claude's face as she descended the stairs.

***

Caroline was enjoying herself enormously. She had made quite an entrance on the arm of the Earl, as she had sashayed down the stairs into the ballroom. All eyes had been on her. She knew that she was the most striking woman there – dressed in her cleverly cut scarlet gown and dripping in rubies about her ears and throat. Sebastian, who was introducing her to all the leading figures of the county set, was leading her around the room. She was in such a good mood, that she found it easy to smile and be charming and attentive to people. She thought that this had to be the best evening of her life. Perhaps Sebastian would propose to her tonight. She imagined him taking her out to the terrace - and then the big announcement. She could hardly contain her eagerness and impatience.

The orchestra was playing a popular tune as Aphra and Claude walked up the stairs to the Ballroom.

"Monsieur Tanquerel and Miss Aphra Chamberlain," announced the Master of Ceremonies.

The words made Caroline clench her teeth.

Aphra felt her face flush with embarrassment. She'd had no idea that she would be announced. Claude took her hand as he led her down the stairs into the Ballroom. "You look very beautiful when you blush," he said with a rather cheeky grin on his face. "Actually, you look beautiful all the time."

There was a hush about the room and everyone looked towards the staircase. Caroline overheard numerous complimentary remarks being made around her, but her eyes were fixed on the beautiful young woman elegantly making her descent. Her evening was ruined and she knew at that moment, that she would hate Aphra for the rest of her life. However, she continued to hide her feelings. As Claude and Aphra made their way through the throng of people, Sebastian smiled and gestured for them to join his group. He paid very little attention to Claude and made a big fuss of Aphra, much to the chagrin of Caroline. Once again, he was getting a great sense of satisfaction at annoying her so much. He told himself that he needed to curb this rather malicious tendency, but continued all the same. After a few introductions and some extremely noisy joking and laughter, they were interrupted as the orchestra began playing a waltz. Sebastian was tempted to ask Aphra for the first dance, just to annoy Caroline, but he felt that even he could not be that mean. He had noticed that she had started looking rather down at the mouth since Aphra had arrived. He suspected that Caroline had made her work right up to the last minute, so it served her right if Aphra arrived late, and unintentionally made a more spectacular entrance than she had done. However, he took her hand and led her on to the dance floor. This seemed to improve her mood and he spent the next hour or so, attending to her and making her feel important.

He noticed that Aphra was in constant demand. For a girl who had never been to a Ball, she showed confidence and accomplishment in her dancing. Although she was a little apprehensive at dancing with a lot of strangers, she hid her feelings and was gracious and attentive to all, even the elderly gentlemen who partnered her. However, she preferred it when she danced with Claude and felt totally at ease with him. She thought that he would have made a wonderful brother.

After an hour, there was a short interval and food was served. She had been so busy dancing, that Aphra had not realised that she was very hungry. She'd had a number of glasses of champagne and felt a bit strange. Claude noticed that she was getting a bit giggly. "I think that you need to eat something and perhaps have a glass of water," he whispered.

"Why do you say that?"

"Because, young lady, I think that you are drunk!"

She was horrified and then started giggling again. He was amused, but at the same time, concerned in case her mistress noticed. She would not need much of an excuse to get rid of this girl who outshone her in every way, so he steered her towards the conservatory and told her not to move. She was used to being obedient and did exactly as she was told, while he disappeared to get her some refreshment. He returned quickly with the water and a plate of delicious food. After she had finished, she realised that her head was clearer.

"Thank you. If my mistress had seen me behaving in a manner that was inappropriate, she may have dismissed me. I sometimes feel that she is looking for a reason to do so. I don't know why this is so, for I work very hard and she pays me a lower than average salary."

"Do you really not know why? Do you not see that you are a threat to her? She likes to be queen bee and she cannot be that with you constantly around. Do you not see that you surpass her in everything and she hates you?"

Aphra was shocked to her core at this observation of Claude's.

"Come now. We must dance some more. Also, you have not yet danced with your host." He pulled her to a standing position.

"No, I cannot - I must not dance with the Earl. She will be enraged."

"Well, dance with me anyway." Holding her hand, he led her back to the dance floor. She was about to have the next dance with him, when the Earl claimed his right as her host. She tried to make an excuse, but he was having none of it, so she conceded. The next dance was a Polka and at first, she was a little bit hesitant. However, she need not have worried, for they danced together exceptionally well. Caroline felt as though a cold hand touched her heart. She tried to keep smiling and appear nonchalant, but she was very uncomfortable, especially when she overheard an elderly lady comment to her friend "what a lovely couple they make."

Although Aphra thoroughly enjoyed dancing with the Earl, she was relieved to see him dancing with Caroline again. One look at her face told her that trouble could be brewing. Sebastian had realised this, so spent the remainder of the evening pandering to Caroline's every whim and paying her compliments. By the end of the evening, she was in a much better mood and when he suggested that the following day, the two of them should take a trip out in his carriage, she had mellowed considerably. Aphra whispered to Claude that she really needed to leave before her mistress, to enable her to have time to change and be waiting in her bedchamber. He discreetly passed this message on to Sebastian, who feigned a desire to spend time alone with Caroline in the conservatory, after they had bid farewell to their many guests.

This ploy worked better than anyone could have expected and by the time Caroline had returned to her room, Aphra was ready and waiting to attend upon her. She was very nervous as to how she would behave towards her, but she need not have worried, for Caroline was in a very good mood. She was convinced that a proposal would be forthcoming on the following day.

However, Aphra felt very uncomfortable when Caroline asked "where did you get that dress? I was very surprised to see you attired so."

"The Countess sent for me and said that I could wear one of the gowns belonging to her daughter, who died. Wasn't it kind of her?"

"Very kind indeed and so unexpected. I was unaware that you had met her.

Well, get to bed now. I want you up bright and early tomorrow morning. Sebastian is taking me out in the carriage. I do believe that he is going to propose to me."

When Aphra went to bed that night, it was with the knowledge that her mistress was content. Before sleep overcame her, she happily relived what was, so far, the most exciting night of her life. She had felt like a princess and was almost conceited at all the compliments she had been paid. She thought that if she never attended another social engagement in her life, nor dressed in fine clothes again, that for one evening when she was young, she had felt beautiful and happy.

"Dear Mama. I wonder if you saw me tonight as I danced with an Earl and a French Count. Did you smile upon me as I giggled from too much champagne? Were you pleased to see me having such a wonderful time and looking so beautiful in a satin gown? I'm now a lowly servant again, but I have my treasure of memories."

It was a bit chilly in the small bedroom, so she snuggled down under the warm covers and was fast asleep in a couple of minutes.

She had been so tired and slept so deeply, that it seemed like only seconds later that she was awoken by one of the servants knocking on her door. "Your mistress is ringing for you Miss."

"Oh no, not her already," she said as she dragged herself out of bed and quickly dressed. "I wonder what time it is."

"Good morning Ma'am." She tried to sound bright and lively. Caroline was already up and ready for the day to begin. The clock on the mantelpiece said five to six.

"Fetch me some tea and then I want you to do my nails. They need to be at their best for the ring."

Aphra headed towards the door.

"And don't be long. There's a lot to do. Just because you were dancing the night away, is no excuse for laxness today. I don't want you taking advantage of my generosity and good nature."

"I'll be as quick as I can, Ma'am." She closed the door and made her way along the passage and down the back stairs. Once in the kitchen, she set to and got the kettle on the boil. As she was pouring boiling water into the teapot, another guest's maid entered the kitchen bleary eyed and yawning. They acknowledged one another, and the other maid mumbled something about bloody selfishness and being up half the night.

As Aphra carried the tray up the stairs, she muttered under her breath. "One fresh arsenic coming up!"

Two hours later, she was back in the kitchen returning the tray. Her mistress had just gone to the dining room to share breakfast with the Earl. Aphra joined the other servants for her own breakfast and was embarrassed to discover that Dorothy had told them about her adventure the previous evening.

"She looked magnificent. You should have seen her. Looked like a duchess, she did."

Aphra thanked her, but that was not the end of it, for three of the staff that had been on duty in the ballroom were determined to have their say too. Two of the footmen went into details about how they wouldn't have minded a turnabout the floor with her themselves and another one made a rather ribald remark, which earned a rebuke from the butler. He, however, closed the conversation by saying that the young lady had looked very nice and had handled herself with decorum. It was said in a manner that made it clear that the subject was now closed, much to Aphra's relief.

As soon as she had finished her breakfast, she went to her mistress's room and waited for her. Caroline flounced in, confident in the belief that she was soon to be the new Countess. Aphra fetched her outdoor clothes and bid her farewell. She remained looking at the door for some moments after it had closed.

"I wonder what sort of a mood she'll be in when she returns," she thought.

***

The carriage swayed and bumped along the country road as the coachman hurried the horses. Miss Grenville tapped on the roof and demanded in a shrill voice that he get a move on.

"Blimey," he cursed to himself. "She's in a stinker of a mood. I wonder what's eating her."

Aphra sat silently opposite her mistress. As they had taken their farewell of the Earl, Caroline had feigned a calm and seemingly happy countenance as she had thanked him for a delightful visit and his generosity towards her maid, but Aphra knew that she was extremely agitated. She knew the cause and it was as she had expected. The Earl had obviously not proposed to Caroline and would not be doing so.

Caroline felt humiliated and cheated. How dare he make a fool of her? How dare he toy with her feelings in this way? God, the whole county would know about this. She would be a laughing stock – especially as she had perhaps unwisely mentioned her expectations a number of times to several of her cronies. Damn him!

But why had there been no proposal? She had been convinced that he cared for her. It was completely incomprehensible to her. She knew that she must put it out of her mind, but how? She would have to think of some diversion to occupy her mind and also she would have to think of some way of saving face. Perhaps she could make some casual nonchalant response if people enquired. Something on the lines of "I haven't made my mind up," or "you'll have to wait and see." Perhaps she could suggest that "we're just keeping things on a friendly basis for the time being." Yes, that should do it.

For a brief while, she contented herself with this solution, but before long the doubts crept in. As she sat looking at Aphra's serene, expressionless face, all the anger flooded back. In her mind, she saw Aphra as she descended that blasted staircase. She had hated her so much at that moment. Why should Aphra have had all the attention and made an entrance like that, when it was Caroline's night? She should have been in her room and carrying out her duties, not sailing down the stairs on the arm of that blasted Frenchie. He got on her nerves as well. He always seemed to be hanging around. If she had married Sebastian, the first thing that she'd have done was send him packing back to France where he belonged. She detested foreigners and what was he doing in this country anyway?

However, she could not let Aphra know how she felt about her. She would not let a servant get the upper hand. She smiled wanly and made some innocuous remark about the weather and what a pleasant stay they'd had at Methuen Park. Aphra nodded and smiled in return. She made a reply that she thought was fitting adding a touch of subservience, which usually helped to placate her mistress.

Caroline shut her eyes and pretended to be taking a short nap. She hoped that she was giving Aphra the impression that she was relaxed, but the constant fidgeting with her gloves told a different story.

***

On their arrival back at Warrington Grange, Aphra was kept extremely busy for a number of days, so had very little opportunity to speak to Emily about the events at Methuen Park, other than very briefly. As the days passed, so her memories faded in importance and found a comfortable resting place at the back of her mind. No one at the Grange knew of Aphra's acquaintance with either the Earl or the French gentleman. Neither had they heard about her attendance at the ball.

Aphra was now completely back in her routine as a domestic servant. She had been thinking for some time that she needed to speak to her mistress about her promise to review her salary. She had now been working for Caroline for more than six months and felt that it was time to discuss this. However, she felt afraid that this might not be the best time to approach her, as she was not in a good mood – although she pretended to the contrary. Aphra knew her too well. She also wanted to ask about having some time to herself. She hardly ever got her afternoon off. Her mistress always kept her far too busy. She decided that she would bide her time and see if Caroline's mood improved. Also, the housekeeper was away again for a week visiting her relative and Caroline was getting Aphra to carry out some of her duties too.

One morning, after breakfast, she gingerly approached the subject of her afternoons off. Quietly but assertively, she added that she had missed quite a number of them. She held her breath, expecting an angry outburst from her mistress. However, she was pleasantly surprised at Caroline's reaction.

"Yes, I've realised that you have missed some of your free time and I have been meaning to speak to you about it. Never, let it be said that I am not a fair employer."

"Thank you ma'am," Aphra said.

"Well, I take pride in treating my servants well. The likes of a girl like you must be the envy of the county.

Miss Salathial will be back from her visit to her sister in a few days, so I suppose that it will be in order for you to take a whole day off for the next four weeks."

"You are most generous Ma'am," Aphra was tempted to try her luck and mention the salary review, but decided to be content with the days off first.

"You can take Thursdays off. That will inconvenience me the least. Emily can do extra duties if necessary. Ring the bell for her now. You may go."

Aphra curtsied and left the room. As always, it was with a mixture of feelings – relief at getting the time off, indignation at the way her mistress often spoke to her, and complete amazement that Caroline seemed to believe that she was some kind of benign benefactor.

Aphra returned to her room and was surprised to find that a very large package had been left on the bed. On the cabinet beside her bed was an envelope. The envelope was addressed to her in a beautiful hand. She opened it. It was from the Dowager Countess.

***

Methuen Park
Somerset

16th March 1885

My dear Miss Chamberlain,

Please find enclosed a few of my daughter's clothes. I know that I must part with these things and who better to send them to than yourself. I do hope that they will come in useful to you.

I was so pleased to be able to assist you on the evening of the ball. You looked very lovely my dear.

I do hope that I will get the opportunity to see you again one day.

With all good wishes for your health and happiness.

Rose Raemond
Dowager Countess of Tawford

***

She opened the package and inside was a collection of beautiful dresses. Some slight alteration might be necessary as she would probably remove some of the decoration so that they were more in keeping with her station in life.

She decided to say nothing to Caroline about the gift and that night she penned a letter to the Countess thanking her and the Earl for the generosity of the gift.

Later, when Aphra was sitting reading in her room by the fire, Emily looked in.

"I'm just going up now. I want to finish my book. You were right. Once I've read a few pages, I feel as though I'm in the story. I've nearly finished. I wonder what happens to Mr Scrooge. Do you think the ghosts frighten him to death?"

"I'm not telling you. You'll have to find out for yourself. It would spoil it for you if I told you what happened."

"What was in that package?"

"It was from a friend that I made at Methuen Park. It contained some clothes that I hope to alter. I could do with a few extra items. The mistress has allowed me to have the next few Thursdays off, so I shall be able to wear them."

"Ooh, can I see them?"

"Yes, when I've altered them," Aphra said. "Goodnight. Sleep well."

***

On Thursday morning, while they were eating breakfast, Aphra said, "have you finished the book yet, Emily?"

"Oh yes. It was wonderful – made me feel so happy. Everything turned out so nice and Mr Scrooge was kind to everyone and buying lots of things. Thank you. It was a wonderful present. You couldn't have given me anything better.

What have you got planned for today?"

"The mistress is letting me take the pony and trap into Westbridge."

"You lucky thing. She's never let me use it."

"Well, there's a downside. She wants me to make some purchases for her, so the whole day won't be my own.

"That's true - doesn't surprise me. She always has to drain the last bit of blood out of us," Emily remarked.

"I may have a meal in that little café – the one that we went to. Do you remember? I'm going to treat myself to something really tasty, but most of all, I'm just going to sit and take it easy. I may do a little shopping for myself."

After breakfast, Aphra put on one of the dresses that had belonged to the Earl's sister. She had removed some of the lace, so that it did not look too ostentatious. As she walked around to the stable, Mickey harnessed the pony to the small trap and she climbed up.

"Are you sure you'll be alright Miss?" He looked worried.

"Yes, thank you. I've driven one of these before."
She turned the trap around and made her way down the drive. It was a bit misty, but it looked as though the sun was trying to break through. She was sure that it would be sunny by the time she got to Westbridge.

She took things at a leisurely pace and just let the pony trot along. As she drove through Watheford, she saw a few of the local people who smiled and waved at her. A couple of gentlemen raised their hats and she nodded. She felt a bit like the lady of the manor and it amused her.

By the time she arrived in Westbridge, it was almost eleven o clock.

Walking past the shops, she stopped to look in the windows and seeing what she was looking for, entered a few of them. When she had completed her shopping, she crossed the road and stopped outside the teashop. She opened the door and stepped inside and walked towards the back of the room.

"Would you like a table, Miss?"

"Yes, please. Would it be alright if I sat here?"

"Of course, Miss. It's nice and warm here beside the fire. Can I get you something?"

"May I look at the menu, please?"

"I'll get it for you," she said, as the street door opened. "I'll just see to these two ladies." She bustled off and greeted the newcomers and showed them to a table by the window. Then she went into the kitchen to fetch the menu. Aphra drew a small book on flowers that she had purchased out of her bag.

The door opened again. Just as the waitress was bringing the menu to her, a very smartly dressed, fair-haired gentleman walked slowly towards the back of the room. The waitress was just about to greet him, when he suddenly exclaimed in a foreign accent "Well, fancy seeing you here Mademoiselle!"

"Goodness!" Aphra said as she looked up. "This is a surprise. What are you doing in this part of the world Monsieur?"

"Oh, I've been looking for a particular book and I'd heard that there was a very good bookshop in Westbridge. Please may I join you? If it would not be improper."

"By all means. It will be very nice to have some company while I eat my lunch."

"But I see that I am disturbing you. You are reading your book."

"Not at all," she replied and replaced the book in her bag.

"Are you sure that this is alright, Miss? If he's annoying you, I can tell the boss."

"No, it'll be in order. I know this gentleman - but thank you all the same," Aphra assured her.

He sat down and the waitress handed Aphra the menu. "I'll get one for the gentleman." She went back to the kitchen. She was not too happy about it and felt quite worried. After all, he was a foreigner. She brought him a menu and then went to serve the other customers.

At last, they could talk without being overheard.

"How are you, Miss Chamberlain?" Sebastian and I have been worried that Mademoiselle is perhaps making life difficult for you. Is it not so?"

"She has been very moody. Probably worse than she usually is, but I know how to cope with her. She was very upset when we returned home. It was a nightmare."

"Ah. That was because she did not go home with a ring on her finger. Am I right?"

"Yes. She'd almost picked out the gown, the flowers and the hymns." They both laughed a little at this. "I shouldn't be unkind, but you know Monsieur, she can be so nasty sometimes, that it stops me having any compassion for her."

"She is a dreadful woman - and please, call me Claude," he said. "Sebastian realised that he could not tie himself to her. What was it he called her? A harpy – that was it. I know not what it means, but I assume that it is not complementary."

"It certainly isn't. Yes, I'd like to call you Claude and you must call me Aphra. We're friends after all.

"My mistress wouldn't be too pleased if she knew that we were dining together. We shall have to keep it a secret," she added.

"Most definitely. If your mistress ever found out, it would not be good for you. I shall never forget the expression on her face as you and I descended the stairs at the ball. Although she did her best to hide it, I have never seen such hatred directed at another human being as she directed it at you. You must be very careful."

"I shall endeavour to do so. Now, that's enough talk about the gorgon," Aphra said. "I'm absolutely famished. Let's look at the menu. The food is usually very good in here."

"Yes, let us not talk about it anymore. It will ruin our appetites. What can you recommend?"

"They do a lovely vegetable soup. I've had that before. Also, the roast beef smells delicious."

The sat in silence for a few minutes and each studied the menu. The waitress returned and they placed their orders.
"Do you have any wine?" Claude asked her.

"I think that we have some Claret," she said. "I'll go and find out. She came back with a dusty bottle in her hand. "Will this be alright, sir?"
He nodded his head. "It really should be allowed to breathe," he said. "But we will make do."

"This really is a treat. Fancy, me, a servant dining and drinking wine with a gentleman in the middle of the day – how decadent," she whispered.

"You will go straight to hell you wicked girl," replied Claude.

"I hope not. I've already been there – more than once," she replied – much to his surprise.

They did not have long to wait for their food. The wine was poured and Claude made a toast to friendship. Although they were a little quieter while they ate, they still chatted a bit and when they had finished, Claude asked to see what desserts were available. They chose two fruit pies with custard, which they ate slowly as they were talking so much.

They exchanged all kinds of information about childhood, parents and schooldays. Claude told her how he and Sebastian had met. Sometimes they spoke in French, but mainly in English for Claude's command of the language was far superior to Aphra's schoolgirl French. They were both pleasantly surprised to discover that they had many likes and dislikes in common. They shared a similar sense of humour and more than once, Aphra had needed to wipe the tears from her eyes as she was laughing so much. When Claude called the waitress over to settle up the bill, Aphra detected an air of disapproval on her face – although the pursed lips relaxed a little when he left her a very generous tip.

Aphra noticed that the waitress was serving afternoon teas to some new diners who had entered the little café. "What's the time?" She had completely lost track. She was having so much fun.

He took out the watch from his waistcoat. "It is five to three. What time do you have to be back?"

"I don't have to be back until six thirty, but I don't want to be out after dark." She didn't fancy driving down country lanes alone.

"Then you should begin your journey back. Would you like to meet again? I have enjoyed your company very much."

"I should like that. The mistress owes me quite a bit of time, so she told me that I can take four Thursdays off in a row. This was the first, so what about next week?"

"I shall be honoured, but we shall have to think of somewhere else. You will be scandalised if we dine here again." As they left the teashop, he thought about it. "Perhaps I can meet you and then we can go on somewhere else."

They walked a little way along the road towards the Ostlers. Aphra saw the carriage with the Earl's family crest on the door. "Well, that will get people gossiping," she said. "Perhaps it would be a good idea to travel in a more modest carriage next time."
"What is gossiping?"

"I need to go. I'll tell you next week."

"I'll find a suitable place to meet. Will it be alright to write to you? Will anyone see the letter?"

"Only Emily and she won't say anything. It should be alright." They discreetly shook hands and Claude watched Aphra go into the Ostler's. He got inside his carriage and waited until he saw her driving off down the road. Then he told the coachman to head back to Methuen Park.

As he sat back in the carriage, he put a rug over his knees. There was a chill in the air. He hoped that Aphra would not get cold in that little trap. He was also concerned for her safety. He did not like to think of her on her own on a lonely the country lane.

A while later as the carriage sped on, he looked at his watch. It was gone five thirty and the sun had almost set. He hoped that she had returned safely to Warrington Grange.

At that precise moment, Aphra was entering the servants' hall. After dinner, when they were enjoying a cup of tea, Aphra showed them her book. Mr Isaacs was most interested and had a good look at it before he went to his parlour. Gracie enjoyed looking at the pictures and Emily showed off her literacy skills by pointing out the names of a few of the flowers.

Gracie handed the book back to Aphra. She had noticed that she had been giggling during the meal. "Your face looks a bit flushed, Aphra."

Aphra was taken aback by this remark and for a few seconds and did not know how to reply. "It must be from the cold wind on the journey back in the trap." As she was saying this, the bell rang.

"I'd better go up and attend to the mistress," she said quickly and darted out of the room.

"Maud, get cleaning those pans," Gracie demanded. The scullery maid reluctantly dragged herself out of the chair and slouched off to the kitchen. When she was out of earshot, Gracie turned back to look at Emily. "Cold wind? My eye. That girl's been drinking while she's been out today!"

Emily said nothing, but her thoughts had been running along the same lines.

***

A few days later, a letter from Claude arrived. Unknown to Aphra, the housekeeper had intercepted it, steamed it open and taken it to the mistress who read the contents and then replaced them inside.

"So," she thought, "there was an attraction between her and the Frenchman. At least it still left some hope that there might yet be a chance for her with Sebastian.

"Reseal it and put it back on the tray and don't inform her that we have knowledge of this. Let's wait and see what happens. You may go. You can bring those accounts up to me later. I've things to attend to at present," she said dismissively.

As the housekeeper walked towards the door, she turned and said "I shall keep a special lookout for her on Thursday, ma'am."

"Yes, do that," replied the mistress.

The housekeeper left the room and went about her daily tasks. Caroline sat quietly for some time and thought about the situation. Into her mind came the expression about giving someone enough rope. This made her feel much better.

The letter had been returned to the tray and Miss Salathial waited until later in the morning to inform Aphra that she had received some post.

"Miss Chamberlain," she said, in that intimidating and disapproving voice that Aphra always felt was especially reserved for her. "There is some correspondence in the hall addressed to you. I cannot begin to think who would be writing to a person in your position."

She replied politely that perhaps it was from her father's lawyer. She went to the hall and picked up the letter and placed it in her pocket.

She continued with her duties and left the reading of the letter until she was alone in her room at bedtime. She knew that it was from Claude and that it would be information on their next meeting on Thursday. She felt that the time could not go fast enough. It was going to be every exciting. If the weather was good, then Claude was going to take her on a picnic.

***

Thursday dawned with promise and Aphra had a spring in her step as she made her way through the woods. It was such a comfort to be with Claude. She loved Emily dearly and she enjoyed the few minutes of time that they were able to spend together. Emily could be most amusing and was quite bright, but Aphra enjoyed being able to discuss subjects that Emily knew nothing about.

Claude was waiting in a clearing under the trees near the village. He walked towards her, both hands held out in warm greeting. "Dearest girl. You look well." He kissed her on both cheeks in a Gallic gesture.

They chatted as he helped her up into the small carriage. Within minutes, they were speeding along in the open countryside towards a part of the county that he knew well. As he pulled on the reins, he spoke softly in French to the horse and it responded by slowing down. Continuing in his native tongue, he turned to Aphra and commented that he thought that this would be a fine place for them to enjoy their picnic.

She had already enjoyed the journey immensely. At first, she had been a little self-conscious about speaking French. It had been so long since she had done so and she thought that she was very rusty, but she soon forgot her initial concerns and they were soon both chattering away. Every so often, Claude helped her when she faltered, struggling for the correct word, or getting the pronunciation right, and they laughed quite a bit when there was some misunderstanding or the wrong word or phrase was used. She cast her eye over the landscape. The breath-taking view across the valley filled her soul with joy. Oh it was so good to get away from the irritations of daily life.

"This is perfect Claude," she responded. "Aren't you clever to find such a beautiful spot?"

"I often ride up here. It reminds me of home."

He tethered the horse to a nearby tree. Then he carried the picnic items over to a flat patch of grass where Aphra was laying a chequered tablecloth over a blanket. They sat down and as Aphra laid out the dishes, cutlery and napkins, Claude opened a bottle of wine.

"What a magnificent spread," she said as she peered into the wicker hamper. "You have been busy."

"This is from my family's vineyard. I hope that you enjoy it," he said as he handed her the glass with the pale liquid.

As she sipped the wine, Claude lent back and slowly savoured the product of his family's chateau with all the familiarity of a connoisseur.

"This is a beautiful wine, Claude," she said. "I had no idea that wine could be so different. This is crisp and quite different from the one that we drank last week."

"That was vinegar. It was an insult to the name of Claret," he said with disgust.

"Well, I'd better not have too much of this," she laughed as he refilled her glass. "I shall be in trouble with my mistress if I return to my duties under the influence of alcohol again. I'm sure that Emily and Gracie noticed that I was rather flushed and giggly last week."

For some minutes, they sat in silence digesting the beauty of the scenery as well as the food. They were very comfortable with one another and felt no awkwardness at all. It was as though they had known each other for years.

"You miss it, don't you? Tell me about it."

Claude remained silent for a couple of minutes. He was leaning forward and resting his chin on his hands. He continued gazing pensively into the distance. He turned and looked at her and she could see the tears in his eyes. He cleared his throat and began to talk.

"The view from up here is similar to the countryside that surrounds my home in many respects and yet it is also very different. If you can imagine that yonder where the road leads down to that little hamlet, and the road meanders through the wooded hills, there is a lake to the far left, which stretches quite a few miles. In the distance, at the far end of the valley, is the chateau. The first things that a visitor notices are the pointed turrets. The light is different there and the white stone gleams in the sunshine and the blue sky is reflected in the water and the windows. To reach the chateau, one drives through acres of vines that disappear up the slopes on each side of the valley. As one gets near to the house, one passes the formal gardens. They were designed as copies of the gardens at Versailles – although not as grand of course. In the summer, the parterre is full of vibrant colours."

He paused for a few seconds and wiped his eyes.

"But my life is here with Sebastian. I love him very much and I have become used to this country and your ways. Somerset is very beautiful – different from my home, but just as lovely in its own way. I suppose that anyone who moves to live in another country will always be torn. It's a case of roots and branches, isn't it? I always have a feeling of longing to be at home, but I could never live away from Sebastian, for I would always be longing to be here. But you know, it is a great comfort to be able to speak my native tongue with you. Sebastian can order wine in a restaurant and count to ten, but that is about it."

Aphra touched him gently on the sleeve of his jacket and he suddenly became a bit embarrassed. "Oh some people are never satisfied," he laughed. "Please, have one of these delicious little tarts that I have had made especially for you. The cook at Methuen Park is very good about trying out French recipes that I give to Sebastian. Of course, they think that it is for him. It wouldn't do for her to be obeying requests from the secretary, would it?"

"These are lovely Claude. I've never tasted anything like it she said as she wiped away a few crumbs from her lip. "Too much of this and I shall get fat!"

They sat in peaceful silence for a few minutes and then Claude said "tell me about your life. You've told me a little about yourself, but I'm interested to know more.

Aphra began to talk about herself. She took up where she had left off the week before. She told him about her life as a child and her parents and grandparents, of life in the village and the house in which she lived.

She was quiet for a few moments, struggling in her mind whether or not to tell him her big secret. "I have something to tell you that I've only ever told one other person. Will you keep it to yourself until the time is right to bring it out in the open?"

He nodded.

"My grandmother was the daughter of the Viscount of Westbridge. The Kingston family have no knowledge of my existence."

"What! Why are working as a skivvy to that dreadful woman?"

"Because I do not want to contact them until I feel that I have made a success of my life. I want to be independent. I don't want them thinking that I'm just some kind of fortune hunter. I want them to accept me and not shoo me away from the door."

"Well, that is most admirable," he said. "But I think that you would have a much easier life if you were to get in touch with them. However, I applaud your honourable intentions, although I think that you are making a very big mistake. I shall not reveal your secret – not even to Sebastian."

"Thank you Claude. Goodness. Haven't I chattered on?"

"It's been fascinating," Claude said. "Your life has been so different from mine – although there are similarities as well."

He looked at his watch. "I need to get you back. I hope that I can see you next week. You have two more days that she owes you."

"I would love to see you Claude. What shall we do and where shall we meet?" She asked.

"I think that we should meet at the same spot at about the same time. I will write with any necessary details, and in case anyone happens to see the letter, I shall write in French."

Just before Aphra stepped down from the carriage a short distance from the Grange, Claude handed her a small parcel. "I hope that you will accept this little gift. Don't open it now. Wait until you are alone in your room."

"Merci beaucoup, Claude."

"Au revoir," he replied. "Till next Thursday."

"Au revoir – and please remember me to his Lordship."

When she got to her room, she opened the small package. Inside was a silver chain and pendant. On the pendant was an inscription.

Pour ma belle Aphra - Je t'aime
Ma soeur et mon amie

She left it on the cabinet beside the bed and went to attend to her mistress. When she had completed her tasks, she went down to eat her evening meal. She noticed that the housekeeper was not present. What she did not know was that the housekeeper had been in her room and had shown the item of jewellery to the mistress.

***

Over the next fortnight, Aphra and Claude met twice more. On the next Thursday, he drove her into Taunton where they had an enjoyable lunch in a small restaurant in a quiet side street, followed by a pleasant afternoon looking at the shops. Aphra took the opportunity to purchase one or two items that were not available in Westbridge. Claude wanted to buy her all sorts of things, but she felt uncomfortable that he had already treated her more than enough and refused to accept anything except a book that he had brought with him. Although he felt slightly offended, he also acknowledged and appreciated her concern for his financial position. Admittedly, Sebastian made him a handsome allowance, but Aphra still felt uneasy about accepting expensive presents and if her own financial position had been better, she would have liked to purchase some small trinket for him.

On the fourth and final Thursday, the weather had turned cold and wet. Aphra's boots were covered in mud as she climbed into the small carriage. They had hoped to have another picnic, but this was out of the question now. However, Claude told her that he had brought a hamper along with him and that Sebastian had given him the key of a small remote cottage that had recently been refurbished in anticipation of a new tenant. Sebastian owned property all over the county, so Aphra was not surprised by this.

The cottage was at the end of a lane and she thought that in sunshine, it must be a very pretty little house. As Claude saw to the horse and the carriage, Aphra unlocked the door. Inside, it was very small, but clean and freshly painted. In the hearth, the grate was made up and ready with kindling. By the time Claude walked in carrying the hamper, she had the fire alight and the flames were licking up the chimney and beginning to give off some heat.

"That looks most welcoming," he said carrying in the hamper and placing it on a chair in the corner.

A copper kettle was sitting on a small trivet in the hearth.

"Did you bring any tea?" She asked.

"Of course," he replied with humour in his voice. "Would I dare to come out on a day like this with an Englishwoman and not bring tea?"

There was an oil lamp on a small table and a couple of candles on the mantelpiece. She lit these and the room began to take on a warm glow.

While Aphra was making the tea, he went out to the carriage. He returned a few minutes later carrying a small box.

"What have you there?" She asked.

"A chess set. Do you play?"

"I haven't played for years Claude, but I would love to. I've probably forgotten how. You'll beat me easily."

As the room became warm and cosy, they took off their wet outer garments and boots and sat down. Hours passed in quiet enjoyment. Aphra reacquainted herself with chess and they played two games. He won the first, but by the time they played a second game, she was back on form and beat him. It was such fun teasing and bantering with each other and then quietly and intimately discussing all their little secrets and worries.

After they had eaten lunch, the heat of the room together with the wine that they had drunk made them sleepy and both dozed together on the little sofa. Aphra felt that it was so nice to lean her head on his shoulder and to feel safe and protected with his arm around her, and not feel uneasy or threatened by him in any way.

When it was time to go home, they cleared up everything, extinguished the lights and the fire, and locked the door. The weather had grown increasingly bad throughout the day and the journey back to Warrington Grange was quite treacherous. As they approached the Grange, Claude said "I shall have to take you nearer to the house. You cannot make that long walk back in this wind and rain."

At first Aphra would have none of this, for she was concerned that someone from the house might see them together. However, he convinced her that no-one in their right mind would be outside on a night like this, so she agreed to his taking the carriage near to the outhouses that the gardeners used.

"I can make my way easily from there," she said.

As she alighted from the carriage, Claude kissed her hand. "It has been a most wonderful afternoon in spite of this dreadful weather," he said. "It was so warm and comfortable to fall asleep together in the glow of the firelight after the fun little games that we played which quite wore me out."

"Well, I must say Claude that I felt quite weary myself. It must have been because the cottage was so warm and cosy. What would Sebastian have said if he had seen us?

"Ooh - such wickedness!"

"Indeed, we are very naughty people," Aphra replied and then giggled. "I must go. I don't want to draw attention to your presence. Goodness, I feel quite light-headed with all that wine. I hope that I do not miss my footing. The ground is very slippery."

"Take care. I know that I will not be able to see you for a while, but I'll try and write in a few days. Sebastian will be away and it will be easier then.

She turned around and lent into the carriage and kissing him on the cheek whispered "You're a dear man – like a favourite older brother. Thank you for all your kindness to me. It has brightened up my life these last few weeks. I shall miss you. Please give my best wishes to Sebastian."
As she went to go, he grabbed her hand. "You know how much you mean to me, don't you? You are a very special and unusual woman and I have grown to love you deeply."

"And I love you too, Claude." Gently she caressed his cheek and then quickly ran around the corner into the wind and the rain.

As Claude turned the horses and steered the carriage down the lane, a sodden figure in a hooded cloak emerged from one of the outhouses. She had seen and heard almost everything.

***

As Miss Salathial never again referred to her receiving correspondence, Aphra had become relaxed about corresponding with Claude. As their friendship grew, so did their familiarity and the tone of their writing - although much of it was in French.

Miss Salathial continued to intercept the letters. After they had been read, the housekeeper resealed them and returned them to the tray. Naturally, the mistress had been told about the incident near the outhouses. The housekeeper had embellished and distorted one or two of her observations, so that Caroline was shocked at what sounded like an afternoon of drunken debauchery.

All this business was vexing Caroline greatly. The last time that Aphra had been out with Claude, Caroline had searched her room, and was irritated to find that she had received a book in French on wine production, as well as the silver pendant. He had written something that she couldn't understand inside the cover as it was in French and this annoyed her even more, as it just highlighted Aphra's intellectual superiority. She also discovered the items of clothing, including the lace underwear that Aphra had received from the Countess. She mistakenly believed that these were gifts from Claude.

She found it difficult to control the rage inside her when Aphra returned from her final day out, she decided that she would put a stop to these outings by not allowing Aphra to have any time off at all for a while. She would keep her busy. One day, she flew into a tantrum because Aphra had been singing some little French ditty that she had obviously learned from Claude. Aphra had been shocked – frightened even at such an outburst. The mistress had almost seemed like a madwoman.

After a few days of her emotions veering from one extreme to another, Caroline realised that she could not stand to have Aphra around. She wanted to dismiss her, but she knew that she would never get another maid anywhere near as good again. So she made a temporary compromise. She would let Aphra think that she was giving her a holiday because she had done well. While she was away, Caroline would take some time to consider the situation. A couple of weeks should help to clear her thoughts.

***

"She's usually so mean about days off. It's like trying to get blood out of a stone," complained Emily. "I feel quite jealous. What d'you think you'll do?"

"I don't know. I thought it might be nice to visit the seaside – perhaps Minehead or Clevedon. What do you think?"

"Why don't you speak to Mr Isaacs? He goes to stay with friends in Minehead every year for his holiday. I think he'd be able to advise you."

***

The following evening, Caroline attended a dinner in Westbridge hosted by some business connections of Gregory. She did not really want to go, but discovered that Sebastian would be going, so accepted the invitation to accompany her cousin. Gregory called for her in his carriage and proceeded to bore her all the way there with anecdotes about people that she did not know. She tried to smile and make the appropriate responses, but she was so irritated by the time they arrived at the Guild Hall, that it was as much as she could do to be polite to those with whom she came into contact. However, her mood lifted when she discovered that she was seated almost opposite Sebastian. During the meal, polite small talk passed between them. However, after the men had finished their port and cigars and joined the women for coffee, Sebastian came over to Caroline and spoke to her.

"How are you Caroline?"

"Well, I'm feeling rather peeved that I've not heard from you for a while. In fact I've heard nothing since I wrote to you after my visit," she pouted.

"I'm so sorry about that. I'm afraid that I've been very busy with one thing and another. Please accept my apologies."

"What is so important that it stops you from finding time to pen a letter to me or paying me a visit?"

"Oh this and that," he replied – somewhat sheepishly she thought, as though he had something to hide. "Come. Let us not quarrel. Let me get you another coffee," he said as he took her cup and went to replenish it.

When he returned and handed it to her, she was more amiable. "Thank you." They chatted pleasantly for a while and then someone came over and asked if the Earl could join another group of people as his opinion was required regarding some financial matters.

"Please excuse me Caroline. It has been nice to see you again." She detected a coolness in his manner.

"Of course. I understand. Please keep in touch. If you're too busy to write, then get that Secretary to do it for you. That's what you pay him for, isn't it?"

"Oh, I can't do that at the moment," he replied as he walked away. "He's taking himself off on holiday for a few weeks. Most inconvenient and inconsiderate don't you think?"

After this, Gregory came over to her and she told him that she had a headache and wanted to leave. Reluctantly, he agreed to this and ten minutes later, they were on the way back to Warrington Grange.

"Did you have a pleasant evening Caroline?" He could see that she was not in a good humour.

"Yes, very nice Gregory. It's just that my head hurts so." She shut her eyes so as to deter him from talking anymore.

Later, as she was being helped by Aphra to prepare for bed, she asked the girl if she had made arrangements to spend her holiday away.

"Yes ma'am. Thank you very much. I was just about to tell you that I will be going to Minehead the day after tomorrow. I very much appreciate your generosity in giving me this time off. I am very excited and can hardly think of anything else," she said as she folded her mistress's clothes.

"Yes, well just make sure that you behave yourself and be sensible with your money. You don't want to find yourself in a state again. Now, leave me. You can go to your room now," she said with a forced smile.

"Goodnight ma'am."

"What. Oh yes," she replied distractedly. As soon as Aphra had shut the door, the smile disappeared. "So, they're going to the seaside together. I hope they both drown."

PART THREE - THE IMPORTANCE OF BEING HONEST

Two days later, dressed in the smart clothes she'd received from the Countess, and carrying a small valise that Mr Isaacs loaned her, Aphra boarded the train for Minehead. He had contacted his friends, Mr and Mrs Hutton, and asked if one of his staff could spend her holiday at their establishment. What Aphra did not know, was that he had sent some money to help out with the costs. He'd written that this was a very hard-working young lady who was in need of a couple of weeks' break.

From the train, she eagerly observed everything as it sped by. She loved all the little stations where the train stopped. She enjoyed watching people getting on and off the train. At one point, when there was no one in her carriage, she leant out of the window and looked at the sea. It was wonderful to feel the wind in her face – although she was less enthusiastic about the smuts from the engine.

She felt very excited at the prospect of this little adventure. She noticed an unusual looking house up in the hills. She had brought some artists' materials, and thought that it would make a good subject. She'd been surprised at the reasonable charges of the guest house, which meant that she would have a little extra money to spend on treats and gifts.

It was beginning to get dark when the train reached the end of the line, so she could see very little of Minehead as she walked down the platform. Although Mr Isaacs had given her clear directions, she checked with the ticket collector that these were correct.

"Just up there, Miss. It should only take you a few minutes," he said pointing up the road that went inland. She found *Channel Views* very easily and smiled at the inappropriate name. The guest house was small but respectable looking.

A diminutive, grey-haired lady, wearing a lace cap and pinafore, opened the door and was very welcoming as she gestured warmly to Aphra. "Come in, my dear. It's very nice to see you. Here, let me take your case. My husband will take it up to your room shortly. Go into the parlour and sit by the fire."

Aphra entered what was a very inviting medium-sized room, full of bric-a-brac and decorated with lots of warm red tones. She sat down on a comfortable wing chair by the fire. Mrs Hutton was busy for a few minutes bustling about making tea and handing her sandwiches and cake.

Aphra stroked a large, fluffy cat that was sleeping in a basket beside the chair. As soon as Mrs Hutton sat down, it jumped straight on to her lap. Mrs Hutton asked Aphra a few questions about life at Warrington Grange and of course enquired after the health of Mr Isaacs. Aphra felt very relaxed and happy.

"I expect that you're tired from your journey," said Mrs Hutton. "I'll show you to your room when you've finished. Here, have some more tea."

Aphra put her hand up. "No, thank you. I've had more than enough. I shall return home fat and unable to work," she laughed.

"Nonsense, my dear. I hear from Mr Isaacs that you've been working very hard. Besides, I like making a fuss of people."

Mrs Hutton told Aphra a little of her time as a cook. "It was a bleak place there at The Hall – just outside Taunton it was. That was where I met Mr Hutton. He was the under butler, and of course, Mr Isaacs was the butler. He was ever so nice to work for. Firm, but always kind."

"Oh I know. He's a lovely man. He doesn't say much, but he's so nice to have as the person in charge. I shouldn't say this, but the housekeeper is a proper tartar. She really frightens me, but Mr Isaacs is always very kind and fair."

"Well, he's a soft spot for you - spoke very highly of you in his letter. You know you are about the same age as his daughter was when she died."

"I didn't know that he had lost a daughter."

"Yes and his wife too. I met them once. They both had auburn hair like you. He adored them and was heart-broken when they died of typhus. It was many years ago."

"Oh, how sad. I had no idea."

"You know, you look rather like the girl. Maybe that is why he is so fond of you."

Aphra smiled at this pleasant revelation.

C'mon, let's get you upstairs," said Mrs Hutton.

Aphra followed her up the stairs and along a narrow corridor, where the light from the oil lamp made dancing shadows on the wall.

"Here we are my dear. I hope you'll be comfortable." She placed the lamp on the table beside the bed and lit another one that was already there. Then she patted the bed. "This is the best mattress in the house, so you should sleep well. Breakfast is at eight."

"I shall be asleep as soon as my head touches the pillow," said Aphra, as she sat on the bed. "Thank you for your hospitality. Good night."

"Goodnight dear. There's an extra blanket in that cupboard if you need it," said Mrs Hutton as she closed the door.

Aphra heard her padding softly down the stairs. There was just enough light to find her nightdress in the case. She quickly undressed and slipped under the covers. As predicted, she was asleep in seconds.

Although habit dictated that she woke early, she allowed herself the luxury of just savouring the pleasure of doing nothing, until the aroma of bacon and eggs wafting upstairs tempted her to get up. She opened the curtains. It looked as though it was going to be a fine day. Just before eight, she closed her bedroom door behind her and went downstairs. Mrs Hutton was carrying a pot of tea through to the dining room.

"Hello dear," she beckoned with her free hand. "In you come."

There were two other guests already seated. They smiled and nodded at Aphra.

"Good morning," she said.

"Good morning to you," said a man sporting large whiskers. "The weather looks promising."

The rather matronly lady opposite him buttered a piece of toast and handed it to him.

"Here you are George. Eat this," she ordered in a bossy, yet maternal manner and then turned towards Aphra. "Nice and refreshed this morning?"

"Oh yes - very well, thank you. I'm ready to do some exploring today –

although I've no idea where to go first."

Mrs Hutton placed a plate of bacon and eggs in front of her. "This looks delicious," Aphra exclaimed.

After breakfast, she set off for her morning walk and was soon overlooking the sea. The breeze was bracing and she decided to step out briskly and head towards the hill at the end of the esplanade. After a few minutes, she came to a wooded area. She ambled along for a while, stopping here and there to look at different things. Slowly she started to retrace her steps. There was a bench and she sat down and looked at the sea.

It had been many years since she had seen the sea. It made her feel sad all of a sudden, for the last time she had been somewhere like this, she was with mama and grandpapa. She sat there for some time in reverie about her childhood. They had gone to Sidmouth, she remembered, and they had stayed at a comfortable hotel overlooking the beach. She remembered playing with her bucket and spade. Mama was always very elegant just sitting watching - her parasol shading her lovely face from the sun. Grandpapa, on the other hand, would be very undignified and roll his trouser legs up and paddle in the water with the little girl that she used to be. He would splash her and they would all laugh. She loved it best when he made sandcastles for her and she would collect shells to decorate them. She remembered them both laughing at her once, when the ice cream that he'd just bought for her, had started to melt and run down her hands. She'd had a fit of pique about it and he'd teased her gently.

"You alright, Miss?" Aphra looked up to see a tall man, wearing a brown suit and doffing a bowler hat, standing over her.

"Yes. I'm perfectly well. Why are you asking?"

""cos you're crying, my dear." He handed her a handkerchief.
"Am I? How strange. I didn't realise." She wiped her eyes and cheeks, and then offered the handkerchief back to the man.

""No, you keep it Accept it as a gift."

"Thank you." She dabbed at her eyes and then her nose. "It's not like me to be so silly and sentimental. I don't know what came over me."

"Do you have any objection if I sit here?"

"Not at all." She moved to one end of the bench, so that there would be a respectable distance between them. "I was just thinking about my childhood – that's all. Perhaps Memory Lane is a place better not revisited."

"I shouldn't think your childhood was that long ago."

"It seems like a different lifetime. So much has happened since then."

"I hate to see such a pretty young lady looking so sad." He looked at Aphra. She turned to look at him. He had the most penetrating blue eyes that she had ever seen. She forgot her sadness for a moment, for she was completely mesmerized by them.

They chatted for a few minutes about the weather and the seaside. Realising suddenly, that this was a rather isolated spot, she said awkwardly "I really should be making my way back."

He stood up and replaced his hat. "I need to as well. Can I walk with you?"

Aphra hesitated. She wasn't sure that it would be proper, but then she thought that it would be nice to have someone to talk to and he was dressed in respectable clothes, although his accent was not refined. "Of course," she replied.

He told her that he was a salesman working for a company in Bristol that made agricultural equipment. "I've been overworking recently and the doc suggested a rest. So here I am - hoping that the sea air will improve my health," he said. "I'm staying in a small lodging house just up North Hill."

"I hope that it isn't too steep for you," said Aphra kindly. "I expect it's quite tiring."

"Very steep indeed. But good exercise."

As they walked back towards the town, he suggested that perhaps they could go for some tea. He mentioned a teashop that he knew. Aphra felt unsure about the correctness of taking tea with a man that she hardly knew. However, he'd been kind, and besides, he was unwell, so there could be no harm in it.

There were a number of tearooms on the main street. He suggested one that was about half way along. He ordered a pot of tea and some muffins.

"I'm very pleased to see you smiling and hopefully, there'll be no more sightings of those tears."

After they had tea, they sat and talked for a long time. Aphra told him all about herself and her life at Warrington Grange.

"I'm most surprised to hear that you're a servant. You look like a real lady in your fine clothes," he remarked.

Aphra briefly mentioned her connection with the Earl of Tawford and related the events leading up to her attending the ball and he seemed most impressed. She felt guilty that she'd said so much about herself, as she realised that she knew nothing about him.

"There, listen to me boasting about my aristocratic connections and not giving you a chance to tell me about your life," she said, but he seemed reluctant to talk about it.

"My life is nowhere near as interesting as yours. I don't like to talk about myself. I'd rather hear all about you. You're a much more interesting topic of conversation."

After a while, Aphra stood up to leave. "I should be getting back," she said looking up at the clock on the wall.

He paid the bill and they went outside. "Thank you for your kindness. It's been most enjoyable," she said.

"What else d'you hope to do while you're here?" He asked.

"I'm not sure. I thought that perhaps I might see if there's a park. Perhaps there's a band that plays there."

"Yes, there usually is in these places. I enjoy that too. Perhaps we'll meet again."

As they said their goodbyes, he took her hand and kissed it. It was really most unseemly of him to do that. They had only just met. However, she felt quite excited by it. It made her feel desired and grown up.

When she returned to *Channel Views,* Mrs Hutton remarked on how flushed she looked. "It's this sea air," she added.

"Mrs Hutton, is there a park here and do they have a bandstand? I should so like to go to listen to it if there is."

"Oh yes, dear. The park is just a few minutes' walk from here." She gave Aphra directions. "I believe that the band plays there on Sunday afternoons. Other guests have said that they're very good. I think that they begin about two thirty."

***

On Sunday afternoon, Aphra decided to take a stroll in the direction of the park. The band had already begun playing and she followed the sound. She saw the gates on a corner of the street and walked into the park. It was not large, but was very pleasing with lawns, trees and shrubs. She was pleased to see that many spring flowers were in bloom and their colours made a cheerful treat for the eyes.

Walking past numerous strollers, she made her way towards the bandstand. There was a large audience and she spent a few moments perusing the scene until she noticed a couple of empty deckchairs. She walked around the perimeter of the seats and sat on the one that was nearest to her to avoid disturbing the people already seated. After a few minutes, she sensed that someone was standing beside her chair. She looked up.

"Good afternoon," whispered the gentleman. "No tears today, I trust? Can I join you?" He asked, lifting his hat.

"Please, do," she replied as she moved along to the next seat making room for him. For the next hour, they listened quietly to the music, only speaking to comment on the performance during the applause. When the band finished up with *God Save the Queen* everyone rose and stood to attention. As the musicians disbanded, the audience disbursed and many began to walk towards the exit.

When the majority of the people had moved away, he said "it's nice to see you looking happier today."

"I'm enjoying myself very much. The music was so cheerful and rousing.

Isn't this a beautiful park? Just look at those trees. I love trees. I look upon them as my friends."

"Do you know, so do I," he replied. They walked around admiring the park, and everything that Aphra said she liked, he seemed to do the same. Aphra watched some children playing with a hoop and a couple of others playing with a ball and running about on the grass. At the further end of the park, she saw a small group of people who were surrounding someone flying a kite. "Isn't this wonderful? I long for the day when I have children of my own and can take them to the park."

"So you don't have any children?"

"I have to find the perfect wife first," he said laughingly. "It's just occurred to me that we have not exchanged names. I'm Thomas – Thomas Weedon." He held out his hand and took hers.

Aphra then told him her name.

"What a pretty name." He said something about it being almost as beautiful as she herself. Aphra blushed at this welcome flattery and this just encouraged more of the same.

She mentioned to him that she wanted to sketch the house up on the hill. "Oh that'll be Channel court near Dunster," he said. "I could enquire about trips up there."

"I could ask Mrs Hutton if there's a coach that goes that way."

"Oh, I could find out – if you don't mind, that is. Maybe we could go together. After all, we're friends now, aren't we?"

"I suppose so," Aphra replied slightly hesitantly. She felt a little unsure of herself. "I'm not sure that it would be seemly."

"I'm so much older than you. It would be like having your father take you out for the day."

Aphra was not sure that she liked this choice of analogy. After all, her own father had never taken her anywhere. Yet there was something about him that did remind her of her father. It wasn't that he looked like him. In fact, he was entirely different in appearance. She couldn't put her finger on what it was, but there was definitely something.

"We'll be with other people on the coach," he added.

Slightly reluctantly, she agreed.

***

Two days later, she saw Thomas waiting for her just outside the station.

"I was afraid you wouldn't come," he said, as she walked towards him. "My day's so much brighter now for seeing you." And he did look pleased to see her. His slightly lined face lit up and she realised how very handsome he was.

They set off for Dunster in the carriage. Before they made their trip to the big house, they strolled around the village looking at the quaint shops and cottages. Aphra would have liked to sketch them as well. They had a light lunch in a little café, and as they ate, they watched the other visitors outside in the street. Afterwards, they left and climbed for a while until they reached the grounds of the big house. There was a bench that afforded a good view of it and Aphra sat and sketched. In the meantime, Thomas took a short stroll and lit a cigar.

When they got back to the village, Aphra went into a few of the shops to make some purchases of small gifts for her friends. She even bought a small souvenir for her mistress. She thought that it was probably a foolish thing to do, but she was feeling so happy, that she just wanted to share this happiness with everyone.

"You're very thoughtful and generous," Thomas said. "Even though your mistress treats you badly, you buy her a present."

Aphra said nothing, but just smiled demurely.

By the time they were on their way back to Minehead, Aphra realised that she was developing an attraction for this man. He had an air of mystery about him that she found most charming. He seemed very quiet – almost shy – which she thought for a salesman, must be a disadvantage. They arranged that they would meet again on the following day.

"We could take the train to Watchet," he suggested. Before he took his leave of her, he kissed her on the cheek. Once again, she had mixed feelings about this gesture, which seemed overly familiar and yet was not unwelcome.

Mrs Hutton was very interested to hear all about her day. Aphra mentioned the drive to Dunster, the big house, looking in the shop windows, and having lunch. She briefly said that people seemed quite friendly in this part of the world.

"I'm glad you found some nice folk to talk to," she said as she served Aphra her dinner.

She told Mrs Hutton that she was very tired and wanted to retire early to her room. However, she just wanted to be on her own to think about Thomas. She did not go straight to bed, but sat beside the window for some time listening to the sound of the sea in the distance and reliving the events of the day. She had never felt like this before.

Next morning, she took extra care with her toilette and could hardly hide her eagerness to leave for the train.

It was a wonderful day. They talked and laughed much and Aphra felt as though she wanted to be with Thomas all the time. She liked it best when they were able to get away from other people, for he did and said things that made her feel special. He had become very informal and familiar with her, but it felt so nice that she didn't think that there could be any harm in this. He was a lonely, sick man who'd had a difficult life. This much, he had told her. Her feelings for him were becoming stronger every day and he talked much about their future.

As they walked along the quayside, looking at the boats coming and going in the harbour, she said "isn't this where Coleridge wrote *The Rime of the Ancient Mariner* or was inspired to write it? I seem to remember something about this from school."

Thomas looked at her with a blank expression upon his face. "I've no idea what you're talking about my dear."

She laughed. "Oh, it doesn't matter. It was just one of the poems that we studied at school."

"I don't know anything about studying poetry," he said with a frown upon his face.

"But, I'd like to study you – in great detail."

She felt rather shocked at this remark, but flattered also.

"I like to see you blush, my dear. You are so young and chaste and it adds to the appeal that you have for me."

She looked down in embarrassment.

"Come, I've teased you enough. Let's go and find some refreshment. I think I saw a small teashop around the corner." He put his arm out and she slipped hers into it.

On their last day together before Aphra's journey home, they met near the church. He told her that he had a friend who lived close by and who had asked him to keep an eye on his house whilst he was away. This was the first that Aphra had heard about his friend. She thought that it was typical of Thomas' kindness to do this for his friend.

"You don't mind if we go there first?"

"Not at all."

"Perhaps we can take some tea there. I know he won't mind if we make ourselves at home. In fact, he told me to do just that. He knows what lodging rooms are like."

As they approached the house, he added that it would be nice to be alone and to feel relaxed. Aphra agreed with him.

"I'm quite tired today, for I have walked for over two hours this morning. It will be nice to rest my feet," she said.

They walked along a quiet road towards the back of the town away from the sea. It was a respectable street with terraced villas, fronted by small gardens. Thomas opened the gate and walked towards a pot beneath the window. He reached beneath it and brought out a key.

"Are you sure that this is alright?" Aphra asked anxiously.

"Oh yes," said Thomas. "I've been here many times. Peter often has to go away on business and I'm more than pleased to help him out." He unlocked the door with the ease of familiarity. For a second, Aphra was confused. She thought that when they had first met, Thomas had said that this was his first visit to Minehead. Then she dismissed the thought, as she reasoned that she must have misunderstood.

He stepped inside and gestured to Aphra to join him. She stepped over the threshold and into the hall. It was a comfortable and well-decorated house. Thomas opened the door to the front parlour and stepped backwards to let Aphra enter the room.

"Now you sit yourself down here and I'll just check round the house."

She heard his footsteps as he walked around upstairs from room to room with the confidence of one familiar with the terrain. He came downstairs and went into the back room – presumably the dining room, and then out the back to the kitchen and the scullery. After a few minutes, he returned carrying a tray which he placed on a table beside the armchair upon which she sat. There was a bottle of Madeira and two glasses. He poured some of the wine into each glass and handed one to Aphra.

She remembered how the wine had made her drowsy before, and initially refused any. However, Thomas overruled her concerns by reminding her that she was on holiday and free to do as she pleased.

"This is your last day of freedom before you have to go back to the dragon," he said.

She sipped at the wine. It was rich and nowhere near as nice as the one that Claude had given her. However, she enjoyed the way it made her feel.

"I found this cake in the kitchen. Have some," he added, handing her a plate. "You need to eat something with the wine. I don't want you getting drunk." She felt really at ease now as she drank a second glass. In fact, she had begun to feel a bit sleepy.

"Would you like to have a look around the house?" He asked. "There's a fine view of the rear garden from the back bedroom window."

She nodded and followed him upstairs. The back bedroom was a bright comfortable room and he held her hand and led her to the window. He was right – the view was very nice. She stood there for some minutes looking at the neat little row of gardens. She was thinking how nice it would be to marry a kind man and live in a little house like this. It would be so cosy and such a homely place in which to rear a family.

"What are you thinking about?" He asked as he put his arm around her. "You look very thoughtful."

"Oh, I was just thinking how delightful it would be to be here all the time. You know - to be married and to have a family."

"Do you know, I was thinking exactly the same thing myself?" He kissed her neck. She felt very gauche and awkward.

"Wouldn't it be nice to pretend that we were for the afternoon? What do you think?" He turned her around and kissed her on the mouth. Her feelings were now very mixed. The intensity of the moment made her feel afraid and yet excited. Before she knew it, she began to respond to his kisses. He led her by the hand to sit on the bed.

"I hope that you don't think I've taken advantage of you – kissing you this way. I'm not used to being with a woman and have allowed my feelings for you to run away with me. I'm sorry,"

He looked so crestfallen, that Aphra's heart went out to him. "You dear, dear man. I could never think that you were taking advantage of me. You have been the perfect gentleman each and every time that we have met."

Her hand touched his cheek. He turned to her with tears in his eyes. "You've no idea what you mean to me. I'm so lonely and am getting on for forty. I've have never had a woman in my arms. I long for it, but it's a dream that won't ever come true"
She put her arms around his neck and began to kiss his lips. "No!" He cried and jumped up. "We shouldn't behave this way. Let me go downstairs to the kitchen and bring up some refreshments to cool our passion." He patted her shoulder and left the room.

She sat on the bed listening to his footsteps as he descended the stairs. He returned a few minutes later with a bottle containing a homemade brew. "This is an elderberry cordial," he said, pouring it into two glasses and handing one to her.

"There," he said as he walked over to the window.

Aphra sipped at the drink. "This is very pleasant. Are you sure that it is just a cordial?"

"Yes my dear. I thought we'd better not have any more wine."

"You're so thoughtful. Please come and sit by me? I can see that you are reluctant to do so, but I want you to."

Slowly, he moved towards the bed and after initially hesitating, he sat down. "You know how I feel about you. D' you feel the same? I feel so embarrassed, but what I'm trying to say is, what I'm trying to ask you – is – will you marry me? I don't feel worthy of such a lady, but…"

"Hush," she interrupted him as she put her fingers to his lips. "Of course I'll marry you. I love you – very much."

He turned his gaze to her face. "You will! Oh darling. I'm the happiest man in the world." He went to kiss her lips again and then withdrew. "No I mustn't." He stood up and paced about the floor. "I want you so much, but it would be wrong."

She walked over to him and put her arms around his neck once more and passionately kissed him on his lips. She began to feel as she had never done in her life. His hands ran up and down her back and slowly caressed her hips. She wanted him to continue – she did not want him to stop.

"Oh, my dear girl, I want you so much, but I'm afraid you'll think that I'm trying to seduce you." He kissed her neck.

"I don't know what that means," she whispered. "I feel so happy and drowsy - yet I do not want to sleep."

"Lay down on the bed, my darling, where you will be more comfortable." He pulled the covers back and gently eased her down, so that soon her head lay on the pillow. She shut her eyes and he walked around to the other side of the bed. Quickly and silently, he removed his jacket, waistcoat and shoes. Slowly he sat and then lay down beside her. His hand caressed her shoulders and arms through the fabric of her gown. As he did so, his arm gently brushed against her breast. She was surprised and delighted at the feeling. Her breathing intensified and her whole body was filled with a warmth and tingling that she had not expected.

She turned and looked into his eyes. "I have such desires for something that I do not understand. I feel such strange sensations. They are new to me and yet wonderful. I want to be really close to you - but I do not want to have a child, if that is how it happens."

"Don't you worry about that," he replied. "I've heard that if it's the first time for both parties, then there's no risk. I wouldn't take any chances with you my dear."

"Are you sure? For I desire you so much," she said innocently. "I'm so naïve and unworldly in these matters. I don't know what is meant to happen."

"Of course, I'm sure. I would never do anything that would harm you," As he said this, he began to loosen his collar. "It's very warm in here."

"Let me help you with that," she said. At the same time, he began to undress her. Then he began to kiss her neck and her décolletage. Within a few minutes, they had removed all of their clothes. Aphra felt uncomfortable at being naked in front of another person. She went to pull the sheet over herself.

"Oh don't hide your beautiful body. You're a woman who was created for lovemaking." His eyes travelled up and down her body and he could not resist a lustful smile full of longing for her. He had never seen such a beautiful woman. As her breathing quickened, he looked at her full breasts and long shapely legs, and the desire within him could no longer be contained. He began to run his hands and his lips over her body. He kissed and touched her in such private places and in such a way as she had never before thought possible. Gradually, he was on top of her, parting her legs. She experienced a slight pain as he entered her and then felt a mounting ecstasy – waves of it that seemed to continue and repeat over and over again. She gasped and moaned in pleasure and when the feeling subsided and they lay quietly together, she felt so happy and peaceful.

"You're a very passionate woman. We're going to have a wonderful life together. When we meet again, I'll buy you a beautiful ring and then we'll plan our wedding."

During the afternoon, they made love numerous times and in such different ways and positions, that she felt rather shocked at how abandoned and wanton she had become. Also, it surprised her that he seemed to be most knowledgeable and adept at pleasing her for a man who had never lain with a woman before.

When they parted later in the day, he kissed her tenderly and said that he would meet her at the station on the following day to see her off.

When she returned to Mrs Hutton's house, she was not hungry and the older lady noticed that there was something different about the young woman, although she said nothing. Aphra did not sleep for a long time. She opened her window before getting into bed and lay listening to the sound of the sea for hours thinking about how wonderful her life had become. She went over and over the lovemaking in her mind – reliving every sensuous second of it. Eventually, she got into bed and drifted off to sleep happy in the knowledge that she would be getting married to such a wonderful man. In the morning, she was awoken by the sound of the gulls circling above the house and looked out of the window full of optimism about the future.

She said her goodbyes to Mr and Mrs Hutton, thanking them for their hospitality. She promised that she would return some day, if she could. In her mind, she thought that perhaps Thomas and she could spend their honeymoon there.

As the whistle blew, and Thomas helped her onto the train with her luggage he said to her. "I must see you again soon. I'll write to you next week and we can make arrangements."

"Yes, send the letter to the post office at Watheford and I'll collect it."

"Please let me know where I can write to you Thomas. It seems as though I know so little about you. I don't know where you live or anything."

"I'm moving to new lodgings and am not sure of the new address. I'll let you know where you can write, and will make all the arrangements for our big day." He kissed her hand as he shut the door and then reached up and kissed her lips as she leant out of the window.

When they parted, Aphra had mixed emotions. She felt a sense of loss as she watched him standing on the platform waving to her amidst the steam, as the train pulled out of the station. However, she also knew that her life was now full and happy. There was excitement and colour in her life. She had no doubt that this was why poets and composers were inspired to write about love.

***

When she returned to Warrington Grange, it was a completely different young woman who walked through the door of the servants' hall from the one who had left there a fortnight earlier. Everyone was eager to hear about her holiday. She said that she was tired from her journey and would tell them the following day. She managed to eat a small supper and had just gone to her room to unpack when the mistress rang for her. She was once again at her beck and call. However, Caroline was surprised and pleased with the small china ornament that Aphra gave her and for a while, there was a slight change for the better in their relationship and in Caroline's treatment of her.

Aphra fell back into the routine of duties and as time passed, she grew faster, even more efficient and competent at her work. Life was pleasant if busy, and on the whole, uneventful. Aphra waited impatiently for an excuse to go into Watheford and check at the post office for a letter from Thomas. The excitement of seeing him again and making plans for their wedding filled every waking thought that she had. One day, an opportunity to go to the post office arose, but she was disappointed that there was no communication from him.

As the days turned into weeks, she began to realise that she had been very foolish, and alternated between thinking of the whole experience as a terrible mistake and then feeling overwhelmed at her loss. There were days when she decided to put the whole experience down to a pleasant interlude. However, in spite of trying to be sensible, she felt very let down and disappointed that what she had thought of as true love, turned out to be nothing of the kind.

She threw herself into her work and Caroline was surprised that Aphra could work even harder than she had done before. Often, she sat up late into the night sewing and was awake and working long before anyone else. Emily had noticed a distinct change in Aphra. She seemed withdrawn and disinclined to spend time with her. At first, she had seemed very happy – elated even, but now she seemed distracted and as the weeks passed, it seemed that something was really wrong.

Aphra didn't get a day off for a while, but managed to exchange a few brief letters with Claude. If she could, she posted them in Watheford, but sometimes, when she was too busy to leave the house, she put them on the tray in the hall. She agreed to his suggestion that they meet at the usual time and place on the following Thursday as the Mistress had said she could take the afternoon off.

As she climbed into the carriage, a very sun-tanned Claude embraced her, and kissed her in his usual Gallic manner on both cheeks.

"How are you my dear girl? I have missed you. Tell me all about your holiday a la mer."

He could see that something was wrong, for she was not her usual cheerful self.

"What is wrong?" He asked kindly as he leaned forward and looked into her face.

She told him what had taken place in Minehead. "You must think that I am a loose woman to behave in such a way. I feel so ashamed."

"Not at all. When one is in love – well ..." he kissed his fingers in a Gallic manner. "Besides, who am I to judge others? You do not judge me for my relationship with Sebastian, do you? So why would I judge you? Sebastian and I are not married. Can you envisage a time when that would be possible – acceptable by society? I think not."

"Thank you. You're a sweet man." She placed her hand on his. "I've been to the Post Office a number of times, but there has been nothing from him. I tried to appear casual about it, for the Post Mistress, Miss Gaffney is very nosy and I'm sure that she is getting suspicious. I think that I have been very stupid.

"Perhaps he's away on business," Claude said, trying to sound optimistic.

"Perhaps," she said with a glimmer of hope, which soon dissipated. "I just feel very foolish to have allowed myself to be manipulated into doing something that was so unwise. How could I have been so naïve as to believe all the things he said to me?"

"It is not your fault. You fell in love and believed him," he said with affection.

"Yes, I did. Those few days that we spent together seemed so special – so wonderful – at least, to me they did."
She leant her head on his shoulder and cried. "I feel so bereft and let down."

He stroked her hair. "You did not deserve this treatment. I should like to kill him, the cad," he said with passion in his voice.

"It's alright Claude. I'll get over it. It helps to have you to talk to. I feel better already." She blew her nose and smiled bravely. "C'mon, let's not spoil our day. What are we going to do?"

"I thought that we would go into Westbridge and have tea at the Royal Hotel. We have not done that before. Will that be in order, milady?" He jested touching his forelock.

"Drive on James!" She ordered. They both laughed and enjoyed the trip to town. Aphra asked him about his trip home to visit his family and he entertained her with all kinds of amusing stories.

Claude told her all about his visit to his family. He asked Aphra if she had thought anymore about contacting her relatives. "It seems to me that your life would be so much easier. I have met Donald Kingston. He is a very pleasant man and his wife, Hortense, is a very kindly woman. I'm sure that they would adore you."

"I know you mean well, Claude, but I just cannot go to them cap in hand. I suppose that I'm too proud."

"Yes, and stubborn too," he added. "Well, have it your own way. I'll say no more."

The rest of the day followed the pattern of previous outings and the time, as usual, passed far too quickly and it seemed that all too soon, she was back on duty at The Grange.

***

When she had first returned from Minehead, she had been in an elated mood and had not considered the possibility of having a child, but what began as a vague suspicion, now became a serious worry. Foolishly, she had believed Thomas when he had told her that as they were both virgins, there was no risk. How could she have been so stupid as to believe such a ridiculous notion?

To begin with, the staff had noticed how happy and light-hearted Aphra seemed. But as the weeks passed, she seemed to be preoccupied with her own thoughts – even ignoring people when they spoke to her, which was quite out of character.

"Penny for 'em," Emily said one day. "What's wrong?"

"Oh, it's nothing - just struggling to get back into the routine of working after my holiday," Aphra said.

Emily didn't believe her but had to accept her answer for the time being. "Well, if you need to talk, I'm a good listener," she said as she patted her friend on the arm.

"Thank you Emily, but I'm really alright."

As the weeks passed, she knew for certain that she was with child. She was being sick every morning and had now missed her monthly flow. She had always been so regular since she had begun them when she was at school. She remembered how frightened she had been, until one of the teachers explained it all to her and told her that it was normal and would happen every month until she was in her forties or fifties. "It means that you are becoming a woman." The only reason that she would not have them would be when a child was expected.

"Oh God! I shall lose my job and then what will I do? Where will I go?" She fell into a troubled sleep where she tossed and turned for hours. She dreamed of her cousin and his anger at her turning up scruffy and dishevelled on his doorstep holding a wailing new-born infant wrapped in dirty rags. "Get off my land you filthy whore and take that brat with you," he demanded. As she walked down the drive, she looked down at her bare bleeding feet. There was a flash of lightening and it began to rain heavily. This time, she really was going to die and so was her poor child.

She awoke sweating and shaking. She could hardly think straight, but she knew that she had to do something. Going over to the small table that she used for writing, she sat down and began to write to Claude. He would help her. She felt so anxious, that she could not think straight. She mentioned how her mother had been the only other person to love her so much and that Claude loved her in the same way. She even made a silly joke about them getting married. She read it through and thought that it sounded somewhat muddled, but he would understand.

The following morning she was extremely busy and would not have time to get to the Post Office. As the contents of the letter were of such a delicate and confidential nature, she did not want to leave it on the hall table with the rest of the post. She had begun recently to suspect that Miss Salathial was watching her more than usual. So she slipped the letter into her pocket and waited till she had an opportunity to speak to one of the girls from the village while she was cleaning the grate in the morning room. Aphra asked her if she could do her a favour. "Of course Miss," came the reply.

"Could you please post this letter for me? It's rather urgent and I won't have time to get to the Post Office today. I would really appreciate it."

"Give it 'ere Miss," she took the letter from Aphra and placed in her own pocket. "I'll do it on my way 'ome."

Aphra thanked her and left the room. While she was in the room, the door had been ajar. She had not noticed that Miss Salathial had been standing in the shadow in an alcove. As Aphra climbed the stairs, the housekeeper went into the room.

"Give me that letter girl," she demanded holding out her hand in an intimidating manner. Nervously, the girl complied with the order. "I'll make sure that it gets to the correct destination," she added. "Have you finished that grate?"

"Yes Ma'am. It's my last one."

"Very well, then get off home. Quickly now. Don't hang around," she ordered. "There's no need to tell Miss Chamberlain that you have given me the letter. Do you understand?" She added in a menacing tone.

"The girl nodded nervously and gathered up her bucketful of cleaning materials and left the room promptly. She didn't like that woman. She scared the wits out of her. She thought that perhaps she should tell the nice pretty one what had happened – then again she thought it might be better to keep quiet. She didn't want to get into any trouble.

The housekeeper put the letter in her pocket where it remained until she went to her room. When she finally read the letter, she felt a great sense of satisfaction to think that the young madam had got her comeuppance. Later, she would hand it over to her mistress.

***

Warrington Grange
Watheford
Somerset

29th May 1885

My Dearest, Sweet Claude,

I am in serious trouble. I have for some time suspected that I am with child. I am now certain of it and very frightened. When my mistress learns of this, she will surely dismiss me. Oh how easily those few foolish moments of passion has led to a situation that will affect the rest of my life. You cannot begin to know how much I value your feelings for me. Only one other has ever shown me such tenderness and love. Oh Claude, I know that we have only known each other a short time, but our intimacy and the secrets that we have shared together go beyond what many people share in a lifetime and I know that I can rely upon you to help me in this desperate situation.

Perhaps it would be wise to reveal my situation to that personage of nobility – for having a title, position and wealth, he could solve my problems, but obviously, my situation must remain secret for the present. I fear that my indiscretion would affect his opinion of me. Unintentionally, I am guilty of ruining the life of another.

If your financial situation was better, perhaps we could marry, but what would Sebastian have to say on the matter! But this is no time for jesting. Oh God, What am I going to do? Only you can save me. Please, do not abandon me. I await your reply in earnest.

With love and affection,

Aphra

***

Caroline kept her own counsel for some time. On more than one occasion, she read the letter trying to piece together the snippets of information to work out what Aphra had been up to. Obviously, she had been conducting an immoral liaison with that French chap and was now expecting his child. She felt quite agitated about it all. Naturally, the girl would have to go. The disgrace and scandal would reflect badly on her own good name.

However, what really bothered her was the reference to the Earl himself. Aphra had written "only one other has shown me such tenderness and love". So it would appear that she had been carrying on with him as well. God, how she hated her! Yet it was not really the morality issue that bothered her so much. It was the fact that both men appeared to want her. Why? But Caroline knew the answer to this question. Aphra outshone her in every way. Yes, Caroline was beautiful and intelligent and could be witty and amusing when she made the effort. But that was the rub. It was an effort. For Aphra, it all came naturally.

Caroline had not slept well since first reading the missive. Dawn would soon break and she wanted Aphra out of the house - now! She pulled the bell cord beside the bed and got up. She walked over to her dressing table, sat down and began brushing her hair. There was a faint knock at the door.

"Enter," she commanded in an imperious voice. Aphra entered the room. She felt very apprehensive – scared even. Why did her mistress want her at this time of the day? Something was very wrong.

She was surprised to see that her mistress was not in bed.

"Are you well ma'am?"

Silently, Caroline continued brushing her hair for a short while. Aphra felt a deep sense of unease. Slowly and with a deliberate movement, Caroline replaced the brush on the dressing table. She continued to stare in the mirror.

"I'm perfectly well. However, I'm shocked and extremely disappointed at your recent behaviour."

Aphra was puzzled. "I'm sorry ma'am. I don't know what you m…"

"You will be very sorry, my girl."

"But what am I supposed to have done?" The pleading in her voice increasing. She had been very sleepy when she had entered the room. Now she was wide awake. "How can I answer for my conduct, if I know not of what I'm being accused?"

Caroline turned, stood up and glared directly at Aphra. "Can you deny that you have been having secret trysts with the Earl's secretary?"

Aphra was now very afraid. How could her mistress have found out about her meetings with Claude? She thought that she had been discreet in this matter. Could she have discovered her secret? Surely, she was not showing yet. It was far too early. Perhaps Caroline had heard her in the bathroom in the mornings. The sickness had been quite bad at times.

"It's true that I have met Monsieur Tanquerel a few times. We enjoy the same activities."

"I should imagine that you most certainly do!" Caroline almost spat the words out. The irony was wasted on Aphra who did not comprehend their significance. "Can you deny that your behaviour whilst on holiday in Minehead was not that of a lady? I think not – and after I was so kind as to allow you all that free time. You have abused my good nature."

Aphra was horrified and did not know how to reply, but her face told all.

"Don't bother to reply. I know the answer already. What a way to repay the Earl's kindness and generosity towards you.

I also believe that you were responsible for the dismissal of Albert. I know that Mr Isaacs took your side, but I have always suspected that you led him on. You're nothing but a deceitful, wanton trollop and I want you off my property before the staff awake."

"Please let me explain ma'am. What happened in Minehead was a moment of foolishness. I realise that I have been very naïve – and as for Alb...."

"I'm the one who's been naïve - in trusting you - in having you under my roof."

As Aphra made another attempt to plead with her mistress, Caroline waved her hand in a dismissive gesture.

"Please spare me the sordid details. I want you to go – now!" She handed her an envelope. "That's your salary up to today. Don't expect a reference from me. Now get out!"

Aphra was about to say something, but thought better of it. She turned and walked towards the door. As her hand reached out for the door handle, Caroline added. "Make sure that you do not take any of the items that I purchased for you."

As Aphra closed the door, Caroline called out "On no account are you to communicate with any other members of the staff - especially Emily. If I find that you have done so, I shall dismiss her also."

***

As Aphra packed her possessions, she thought about the encounter that had just taken place. Her emotions were in turmoil. Anger, fear and sadness all jostled for superiority. She was also bewildered as to why her actions in Minehead should have anything to do with the Earl. Why did the mistress make that comment about all his generosity towards her? What had that to do with her relationship with Thomas? None of it made sense.

"At least, I won't ever have to see that hateful woman ever again. That is some consolation I suppose." But she felt terribly sad at leaving her friend and not being able to tell her what had happened. Emily would wonder where Aphra had gone and why she had not said goodbye.

As she descended the stairs, another thought came to her. Perhaps the mistress would distort the truth and say that Aphra had just walked out and deserted her post. She was absolutely right. Caroline would do exactly this.

Within a few minutes, she was walking towards the woods. Before she entered them, she turned and took one last look at Warrington Grange. It looked so beautiful in the early morning light. She remembered how desperate and destitute she had been when she had first arrived – she had feared that she was going to die if she had not got the job. But she had been successful and had made a full recovery. She knew that she had worked well and that Caroline would have difficulty in finding someone to match her high standards. She thought about the wonderful Christmas, the affection from the other members of the staff and the gifts that they had exchanged. She tried to keep the unpleasant memory of Albert from her mind. That was now a thing of the past – and yet her mistress blamed her for the incident. It seemed that once again she was alone and friendless. Her sadness felt so great. But the saddest thing of all, the thing that was breaking her heart, was that she could not say goodbye to Emily.

***

Sebastian was engrossed in *The Times* and was unaware of Claude's anxieties. Every now and then he made some comment or other regarding an item of news that interested him. After a while, he became aware that Claude was not paying attention – in fact, he seemed rather distracted. Eventually, Sebastian looked up. "What's the matter?"

"I was thinking about Aphra. I haven't had any reply to my last three letters. I think something's wrong."

"What makes you think that?"

"Well, it's not like her. She's always so meticulous about writing back promptly."

"It sounds odd – I must admit. Would you like me to look into it? Perhaps I could visit Caroline and find out what's going on."

Claude thought about it for a few moments. "On the face of it, it sounds like a good idea, but don't you think that re-establishing contact with her might lead her to think that you are still interested in her?"

"You're right. I'll need to tread carefully. However, buttering her up a bit might prove useful in obtaining information about Aphra. Send a short missive and say that I'll be paying her a visit on Thursday afternoon.

***

Sebastian followed Emily along the corridor to the drawing room. She opened the door and stepped backwards to let him pass.

"His Lordship, Ma'am," Emily said, trying to sound confident. She always felt in awe of the Earl.

"Caroline," he gushed, making a great show of kissing her hand. "I trust that you're keeping well. You look marvellous."

"Well Sebastian, I should be much happier if you bothered to keep in touch. I've not heard anything from you for months. You're very naughty. I feel quite hurt," she said with an exaggerated pout.

"Nonsense," he replied stepping towards the armchair. "You're not the kind of woman to get hurt. You're much too tough for that."

"I'm not sure that that's a very complimentary remark, but I shall overlook it. Now come and sit next to me," she ordered as she patted the cushion beside her.

Reluctantly, he joined her and continued paying her compliments, steering the conversation away from her petulant annoyance and towards generalities and gossip both local and national.

After a few minutes, Emily returned bearing a tray with the tea things. This, she placed on the table beside Caroline, who impatiently dismissed her. Emily curtseyed and noticed the kind smile that the Earl gave her.

Sebastian stood up and took a couple of paces towards the tea tray. "Let me be mother."

As Emily shut the door behind her, she overheard him say to her mistress in a bad attempt at a casual voice. "Where's your other maid – the one who accompanied you when you visited me?"

"I had to dismiss her."

"What!" Sebastian realised that he was showing too much interest. "I mean why, what for?" He struggled to sound disinterested, but did not fool Caroline who almost snatched the cup and saucer out of his hand. He felt that he was stepping on dangerous ground.
"She was unsuitable – not up to the job," she replied sipping at her tea.

"That sounds most unlikely. In fact, you told me yourself that she was exceptionally good at her work."

After pouring out his own tea, he walked over to the armchair and sat down. He no longer felt the need to ingratiate himself with her.

"What was the real reason you dismissed her Caroline? Please tell me the truth."

Caroline stood up and began to pace the room. This was not going the way that she had hoped. Why did he have to start talking about that wretched girl? She walked to the window and looked out onto the parterre and made a feeble comment about how lovely the display was.

"Please don't change the subject Caroline. I want to know the truth." His masterful voice reminded her of his superior social standing.

"Perhaps you should ask that Frenchie chap that you employ," she almost spat the words out.

"Why should I ask Claude, and please do not refer to him in that derogatory manner. He happens to be a very good friend of mine."

"He may not be such a good friend when you hear what he's been up to behind your back!"

"What do you mean?" He was completely baffled.

Caroline ignored his bemused face "Oh c'mon Sebastian. I know what's been going on and why you haven't been in touch with me all these months. I saw the two of you walking around arm in arm, engrossed in a very cosy tete a tete. But you haven't been the only one. Where do you think he's been going on his days off? He's been having secret trysts with that hussy behind your back and now she's expecting his child."

"Don't be ridiculous."

"I'm not being ridiculous and I would appreciate your not telling me that I am."

"I'm sorry. I didn't mean to offend you, but these allegations are nonsense. Do you know where she's gone? Does she have any money or any relatives?"

"I neither know nor care. If she cannot behave with more decorum then she must suffer the consequences. She has been paid her wages and I've washed my hands of her. This whole business has been of great inconvenience to me. I still haven't found a replacement. All this advertising and interviewing most unsuitable people is very vexing, not to mention the backlog of outstanding work to be done. Isaacs is on holiday and one of the girls who normally comes up from the village is feigning some kind of illness. I'm the one who's been inconv ..."

"I feel that I must do something to help her." Sebastian cut her tirade short. "Whatever makes you think that Claude is the father?"

"Sebastian, she more or less admitted that she was carrying on with both of you and that she was pulling the wool over your eyes and deceiving you.

In fact, I'm most surprised that she hasn't turned up on your doorstep."

This was all quite a shock to him. He did not know what to make of it. The allegation was absurd, but he was intrigued to know who the father was. Perhaps Aphra had become involved with one of the other servants and did not want to name him in case he was also dismissed. It was certainly a mystery.

"I haven't heard anything from her." He did not add that Claude was very worried and had discussed this with him. Tactfully, he changed the topic of conversation and the atmosphere improved slightly - although Caroline was still rather prickly.

After a few minutes, he managed to bring the visit to a close and made some excuse to leave. He could see that Caroline was none too happy, but managed to placate her by giving the impression that he would be in touch again without making an actual commitment.

After bidding Caroline farewell, he followed Emily down the stairs. As she handed him his hat and cane, he thanked her and made some pleasantry about the weather adding "I understand that Miss Chamberlain no longer works here. Do you have any idea where she has gone? Perhaps she has gone to stay with relatives. Did she tell you anything?"

Emily bit her lower lip and started to fidget with her hair. "I'm sorry sir. I don't know where she's gone. I'm right upset about it. She didn't even bother to say goodbye. I thought that we were friends."

"I'm sure that's still the case. Perhaps she was not in a position to speak to you before she left. It may not have been up to her."

Emily was surprised at this and appeared to be thinking about it.

"Did she ever mention any family?" He asked as she opened the door.

Emily coloured. "It's not for me to say sir." She was obviously hiding something.

The Earl stepped outside and was about to bid her a good day, but then he turned around. "Emily, I think that your friend is in serious trouble and I want to help her. Please tell me if you know anything." His voice was kind but forceful.

"Well sir, she did tell me that she was distantly related to some toff with a title, begging your pardon sir, but I can't remember what 'is name was. I know I was surprised and wondered why she was doing this job if she had rich kin. She said her grandma had run off with her grandpa. He was a parson or something, and she had been cut off from the family. I feel bad telling you this. I gave her my word not to repeat it and now I'm breaking my promise."

"Emily, rest assured that you are doing the right thing." Sebastian already knew that Aphra was an exceptional young woman, but he was rapidly discovering that she was a woman of many surprises and secrets. "If you remember anything at all, please let me know. Perhaps it would be best not to mention it to your mistress. In fact, I would prefer that we kept this conversation between ourselves. I know that I can trust you."

"Oh, of course sir." She brightened up at the idea of excluding her mistress from this information. "I shan't say a word."

"Goodbye Emily. We'll speak again soon." He lifted his hat and turned and walked down the steps to his carriage.

As she closed the door, Emily felt better than she had done for some time. In fact, she felt quite smug that she had a secret with the Earl and that he had asked her not to tell the mistress!

***

When he returned to Methuen Park, Sebastian marched into his study where Claude was sitting at the desk dealing with some correspondence. "Well?" He said as he looked up inquisitively.

"This has been a most educational afternoon," Sebastian said as he flung himself into an armchair.

Claude put down the letter that he was reading. "What's happened? Is she alright?"

"No, she's not!"

Claude could see that he was angry and walked over towards him. He was really worried now.

"She's expecting a child and Caroline has dismissed her. She's convinced that you're the father." One could not fail to detect the irony in his voice.

"What! You're joking."

"No I'm not. God knows what Aphra has been saying or writing. I suspect that Caroline has been intercepting letters. Apparently, the girl more or less confessed to affairs with both of us. If it wasn't such a bloody mess, it would be funny!"

"She would never tell a lie like that. Caroline must be making it up or else she has misunderstood what has been written."

"Did you know that she's related to a member of the aristocracy?"

"Yes, Viscount Westbridge. Why?"

"What! Old Donald Kingston? How long have you known about this?"
"She told me a while ago. Is it important?"

"Why didn't you tell me about it?" Sebastian was obviously quite put out.

"I'm sorry but I couldn't tell you. She told me in confidence. Besides, I didn't think that you'd be particularly interested. She's more my friend after all."

"I suppose so," Sebastian replied grudgingly. "I wonder why she didn't turn to him for help rather than be enslaved by that dreadful woman."

"I asked her more or less the same question when she told me. I suggested that perhaps he could have helped her financially, but she was determined not to ask for help and wanted to become financially independent before informing him of her existence. Apparently, the Westbridge family have no knowledge of her mother's existence – let alone hers."

"I think that I had better write to old Kingston and ask if I can pay him a visit. I haven't seen him for a while. He rarely sits in the House these days. If I remember correctly, his health isn't too good. I wonder what age he is now. He must be over seventy."

"You're not going to tell him about her condition are you?" Claude asked anxiously.

"Of course not. I shall be very discreet. In fact, we both need to be very discreet and not say anything about this whole matter to anyone. Perhaps we can keep this between ourselves and help her before matters get any worse. I suppose that there's a possibility that she has gone to him for help."

Claude shook his head. "I very much doubt it. It would not be in her nature. She's too proud." He walked over to the desk and sat down, but before he could reach for a sheet of paper, Sebastian said "I think that I'll write this myself." Claude got up from the chair and Sebastian sat down and dipped the pen in the ink and began to write.

Claude wondered aimlessly around the room. "I know what's happened. She told me that she met a man when she went on holiday. She began to tell me something about him. He seduced her. She seemed rather anxious and upset. However, I had no idea that she was expecting a child." He sat down beside a small table and stared vacantly out of the window. Where on earth had she got to, and was she in danger?

***

The Earl was shown into the study.

"Sebastian! Must be ages since I saw you," said Donald Kingston as he hurried forward to shake hands. "Fancy a snort?"

"Don't mind if I do," replied Sebastian. "Not interrupting anything am I?"

"Not at all. Nice to see you. Just writing a short missive to my tailor. Scotch?"
"Just the thing."

"Got a fine malt here." Donald poured the whisky into two lead crystal tumblers and held up a matching jug containing water, with a questioning expression on his face.

"Just a dash please," replied the Earl who was pacing about the room. "How is Hortense these days? Still hard at it saving the world?"

"Oh yes. Hardly see a thing of her – today she's addressing a meeting for the Educational Board – something to do with literacy for the masses – not sure whether it's a good idea or not – gives 'em ideas above their station, y'know.

Have a seat," he said as he indicated a leather Chesterfield armchair. He handed Sebastian his drink. "What can I do for you ol' chap. Must be a reason for your visit. Not just social I assume?"

"Quite correct." Sebastian cleared his throat. "Actually, you'll probably think this rather an odd subject, so I'm not sure where to begin."

"The beginning always seems a good place to me."

"Do you know anything about Lady India Kingston? I understand that she was your great aunt."

"Good Lord! – haven't heard mention of her for years. Now what did father tell me about it? Let me think. Ah yes. She ran off with a village parson or something and my great-grandfather cut her off - seems a bit extreme."

"Yes, that's what I thought. I don't think that there was actually any scandal attached, was there?"

"Not as far as I know. Just the ol' chap flexing his muscles probably. He was a bit of a martinet by all accounts. Apparently, he regretted it afterwards, but was too proud to lose face. Died a broken man. Bloody silly, if you ask me. Why are you asking? It's all ancient history now."

"India died many years ago, but she had a daughter called Ellen."

"Really! You mean I have a cousin?"

"She'd be about forty if she was still alive. Unfortunately, she died some years ago."

"Oh - too bad. It would've been nice to have a blood relative. Hortense has kin in spades, but I've no one." He looked a bit dejected. "Ah well."

"She had a daughter and she's still alive – at least she was a few weeks ago."

"Well I'm dashed," said Donald. "What do you mean 'a few weeks ago'? What's happened?"

"Well, I'm not sure. She seems to have disappeared and - 'er well I was asking about - well what I mean is, I called to see if you'd heard from her, but obviously you haven't."

"Do you think that she's in a spot of bother and might turn up looking for a handout?"

"No, no - quite the contrary. She's known about you all her life, but is too proud to ask for help. She's a friend of mine and she's had quite a tough time with one thing and another, but is very resourceful and, as I say, very proud. Apparently, she didn't want to inform you of her existence until she was in a stronger financial position."

"Sounds like a good egg to me. What do you want me to do - make some enquiries amongst my cronies?"

"I don't think that'll be necessary. I'll see to all that myself. Don't want to put you to any trouble. Besides we need to be careful that we don't cause her any embarrassment when she returns to society."

"Naturally 'ol boy. Whatever you say. Shan't breathe a word to a soul - not even the guv'nor," he said with a wink and tapping the side of his nose.

Sebastian drained the glass. "Well, I won't keep you from your affairs any longer. You and Hortense must pay me a visit sometime soon. It would be nice to talk about old times. We haven't done that for years."

"Shoot the breeze - isn't that what the Yankees call it?" He said. "Could make it during the grouse season - expect you've got plenty."

"Oh I keep shooting to bare necessities at the Park, but you're both welcome at any time. Next time, we're in the House, we'll check our diaries."

"Capital idea."

Donald walked Sebastian to the door which was held open by the butler, and they continued their conversation about various mutual acquaintances and items of news. As Sebastian's carriage went down the drive, Donald stood waving and then turned to walk back in the house. "Well, fancy that - I've got a cousin. I wonder what she's like. Probably all horsy and plain, with big feet."

***

Aphra stood and looked up at the dark, forbidding building. Every fibre of her body rebelled against her taking another step. She looked through the railings and contemplated her desperate plight. She needed shelter and nourishment – especially for the child. She put her hand to her side and felt the brooch pinned to her undergarments. If she sold it, she would have a fair sum of money, but she could not. It felt like a betrayal of her mother. Besides, who would have believed that she had come by it legally? If she tried to sell it, in her present condition, her appearance would no doubt get her arrested.

No, she would have to give in and enter the workhouse or she would starve to death. It was beginning to get dark and she felt a few drops of rain on her face. She could not face another night out in the open. Reluctantly, she trudged down the path towards the front door. Her back ached and the thought of the growing child within her reminded her that she must do this.

She rang the bell at the side of the large double doors. After a couple of minutes, she heard echoing footsteps approaching. The doors opened and a short, rotund man wearing a frock coat, tall hat and spectacles looked at her. "Yes, what d'you want?"

"I've nowhere to stay and no money. I'm with child and haven't eaten for many days."

"You'd better come in," he said curtly, stepping aside to allow her to pass.

The large doors banged shut behind her and the sound echoed down the long dark corridor. There was a damp chill about the place that made it feel even colder than outside. Aphra wondered what it would be like once winter set in, and shivered. Coming from a distant part of the building, she could hear screaming and crying. It terrified her and she secretly questioned whether or not she was doing the right thing.

"Follow me," ordered the porter, picking up an oil lamp from a small table beside the door. His name was Mr Davidson. As Aphra walked behind him, she suspected that he was one of those people, who, given a tiny amount of authority, became full of their own importance.

The light from the lamp did not penetrate the sides of the passage and the eerie gloom frightened her. At the end of the corridor, he entered a room.

"Wait here," he ordered and walked off. Aphra paced back and forth in the room, stamping her feet and rubbing and blowing on her hands.

"Come, this way," said a sharp voice. Aphra turned to see a woman who reminded her of Mildred Salathial. As they walked, she laid down the law about rules and regulations that Aphra found very hard to absorb as she was so tired and hungry.

"In here. This is the receiving room. Strip down to your undergarments, so that I may search you."

"Why do you need to do that?" Aphra asked.

"Union Workhouse regulations. If you don't like it, you can leave," the woman said in a tone that was a mixture of spite and indifference.

"No, no. I just wondered why," she said as she placed her bag on a chair by the wall. Surreptitiously, she unpinned her brooch and popped it in her mouth, while the woman went to a cupboard and removed some items of clothing and a pair of old boots. She threw them on the floor next to Aphra's belongings.

Roughly but swiftly, she searched Aphra's whole body. Fortunately, she did not look in her mouth. She then proceeded to look through the bag. "What are you looking for?" Asked Aphra, trying not to swallow the brooch.

"Anything that you shouldn't have according to the rules," she snapped back and then went on to repeat the list of rules. "Come, bring that lot with you," she said, gesturing towards the pile of clothes and the boots. Aphra picked them up and went to retrieve her bag. "Leave it," said the woman. "You'll get it back when you leave."

Aphra followed the woman up a flight of stairs and along another dark corridor. At the end of it, the woman entered a room. Inside were four baths.

"Get in!"

Aphra was about to protest and to ask the woman to leave, but then thought better of it and just did as she was told and undressed. The water was not very warm, but Aphra did not complain. She sensed that this woman wanted to break her spirit. "As if it isn't already broken," she thought. She picked up a small piece of soap in a dish at the end of the bath and a small grey rag and began to clean herself. Suddenly, a jug of ice cold water was poured over her head. Aphra screamed in shock.

"Wash your hair," demanded the woman. "We don't want the likes of your kind bringing lice and nits in here." After she had got over the shock, Aphra rubbed her hair with the soap before another jug of water was tipped over her to rinse it.

"Get out and dress, and when you've finished, clean the bath. This isn't the Grand Hotel."

The woman left the room muttering loud enough, so that Aphra could hear her. "I expect that's what you're used to my fine lady."

Aphra dried herself with a worn towel and put on the heavy, drab garments and laced up the boots that rubbed against her heels. She then took the brooch out of her mouth and pinned it to her petticoat.

When the woman returned, she was carrying a pair of large scissors. Pulling a chair into the centre of the room, she ordered Aphra to sit.

"What are they for?" Aphra was beginning to feel rather alarmed.

"Workhouse rules."

"Aphra knew what was about to happen. As her lovely hair fell to the floor, the tears rolled down her cheeks. So it had come to this. She felt completely degraded and dehumanised - but then that was the intention. "Put this on." The woman handed Aphra a bonnet of some kind of cotton material. It didn't look very clean and felt scratchy to the touch.

"You're too late for dinner. You'll have to wait till the morning."

"Isn't there anything I can have now? I haven't eaten for days and feel very weak."

"I just told you. You're too late. Now follow me."

"This is the dormitory where you'll sleep. Your bed is that one over there. No talking. Go straight to sleep." With that, she turned around and left the room, shutting the door hard.

Aphra walked over to the bed that the woman had indicated. By the light of a single candle on a cabinet next to the bed, she could see that it was a utilitarian metal structure with a stained tuck mattress. Folded at the bottom of it was a pair of sheets and a blanket. All the items had seen better days. Quickly, she made up the bed and undressed and put on the nightdress. She laid the dress and jacket over the blanket to try and add some extra warmth. Slipping under the covers, she blew out the candle and shut her eyes. In spite of her hunger, she was so exhausted, that she fell asleep in a few minutes.

The next thing that she heard was a bell ringing. There was a sudden commotion in the room. She sat up and saw that the other occupants of the room were hastily getting dressed.

The woman nearest to her said "you'd better hurry up. Matron will go mad if you're late."

Sure enough, a few minutes later, the unpleasant woman from the night before came in. Aphra thought that her face would curdle milk. She glared at Aphra. "Sorry milady. No breakfast in bed this morning."

Aphra attempted to get dressed as quickly as she could, but it was not fast enough for the matron and she began to make more sarcastic comments. "I bet you weren't this slow when you took your clothes off and got yourself into the condition that you're now in. Now move it."

The women followed her down the stairs to the chapel, where morning prayers were said. After this, they filed into the dining room, where each woman was given a bowl of thin gruel and a mug of watery tea. They ate in silence and when Aphra whispered to one of the other women asking if this was all they were getting, the woman furtively looked up before answering her. "We mustn't speak. We'll be punished if we're caught and that means no rations for two days."

Aphra indicated her understanding and ate the rest of the meal in silence. The food was dreadful, but at least it lessened the terrible hunger pains that she'd had a few minutes earlier and she did not feel quite so faint. She was just finishing the last of her tea, when the bell was rung again. All the women stood up and filed out of the room. Aphra followed them out to the corridor. They all went different directions and she was unsure what to do next.

"Come here girl." It was the nasty woman again. "In here." She indicated a room behind her. Aphra went in. It was a kind of office. "Now, you arrived at a very inconvenient hour last night and there was no time to record your admittance. The woman sat down behind a desk and opened a large ledger.

"My name is Mrs Robinson and I'm the matron. The master is called Mr Griffiths, but you won't be seeing much of him. You've met Mr Davidson, the porter.

Now can I have your full name and your details?"

Aphra told the woman that her name was Mrs Taverner and that she had been abandoned by her husband. She hated lying, but it was necessary and as near to the truth as she could get.

"So have you been carrying on behind your husband's back?"

"Sorry?" Aphra did not understand the question.

"I've read the letters in your bag from the French chap. It appears that you were rather familiar with him – creeping out to meet him in secret. I'm not surprised your husband abandoned you"

"How dare you read them! They're private. You've no right," Aphra protested indignantly.

"I have every right my girl and if you speak to me like that again, I'll put you on a punishment charge and you'll get no food for two days.

Now do you have any proof that you're married?"

Aphra said nothing – just shook her head.

"I thought as much. You fall into our category C group."

"What does that mean?"

"Unmarried mothers, prostitutes and refractory women. You're the least deserving group and as such, will not be allowed privileges and your diet and clothes will reflect this. I thought as much last night when you arrived, and that is why you wear the uniform that you have to distinguish you from the respectable women."

Aphra knew when she was beaten and just accepted what was meted out to her.

"Right now. You'll be working in the laundry. I trust that it isn't beneath you."

"I'm used to hard work and will do my best."

"See that you do. Right, I'll show you where the laundry is and you can begin earning your keep. This way."

The laundry was hot and steamy. When she first entered the room, Aphra was pleased to be warm again. However, she soon found that the hot, steamy atmosphere, together with the heavy fustian dress and jacket that she had to wear, made it very unpleasant to work in.

One of the paupers, a woman called Louisa was in charge of the laundry. She was a slim, fair-haired, capable person. Mrs Robinson called her over. It was very noisy in the room, so she had to shout.

"This is Aphra Taverner. Show her what to do. Make sure that she doesn't shirk her duties. She's a category C, so she's probably a slacker – more used to working on her back I should imagine!"

Aphra was deeply shocked and hurt by this remark. However, she knew better than to say anything.

"I'd have thought that someone so hoity toity as her would have had more sense than to get in the family way. Anyway, see that she learns her duties and report back to me if there are any problems." As she walked off, she gave Aphra a look that left her in no doubt that life in here was going to be very difficult.

Once the matron was out of earshot, Louisa said "Just ignore her. She's a really nasty piece of work. She's spiteful and cruel to everyone. Mind you, she seems to have it in for you especially."

"I feel as though I've committed a terrible crime. All I did was to be stupid enough to believe that a man loved me and was going to marry me. I haven't hurt anyone or stolen anything. I don't know why she's being so vindictive. I've done nothing to her."

"Try not to think about it. Now, I'll show you what you need to do and then leave you to get on with it. We're very short of able bodied women at the moment, so those of us who are able to work, are rushed off our feet. The infirmary's overflowing and so is the lying in ward, so there's a lot of laundry." She explained what needed doing and left Aphra to get on with it. It was not difficult for Aphra to understand the process, but it was back breaking work and by the end of the first day, she was exhausted and her hands were red raw.

After the first week, she had got used to the routine and Louisa was very pleased with her progress. "You're the best worker I've had in here for a long time. I'll be able to give the ol' bat a good report on you."

"Thank you," said Aphra – although she doubted that it would improve the woman's opinion of her. She had made her mind up that Aphra was no good.

The two women had established a sort of friendship, or as much as was possible considering that they were not allowed to talk much. However, the inmates were allowed a half hour of free time after their evening meal. It was during this time that Aphra learnt about Louisa's background. She was a married woman. Her husband had been a stevedore in Bristol docks and had been injured by a shipment of cargo that had fallen on him and was now unable to work. Louisa had tried all kinds of jobs to keep them from destitution, but things had got very difficult and then her work had dried up. There were two grown up married daughters who had tried to help, but had their own money worries – one had a sick little girl and the other was expecting her fourth child. So, in the end, Louisa and Jack had lost their home as well as everything else.

"There was nothing for it, but to come here. Jack's in the infirmary. I'm allowed to visit him at the weekend. If the weather's nice, I try and take him out for a short walk in the yard." She looked very sad and then added. "He'll never be the same. He's a shadow of his former self."

Aphra commiserated with her problems and then told her about Thomas and also about being sacked and the various incidents that had happened to her. They were both sympathetic to each other and Aphra knew that the friendship of this woman would help alleviate her difficulties while she was in the workhouse.

One evening while they were chatting, Aphra told her about life at Warrington Grange and happened to mention her sewing duties for her mistress. At this, Louisa looked very interested. "We need some sewing done here. The bedding is in a terrible condition. I'll speak to matron."

"I'd love to do that," said Aphra. "I find sewing so easy and I know that I'm good at it."

"The sheets really need replacing, but this would be too expensive. Between you and me, I wonder where the money goes in this place. I wouldn't be surprised if someone's skimming off some of it. Anyway the sheets need to be turned and repaired."

The following morning, when Aphra walked into the laundry, Louisa told her that matron had said that she was to make a start on the sheets. The pile was enormous and the matron thought that Aphra would never get through it all. However, Aphra found the work very easy and it also meant that she could sit down whilst working. For this, she was most appreciative. Aphra worked very hard and Mrs Robinson reluctantly had to admit, to herself only of course, that Aphra was doing a first rate job.

However, the work was so easy that it required very little mental effort on Aphra's part and it left her mind free to roam. She thought about the events leading up to her entry into the workhouse.

After leaving Warrington Grange, she had walked to the village. When she got there, she had gone into the little church and knelt down at the pew nearest the door. She tried to pray, but her thoughts were in turmoil and she was shaking and shivering in spite of the mildness of the morning. She remembered Christmas morning and singing carols with her friends. The memory brought tears to her eyes. She would probably never see any of them again. She felt nauseous - although she knew that she would not be sick again. She had already done so twice this morning - once in the bathroom and again in the woods. She had nothing left inside her.

After a while, she sat back in the pew. How had Caroline discovered her secret? Did she know of Aphra's condition and why was she so angry about her meetings with Claude? She had done nothing wrong – and what had Caroline meant by that comment about Claude and her enjoying the same activities? Did she think that they had been physically intimate? Suddenly Aphra realised how bad her behaviour might appear. Did Caroline think that she was leading Albert on and carrying on with different men? How could she have thought such a thing about her? She was appalled.

However, the thing that worried her most was that Claude seemed to have abandoned her when she most needed him. She could not understand it. Perhaps, he had gone away, but thought that was most unlikely. Neither Claude nor the Earl would be shocked to discover that she was expecting a child.

Then it crossed her mind that perhaps Caroline had written to the Earl, naming Claude as the father, and the Earl was furious and jealous of her - but surely not! Maybe the Earl had told him not to see her anymore and to cut all contact with her. Yet, she could not believe that he would take Caroline's word. He knew her too well and disliked her intensely.

She decided that she needed to put these ideas from her mind and focus on the practical problems now facing her. She was unemployed, unmarried and expecting a child. The first thing that she needed to do was to get as far away as she possibly could from Watheford and make a new start.

First, she would have to walk to Westbridge. She felt that this would not be too difficult. The weather was good and it was not too warm yet, for it was only just getting light - and despite the weight of the books and other possessions that she was carrying, she was fit and strong. She'd also had the foresight to help herself to some food from the pantry for her journey. She smiled when she imagined Gracie's face when she discovered a couple of items missing from her larder. Aphra knew that she would not mind. Besides, she was more than entitled to the food as she had worked up to the last minute on a paltry salary for that dreadful woman.

As she walked, she contemplated what she would do when she arrived in the town. First, she would go to the bank and withdraw her savings. Then she would travel to Bath. It was a large city and she would be anonymous there. She would call herself Mrs Taverner and say that her husband had died. She would need to get another position as soon as possible, but it would not be so easy without a reference. It suddenly occurred to her that Caroline still had her reference from Mrs Brookes and her school report. She was annoyed at herself for not asking for them back before she left. Although she thought that it was most likely that they had already been destroyed.

She broke her journey in Wells, as it was quite late in the evening when the coach arrived there, and she decided to spend the night at the inn. This time, being more worldly wise, she pulled a large heavy table in front of her door, placing a china jug on the corner of it. She remained dressed and slept with her possessions in her arms. Although she was very tired from the arduous journey, it was some time before she managed to sleep, as troublesome thoughts flitted around in her mind.

She thought about her letter to Claude. Did he not understand the urgency and seriousness of her situation? She wondered whether she had been unclear in what she had tried to convey to him. She had been so distressed and distracted that she was sure that it was all a bit muddled. Obviously, she had mentioned the baby. She had referred to the depth and intimacy of their friendship, pointing out that only her mother had shown her such love and kindness as he had done. Also, she knew that he would tell her to go to see Viscount Westbridge, but she had written that she did not want that person of nobility to think badly of her and was determined not to contact him, for she felt that they may disapprove of her even more – especially after the history of her grandmother's elopement. Thinking of it now, she should not have made that silly joke about marriage and the Earl and jealousy – perhaps it was in bad taste or even dangerous considering the nature of their relationship – but surely Claude would not take this the wrong way. It would not be in his nature. Over and over she mulled these matters in her mind until eventually she fell into a deep sleep.

It was the nausea that woke her early. Once it had subsided, she lay back on the bed and reflected on her current situation. She knew that she had to overcome her anxieties and get on with the task in hand. Fretting was not going to get her anywhere. She worked out that she had enough money for food and accommodation for a while, but she did not want to dip too far into her savings. She was going to need as much money as possible for the child. She made a few calculations in a notebook and jotted down some ideas as to how she should proceed. As she was doing this, her hand went to the brooch, for she had a tendency to keep checking that was still there.

"Oh, Mama I have been so foolish. I forgot your sound advice about men and now I'm in this dreadful situation. What is to become of my poor baby, your grandchild? I've let you down. Please forgive me."

The following day, she was making her way along one of the fashionable streets of Bath dressed in her smartest clothes, and optimistic about something turning up. She deposited most of the money that she had withdrawn from her previous account into another bank in the city. However, by the end of the week, her buoyant mood had plunged. Without Mrs Brookes' reference and her school report, and her vagueness regarding answers to questions about her most recent employment, her prospects were not good. None of her enquiries had borne fruit. She felt quite despondent as she returned to the small room that she had rented.

However, a few days later, she obtained a post as a maid of all work to a woman living on the outskirts of the city. It was not what she really wanted and the wages were low, but it meant food and shelter for the time being. Miss McDonough was aged about fifty and Aphra saw that she was very cantankerous and would not be easy to please. Her home was a small terraced villa. It was cluttered and old fashioned with no modern plumbing or facilities.

When she arrived at Miss McDonough's house, the welcome was not friendly.

"My goodness, you have got a lot of baggage."

"Yes, I have quite a few books," Aphra replied.

"Well, you won't get much time to read them. You're here to work."
This was not an auspicious start and Aphra knew immediately that she was not going to like this woman.

"Follow me," Miss McDonough said in a cold voice. "I'll show you your room." She proceeded to climb the stairs and Aphra followed her – noting how dusty everything was.

"The last girl was useless. I had to dismiss her. I hope that you'll prove to be a better worker. I've noticed that your hands aren't used to manual labour. A few days here and you can forget those manicured nails!"

"I'm not afraid of hard work," Aphra replied. "I'll do my best. I assure you."
"Let's hope that your best is good enough." She opened the door to the bedroom, which was in the attic. It was stark with a narrow bed, a small table and a hard backed chair, bare floorboards and faded peeling wallpaper. Aphra stepped into the room and put her bags down.

"Unpack and come down. I'll show you where everything is and what needs doing."

Miss McDonough shut the door and went downstairs. Aphra went and looked out of the window. The view was of rows of similar houses and gardens. She sat on the bed which felt lumpy and uncomfortable.

"How did I end up here?" She examined the bedclothes. They were thin, worn and badly stained.

"Thank goodness it's summer. At least I won't be here in the winter. But where will I be?"

She quickly unpacked and went downstairs.

Miss McDonough was getting agitated. The girl had been at least ten minutes and she wondered what she could be doing. As Aphra reached the bottom step, she overheard her mutter "and about time too!"

Later that night, as Aphra carried a candle up to her room, she knew that she was going to find it tough working for this horrid woman. Fortunately, the months of running up and down stairs for Caroline, together with the good food and country air, meant that she was more than capable of doing the job well.

However, it didn't matter how hard or fast she worked, there was just no pleasing her mistress. She constantly hovered, inspected, criticised and complained. Aphra did her best to detach herself from the complaints, but it was not always easy to do this. She tried to concentrate on the fact that it was for a short time only and that every penny she earned went into her savings. She put out of her mind the reality of what she would do when she could no longer work, or when the child was born. For now, she just kept busy.

The morning sickness had been a problem that was difficult to hide. Miss McDonough always seemed to be around poking and prying and watching her every move. However, after a few days, she seemed to realise what a meticulous and conscientious worker Aphra was, and spent less time watching her, and more time in her drawing room reading her bible.

The morning sickness disappeared and was no longer a problem, but her expanding waistline was becoming one. At first, it was not noticeable and her skilful adjustments to her clothes concealed much, but one day, the mistress commented on how Aphra appeared to be putting on weight.

"I must be feeding you too well," she said as Aphra carried a tray out of the room. She felt scared, for it would not be long before she would have to leave.

Whilst out on errands, or on the rare moments of free time, she began looking around for accommodation and employment that she would be able to do in her condition. She scoured the local newspapers and made numerous enquiries, but without success.

One morning, when she was dressing, she knew that her secret would be detected very soon, and she was right. Later, she caught a reflection of herself in Miss McDonough's mirror whilst cleaning her bedroom. There was little doubt now of her condition. Her back had started to ache a little and she had developed the habit of leaning backwards with her hand at the small of her back when very tired.

"What's wrong with you girl?" Miss McDonough snapped. "You're always standing like that these days. You look like an expectant mother." As she said the words, a look of realisation came into her eyes as she slowly considered the possibility and then the fact of her maid's condition. Aphra was horrified at the discovery of her secret and it showed on her face.

"You are, aren't you?" Miss McDonough demanded with disgust on her face. "I bet you're not really married, are you? You're a trollop."

***

"Oi! Trollop. Did you hear what I said?"

Aphra looked up from her sewing. "I said, there's another pile for you to be getting on with," snapped one of Mrs Robinson's cronies. "You're taking your time. Matron said to get a move on."

Aphra said nothing, but just nodded and continued with her work. As her needle went in and out of the fabric, so her mind wandered again into the past. She spent hours in reverie about her lost family and wondered what her mother and grandfather would have been like with her child. Would they have been disappointed at her foolishness at getting into this predicament? She thought not, for her grandparents had been in love and eloped, and her mother had fallen in love with her father – although he turned out to be no good. No, they would not have chided her. They would have loved her and the child, and they would have understood.

She missed Emily and their warm friendship very much. She wondered what Emily would be doing now and how she must feel about Aphra's sudden departure without explanation or farewell. This caused Aphra much heartache, but what really hurt and confused her was the total abandonment by Claude. It seemed somehow so out of character – and yet there had been no response to her letter.

One day, when she was thinking about it yet again, it suddenly occurred to her that perhaps the letter never arrived at Methuen Park. Maybe it had got lost or gone astray – these things happened from time to time, didn't they? Then she realised something that had not occurred to her before. How could she have been so stupid? Of course, that was how Caroline knew of her condition – the letter had been intercepted. "My God! I've been such an idiot. Why didn't I think of it before?" She had thought that the letters were not being noticed and that the contents were safe from prying eyes. "What had she written, and how many letters had Caroline read?" Aphra had been so careful to conceal the true nature of Claude and Sebastian's relationship, that she had omitted to pay attention to other things that she had written – especially in regard to herself. Could this be the reason that Caroline thought that Aphra was carrying on with Claude and the Earl – and hence the remark about Albert? Days passed and she contemplated these matters as she sewed. That last letter had been handed to the girl from the village - but supposing somehow Caroline had got her hands on it. Perhaps she or Miss Salathial had seen her give it to the girl and had forced her to hand it over.

She reached for another sheet and rethreaded her needle.

Her thoughts returned to the day that she was dismissed by Miss McDonough. Her bags seemed much heavier than they had done a few weeks earlier. As she trudged down the road, carrying all her possessions, she tried to decide what to do next. Once again, she needed to find somewhere to spend the night. She walked towards the centre of the city and found a small guest house and rented a room for two nights. She spent the days searching for employment, but by the end of the second day, she knew that it was very unlikely that she would find a post in a respectable establishment. For the present time, she had enough money to survive, but it would not last long if she was paying out rent at this level, so she moved to a place where the rent was much lower. She spent a few more days searching for work.

She decided that it would be wise to try and sell some of her possessions - mainly the books, as they weighed so much to carry around. As the days passed, she also took her best clothes to a dealer. She did not receive their true worth, but it meant that she could travel lighter and it paid for food and lodging for a few nights.

Finally, she obtained a position in a very rough inn - cleaning, and working in the kitchens. The work was back breaking and the hours long. The kitchen was hot, steamy and uncomfortable, but it was employment - albeit with very low pay. She had a small room in the basement – adjacent to the kitchens. The staff and the men that stayed at the inn were uncouth and bawdy and she was constantly afraid of being accosted. On more than one occasion, she was touched inappropriately, so, at night she slept with furniture pulled in front of the door.

As she worked at her sewing, she continued to contemplate the past. She remembered the fear and desperation that she felt whilst working at the inn. She did not earn enough money to save and although she had her board and food, the quality of both was far from desirable. At nights, the few hours respite was plagued with terror as drunken men tried to get into her room.

Finally, after one particularly nasty incident, she knew she would have to leave for her own safety. Again, she found herself forced to trek from one establishment to another trying to find work while she dipped more and more into her savings to pay for rent. She became increasingly aware that it was going to be impossible to make her money last. She wondered what she was going to do when the money finally ran out. She sold the last of her possessions until all that she had left were the clothes that she stood up in, her correspondence with Claude and the brooch. Her shoes were very worn, and her expanding waistline meant that she had needed to sew panels into her dress.

By the end of September, her money was all gone and she found herself spending the nights sleeping rough. She remembered back to that day more than a year ago, when she had arrived at Warrington Grange and the state that she had been in then. She was exhausted and nearly starving. Now she had her child to think of and she could not risk getting into that state again, for if she died then her child would die too.

It was at this point that she once again thought of the workhouse. She shuddered. No, she could not go there. By all accounts, they were terrible places – but after a week of sleeping rough and the autumn leaves beginning to fall, she knew that for the sake of her unborn child, she would have to give in.

So here she was in this grim establishment trying to fight off feelings of melancholia. She cut the thread that she was using, placed the completed article on the pile to be ironed and then selected another sheet from the growing pile awaiting mending. It seemed to be never ending and she sighed with weariness as she threaded the needle once more and continued her work.

***

It was a couple of weeks after Aphra's arrival that the matron fell down the stairs and broke her ankle and wrist. Most of the inmates wished that she'd broken her neck. However, although the woman was a mass of bruises, and had concussion, the injuries were not life threatening. But it did mean that she was going to be laid up in the infirmary for some time.

Mr Griffiths, the master, was concerned that her administrative duties would be neglected. Unlike her, he was a fair person. He tried to keep an eye on what was going on in the women's section, but was usually so busy that he left much of the everyday management of things in that part of the workhouse to Mrs Robinson. Her absence put him in a quandary. He decided that he'd have to ask one of the inmates to take over her duties until she had recovered. He had a word with a few of them. It seemed that a young woman who had recently arrived was quite intelligent and well educated. He asked for her to be sent to him.

Aphra was most surprised to be summoned to his office.

"You wanted to see me sir?"

"Ah, Mrs Taverner. Please take a seat," he gestured with his arm.

Aphra had got so used to being shouted at and ordered about, that she was quite taken aback at his courtesy.

"As you know, Mrs Robinson has had a nasty accident and it has meant that some of the office work is piling up. Bills need to be paid and orders need to be placed for provisions. I understand that you've had experience in this area."

"No sir. I was a lady's maid and dealt with correspondence for my mistress – usually of a social and personal nature."

"Yes, I see, but you have had a good education and I think that you are an intelligent woman. Do you think that you could take over the running of things until Mrs Robinson is able to resume her duties?"

"What does Mrs Robinson say? She does not think very highly of me and I do not want to antagonise her further."

"That is irrelevant. What is important is the smooth running of the workhouse. We do not want to be running out of food or fuel – especially as the winter is upon us."

"I'll do my best sir," she said.

"Thank you. You may go now."

She curtseyed and left.

For the next three days, she spent her time familiarising herself with the ledgers. At first, it seemed very complicated, but after a while, she became confident in her work. However, she kept finding that things did not add up. As she checked tradesmen's invoices and receipts, she found that she could not make the figures tally. It took a few sleepless nights before she realised that Mrs Robinson was stealing. Louisa had mentioned that she thought something was not right and had wondered where all the money went. According to this paperwork, new sheets and blankets had been purchased, but this was obviously not the case. The sheets were worn and there was a severe shortage of blankets. She only had one on her bed. In fact, on colder nights, the women were sharing their beds and blankets, in order to keep warm. The food accounts did not match either. According to the paperwork, the food order should have been for meat and bread and vegetables. There were items on these invoices that had not been served for meals while Aphra had been there. So where was the food going? Was she selling it? Aphra was undecided what to do. Should she tell the master? She had to be absolutely sure of her facts. If she was wrong, then Mrs Robinson's fury would be terrifying.

One night, she lay awake for hours pondering what to do. She finally fell asleep having made the decision that she would point out the discrepancies to the master and ask him if he could explain them to her. That way, it would not look as though she was making any accusations, but just telling him that she was confused.

When she awoke to the usual noise of the bell being rung, she quickly dressed and went down with the other women to the dining room. To her dismay, Mrs Robinson was standing leaning on a stick. She was obviously back on duty and as formidable as ever. She made it quite clear to Aphra that her services were no longer required in the office and advised her that anything that she had dealt with was confidential. Aphra said nothing, but returned to her sewing.

After this, Mrs Robinson made her life even more difficult. Aphra was now expected to help with the laundry as well as doing the sewing. This meant that she was often working later than the other inmates and missing meals and the small amount of free time that they shared together. She suspected that this was so that Aphra would not have any opportunity to discuss with anyone else what she had seen in the office.
She tolerated this ill-treatment, for there was nothing that she could do about it. She had witnessed punishments being handed out unfairly to inmates on numerous occasions and she was in no position to protect herself from this cruel woman. There were a few women that Aphra had come to know reasonably well besides Louisa. One of them, a large, slow-witted woman called Bertha was often the recipient of cruelty. The poor woman was even less able to defend herself than the other inmates. On more than one occasion, Aphra had tried to comfort the woman at night as she cried herself to sleep. "I can't 'elp being large and clumsy. I do my best, but she still makes fun of me in front of all the others. I know I ain't very bright, but I do my best."

Aphra did not know what to say. She was so young and was encountering things, the like of which she had no experience. She tried to say something soothing, thinking of the things that might make Bertha feel better – although she thought that they were totally inadequate and crass.

There was another inmate that Aphra had got to know. Her name was Holly and she was little more than a child herself. Aphra had found her crying one day and when she asked the cause of it, Holly told her that the matron had said some really spiteful things and called her an unnatural and evil slut. Also, she had now been put on to floor-scrubbing and was finding the work very hard on her. "My baby is due any day now. You'd think that she would understand and let me do some easier work – but no, she gives me even harder work to do."

"Why did she call you unnatural?"

"It's 'cos my dad's the father of the child. I told her when I first came 'ere that I didn't want to do that with 'im, but he made me. E's a big man with a bad temper – especially when he's been at the ale. I was only fourteen when I got with child. I was thirteen when he started it."

"Good God! I've never heard anything like it in my life."

"It goes on a lot."

"I had no idea that people behaved in that way. He should be in prison."

"'Yeah, but no-one's going to put 'im there – if they did, ma and the other kids would just end up in 'ere."

The following day, Aphra spoke to Mrs Robinson. "Can you not take the girl off such arduous duties? Her time approaches. She has done nothing wrong. She's the innocent victim of a terrible abuse by her father."

Mrs Robinson said nothing for a moment. Her mouth twitched and a nerve on the side of her forehead pulsated. She was obviously furious that this inmate should have the audacity to speak to her thus.

"Very well. I shall put her on lighter duties. You can take her place and don't think I'm letting you off the sewing or your shift in the laundry. I want those sheets finished by next week at the latest. If necessary, you'll work through the night."

"But you can't do that," Aphra protested. "I'm already exhausted."

"I can do as I like, and if you continue to argue with me, I'll put you on a punishment. I already have you marked down in the register as a refractory woman. You're a troublemaker."

"That's not true." Aphra was about to mention what she had learned about the book-keeping, but then decided to keep her own counsel. Innocent and naive as she was, it had not occurred to her that she had the power to bring this woman down. She could have threatened to report her, but instead she was too frightened of the consequences.

From that moment on, her life became even worse. She was scrubbing floors and washing linen first thing in the morning and late into the night. The sewing was carried out during the part of the day when there was the best daylight. She was getting very little to eat and less than three hours sleep a night. Often, she found herself falling asleep while she was sewing.

One morning, she overheard one of the women talking to another one. "Born dead it was. Probably just as well. What sort of life would it 'ave 'ad? Poor little bugger."

She looked up from her work. "What's happened?"

"Holly lost the bairn."

"Oh, how sad," said Aphra. "But as you say – perhaps it's for the best. Their lives would have been very difficult." She wanted to go and visit Holly in the lying in ward, but knew that Mrs Robinson would not allow it.

The next topic of conversation was news that one of the guardians was shortly to be paying a visit to the workhouse. Aphra was not interested, as it didn't concern her.

"It's another one of these toffs. I expect that ol' Robinson will have everything looking spick and span. At least we might get some decent grub and some heat for a day or two."

"Yeah, and then it'll be back to normal afterwards as usual," replied the other woman.

"She'll probably cut down even more to make up for it."

Just as the woman had predicted, things improved. Welcoming fires burned in the grates, and there was a lot of activity - cleaning, laundering, cooking and generally making things appear much better for the inmates. In the entrance hall and the dining room, some chrysanthemums were placed in vases in attractive arrangements with twigs and leaves.

On the day of the visit, the aroma of a hearty beef stew wafted through the building. There was a rice pudding for afters and there was to be a choice of ale or cider to wash it down. Baskets containing bread were to be placed on each table. The children had been taught a cheerful song to sing and the inmates were all allowed to take baths, their boots were polished and some were given cleaner, although still threadbare, uniforms. Also, bowls of apples from the orchard were placed on some of the window sills, giving the impression that the inmates could just help themselves between mealtimes.

Everyone except Aphra was given a hearty breakfast of milky porridge, toast and jam, and tea with sugar.

As the visit began, Aphra sat sewing by the window in a small room at the rear of the building far away from where the visitor would be shown around. She was having difficulty keeping her eyes open. She was so tired and hungry that she felt faint. Also, the room was so cold, that she could hardly feel her fingers.

PART FOUR - AN IDEAL WIFE

What a strange few days? I cannot sleep for the excitement that I feel. My brain seems to be racing with a thousand ideas. My life has changed beyond anything I could have imagined.

I was sitting sewing sheets in that horrible little room. I knew that I was being kept as far away as possible from the rounds that the dignitary would be taking, for Mrs Robinson intended that I should not be seen by him. I suspect that she didn't want me saying anything about her little secret.

So worried was I about what was to become of my unborn child and me, that with each stitch, I prayed for some resolution to my problems - a release from that dreadful place. I did not expect my prayers to be answered – and certainly not that quickly.

I must have blacked out, for the next thing that I knew, I was on the floor. I have no idea how long I had lain there.

From what seemed a long way off, I heard voices. "What's in this room?" It sounded like a man's voice.

"Oh, it's nothing but a store room, Milord. You don't want to go in there." It sounded like the matron. I must have blacked out again. Then I heard the man's voice say "however, I should like to see in here, all the same."

The room was very cold and the stone floor was even colder. As consciousness returned, I was shivering and sweating. I was so engrossed in my own misery, that I was unaware at first of a sudden commotion in the room.

"Stand up woman. You're in the presence of the Earl of Tawford!"

What a shock to see Sebastian.

"My dearest Aphra," he exclaimed as he rushed to help me up from the floor - no less shocked than I was. "What are you doing here? Claude and I have been so worried about you." I attempted to stand up as he helped me back to the bench. He sat down and embraced me. I feel embarrassed now to think of how the tears welled up and flowed copiously. The weeks of trying to keep my feelings and fears in check seemed to have acted like a dam which now burst at the relief of seeing this kind man again and having his warm gentle arms around me. Mrs Robinson had been about to scold me for my behaviour, but changed her mind and her attitude towards me when she saw the affection and esteem with which the Earl held me.

I started to feel faint again and suddenly Sebastian lifted me up in his arms. "This woman is frozen. What do you mean by allowing her to sit and work in a room with no heating?" He carried me out to the dining room and sat me by the fire. "Someone fetch some blankets!"

He turned to look at me. "Have you eaten today?"
I shook my head.

"Get her some hot food immediately!"

One of the inmates scurried off and returned with some of the beef stew in a bowl. Sebastian pulled up a chair and began to feed the nourishing food to me. A minute later, two thin grey blankets were placed over my knees. After a few minutes, I began to revive.

"Thank you," I said, and I know that he could hardly hear me as my voice was so weak.

"You must return with me to Methuen Park immediately. I started to protest, but he would not listen to any refusal.

"I'll get someone to get your possessions and I'll continue with my rounds," he said.

He continued with his inspection of the workhouse with Mrs Robinson running after his great striding figure. As he left the dining room, I could hear him chastising her about my treatment and she in her turn was saying that she'd had no idea that I was in an unheated room and could not understand why I had not eaten any breakfast.

"Well, you should know. You're in charge of the women's section. Ignorance is no excuse!"

Another one of the inmates handed me my bag and old clothes and helped me to a small room off the corridor, where I changed into the dress that I had been wearing on my arrival. I had expected that it would be too tight, for my pregnancy was now a few more weeks advanced, but to my surprise and shock, the dress hung on me. I had obviously lost a lot of weight.

Dear mama's brooch was still with me - hidden in my under garments. What a dilemma it had been to hold on to the only thing left of her, my most precious possession and yet knowing it to be so valuable and so could provide for my child. Thank God that I am not faced with that choice now.

I hope that you can forgive me Mama for considering selling it, and also for my smugness as I stepped into Sebastian's grand carriage. Yes, I gloated heartily at the look on Mrs Robinson's face with its fixed smile, and her resentful subservience to me, after all the weeks of spiteful cruelty and catty remarks. It is not an attribute of which I am proud, but I should like to see her face when she learns of her dismissal. I have told Sebastian about the true conditions there and he is going to insist on an investigation into the management of the place. It may be that criminal proceedings will follow, for he tells me that there should be enough money for adequate heat and food. I wonder how she will enjoy the facilities when she is in prison and at the receiving end of possible ill-treatment herself.

I have suggested to Sebastian that Louisa be given her post at the workhouse. She is a capable, intelligent and honest woman with compassion, and I believe that her experience will prove invaluable. I know that she will do her best for the other women there - especially Bertha. Sebastian has agreed to my suggestion and will arrange for Louisa and her husband to share the accommodation that was previously Mrs Robinson's.

I have also requested that a position be found for Holly. "Perhaps you know of a fair employer who would take her on. If she returns home to her family, she will be in danger from her father," I said. He assured me that he would find a place for her. As the carriage sped away, I relaxed for the first time in months. I must have fallen asleep for a while. I opened my eyes and saw that it was growing dark. Sebastian was lost in thought. He became aware that I had awoken and smiled at me. He seemed pensive and distant.

"What's wrong?" I asked nervously. "Have I placed you in an awkward position?"

"Not at all" came the reply. "I'm hatching a plan, but it may not be to your liking."

"A plan - what kind of a plan?" I was rather curious.

"The nuptial kind," he replied with a wry grin on his face. I said nothing, but just stared at him, not comprehending.

"I think that we should marry – and soon."

"What! You're not serious - but what about Claude?"

"Oh, he can be best man," he said chuckling to himself.

"Don't you think that you should discuss this with him first?" I asked, adding that he may not be too keen on the idea.

"Of course, you're right my dear and I will talk to him as soon as we are home. But what do you think about the plan?"

"I don't know and to be honest, I'm somewhat perplexed. I'm extremely grateful for being rescued, but did not expect a marriage proposal," I replied.

"Let me put my idea to you and then you can tell me what you think," he said as he leant forward and took both of my hands in his.

"I did consider marrying Caroline. She has most of the attributes to be the perfect wife for me and to provide me with an heir. She is beautiful, clever, and healthy and would make an excellent hostess and consort. Besides, her cold and calculating nature would avoid my having any twinges of guilt about using her. However, I realised that this negative side of her character meant that I could not tolerate a lifetime of such close connection with her. However, my main objection to marrying her was that she would be unlikely to be warm and caring towards any children that we may have. I could not inflict such suffering on an innocent child.

Whilst you have been asleep, I have been thinking about your predicament and have come up with the ideal solution. If you become my wife, you will become the Countess of Tawford and I will claim that your child is mine. If it is a boy, he will become my heir."

I immediately protested. "That cannot be right, Sebastian. There is no blood connection." He put his finger up to his lips and gestured to me to lower my voice in case the coachman heard.

"It is what I want," he whispered. "I think that this plan will suit us all admirably. You and I share a warm affection for each other and I think that you'll agree that we are always at ease together. Claude is also very fond of you and enjoys your company enormously. Besides, it will be fun to have a child in the house.

As for you, I will arrange an allowance for your clothes and personal needs. You can employ a maid and a nanny. I shall leave the choice of candidates up to you, but if you need assistance in this matter, then I'm sure that my mother would be only too happy to advise you."

He continued to relate all the benefits and advantages that would be mine.

"But I feel guilty about the deceit. It isn't honest."

"Who would we be hurting? Let's face it, much of the aristocracy can trace its ancestry back to medieval times when probably most of them got their positions and wealth from ill-gotten means."

"Yes, but ..."

"In fact, we need to say very little, for people will make up their own minds."

"I suppose so. But what about your mother? What will she say?"

"Ah. That's one area where I do feel uncomfortable, for I do not like the thought of deceiving her." He was quiet for a moment and then continued. "However, needs must. Maybe you will have a girl and that will solve the problem to some extent - for a while at least. Perhaps we could try for a child of our own at some later stage"

I felt uneasy about the situation and Sebastian saw this. "She's getting very old and frail and will just be happy that I am getting married and that a child is on the way. I doubt whether she would understand the relationship between Claude and me. I don't want to hurt her."

I was quiet for a moment but reluctantly agreed that it would be best not to tell her.

"Anyway, I'm sure that she'll be delighted. She took a real liking to you. She couldn't abide Caroline."

"Won't she be concerned about my having been a servant? Surely, she would prefer that you marry someone from your own sphere."

"I will be. I've learned of your family connections. I forced the information out of your friend, Emily. She was very reluctant to break her word to you, but when I pointed out that I thought you were in trouble, she told me about your connection with an aristocratic family. Claude filled me in with the name. I've already been to see your cousin and he is anxious to meet you."

I did not know what to say. It was all too much for one day.

"I'll arrange with mother for you to have some of the family jewellery made available. Perhaps, we should start off with some of the smaller, simpler pieces, until you feel more comfortable. Some of it is a bit grand and on the large size! I expect that at the moment, jewellery and the like seems somewhat trivial, but these are things that we'll need to consider for the future.

The first thing that I'll need to set in motion will be for some clothes to be made for you."

"I seem to have lost weight recently, but I expect that I shall soon be expanding fairly rapidly. The seamstress will need to allow for my getting bigger."

"That will all be taken care of, but for now, you need to rest and get yourself well. You've been through a bad ordeal. In time, when you feel ready, you can take over the running of the household. Mother and I share the responsibility of it, but I'm sure that she will be glad to relinquish the duty. I know that I shall."

He continued in this vein, telling me of all the advantages that I would receive. It was a heady potion that he described.

"But surely I can't just take all this from you. What can I give you in return? There must be something that I can give you or do for you in return. Please tell me that there is something – anything that I can do to repay you for all your generosity."

"There is only one thing that I ask of you. I need your solemn promise that you will never reveal the truth about Claude and me, the child's true parentage and the nature of our marriage."

I promised. It was such a little thing that he expected of me. It was such an easy thing for me to do. He was giving me so much and I was giving so little in return.

He went on to say that if I wished to have the odd discreet liaison, as he called it, then that would be acceptable to him. However, I had to bear in mind that there could never be any question of a divorce.

When we arrived back at Methuen Park, it was dark and I was quite exhausted. However, I forgot my tiredness as the carriage pulled up at the base of the steps to the portico, and there standing at the top was Claude. As soon as he saw me looking out of the window, his expression changed and he ran down the steps shouting "Ma cherie, ma soeur – at last you are found." As I stepped down from the carriage, he kissed and embraced me as once my own dear mother used to do. "Welcome home, my dearest girl. Where have you been? What has happened to your lovely hair?"
"I found her in the workhouse," said Sebastian. "What a stroke of luck that I went there today." He turned to me and held out his hand to guide me up the steps. "Welcome home, Countess."

And I was.

I must have looked a pathetic sight as I entered the palace – the place that was to be my home for the rest of my life. After the weeks in the workhouse, it seemed grander than ever. Travis was standing awaiting instructions.

"Can I be of service, Milord?" He asked, giving me a swift, slightly disapproving appraisal.

"Yes Travis. Can you please ask Dorothy to run a bath for Miss Chamberlain and to find some suitable night attire for her? Thank you."

"Certainly Milord."

Ten minutes later, I was in a warm, scented bath with Dorothy washing my hair.

"Oh Miss, what have they done to you and your lovely hair?"

"It'll grow again and I expect a good cut will make it grow all the better – rather like pruning a rose bush."

We both laughed at this. It was so good to laugh and to be with someone friendly and kind again. She had spoken to the Countess who had told her that I could use some of her daughter's things. She was very distressed to hear of my ordeal. Sebastian had told her what had happened and about the baby. He was concerned that she would be shocked, but was pleasantly surprised at her positive reaction to all the news. The one thing that made her angry was Caroline's behaviour regarding the letter and Aphra's dismissal. "Just the sort of underhand behaviour I'd expect of that jumped up nobody."

***

So here I am sitting in this beautiful room – for the first time in many months with the leisure to just sit and pen my thoughts. Oh how fortunate I am. As I sit here at the desk writing, I look around the luxurious bedroom and count my blessings. What a wonderful life I am going to have – such wealth and status. How will Caroline react? I must not be so malicious as to gloat at the change in our fortunes, but it is tempting and I do long to see the look on her face when we next meet. Oh Mama, I must kerb this tendency for vengeful spite. It is an unattractive trait.

As I write this, I am feeling something familiar – yet not unpleasant in my abdomen. What used to be a slight fluttering, has now become a very strong kick.

My child is letting me know that it is safe and well.

That first night, I thought that I should never sleep, but I did. Shall I sleep tonight with all these thoughts racing around in my head and my child becoming more boisterous inside me?

I am very fortunate to be receiving so much and having to give such a little in return. It is going to be so easy for me to keep my promise. I have certainly got the best part of the bargain. I really do thank God for all his blessings.

***

Over a week has elapsed since I last wrote in this journal. My husband - how strange that sounds - has not long left my chamber. He said that for the sake of appearances, it was best for us to spend the wedding night together. That way, we would reduce the chance of any suspicion or subsequent gossip. We enjoyed a light breakfast of coffee and toast together before he left to attend to some estate business with his land agent.

It is a shame that two days before the wedding, I began to feel a little unwell. It was nothing serious, but my throat was becoming increasingly sore and speaking was becoming very difficult.

It has been a hectic time with all the preparations for the marriage. Seb (I am getting accustomed to using this shortened version of his name - he says that it is what he wants) made arrangements for a dressmaker to call and speedily supply me with a suitable gown.

The dress is beautiful and the height of fashion. I have never worn anything like it. The dressmaker is ingenious and made the dress in such a way as to conceal my expanding waistline. Also, I am now the owner of a very fine trousseau that includes a pair of white satin buckled slippers, undergarments and night attire.

The jewel encrusted tiara, and the Honiton lace veil once belonged to his mother, as did the family jewels of emerald necklace with matching bracelet and earrings. Seb told me that when he first told his mother about our forthcoming marriage and that it was to be a quiet affair in the chapel, she was not too happy. I think that she had wanted a grand affair with many important guests for her son's wedding. However, when he explained about the baby, she seemed to be very excited at the prospect of becoming a grandmother and agreed that a quiet wedding to take place as quickly as possible was the best idea.

I remember her kindness to me when I first met her. She disliked Caroline immediately and did not want her son to marry her, but I knew that she liked me, so I was not concerned that we would not get along. Besides, I suspect that she has had some concerns regarding that other matter, so she is probably just relieved that he is getting married and that an heir is due.

She got very involved in the arrangements and I think that she has thoroughly enjoyed herself. She took charge of the small wedding breakfast, the flowers for the chapel, and all those last minute little extra details that always seem to need attention. This included a thorough clean and minor refurbishment of the small chapel in the woods. It is hardly ever used these days, as the family and staff tend to worship at the village church. The chapel is mainly a burial place for their ancestors. However, it has been sanctified, and is therefore, suitable for a marriage service. I am very grateful to the Countess, (who, incidentally, has asked me to call her Rose.) for all the help, for I have been quite tired and have often needed to rest. I just hope that she has not over-tired herself, for her health is not robust.

Yesterday morning, I rose quite early. Dorothy came to my room and helped me to dress and do my hair (despite the shortness of it), and fitted the tiara and veil. It seemed so strange to have someone helping me with my toilet and preparations, when I have been so used to being the one carrying out these tasks for someone else.

There was just one more item to add and my ensemble was complete. I went to the drawer and took out Mama's brooch and pinned it onto my dress.

Dearest Mama, I wonder if you watch over me, and were you smiling yesterday to know that at last I would be safe and happy for the rest of my life and that your grandchild was provided for as well?

My toilet now finished, I descended the stairs with Dorothy beside me. A few of the servants were waiting in the hallway. They all clapped, which I thought was rather sweet. What a happy household this is. We made our way down the steps to the carriage which was waiting to take us the short distance to the chapel. Rose was already seated inside and smiled as I climbed in.

"You look lovely my dear," she said. "Sebastian could not have chosen a better bride." I smiled and nodded, but did not respond for my throat was very sore and I was trying to preserve my voice for the service.

We set off towards the woods. It only took a few minutes. Rose and Dorothy entered the chapel first and I followed, allowing a small distance of time to give a sense of ceremony to this very informal occasion. The Chaplain stood in front of the small altar and Sebastian and Claude were next to him. At the back of the four small pews, sat Travis, the butler and Mrs Williams, the housekeeper. Rose sat in the front pew with Dorothy beside her. As I walked in, they all stood up. It was only a matter of a dozen or so steps and I was standing beside Sebastian, who had his hand outstretched to me. He seemed very relaxed and happy. The ceremony was very short and simple. First a hymn was sung, and this was followed by a prayer. Then the chaplain began the proceedings proper. It is odd now when I think of it all. At one point, I could hardly utter more than a few words, due to my laryngitis and Claude had to speak most of the vows for me. How strange - yet fitting! Within a few minutes – certainly no more than twenty, it was all over and I was Seb's wife, and a Countess.

We returned to the house where the five of us, including the Chaplain, sat down to an informal yet sumptuous wedding breakfast. Travis, Mrs Williams and Dorothy all left to continue with their duties. I did not eat very much, for I was too excited and my appetite seemed absent – probably due to the throat infection. Oh how I wish that my mother, grandfather, and Emily had been here to celebrate this occasion. If they had, then my happiness would have been complete. A few toasts were made, and altogether, it was a very happy occasion. At the end, Sebastian said that he preferred for no announcements to be made about the wedding for the time being and said that he had given these instructions to the staff also. This has comforted me, for I would prefer as little fuss as possible for I do not want to draw attention to my condition.

When we'd finished the meal, the Chaplain left to carry out his clerical duties elsewhere. Seb said that he had some letters to write, so he and Claude went to his study. Actually, I think that they just wanted to be alone. Rose was looking quite tired and excused herself. As I was feeling much the same, I was grateful to be able to retire to my room. I lay down on the bed and slept for about two hours. Late in the afternoon, the four of us took tea together in the drawing room. It was very relaxed as we sat and chatted.

Last night, just before we retired, the butler brought a bottle of champagne on ice to my bedroom and placed it, with two exquisite crystal glasses, on a table in an alcove. As he was doing this, Sebastian made a big show of pretending to be amorous towards me – so much so, that the poor man was extremely embarrassed and left the room as quickly as possible.

Obviously, there was no re-awakening of the passionate experience that I had in Minehead – yet it was pleasant – comforting, although strange and probably an unusual wedding night. We spent much of the evening getting to know each other – swapping life histories, likes and dislikes, jokes, anecdotes and so on - although I found it hard to make myself understood at times, due to my voice being so faint. At one point, Claude joined us to drink the champagne. Shortly before midnight, Claude took his leave of us. Sebastian briefly left the room with him and then returned. I imagine that they wanted some privacy to wish each other good night.

I slept very well and was awoken by the butler carrying a tray of coffee and toast. It felt very strange to have this man entering my bedchamber with me in bed with a man. I was not accustomed to this and, to tell the truth, was most uncomfortable.

So, here I am sitting at my desk. It seems so strange to have nothing to do. I am so used to being busy that this inactivity seems most peculiar. I shall just have to see what the days ahead bring. But for now, I shall rest. I feel that after the ordeal in the workhouse, my body needs to recuperate.

Last night when Seb and I were finally alone, I felt unsure and afraid – what to do and how to behave. I need not have worried. We undressed separately – each in private. We sat in bed – Seb enjoying a nightcap – as he called it, with me next to him, with my hands nestling a cup of warm milk that he had fetched for me. What strange bedfellows we made!

Gently, he put his arm around my shoulders and having finished the milk, I replaced the cup on the saucer and leant my head on his chest. When I awoke this morning, his head was back against the pillows. We had spent the entire night in this tender embrace.

Oh that my own father could have held me like that – just once!

***

Two days after the wedding, Sebastian entered the study of Viscount Westbridge.

"Nice to see you ol' chap," said Donald, indicating a leather armchair. Walking over to a Tantalus on a Chippendale cabinet, he picked up a crystal decanter and held it up with a questioning glance on his face.

Sebastian nodded and his host poured out two whiskeys, adding a dash of water to each. Handing a glass to Sebastian, he asked "so what's all this about? Have you some information about my cousin?"

Sebastian took a small box out of his pocket and placed it on the desk in front of Donald.

"Open it," Sebastian said. He watched for the reaction.

Slowly, the Viscount opened the box. His face went pale as he looked at the brooch. "You've found her!" He recognised the family heirloom from a few of the portraits of his ancestors.

"Yes, she's my wife."

"Your wife!" Exclaimed Donald.

"We married two days ago."

"Why didn't you tell me? I could have given her away." He sounded peevish.

"It was a very quiet ceremony. We had to act with speed." Sebastian looked contrite. "I'm sorry."

"A child?"

"Yes. It's a long story, but I won't bore you with the details."

Donald, who was not one to harbour a grudge, held out his hand. "Well, it would seem that congratulations are due on two counts." They shook hands.

"Thank you."

"When is the child due?"

"Oh, in about three or four months. I'm not too good on these things." He sounded a bit vague. "We're going abroad very soon. The child will be born abroad and that will make things a bit easier - you know – a bit more discreet."

"Of course, I understand. When can I meet her? Before you go, I hope."

"Of course. She's very excited at the prospect of finding her relations – although unsure because of her condition."

"Oh tell her not to worry about that. Another Westbridge – or two for that matter - is very welcome."

"What about lunch this Sunday?"

"I'll check with the boss, but I'm sure that it will be most agreeable."

As they walked out into the hall, Donald pointed up the stairs to a painting of a very beautiful fair-headed young lady wearing a magnificent blue satin ball gown and a sapphire and diamond tiara and necklace. "Look," he said. "That is India Kingston. She was a real beauty. See the brooch."

Sebastian rapidly climbed a few steps to get nearer. He turned, and Donald could see the shock on his face.

"What is it?"

"That's her! Apart from the difference in the hair colour, that's Aphra!"

***

I was so nervous and excited that I slept little last night – perhaps just two or three hours. I was up and dressed long before Sebastian awoke. It was a beautiful morning and I decided to go for a long walk down by the lake.

When I returned, Sebastian and Claude were taking breakfast.

"Good morning wife. And where did you get to?"

"I couldn't sleep, so took a turn down by the lake. It's so peaceful and beautiful. The leaves are such vibrant colours. I walked right around to the folly. I think that it's very interesting and unusual."

"A bit grandiose for my taste," Seb laughed. "One of my ancestors was rather pretentious."

"Well I like it. It's rather Arcadian," I replied. "It will be a lovely place to sit with the baby and look across the lake. The ducks and swans were all around me. It will be fun for us to feed them when our child is growing up."

At this, Seb smiled.

"This is a big day for you, I think," said Claude, as he buttered some toast.

I helped myself to some scrambled eggs. "To think that I have a blood relation. I feel so fortunate. To think that only a short while ago, I was alone in the world and now I have you two who are so kind to me and your wonderful mother - and today I'm to meet my cousin and his wife. I do hope that they will like me and not disapprove of the situation."

"I have no doubt that they will adore you. Remember, I saw his reaction when he saw your grandmother's brooch," Sebastian said, trying to reassure her. "He was delighted. You are his only living blood relation too. They are quite old now, so there will be no children or grandchildren. Besides, you are almost a double of your grandmother, India."

"But perhaps he will think that I've behaved in an unseemly manner and have disgraced the family."

"Rest assured my dear, he will not judge you. He is a kindly man and I believe that he'll be very happy to welcome you and the child into the Westbridge family. Please try not to worry."

After breakfast, I spoke with Mrs Williams about the menu for lunch. She is so very kind and is helping me to learn about the routine of the house. When we return from our trip abroad, I must take control of the running of the household.

The thought of this is daunting. "I'm afraid that my lack of experience will prove to be a handicap," I said to Sebastian.

He dismissed my fears with a wave of his hand. "You have more experience than you think and if nothing else, your time working for the gorgon will stand you in good stead. It will certainly have taught you how to treat people."

"Yes, but ..."

"Hush, I'll brook no more of these doubts and insecurities. Just give it time and be yourself." With that, he kissed me on the forehead and smiled benignly at me.

Shortly after eleven thirty, Travis knocked at the door of the drawing room. As he opened it, he stepped to one side and solemnly announced "Viscount and Countess Westbridge."

I was to learn that Travis loved anything that gave him a chance to practise formality and protocol. It was something that amused Sebastian and Claude greatly and they often had great difficulty in not bursting into great guffaws of laughter. However, on this occasion, they were more concerned with how I felt and were very subdued and well behaved.

Sebastian leapt up out of his chair and rushed forward to greet his guests warmly.

"Donald, wonderful to see you both. Come on in." They shook hands. "Hortense, it's been a long time. You're looking well." He kissed her hand.

I felt very nervous and the palms of my hands became very damp. That was all I needed. Sebastian was about to introduce me when the Viscount looked me straight in the eye and said. "I don't believe it. The resemblance is incredible. My dear girl, you're the image of your grandmother."

I stood up slowly and was about to hold out my hand, when he gave me the most enthusiastic embrace. It almost took my breath away. As he released me, he held both my hands and stepped backwards. "Let me look at you." For a few seconds, he silently studied me in what seemed like great detail. "My goodness, I can't get over it. There's no doubt about it, you're a Westbridge."

I was surprised to see the tears well up in his eyes. "My father loved his aunt very much. It was such a shock when she left. His grandfather was such an ill-tempered man. Everyone was terrified of him. To think that India and your mother were living in Wiltshire all the time. If only we had known, we could have visited you."

Hortense placed her hand on his arm. "Dearest, please do not upset yourself. This is a happy day for us all.

All my anxieties now vanished. Hortense greeted me just as warmly – though with less exuberance than her husband. "It is wonderful to meet you my dear. I'm sure that we will be seeing a lot of you in the years to come and we both congratulate you on your marriage – although you were very naughty not to let us give you a big do. However, we do understand."

She embraced me gently and for the first time since I was twelve, I felt the comfort of being held – as though by a mother.

We sat and chatted for some time and Travis served glasses of sherry for Rose, Hortense and me, and whisky for the gentlemen. Just before we went into lunch, Donald handed me a small red leather box. "Go on, open it," he said. Slowly, I did as I was told. I gasped when I saw the contents. Inside sitting on the plush velvet was a pair of earrings that perfectly matched mama's brooch.

"Mama told me that her mother had left these behind when she had eloped. Thank you so much. I shall wear them with pride."

"You are very welcome to them my dear," said Hortense.

Luncheon was a very enjoyable occasion and although it was more formal than I was used to, it was also very relaxed. The time passed all too quickly, and in no time, our guests were leaving with promises to get together soon.

As I write here, I know that I am blessed, as will be my child.

In a few days, we leave for the continent. I'm very excited, for I have travelled very little. However, before that, there is something that Seb is doing for me and I count the hours until it is sorted. I shall sleep well tonight.

***

The mistress wishes to see you at once," the housekeeper said in a very menacing tone.

Emily could not understand why this was so and her first thought was that she must be in some kind of trouble. She could not think of any recent transgression, but it required very little provocation to upset the mistress, and she had been even more moody of late.

"C'mon girl – don't dawdle," snapped Miss Salathial as she marched ahead up the stairs.

Emily followed her into the morning room. Her mistress was seated at her desk, and as Emily approached, she noticed that the mistress was holding an envelope of very expensive paper. It looked as though it might contain a very important document. Although the mistress was trying to conceal her emotions, the way that she was fiddling with the object indicated that she was extremely agitated. Emily recognised the signs and her feeling of alarm increased immediately.

As the envelope was turned over and over, she recognised the familiar seal of the Earl of Tawford. There was nothing unusual in this, for the mistress had often received correspondence from him. However, what was unusual was that the envelope was handed to her.

She looked at it and then her glance passed from the mistress to the housekeeper and back again. "But I don't understand," she faltered. "It's addressed to me."

Caroline sighed impatiently and drummed her fingers on the desk. It was obvious that both she and the housekeeper expected Emily to open the envelope in their presence and then to hand the contents to the mistress to read. Emily would have preferred to have taken it to her room and read the contents in private, but she didn't dare incur further wrath.

"Don't keep the mistress waiting girl. Open it!" Miss Salathial demanded.

Emily drew out the contents which were brief and to the point.

The other two women were surprised to see that not only could Emily read, but quite quickly too. However, they were even more surprised at what she had to say. The girl looked up and announced "his Lordship has summoned me to Methuen Park."

"What! You've misread it." Caroline snatched the letter out of her hand. But there was no mistake. There it was on the page, in the familiar hand of Sebastian himself.

***

Dear Miss Frances,

It would be appreciated if you would make yourself available to attend at Methuen Park immediately.

I wish to speak to you in relation to an urgent matter.

Yours sincerely,

Sebastian Raemond
Ninth Earl of Tawford

***

"I don't understand," Emily said with a perplexed expression on her face.

Caroline got up and paced the room for a moment or two. She could think of no reason why Sebastian should wish to see her parlour maid. It was all most peculiar and vexing. However, there was nothing for it, but to accede to his request and let the girl go.

She turned to face Emily. "Well, you'll have to do as he says. If the Earl has demanded your presence immediately, then you must go this morning. His carriage is outside."

As Emily curtsied and turned to leave the room, the mistress continued. "Take a bath and make yourself presentable. Do you have something smart to wear? I don't want you showing me up."

"Yes, ma'am. I can wear my church clothes."

"Very well. Then go and get yourself ready. Pack a bag. You'll probably have to stay overnight." At this, she dismissed Emily with a swift gesture of the hand.

"Make sure that your shoes are polished," added the housekeeper in a waspish tone.

Emily ran quickly down to the kitchen to tell Gracie and Maud the incredible news.

***

Emily was looking out of the carriage window and enjoying the view as well as tucking in to a tasty beef and mustard sandwich that Gracie had made for her. It was grand to be riding in such style. "I feel like lady muck," she thought and although she was quite nervous, she was also quite excited. "What an adventure - and it's got me out of two days' hard graft."

She closed her eyes and tried to imagine what the Earl's house would be like. Obviously, it would be much grander than Warrington Grange. She wondered if the servants there would look down their noses at her and she felt a bit apprehensive. It was all such a mystery and she kept going over in her mind what could be the reason for the summons.

Then she remembered the conversation with the Earl shortly after Aphra had disappeared. She still felt a mixture of uncomfortable emotions when she thought about Aphra. She was very sad that she had never heard from her, but she was also very put out that Aphra had just left without speaking to her or saying goodbye. She had noticed in the weeks that had preceded her departure, that Aphra had not been herself. In fact, she had not seemed the same girl when she had returned from her holiday in Minehead.

Her reverie was interrupted by the carriage turning off the road and stopping in front of a pair of ornate gates. The lodge-keeper came out of the small building just inside the wall, and the coachman spoke to him before the gates were opened and the carriage made its way up the curving drive.

Although she was used to the elegant and lavish lifestyle of her mistress, nothing had prepared her for the grandeur of Methuen Park. When the carriage stopped in front of the entrance, Emily looked up at the imposing edifice. She had never seen such a huge building. She wondered how many windows there were. It was certainly impressive. She thought that it must be a wonderful place in which to live.

She hung her head out of the carriage window. "Why've you stopped here?" As she was asking these questions, a liveried footman descended the steps and proceeded to open the carriage door and fold down the step for her. Then he held out his hand to assist her as she stepped down. It was all she could do to stop herself from bursting into laughter.

The footman said "please follow me miss."

Emily was taken straight to his Lordship's study. Although her mind was full of the forthcoming interview with the Earl, she couldn't help noticing the magnificent Portico, as she passed through it. She walked through a large lobby and saw the grand circular staircase and numerous large oil paintings – presumably of the Earl's many ancestors.

The footman knocked and opened the door to the study. The Earl was seated at his desk.

"Ah, Emily, my dear. How are you?" He put down his pen and stood up. Emily was most surprised as he shook hands with her. "Welcome to Methuen Park. Please take a seat." He rang for tea. "I trust that you've had a comfortable journey."

"Very nice, thanking you kindly Milord." This all seemed very odd.

"I hope that you're not too tired. I always say that a cup of tea really revives one – don't you think?"

Emily didn't know what to say, so just smiled politely.
There was a knock at the door and a maid bearing a tray of tea and biscuits entered the room and placed it on a small table by the fireplace.

"Thank you Betty," the Earl said. "Have you had your tea yet?"

"I'm just about to do so Milord," she replied in a relaxed manner. "Cook has just made some of her lovely scones."

Sebastian leaned forward and in a conspiratorial manner said. "Well you go and enjoy them. But before you do, could you please inform her Ladyship that our guest has arrived."

Emily was surprised and impressed at the friendly relationship that the Earl had with his staff. She thought that it must be a happy household.

As he handed her a delicate bone china cup and saucer, Emily thought how amusing it was to be waited upon – especially by one of the toffs.

He took a sip of his tea and then put down the cup. "I'll be quite honest with you Emily. It's not me that requires your presence here. You'll not have heard of this yet, as it isn't common knowledge, but I have recently become married and it's my wife who's expressed a wish to speak with you."

Emily suddenly realised that she was sitting with her mouth open.

"A new post has been created here, due to my recent nuptials and my wife wishes to offer you the position – that is assuming that it would be suitable from your point of view. When you see the Countess in a few minutes, all will become clear."

"About as clear as mud," Emily thought to herself. "Sir – I mean Milord, I don't understand. You say your wife, but I had thought that Lady Caroli…"

"Ah –Yes. Well, that was what she'd thought, I expect," he said, ringing the bell again. "No. I did vaguely consider making a proposal of marriage to your mistress, but decided that it might not be a wise choice."

Emily gave a knowing smile, but said nothing.

"I see that you understand me perfectly," he smiled. "We're going to get on very well, I suspect. Actually, I'd developed strong feelings for someone else, so it wouldn't really have been appropriate."

Emily nodded, as she didn't know what to say. This was certainly a strange, yet interesting conversation. There was another knock on the door and another maid entered the room.

"Milord?"

"Yes Polly. Could you take Miss Frances here to see the Countess please?"

"Of course Milord." The maid turned towards Emily. "Please follow me

Miss." Emily stood up and began to follow her out of the room.

"I'll see you this evening at dinner," the Earl called up after her.

As the two girls walked along the corridor, they made polite small talk with one another. Emily's nervousness had completely disappeared and had been replaced with eager curiosity. She wondered whether or not she was going to wake up in a minute only to find that she had overslept and was in trouble with the mistress.

When she entered the bright, sumptuous room, she realised that she was staring with her mouth open.

"Aphra!" She ran to embrace her dear friend. "I thought I'd never see you again. I'm so happy."

"My dear, dear friend. Thank God you're here at last. I've missed you so much."

"Why did you leave so suddenly? Where have you been?" Emily asked with tears in her eyes. "And why didn't you say goodbye to me? I've been so worried and hurt." Then she added "and very, very angry with you too."

"I know – and quite rightly so. It's a long story. Later, you shall know all about it, but for now, let me just look at you and enjoy your company again."

"It hasn't been the same without you. I've missed you so much."

"And I you." Aphra led Emily by the hand and the two young women sat down on a small sofa.

"How are all my dear friends at the Grange? I've missed them too. Are your parents well and what is the latest mischief your naughty brother has been up to?" Aphra asked, and Emily brought her up to date with some of the news and gossip from Watheford.

"Emily, I want you to come and live here with me and be my companion. What do you say?"

"The answer is yes. I can't wait to start," came the prompt reply.

After a while, Aphra stood up. "I expect that you'd like to freshen up before dinner, so I'll take you to your room. I have a couple of things to attend to."

She showed Emily into a lovely chamber. "This will be your room."

Emily wandered around the room touching everything and looking out of the window. "Oh Aphra, it's so pretty. Will it really be mine? I can't believe it."

"I'll see you in a while and we'll talk in detail after dinner. There's a dress in that wardrobe. I'm sure that it will fit. I think that the colour will suit you very well."
Emily looked in the wardrobe and took out a pretty blue dress. It was much nicer than anything that she had ever worn in her life. When she came down to dinner with Aphra, she felt very grand as they entered the dining room and sat at the huge polished table. At one end sat the Earl. Next to him sat a plump, elderly lady. She nodded to Emily as they were introduced. "This is my mother," said Sebastian. "Countess Rose."

Emily curtsied. "Pleased to meet you, Milady." She felt rather nervous. Was she saying the right thing?

"And I'm very pleased to meet you my dear. I do hope that you will be joining us. I expect you can't wait to get away from that nasty harpy! I expect that she works you to death," she chuckled to herself.

Next, Sebastian introduced his secretary, Claude Tanquerel. "Everyone calls him Monsieur," he said.

The Earl and his mother were excellent company, as was the Frenchman. Emily thought that they were all very nice – and quite down to earth for toffs.

There were a number of courses, and one or two things that Emily had never heard of, let alone eaten before. However, she was prepared to try everything and persevered with them even if she didn't like them all. She followed Aphra's lead with the cutlery and glasses and thought that she managed quite well for her first time.

When the meal was finished, the two men went off to enjoy their port and cigars. The three women sat and chatted for a few minutes and then the Dowager Countess asked to be excused, for she was very tired and wished to go to her room. Actually, she wanted to finish a book that she was reading – besides, she had an excellent cognac waiting for her.

"Come Emily," said Aphra. "Let us go up to my rooms and we can talk.

"Now to explain all the mystery. Firstly, please forgive me for leaving without saying goodbye, but I couldn't speak to you. The mistress had dismissed me, and she threatened to dismiss you as well if I had any communication with you."

"But why did she dismiss you? What had you done?"

"I suspect that Miss Salathial had been intercepting and steaming open my letters and discovered that I'm expecting a child. I sent a letter here, but it never arrived. When I heard nothing in reply and the mistress dismissed me, I didn't know what to do. I suppose it would have made sense to come here and speak to Sebastian, but I wasn't thinking clearly. I ended up in the workhouse."

"Well, all I can say is that you're a dark horse. When's the baby due?"

"In the new year. It was a very quiet wedding for we had to act swiftly, as I'm sure you'll appreciate. Only Sebastian's mother and Claude were present as witnesses as well as three members of the staff."
"I wish that I could've been here as well." Emily sounded a bit peevish.

"I wish you could too. But it had to be a very quick and private ceremony." Aphra gently laid her hand on Emily's arm. "Can you forgive me for all of this?"

"There's nothing to forgive now that I know what has been happening. By the way, did you know that the Earl came to see the mistress? He was searching for you. He must love you very much."

"You know, I think that he does care greatly for me. He is a most affectionate and caring man."

"Actually, I have a confession to make." Emil looked very contrite.

Aphra raised her eyebrows in enquiring anticipation of the revelation that she knew was about to come. "Tell me what dreadful thing have you done?"

"I told him about your family. I'm sorry, but I didn't know what to do." Emily looked as though she were about to burst into tears. "I thought something terrible might've have happened to you."

"It's alright Emily. Sebastian told me. You did the right thing," she reassured her. "I met my cousin, the 13th Viscount of Westbridge the other day. His name is Donald, and his wife is called Hortense. They are very nice people and have welcomed me into the family."

Relieved, Emily decided to change the subject. "So tell me about the position?" Emily was eager to learn all about it.

"Well, what d'you think, silly? Apart from being my companion, you're going to be nanny to my baby. There's no-one in the world I'd trust more to care for my child. Will you do it?"

"Oh Aphra, this is the best day of my life. I'm so excited. I can't wait to start. But I don't suppose you'll want me here until your confinement."

"I want you here as soon as possible. We're going abroad in a few days and you're coming too," Aphra replied. "When you return to the Grange tomorrow, Sebastian will give you a letter asking Caroline to release you immediately. Hopefully, that will make things a bit easier for you."

"She's going to have a fit."

"I know."

"This is too much for one day. I'm to be going over the sea. Where are we going?"

"Sebastian hasn't formalised the plans yet, but we'll definitely be going to France and Italy.

They chatted for a while and Aphra told Emily what her salary and conditions were to be. Emily couldn't believe her good fortune. It would mean that she would be earning so much more than at present, leaving her plenty to save for her future and also for some to send to her family.

"It goes without saying, that as you're my friend, my best friend, you won't be considered a servant, but one of the family. I look upon you as my sister and you will be treated accordingly by Sebastian and Claude. Also, I know that the Dowager Countess will treat you well. You'll find that this is a very happy household. Sebastian insists that everyone is treated with respect. He has a very relaxed manner with everyone."

"I've already noticed that. I like him very much. Perhaps, I'll have to get myself a toff. What about the Frenchman? He seems rather nice too."

"Behave yourself Emily," Aphra scolded and they both laughed.

Just before bedtime, they took a short stroll on the terrace. Emily noticed the Earl and Monsieur emerging from the woods. Aphra noticed too, and it reminded her of Sebastian's strict rules. She casually told Emily, and tried to emphasise the importance of sticking to this rule without trying to draw too much attention to it. "Just look upon it as one of the many strange eccentricities of the aristocracy," she giggled.

"What else happened to you after you left?" Emily asked. Aphra related the events up to her entry into the workhouse and then the terrible time that she had at the hands of Mrs Robinson.

"Oh Aphra. How awful. Especially after you'd been through such a tough time before you arrived at Warrington Grange. It must've been terrible for you."

"It was hard to cope with at the time. So imagine my joy when Sebastian walked in and spoke to me."

"How romantic!"

"That's one way to describe it. My life and fortunes changed overnight," she said. "Just think, only a short while ago, I was a pauper - a refractory woman is what I was called in the workhouse, and look at me now – a Countess."

Both girls were laughing as the two men mounted the steps to join them. "This is a new sound that we'll have to get used to now, my friend," said Seb to Claude.

"And what sound is that?" Asked Claude.

"The musical sound of female laughter," said the Earl. "And very welcome it is too."

Emily made a cheeky retort, to which everyone was still laughing as they entered the house. Goodnights were said and the Earl kissed his wife on the forehead. "Sleep well my dear. See that you get plenty of rest. I'll see you in the morning."

Emily thought that this seemed a little odd. She knew enough about the facts of life from the village and her own family to know that newlyweds couldn't wait to get into bed together. Perhaps the upper classes were different.

When Aphra walked Emily to her room, Emily made a casual remark about the Earl's not coming to her room. "Aphra was taken aback and it was only quick thinking that got her out of a difficult situation. "Oh, he thinks that because of my condition, I'm very delicate now."

Emily thought that he must be most thoughtful and considerate – not like some of the men that she knew in Watheford.

Aphra laughed and said that men were really quite innocent and ignorant about these things.

"Well, I think that you're very lucky to have bagged one like him."

"I certainly am. Goodnight my dear friend. It's going to be wonderful having you here. We are going to have such fun."

"Sleep tight. Don't let the bed bugs ….,"

"Goodnight Emily," Aphra closed the door.

Once Emily was tucked up in bed, she lay and thought about the incredible events of the day. She was so excited with her mind racing from one idea to another, that she thought she would never get to sleep. However, one minute, she was thinking about how she would cope with people speaking foreign languages and worrying about meeting all sorts of odd foreigners, and the next thing, Aphra was sitting on the bed and the sun was streaming into the room.

"Come on sleepyhead – time to get up. Are you hungry?"

Emily rubbed at her eyes. "What time is it?"

"Nearly eight fifteen."

"Gosh. I slept like a log in this lovely bed," said Emily, as she scrambled to her feet.

"We'll have breakfast, then you can go back and take your leave of the monster," said Aphra. "I'll see you downstairs in the dining room."

After they had eaten breakfast, Aphra bid Emily goodbye and watched until the carriage disappeared around the curve of the drive.

***

Emily knocked on the door of the drawing room.

"Enter."
As Emily stood in front of her, trying to appear confident, her mistress spoke.

"Well?"

"Ma'am?"

"Don't be stupid girl," she snapped. "Why were you summoned by the Earl? You've got a tongue in your head. Use it," she demanded.

"Yes ma'am. I'm sorry," she gulped – then continued. "I have a letter for you from His Lordship. He wants me to work for his wife, the Countess. I'm to be ..."

"He's married?"

"Yes ma'am." Emily nervously stepped forward and handed her the Earl's letter. For a few moments, she stood silently while Caroline read it. The letter was brief and to the point. There was no mention of his recent marriage – only a polite request that Emily be released straight away, as her presence at Methuen Park was required immediately. Caroline was furious. How dare he write this letter to her – with no apology – no explanation of his behaviour.

"I don't understand why he sent for you. It doesn't make sense." She looked at Emily in a calm but intimidating way. "Did you meet her?"

"Yes ma'am."

"I see." Caroline got up and paced around the room. "What's she like? Is she attractive?"

"Yes ma'am – very." Emily did not like the direction that the conversation was taking, but she wanted to get it over with as quickly as possible. She almost stammered, she was so nervous. "I've accepted the position ma'am and wish to commence as soon as you can let me go. In fact, his Lordship's carriage is outside. He's expecting me to return straight away."

Caroline returned to her seat.

Emily knew what was coming.

Very quietly, Caroline asked "What's the position?"

Emily knew from experience that this was the calm before the storm.

"My duties would be many ma'am."

"Don't be obtuse."

Emily trembled. She didn't know what the word meant, but this was becoming as bad as she'd dreaded.

The mistress stood up and leant forward - her face pressed close to Emily's. "Who is she?" The tone was now menacing.

The moment that Emily had dreaded had arrived. She took a deep breath. "Aphra ma'am."

There, she'd said it.

"I knew it," Caroline said calmly, but inwardly she raged.

"I'll ask you once more. What's the position?"

"I'm to be nanny to their child when it's born." She wanted this interview to end as soon as possible, so she moved it on. "I don't want to inconvenien…"

"I couldn't care less," Caroline screamed. "You're dismissed as from this moment. I want you out of this house within the hour. Miss Salathial will give you your wages to date."

"Thank you ma'am." Emily curtsied.

"I don't know about 'thank you ma'am'. You'll receive no reference and I shall say to all who enquire that you've been dismissed for dishonesty and lewd behaviour."

"Then those people will find it incredible that the Earl should employ such a wayward servant," Emily replied with sudden confidence.

"Remember that when it all goes wrong and he divorces that jumped-up trollop from the gutter, don't come slinking back here expecting your job back. Get out!"

Emily suddenly felt enraged at the way that this woman was speaking about her friend. "How dare you speak of Aphra in that manner? She certainly isn't a jumped-up trollop. In fact, she's back where she belongs. After all, she's an aristocrat by birth." The mistress looked shocked. "No, you didn't know that, did you?" Emily added smugly.

Suddenly, she became very brave – after all, she had nothing to lose now. "You've always hated her, haven't you? And everyone knows why. It's because she's everything you'll never be. She's prettier than you, cleverer than you and most of all, she's a lovely person – admired and loved by all who meet her. No wonder, the Earl's married her." She couldn't stop now. "You'll just end up a bitter old maid. I'm glad I'm leaving. You're horrid to work for." And with that, she flounced out of the room, slamming the door behind her.

Outside in the passage, the housekeeper moved away from the door and seemed to be engrossed in checking the water level of a vase of flowers.

"Find it interesting, did you?" Emily said as she pushed her face close up to the housekeeper. "I'll be coming for my money shortly. Make sure that it's ready in time." She could not believe her own courage and neither could the other woman.
"How dare you speak to ..." she said.

"Oh, go and stick your head in one of Gracie's stew pots!" Emily shouted as she threw her apron at her.

It was only when she was bidding goodbye to her friends in the kitchen that Emily became tearful. "I'm going to miss you all. Don't forget that

Aphra has invited you all to visit whenever you can, so we'll be able to stay in touch."

"See that you do young lady," said Mr Isaacs. He was pleased to hear of the fortunate changes in Emily's life, but more than this, he was relieved to know that Aphra was safe and well. He had always admired her and even though he never shared his feelings with anyone, he was very fond of the girl. "Perhaps it will be wise to address any correspondence to me and care of the post office in the village, for the mistress may not be comfortable about letters arriving from Methuen Park," he added diplomatically as he helped her into the carriage.

The coachman stopped by Emily's home, allowing her to say goodbye to her family.

"You know, you can visit me and I'll come and see you all regularly. I know that Aphra will be most generous about time off," she told them.

"Fancy you being a companion to a Countess," said her brother.

"I can't quite believe it myself."

"Goodbye," she said with tears in her eyes. Her entire family stood waving long after the carriage was out of sight.

For the second time in her life, Emily was driven up to the grand house where she was now about to begin a new life. She felt overcome with all kinds of emotions, but tried to appear nonchalant. She suppressed a giggle as a footman assisted her from the carriage in front of the vast portico, and carried her luggage up the steps and into the house. Tentatively, she followed him into the vast entrance hall, where Travis the Butler awaited.

"Good day Miss Frances." He seemed slightly uneasy about addressing her as such. Her position in the house was a strange one. She was an employee - a servant - and yet his Lordship had stressed that she was to be treated as one of the family. Travis did not approve of anything undermining propriety. However, he would do as his master had requested.

***

It is two days since my dearest Emily joined us here at Methuen Park. I am so very happy – the happiest I have been for a very long time – if I exclude the foolishness in the earlier part of the year. The maids here worked extremely hard making her room comfortable. It is a lovely cheery room at the other end of the corridor and has a sunny aspect first thing in the morning. I know that Emily will be very content having such a spacious and grand room. She had remarked, on first seeing it, that it was bigger than her parent's entire cottage – including the garden.

When she entered my sitting room, we hugged and hugged each other and laughed and danced around like two silly schoolgirls.

A few minutes later, one of the maids entered the room carrying a tray with tea and scones. I am trying with some degree of difficulty to remember the names of the staff. This one was quite easy for she is very tall and thin, and there is something about her that reminds me of Maud.

"Thank you Daisy. Can you put the tray here on this small table please? This is my dear friend, Miss Frances, who is going to be living here."

"Pleased to meet you Miss," said Daisy – and she curtsied. I could see by the expression on Emily's face that she was torn between surprise and suppressed laughter.

"Thank you for doing such an excellent job on Miss Frances' room. Can you please mention my appreciation to the other girls who were involved? The flowers looks lovely."

"Yes Milady," said Daisy, obviously very pleased to be complimented. Emily also thanked her.

"Will there be anything else milady?"

When I replied that there wasn't, she curtsied again and left the room.

Emily looked at the contents of the tray. "Ooh, my favourites."

"I'll pour the tea milady," She joked in a mock deferential voice as she curtsied.

"Oh no," I Groaned. "Don't you dare start that."

As we buttered our scones, I said. "So, tell me all."

"Well, you should have seen her face. It was purple. She looked so – so ugly."

She related the events that had taken place at the Grange. When she concluded her story with the account of her dealings with Miss Salathial, we were laughing so much, that tears ran down our faces.

"Fancy you telling her to stick her head in a stew pan," I said. "However, I expect that everyone downstairs was sad to see you go."

"Yes, I think they were. Gracie was in tears and so was I."

"Did they think very badly of me?"

"No - not at all. Mr Isaacs was really happy to hear about your good fortune. He said that you deserved to be happy. He had been very worried about you."

"Well that is very nice to hear. I shall write to him soon. He's a dear man"

"Tell me Aphra – why didn't you go straight to the Earl for help? It's so obvious that he cares for you very much. It seems so unnecessary to have suffered as you've done these last few months."

"Well, as I said the other day, I did send a letter mentioning the baby. I now realise that it never reached Methuen Park. It was silly of me not to come straight here, but I was very upset and thought that perhaps – Oh I don't know. You're right – it was very silly of me."

I needed to be careful. I nearly said that I had thought that Sebastian might be disapproving of my condition and shocked at my behaviour, but realised just in time that would not make sense, as Emily believed Sebastian to be the father.

"It is only recently that I have surmised that my correspondence may have been intercepted by Miss Salathial and passed on to the mistress. Why do I still keep calling her that? From now on, we will call her by her name. She is no longer our mistress. Anyway, I can just imagine that ghastly woman steaming them open and reading all about my private business. I wonder how many times that was done. I was often too busy and so didn't always take my letters to the post office in the village. I suppose that they read any letters that were sent to me as well. How awful. I suspect that's how my condition was discovered and that the letter mentioning the child is secreted in the bureau in the morning room."

"Don't you think that you should ask her for it back?"

"I suppose that I could, but Caroline is never going to admit that she has it, so I shall just have to put it out of my mind."

"But she might use it against you. You know what she's like."

"I can't see what harm it can do now that I'm married to Sebastian and everyone will be able to work out the dates. It's not going to be a big secret that I was expecting a child before the wedding. Besides the aristocracy don't seem to worry as much about these things as other people. However, Sebastian wants us to go to Europe for a prolonged trip until the baby is born. He thinks that for my sake and the child too, it will be more discreet."

"Well I don't trust her and she could make trouble for you in the future. Please be careful Aphra. She really hates you."

"She always has." .

"Seriously Aphra, she really detests you with a vengeance and if she can do you any harm, she will. You did not see her this morning. Her eyes were almost those of a mad woman," Emily said "It quite frightened me."
"Let us forget such unpleasant thoughts and turn our minds towards our forthcoming trip."

We have been so busy that Emily and I are both quite worn out and will be glad to be on our way. Claude has gone on ahead to make all the arrangements. Sebastian says that it will be better for appearances sake. He will meet us once we arrive in France. I am thrilled to be having the opportunity of speaking French. It will give me the chance to really improve.

Now I really must get some sleep for we have an early start. I am so fatigued, that I'll probably fall asleep straight away.

***

So here I sit beneath a canopy on our terrace looking out where the sapphire blue sea meets the clear azure sky. In the distance, there are cliffs with crumbling rocks that fall onto the deserted sandy beach. There is little sound other than the gentle lapping of the waves upon the sand, a chirping bird in a hibiscus close by and the soporific droning of bees. I must ask Claude what the bird is called. He is like mama and knows much about nature.

I move Sophie's little crib out of the sun. I'm concerned that the heat will harm her delicate pale skin. She snuffles slightly and rubs at her face and then is at peace again.

This is the first opportunity that I have had to sit and write my journal since we left England. I enjoy being able to write down my thoughts and feelings. I used to do it when I was at school and when I was with Mrs Brookes. I wonder why I did not do it at Warrington Grange. Perhaps it was a combination of being too busy and also not wanting to have Caroline or Miss Salathial read about my private thoughts. Now I have lots of leisure time and many happy things to write about and it gives me great pleasure to do so.

As I contemplate the vibrant cerise colour of the Bougainvillea that tumbles over the staircases, I think that it should clash with the scarlet geraniums in the terracotta pots – but somehow they complement each other – what a delightful contrast to the brilliant white of the wall – and as I watch a sailing boat near the horizon, I reflect on recent events.

A few days after Emily arrived at Methuen Park, we set off on our journey to mainland Europe. The crossing to France was terrible and poor Emily was so seasick. Sebastian and I were not too bad, but she suffered terribly. I tried to do what I could to nurse her, but nothing seemed to help. However, within less than an hour of reaching terra firma, she was much improved. I thought that it was such a shame to be ill like that on her first voyage, as she was so excited about going abroad.

When we walked down the gangplank in Calais, Claude was waiting for us with a carriage to take us to the Paris-bound train. His face was full of joy as he waved to us. He shook Sebastian's hand in a mock formal gesture, but I saw the extra tender caress that Sebastian gave him with his free hand and I tried to distract Emily, by pointing out something that I thought would be of interest to her. Then Claude spoke to me. "Bienvenu ma chere. So you have finally arrived in my country." He gave me a gentle embrace and kissed me on both cheeks.

"And bonjour to you too Mademoiselle Frances." He took her hand and kissed it. She blushed. "Thank you sir."

"Merci monsieur," he corrected. Nervously, she repeated the words.

"Ah! Tu parle Francais, oui?" He jested. I explained to her that Claude was saying that she spoke French. At this, Emily seemed very pleased with herself.

"Emily's had a terrible ordeal, but hopefully will soon recover. It was so choppy."

"Ah, the mal de mer," he said with compassion. "I have experienced it before – many times. It is terrible, is it not?"

Emily nodded. As we made our way to the carriage, two porters carried our luggage and between them, secured it on the top and the back of the vehicle. The cases were mainly full of Sebastian's clothes, for Emily and I had only a few items. Sebastian said that when we got to Paris, he would arrange for me to have a wardrobe suitable for the months ahead and for the seasonal and climate changes. Of course, we would also be buying some new clothes for Emily in keeping with her new position.

Paris is a beautiful city and I hope to return one day when I will be able to appreciate it fully. Our first sighting of the city when we were some distance away was of the new tower dominating the landscape. We had read about its construction in the newspapers. Emily was enthralled and Claude said that he would take her to see it. "Perhaps go up it," he suggested.

"I don't know about that. I might be scared," she replied, looking a bit worried.

"You would get a wonderful view of the city,"

I would have liked to do this also, but not while carrying a child. So that could be something for the future. Perhaps one day, I would take my child and together we would look out over the river, the boulevards and the parks of Paris.

I was extremely tired by the time we arrived at our hotel.

We spent a week in Paris and most mornings were taken up with the purchase of new wardrobes for Emily and me. It was great fun to be treated in this way, but what gave me the most pleasure was the delight on Emily's face as she tried on elegant gowns and hats. There was not enough time for us to have things made, so we bought just enough readymade items for our trip. Sebastian said that we could think about further purchases on our return, when, hopefully, my waistline would have returned to its normal size.

Some afternoons, we did the rounds of visiting the famous sights. Claude acted as our guide and gave us a lot of information about French history – especially about the revolution and the storming of the Bastille. We spent a whole day at Versailles, which was the most spectacular sight that I have ever seen. Emily was enthralled to hear about the Sun King, Louis XIV.

"Puts our little cottage in the shade," laughed Sebastian, as we strolled through the magnificent hall of mirrors.

As promised, Claude and Sebastian took Emily up the Eiffel Tower. I sat and had coffee in a small cafe, while they made their ascent. When they returned to earth, Emily was so excited and thrilled by her adventure. In fact, I think that she felt quite pleased with herself that she had had an adventure that I had been denied, due to my condition. I felt very happy for her to have this feeling of superiority over me.

In the evenings, Emily and I would retire to our rooms to read and sew, but Sebastian and Claude went out on the town. Seb said that they went to cafes and places of entertainment. I suspect that some of these establishments were a bit on the racy side. I have heard stories of people imbibing rather a lot and there is something called Absinthe – I don't know what it is, but it sounds rather dangerous to me. I do not think that I should like to visit one of these places – far too noisy and too much cigar smoke.

What Emily and I preferred was sitting at an outside pavement café drinking coffee and watching the hustle and bustle of Parisian life. I enjoyed listening to the people going about their daily lives and chattering, arguing and shouting in their native tongue. It stretched my mind trying to understand what they were saying.

On Sunday morning, we attended mass at Notre Dame. I loved the sound of the choir echoing up through the vaulted ceiling, but I think that Emily was uncomfortable with the litany spoken in Latin. As we left, she asked "what was all that about? I think that I'd rather be saying my prayers in the village church in Watheford. I don't hold with all this papist nonsense," she said primly. I had to smile as I thought that my dear friend needed to learn to open her mind. I'm sure that this trip will help to broaden her horizons.

We continued our journey south to Marseilles, where we took another ship to Italy. Emily was rather apprehensive – not surprising really, after the crossing of the Channel. However, we need not have worried. The weather was mild and sunny and the sea was calm for the entire trip. It quite altered Emily's views on sailing.

We visited a number of Italian cities, including, of course, Rome, Venice, Florence and Naples, but after a few weeks of this, I felt that I needed to take it easy.

My confinement was surprisingly easy and Sophie was a small yet very healthy baby. Emily assisted me along with a local doctor that Sebastian insisted we call. Actually, Emily seemed to be more help than the doctor. She had plenty of experience of babies being born when she was at home in Watheford, so it was all in a day's work to her.

Sophie has been no trouble and is the joy of my life. She has no hair whatsoever and is becoming quite chubby in a very attractive way. Her eyes are huge and bright blue. I hope that no-one ever notices, for Sebastian has brown eyes, and mine are green. She has her father's eyes.

As I sit here, I have just realised something. When I met Thomas, I thought that he reminded me of my father – not to look at, but there was something else. I now realise that it was his manner. It was the superficial charm and the way he manipulated me and appeared to be caring to get what he wanted. In actual fact, he did not care at all. I now remember that so clearly about my father. Also, this memory has made me aware of something else. Thomas and Claude share a similarity of appearance in colouring – especially in the eyes – that bright, penetrating blue. In fact, it is strange how much Sophie's looks resemble Claude's. He is fast becoming the doting uncle and just adores her and needs little excuse to cuddle her. Oh how much better a father Claude would make than Thomas or my own father.

Once Sophie was a few weeks old, we moved here to this marvellous villa on the coast. We have been here three weeks and Sebastian says that we will stay here for a few more and then make our way back home through France. We shall take a different route, which will allow us to spend a short time with Claude's family.
Sebastian is concerned that there are outstanding matters to be dealt with in England, although he has managed to deal with the more urgent matters as he has had some papers forwarded. Also, he has kept in contact as much as possible – or as much as the telephone and telegraph systems on the continent allow. There were times, when connections could not be made and he got rather hot under the collar. Emily commented the other day that she had noticed that he has quite a fiery temper. I laughed as I remembered that encounter with him in the woods at Methuen Park.
"Yes," I replied. "He can sometimes fly off the handle. I've experienced it myself. However, most of the time, he's a pussycat."

I have mixed feelings about our return to England. On the one hand, I look forward to being back in my own country and to Somerset - to the Mendip Hills and the Levels with sheep and cattle grazing in the fields - to the culture and climate with which I am familiar – although, I know that I shall miss the brilliance of the sky, the light and the colours and the sense of freedom that there is here.

However, I am apprehensive about my new role in life and how well I shall carry out my duties as Countess. These last few weeks have given me an opportunity to "practice" away from home, but I feel like a child playing at fairy tales. It seems unreal. I know that Sebastian and Claude will make my transition from servant to an aristocrat's consort as easy as possible, but in truth I am very frightened – especially of Caroline's reaction. I fear her wrath. She could make life very difficult for me amongst the aristocracy and the gentry of the county. I hope that they will accept me.

Ah – I see Seb and Claude walking back from the beach. I expect that they have enjoyed their swim together. I wish that I could join them, but it wouldn't be seemly for a woman in my position. Also, I suspect that I should be playing gooseberry, although they would pretend otherwise. It is nice for them to have the freedom to be alone together.

As they walk up through the gardens to our villa, I can see how relaxed and happy they are here. I know that they would like to remain here permanently, but we must soon return to England. There is much for Seb to attend to and his presence is required in the House. He is so conscientious and has a real sense of duty. I know that he feels guilty about his long absence from home – although he and Claude have spent many hours working very hard into the small hours of the night.

They are mounting the steps now and Sophie has awoken. No tears, just smiles – what a treasure she is, my darling baby. It is time to feed her. (Sebastian has given me a free hand in this and I'm so grateful to him. I did not want a wet nurse.) I do so enjoy these times that I spend with her and I reflect on what our lives would be like if Sebastian had not rescued me from the workhouse.

I think that I shall finish this entry, for I hear Emily approaching. She has been having a siesta in her room – although, I suspect that she has been reading. She has become an avid bookworm and for that, I am very pleased. She has even learned a few words in French and Italian which has increased her confidence in herself. This will be very important for her in the days to come. I should hate for her to feel inferior to the people with whom she will have daily contact at Methuen Park.

I smile with pride remembering the times that we have sat together writing postcards to our dear friends back in Watheford. (We even contemplated sending a card to Caroline. It made us laugh so much.)

I believe that this has all been a wonderful experience for Emily. I shall never forget her kindness to me when I first arrived at Warrington Grange, and I am so glad that I was able to give her this opportunity.

**

I discovered on our return to England that my fears had been quite unfounded. It was with mixed emotions that I had embarked the Channel steamer at Calais. Our time abroad had been most enjoyable – wonderful actually - and I had got to know Sebastian and Claude very well during this time. They, in their turn, had got to know me - and Emily too - and had shown such kindness and consideration towards us. They must be the most considerate men in the world. Of course, it was sometimes wearying for the three of us – keeping up the pretence whilst in the company of others – especially Emily. However, the freedom that we felt when we were alone was relaxing and for me it meant that for the first time since the death of my mother, I felt that I had a real family – and a warm and loving one at that.

Of course, the biggest joy and delight for the four of us was the gift of Sophie. From the moment of her birth, she bonded us all in our love for her. Sebastian fell into the role of father easily and with such enthusiasm – how unlike the cold indifference that I experienced with my own father. Many has been the time that I have observed him and Claude cooing and chuckling at her – completely unaware of my study of them. Sometimes they seemed like a couple of maiden aunts and it so amused me. Claude considers himself to be an honorary uncle.

When we arrived in Florence, shortly before her birth, Sebastian ordered a substantial layette that included everything that a new-born infant could require. I was very grateful for Emily's help too, for I was completely ignorant of what needed to be done. In each place that we visited, both Sebastian and Claude spent far too much money on purchases for Sophie – especially Claude, who could not resist little silk nightgowns, embroidered shawls, bonnets and bed linen – all exquisitely beautiful, yet totally impractical as regards laundering (which I have discovered is a large part of the daily routine with an infant). When we were in Rome, he purchased an ornate silver rattle, which Emily told me was most unsuitable, as small children tend to put things in their mouths. I will need to be very diplomatic with him so that I do not offend him.

The few days that we spent at the Chateau were wonderful and Claude's family made us very welcome. Emily really enjoyed learning all about viniculture and began to get quite a taste for the wine. More than once, while we were there, she got a bit tipsy.

Sophie enjoyed all the attention. She is the kind of child who smiles at everyone. Every day, she grows more beautiful. She has started to get some hair. It is blonde and curly.

Our final visit in France was a return to the capital, where we stopped for a few days to make some purchases of clothes and accessories for Emily and myself. We also bought a number of items for Sophie - including clothes and toys. As usual, Claude could not resist treating her to all manner of things, including a doll which was about three times the size of her!

"She won't be able to play with it until she's about five," I said laughing.

He took no notice of me and held it out in front of her and she began to cry with fright. He was quite disappointed until I said to wait a few months and see how she reacted.

"I'm sure she'll love it when she's bigger," I reassured him.

It is very pleasant to be back here in Somerset. I have missed the lush green of the landscape and the softness of the rolling hills standing like sentinels over the levels. Spring is now in full flow with carpets of bluebells in the woods, and little lambs frolicking in the fields.

When we arrived at Methuen Park, both the inside and the outside staff, and those from the surrounding estate were lined up in front of the main steps and portico. Claude and Emily had gone on ahead to instruct Travis to prepare the house etc. I am in no doubt of the feelings of these people towards their master, for we were greeted with much warmth and kindness by everyone. Sebastian, in turn, was so pleased to see each and every one as he went along the line. In most households this would have been to inspect the ranks, but at Methuen Park it was an opportunity for Seb to stop and greet each person individually – shaking hands and asking about their health and their families. I was amazed at how well he remembered so much detail. I am sure that in many large households, the master probably doesn't know anyone's name – and it is most likely that they would not even recognise faces, but Seb took a genuine interest in his employees and not only knew their names, but many of the day to day problems of their families. I wondered how on earth I was going to manage to remember all this, but decided that I would just take my time and do my best.

He introduced me to everyone. I do hope that I put them at their ease, for I do want to be a good mistress. I know, only too well, how it feels being on the other side.

Behind us, Emily, who had met us at the carriage, entered the main hall carrying the small wicker travelling crib in which Sophie lay sleeping.

When Seb had finished engaging with the staff, the women – young and old – moved eagerly towards the crib and jostled for position to peek inside. Perhaps it was the noise of the enthusiastic, bustling crowd that awoke Sophie or maybe it was the cessation of the rocking of the carriage which had prolonged her slumber. Whatever it was, it disturbed and frightened her at first. I try to imagine what it was like for her – such a little person and all these strange people pulling faces and making silly noises as people always do with babies. Her tiny bottom lip trembled as her big sapphire eyes filled with tears and searched for a familiar face. As her cries became louder and her arms flailed in panic, Sebastian gently pushed his way through the throng and two strong hands whisked her up out of the crib.

Instantly, the crying stopped and her face was full of sunshine and smiles. Instantly, she had won the hearts of all at Methuen Park and I overheard one of the women remark how much she loved her daddy. I knew then that it was going to be alright.

***

After their arrival home, life settled into a routine. Sebastian was constantly busy with the estate, his business affairs and his philanthropic causes. His long absence from England had meant that certain things had piled up. Because of this, he was not able to spend as much time with Sophie as he would have liked. However, Claude, whose duties were less, managed to spend quite a bit of time with Aphra and Sophie.

In spite of Travis' initial, haughty attitude, Emily settled in well and in time, he mellowed and decided that she was a very nice young lady - if something of a rough diamond.

She counted her blessings constantly, still hardly believing her good fortune to be in this position. Her employer was her best friend and her duties consisted of caring for this darling little baby and keeping her best friend company.

Her room was very luxurious with a large bed beneath a dark blue satin coverlet. The walnut furniture consisted of a commodious wardrobe, two large tallboys, two bedside cabinets, and a comfy chintz armchair by the large stone fireplace, and in the window a small writing table together with a pair of delicate antique chairs. The carpet was a matching blue, as were the heavy damask curtains that draped the large windows.

When she had left Warrington Grange, it had been something of a rush to gather together all her possessions. Although she left her plants for Maud, who was delighted with them, she had struggled to carry all her bits and pieces down the steep stairs from her attic room. However, when she had brought them into this room, it had seemed as if she had very little. She only had two or three items to hang in the wardrobe and everything else fitted in two drawers. Now she had all the lovely items of clothing and souvenirs that had been bought in France and Italy. Not only this, she was beginning to acquire her own little library and she proudly displayed her books on some shelves that were built into an alcove.

She found the other servants to be friendly towards her, although she spent much of her time in the nursery with Sophie or with Aphra in the drawing room. Sometimes, they would take a walk in the grounds, or sit on the terrace if the weather was fine. One of their favourite places to sit in fine weather was the Arcadian Folly and feed the ducks, geese and swans. Sophie was starting to take a lot of notice of everything and would shout and wave at the birds.

Aphra had not been this content since she had lost her mother. She had placed the cot next to her bed as she was nursing Sophie herself. She would just pick her up and have her in bed with her when she cried during the night.

As she managed to wean Sophie, so the little girl began to sleep in the nursery, which adjoined Emily's room. Emily was delighted to have her so near in the night. She had been used to being an early riser when in service to Caroline, so it was nothing new to be up and attending to Sophie when Aphra walked into the nursery.

Sophie was everyone's darling - family and staff alike. As the months passed, it was clear that she was a bright and beautiful baby. She was nearly always happy and delighted in everything that was going on around her. Aphra and Emily developed a routine that suited them both, allowing Aphra time to become used to her position as Countess and running the household.

So Aphra spent more and more time with Rose, who gently instructed her in the running of the house and the requirements of her position. Aphra found that she enjoyed this very much and threw herself into her new role with enthusiasm - much to the relief of the ageing dowager, who had lately become very frail and was glad to relinquish some of the wearying duties that she had carried out for decades. Both women enjoyed each other's company and Aphra valued her advice. They discovered that they had much in common and each felt that the other filled an empty place in their lives.

Aphra also found that Mrs Williams was a great help in guiding her in the running of the household. She did this in a very diplomatic way and it was not long before Aphra realised how much she relied upon this woman and how fond of her she had become.

One morning, when Aphra was sitting in the morning room dealing with some correspondence, Mrs Williams knocked at the door. She had come to inform Aphra that she needed a few days' leave to visit her elderly mother who was becoming increasingly frail and confused. It appeared that Mrs

Williams' elder sister had been looking after the old lady, but was unwell herself.

A few days later on her return, she informed her mistress that she would have to give notice as things had become very bad and her sister was very sick. Aphra was very sorry to lose her as she was so essential to the smooth running of the household. She was released from her duties immediately with a sum of money to help lighten her load.

Aphra consulted Rose about advertising for a new housekeeper. They interviewed a number of candidates, and eventually settled on a middle aged woman called Hetty Drake who had excellent references and was able to take up the post immediately. She settled in to the routine easily and was a quick learner, which was a great relief to Aphra and Rose.

In spite of her days being very busy, Aphra still allowed much of her time to be spent with her daughter. She was determined that Sophie would receive as much maternal love as possible. The dowager, too, enjoyed her role as grandmother and was quickly establishing a bond with both Aphra and Sophie.

Emily doted on the baby as if she were her own. If anything, Aphra was concerned that the child might get spoilt, but decided that it was far too early to be worrying about that.

Aphra noticed recently that Emily's speech had changed and that her West Country burr was less distinct. The girl had decided that if she was to be the nanny of an Earl's daughter, then she needed to improve her speech. This was not due to anything that Aphra had said, but was part of Emily's desire for self-improvement and enlightenment. Since Aphra had taught her to read, she had made great strides. Emily wished to be able to read stories to Sophie as she grew up and to teach her things. Sebastian had told her that if she wished to borrow books from the library, she only had to ask him and he would assist her. Often Aphra came upon her reading geography or history books. It was a great pleasure to see that the seeds she had sown in Emily's mind were bearing such rich fruit.

As for Sebastian and Claude, their life had more or less returned to how it was before the wedding. Often, they were busy with the day to day affairs of the estate. Sebastian could regularly be seen consulting and walking around the grounds with his steward or riding out to the various farms to visit tenants. Sometimes, he would be in London – either sitting in The House, or dealing with his financial affairs, and Claude would spend much of this time with Aphra and Sophie. Aphra enjoyed this very much. Claude would attend to any of Sebastian's needs as and when required. Both men visited Sophie as much as possible and played with her – especially Claude, who had more time and who absolutely adored her. As the months passed and Sophie began to utter her first words, Aphra was delighted to hear that some of these were in French.

***

Dear Mildred,

I trust that you are in good health. My apologies for the delay in writing, but much has been happening in my life and this is my first chance to do so.

Do you remember how unhappy I was with things at Grosvenor Court? Well, you'll be surprised to hear that I've got myself a much better position. Three weeks ago, I was engaged as Housekeeper at Methuen Park. Can you believe it? I feel so fortunate.

The house is very grand and I'm sure that I shall be forever getting lost. It is very beautiful with lovely paintings, porcelain and chandeliers. The grounds too are magnificent. The Earl is a very nice man and quite free and easy with the servants, but he has a very strange rule. No one is allowed in a particular area of the woods. The Countess stressed this point at my interview. Apparently, anyone breaking this rule will be dismissed immediately.

She's a real beauty. I have never seen anyone with such perfect features? I think that I'm going to like her. She seems most friendly - not at all haughty.

There is something that I do find rather odd and makes me feel a bit uncomfortable. The Earl has a secretary – a French chap. He seems alright – considering that he's a foreigner, but I have noticed that the Countess spends a lot of time with him. They seem very close. In fact, I know that I should not be saying this, but it would seem that when the master is away, they spend even more time together. He is also very fond of the little girl, and the Earl and the Countess joke that he is her second papa. That does not seem right, but who am I to understand the strange ways of these aristocrats.

Well, I must check the linen. I'd like to be able to criticise my predecessor, but have to admit that everything here was left in very good order.

I'll write again soon. Please write to me soon. I should love to hear about how things are at Warrington Grange and your lady there.

With fond wishes, your friend Hetty

***

In November, to celebrate Aphra's Birthday, Sebastian planned a grand dinner party to mark the occasion. Various dignitaries and people from around the county were invited. Sebastian thought that it would be a good opportunity for Aphra to begin her public life as Countess. Aphra asked Emily if she would like to attend, but Emily declined.

"I do appreciate your asking me, but I feel much more comfortable keeping in the background and I would much rather be with Sophie. I hope you don't mind."

"Not at all. I understand and perhaps it will be easier in the long run. But please tell me if you wish to attend anything in the future. I shall miss your company tonight, but maybe I need to concentrate on my role and talk to the guests and get to know them."

"That's what I was thinking. Besides, what would I say to all those toffs? I'd rather be up here in the nursery with my darling and reading a good book."
"Very well. However, perhaps we can celebrate my birthday on our own – just the three of us. What do you think?"

"I'd love that. I feel alright with the Earl and his mother, and of course Monsieur Claude is so down to earth and likeable, and I'd like to come to some of the family events like when your cousin and his wife visit, but not big, posh affairs."

"I have to admit that the whole thing feels quite daunting to me as well."

"Oh you'll walk in the room and they'll all love you. You've nothing to worry about. Besides, you're educated and clever. I don't feel right in that sort of company. I'm really very happy doing what I'm doing – and hopefully, doing it well."

"You certainly are, dearest Emily. No one could do it better than you."

At breakfast, on the morning of Aphra's birthday, Sebastian presented her with a gift. She unwrapped it, to find that he had bought her a beautiful diamond necklace. "Oh Sebastian!" She exclaimed. It's beautiful. How good you are to me."

"Here – let me put it on for you," he said as he took it out of its red velvet covered case. He stood back and admired her. "You look lovely, my dearest girl. Happy birthday."

"Thank you Sebastian. I shall wear it tonight." She kissed him gently on the cheek.

"You deserve it. I hope that your day is truly happy and the year ahead of course," he said touching her hand lightly. "Well must get on. Claude and I have much to attend to today. I shall see you this evening, my dear."

Later, when she took her leave of Sophie and kissed her goodnight, she went to her room to get ready. Dorothy was waiting to attend to her. Aphra had recently taken delivery of a satin gown especially for tonight's party. It had been made for her by the London dressmaker that Sebastian's mother and deceased sister had used for many years. Tonight's gown was magnificent – surpassing anything she had worn before - even the gown that she had worn at the previous ball, paled into insignificance in contrast to this dress. Cut low at the front and fitting perfectly and then filling out and sweeping behind her, the layers of glossy scarlet fabric trimmed with black lace enhanced the perfection of her figure which had even improved on what it was before she had Sophie. Most people would say that red should not be worn with titian hair, but on Aphra, the effect was breath-taking. Her hair now reached below her shoulders, and Dorothy dressed it in a similar fashion to what she had done a year before – only now she allowed tendrils of ringlets to cascade around her neck in the way that ladies wore their hair in ancient Greece or Rome. The diamond necklace and some matching earrings were added. The finishing touch of a dab of French perfume, a daring brush of rouge, and the careful pinning of her mother's brooch and the effect was complete.

Dorothy stood back and admired her. "The Earl is a lucky man. You look wonderful. All the other men are going to be very jealous of him," she said cheerfully. "Off you go and enjoy yourself."
The evening was a grand affair. Forty guests arrived for the banquet and when Aphra descended the staircase on Sebastian's arm, there was a universal gasp and then a hush, as he introduced his wife. Aphra knew that she would never remember the names of all these people. She felt

overawed by their grand titles, and socially inferior until she reminded herself that her status was now actually higher than everyone else – with the exception of Sebastian. She found this very amusing. Sebastian was wonderful at putting her at her ease and constantly praised and encouraged her on her success. When she went to bed in the early hours of the morning, she felt that she had made her first real step into her public life as a Countess.

***

Dear Hetty,

What a nice surprise to hear about your good fortune. I expect that it will be a lot of hard work, but I'm sure that you will cope. You must be sure to keep on top of the maids. I know how these young girls will take advantage given half the chance – and will get away with all sorts if not checked.

I agree with you about the Earl. I met him briefly a few times when he was courting my mistress and he was always very polite. Of course, he did not treat her well. I expect you know all about the carry on with her maid – now the Countess. I admit, she's quite an attractive woman, but don't let that blind you to the real character beneath. I saw a very different side of her.

As you know, I'm not one to gossip or cast aspersions, but she behaved in a shocking manner – especially with the Frenchman. They were always writing to one another and she was forever creeping out to meet him. But I must say no more. She is now your lady and new employer and I should hate to turn you against her.

Life here is much the same and I am hard pressed to get the right calibre of girl to work here. Mr Isaacs is still the butler and Mrs Flowers still does the cooking – although she does tend to eat too much of what she cooks. She seems to expand by the day!

Well I too must return to my duties. Our work is never done.

I look forward to hearing your news about life at Methuen Park and the interesting things that go on there.

Mildred

***

Months passed and Aphra attended a number of social events with Sebastian and began to feel really confident and assured. Life felt good and in spite of the occasional feelings of loneliness that she felt when in her chamber at night, she counted her blessings daily.

Sebastian told her that he was very pleased with her progress at taking over the task of running the house and thereby relieving his mother of what had become a chore for her. He also commended her on how well she had adapted to the role of his consort.

Aphra was also pleased at the decision to hire Mrs Drake. She was proving to be very efficient and ran things very smoothly, so that there seemed to be a minimum of problems with the staff.

In early April, Sebastian informed her of an invitation that they had received from some old friends of his who lived some miles away. Aphra detected a note of concern in his voice.

"Is there a problem?" She asked.

***

Dear Mildred,

Thank you for your letter. I've been so busy these last few weeks and never seem to have a moment to spare, but I'm not complaining. I really enjoy the work and my salary is very generous.

I have got to know the staff here very well now and find them all very nice. Mr Travis, the butler, is a rather serious man, but I find working with him no problem – although he is a stickler for protocol and correctness, but that is how it should be.

I found what you said about the Countess most intriguing. As you know, my previous post was some distance away, and with all the problems there, I was not aware of much that was going on outside my own little world. I had no idea that she had been working as a maid before she married the Earl. I have since spoken to one of the kitchen maids who confirmed what you said. This does seem strange, for she is a cousin of some kind to Viscount Westbridge, but as I've said many times, I do not understand the ways of the aristocracy.

I have recently discovered that Miss Frances, her companion, and nanny to the child, was also a servant at Warrington Grange. I suppose they were friends when they worked there. I should be interested to know about her. I expect that you knew her well, for she would have been under you. She seems pleasant enough, although I have few dealings with her, for much of her time is taken up with the child. Obviously, she does come below stairs sometimes in connection with her duties for Lady Sophie, and I see her pushing her about in the grounds in her perambulator.

The little girl is very bonny and a real smiler. She has the most enormous blue eyes and I think that she is going to be very fair for she has a little golden cap of curls, which is so becoming. Everyone loves her and I suspect that she is going to be very spoilt. I have never really been interested in children, but this one has touched my heart, especially when she chuckles.

I have had few dealings with the Dowager Countess, for she wishes to be less involved with the running of the house and keeps to her own quarters much of the time. She is getting on in years and very tired. She is a very dignified old lady and I like her very much.

Before I finish, I must add that the Countess does spend a lot of time with Monsieur, as we call him. Like you, I don't like to gossip, but have noticed that when the master is away, they seem to be together even more. I'm sure that it is all very innocent, but does give the impression of too much intimacy! I'll finish up now, for I do not want to miss the post.

Yours Hetty

***

"I don't know how you feel about attending this gathering," said Sebastian. "It will be a weekend house party. In some ways, it will be very pleasant, for our hosts are both charming people. I went to school with George and he is a thoroughly decent chap. His wife, Katherine, is very quiet and unassuming. However, there is a drawback and you may wish to decline," Sebastian said, as he poured himself a glass of Scotch.

"What could be so dreadful, that I should not wish to accept the invitation?" Aphra asked. "Is the house haunted? Are we to be terrified by ghouls and monsters?"

"Much worse than that," he replied. "Caroline will be there."

"Ah." Aphra was very quiet for a few moments. "You know. We're going to have to face her at some time, so perhaps we should get it over and done with as soon as possible."

"That is very brave of you, but you're right. We need to deal with her. I'll get Claude to reply today," he said reluctantly. "We'll order you a new gown to give you added armour."

"I think that it had better be made from chain mail."

***

And so it was that on a chilly afternoon with the pale sunlight fading in the west, Sebastian and Aphra sat in the carriage making their way towards the countryside that was becoming increasingly familiar to her. Lambrook Hall was but a short journey from Warrington Grange. Aphra seemed to remember that Caroline had mentioned it in the past. She was dreading the moment when she would finally come face to face with her old adversary.

As their carriage approached the entrance to the Lambrook estate, so another carriage was about to do the same thing, but coming from the opposite direction. Aphra recognised the driver. It was Mickey, and her heart sank as the two carriages made their way up the drive to the house. She was in such turmoil, that she took very little notice of her surroundings. As Sebastian helped her from the carriage, he turned his head slightly and greeted Caroline.

"Isn't this nice? I was just saying to my lovely wife here how pleasant it is to be back in this part of the county."

Aphra was relieved to have him take charge of the conversation, for she felt so agitated that she absorbed little of what Caroline replied to this small talk. Fortunately, there was something of a commotion as more carriages were arriving, and instructions were being given to the drivers and servants to attend to luggage and horses etc. As the party made their way into the house, there was much conversation as guests were being greeted by their hosts, and introduced to one another.

A short time later, when Sebastian and Aphra were settled in their room, she thanked him for his kindness.

"You handled it so well, Seb. It saved me having to make any effort whatsoever. I am such a fortunate woman to have you as my husband," she said giving him a gentle kiss on the cheek."

"It was my pleasure, dearest girl. Now, let us make haste or we shall be late for dinner," he said fixing the clasp on her necklace. "May I add how charming you look – as usual? I shall be the envy of every man present." He held out his hand and led her from the room and down the stairs.

As was the case at every function they attended, Aphra was the centre of attention, which made Caroline seethe inwardly. The host and hostess led their guests into the dining room, where the table was laid for a small party of a dozen people.

The evening progressed in much the same way as many before. Aphra found it very difficult to concentrate on the conversations around her. This was due to a mixture of anxiety at the close proximity of Caroline and just sheer ennui at the repetitious nature of the subjects being discussed. Topics included general gossip about various neighbours within the county as well as some about the Prince of Wales and his latest dalliance. Some of the men were discussing a shooting party attended the previous week. The mere idea of killing for pleasure disgusted her.

There was talk about this year's "Season" and who would be coming out, and the latest fashions in hats. She had heard it all before and felt that she could contribute nothing. If she did happen to join in and talk about clothes, she found that she tended to talk about the making of the garments. One woman was complaining about her dressmaker. "The costs are so high and it takes her so long to get it done. I had to wait almost a week," she complained. Aphra leant forward and suggested that a week was a very short time and that perhaps the person in question had other commitments. This was not received well and Aphra found it all far too tedious.

Suddenly, a shrill voice from across the table added. "I think that some of these seamstresses get too much above themselves. In my experience, many of them are nothing more than trollops - and they are far too well paid. You have my sympathy Daphne. The stories that I could tell you about seamstresses, and servants too - but it would not be suitable in polite company."

Aphra was about to make some retort to this catty remark, when Sebastian saved her the task. "Come now Caroline, what a thing to say. Let us change the subject and talk of more pleasant things. After all, this is supposed to be an evening of enjoyment and not one of complaints, when we all have so much for which to be grateful."

Aphra looked down at her dinner plate and tried not to laugh. She knew that Caroline would be furious at this. Their host began talking about having another wing added to his house and some changes to his garden. This helped to improve the atmosphere a bit and soon afterwards, the ladies withdrew to the parlour to have their coffee, whilst the men enjoyed their port and cigars. Aphra tried to sit as far away from Caroline as she could without drawing too much attention to this. As it was rather warm and stuffy in the room, the French windows were open slightly onto the terrace. Aphra accompanied Katherine outside as they both carried their coffees.

"You have a lovely, comfortable home," Aphra told her host.

"Thank you. It isn't as grand as your home, but we love it."

"It is much more homely than ours and I'm quite envious of you. I'll let you into a little secret. I'd love to live in a pretty little cottage, but I think it unlikely that I shall ever do so."

"I've often thought much the same thing - although I expect that I'm being quite unrealistic. It would probably be dreadful and I don't think that I'd be very good at making do." They both laughed at this idea. "I see that the gentlemen are joining the ladies indoors. I had better go back in," said Katherine shivering slightly.

"I'll join you in a few minutes. I'll just finish this out here."

"You take as long as you like my dear. I would if I didn't have to go back in and play hostess." She patted Aphra's arm affectionately.

After the older woman had gone back into the house, Aphra finished the coffee and placed her empty cup and saucer on a small table and decided to take a turn in the garden. She walked down a few steps to where there was a stone fountain with some cherubs playing harps. She sat on the edge and dangled her fingers in the water. Suddenly, she heard a sound behind her. She knew it was Caroline.

"Was it necessary for you to be quite so nasty?" She said without turning around.

"I was just stating a fact. My own maid turned out to be nothing more than a woman of the night."

"Oh, don't be so melodramatic Caroline. I'm an ordinary, decent woman who made a very foolish mistake."

"Made a mistake!" She shrieked. "You were carrying on with the pair of them and leading on that poor lad – Albert, wasn't it? I don't know how you've the gall to come into respectable society after the way you've behaved. Talk about jumped up! You're a brazen hussy and when Sebastian discovers the truth about you, he will file for divorce and throw you back in the gutter where you belong – and don't try to impress me with this nonsense about being related to the Westbridges. Your grandmother eloped, didn't she? It sounds as if she was a trollop too. It must be in the blood.

Sebastian was going to propose to me, until he met you. When he turns his back on you, it will be to me that he will come. Just you wait and see. One day, he will be mine – like he should have been in the first place."

"You think you have all the answers, don't you, Caroline? But you see, Sebastian and I have no secrets from each other. We have told each other all manner of private things that many other couples would not even discuss. And, as for the notion that one day you'll win him back – well, firstly, he was never yours."

Aphra got up and began to walk towards the house. She mounted the steps and turned around at the top, looking down on Caroline. She paused for a few moments. "And secondly, I can assure you Caroline that no woman will ever take Sebastian away from me – of that I am absolutely certain." And with that she turned and walked briskly across the terrace and back into the house.

PART FIVE - THE UNHAPPY PRINCESS

As Aphra looked up at her husband, she smiled. She often watched him as he quietly read. His cigar was suspended over the ashtray and he seemed to be unaware of its existence, so engrossed was he in his book. However, she knew him so well that she was not surprised that at just the right moment, his forefinger tapped the cigar to remove the build-up of ash, before he raised it to his lips again.

Dear Sebastian, she thought. Their marriage had been one of harmony, companionship and affection formed on a foundation of honesty between them. During their years together, they had shared few cross words. There had been so little to disagree about, for they were totally at one in their feelings and opinions about most things.

She knew that she was a very fortunate. He had been an ideal husband in so many ways. He was kind and generous. There were so many positive aspects of his character and personality that she admired. She smiled to herself wondering how long it would take to list all his qualities. He, like Claude, had become a dear friend and he had remained true to his word in everything that he had promised. So why did she feel like this?

Her gaze moved towards the terrace, where Sophie sat holding her kitten - behind her, stretched a vista of peace and tranquillity. The gardens of the estate were luscious and a myriad of colour. Aphra looked down at the garment she was embroidering. She pushed the needle through to the reverse of the fabric and made the end of the thread tidy and snipped it off. She held up the little dress. "Sophie will look beautiful in this."

Sebastian looked up from his book and smiled fondly. "Is it possible that mere clothes could make either of you look more beautiful?"

"You're just an old flatterer," she laughed. "Shall I ring for tea, or would you like something cold? It's very warm today and I could do with something refreshing myself."

"Yes, perhaps some cool lemonade would be most welcome," he replied. His fond gaze shifted to the little girl on the terrace, who was giggling and chattering to the kitten. "We chose the right gift. She adores it."

"She certainly does," said Aphra, ringing the bell by the fireplace.

***

It is only after Travis has finally departed our private rooms at the end of the east wing that Sebastian and Claude, free to display their deep affection for one another, are able to fully relax and be themselves. They are usually seated by the fireplace finishing their port and cigars. Travis always says to Sebastian "Will there be anything else Milord?" and the reply is always in the negative with Sebastian trying hard to conceal his impatience and desire for time alone with Claude.

Travis then leaves the room silently, walking backwards in an overly deferential manner. Sebastian has long ceased trying to stop this absurd nightly ritual, for he actually dislikes it. However, for the butler, formality and protocol are of supreme importance and the social hierarchy has to be maintained. After his footsteps in the passage have died away and we know that he is well out of earshot, his behaviour has sometimes reduced us to fits of giggling like schoolchildren, and takes some time to restore a sense of decorum and dignity befitting our social positions.

The two of them usually sit some distance apart, but as the door closes behind Travis, they move closer together and for me this is the signal for my departure. They never do or say anything to make me feel unwelcome, but I know that these few short hours are precious to them. I rise from my seat and walk over to them. Each one stands up and embraces me warmly. Sebastian kisses me on the forehead like an affectionate father and Claude kisses me numerous times on my cheeks in his usual flamboyant, Gallic manner.

Many a night, Sebastian takes Claude's hand and they walk towards Sebastian's room, smiling with the light of the candles in their eyes - eyes that are filled with longing and love for each other. I am glad that they are safe for a few hours in the protection that my presence affords them. I have no knowledge or understanding of what takes place in that room and I have no need to know, but I imagine that the joy they share is much the same as that between a man and woman who are in love.

I can only imagine the joy of love, because so far, it has eluded me. I once experienced sexual passion and physical ecstasy, and although it was very pleasurable, there was no love – at least, not on his part.

Tonight, I bid them both "Goodnight and God Bless", and once again walked towards the doors of my own silent and empty chamber. There are times when I feel such a terrible envy – that it gnaws at my insides like a starving maggot.

Soon I will curl up in my bed with only the soft, coolness of the pillow to caress my cheek, the warmth of the covers to embrace my body and only the night air to kiss my lips.

How many nights have I spent alone like this? And how many more do I have to endure?

Today, it felt as though a black mist came rolling down the hills, in through the windows and descended from the ceilings and completely engulfed me. Why does it keep doing that when I feel like this? I see my future life – empty years stretching out, full of luxury and ease, days that are busy with duty and overcrowded with loneliness.

Next week, Sophie, Emily and I will be going to the cottage and I must make the effort to cheer up for I shall spoil it for them if they detect this black mood that I am in.

***

At the moment, Emily and Sophie are down by the river. I know that they will have removed their shoes and stockings and Emily will have hitched her skirt up in a most undignified manner. They will be paddling and fishing for tiddlers. Perhaps, tomorrow I'll join them, but at the moment, I seem to have this feeling of lethargy – torpor even. I don't know what is wrong with me. Perhaps I've become far too self-absorbed.

Sophie, Emily and I are having a little holiday in our cottage on the estate. It has become quite a regular occurrence with us. We all enjoy it so much. For me, it is a chance to have my dream – a little home from home where we can "play house" and pretend to be ordinary people – goodness, I sound like Marie Antoinette! I shall need to be careful, or I shall lose my head. Actually, I sometimes think that I shall lose my mind. I know that I have so much for which I am very grateful, but at times, I feel so sad and lonely.

I suppose I can trace it back to when Emily began walking out with Henry, one of the footmen. It was probably about eighteen months ago. I am very happy for her and I know that they are deeply in love, but it has brought into stark contrast, my own empty situation. When she has been out with him, she comes back glowing with joy and full of details about what they have been doing – although, I suspect that she leaves much out of the narrative! It reminds me of how I felt when I met Thomas. I remember the excitement of it all – feeling as though I could not breathe, eat, nor sleep – I was so much in love with him. Oh how I have longed for that feeling again – but not only that. It is the feeling of being at one with another person – someone with whom one can share secrets and joys and sorrows –

someone to laugh at silly jokes that only we understand. I am very happy for Emily, and am glad that she has found such happiness. But am I never to feel that in this life? Am I to be alone forever? And of course, I can tell no-one how I feel. To the outside world, I have everything.

This all sounds so selfish, but I long to feel the warmth of a man's arms around me and his kiss on my lips and to feel those physical emotions - that ecstasy, the joy of … I need to stop this, for I shall drive myself mad. I must concentrate on uplifting thoughts.

I shall focus my thoughts on the cottage and describe it, writing all the things that make me feel happy about it.

There are three good sized bedrooms upstairs under the eaves. Sebastian has had them all decorated with pretty wallpaper covered in little pink flowers. Sophie's room is full of toys that are kept here. There is a little wooden cot, where her dolly, Bessie sleeps. Sophie is very particular about her care. Bessie is not allowed to go outside the cottage, in case she gets her clothes dirty. There is a blackboard and easel. Sophie and Emily play games and draw with the different coloured chalks that are kept in a colourful wooden box. A rather dog-eared rabbit sits forlornly on the patchwork counterpane on the bed that Emily and I stitched while we were in Italy awaiting Sophie's birth. The rabbit is kept company by an equally tatty looking rag doll. Both of these toys will accompany us back to Methuen Park.

There is a box under the window, where Sophie keeps her treasures. Emily and I are not allowed to open it. We have obeyed the rules, but we worry that there may be some rather unsavoury items lurking in there. I must speak to Sophie and see if I can persuade her to clear it out before something starts breeding!

My room is quite different and includes a table where I sit and write my journal and letters – usually to Sebastian and Claude or Donald and Hortense. I tend to spend too much time in my room, although I do like to be outside with the other two.

Also, I still have matters to deal with in connection with the various committees upon which I sit. In the last few years, I have become involved with a number of charitable organisations. These include being a governor of the local cottage hospital and the workhouse where Sebastian found me a few years ago. I have found that my own experience there has proved to be invaluable. I do hope that I make a difference to the poor people who have to spend time in these institutions. I know that things are now much better in the workhouse since Louisa became the Matron and I am so glad to have been able to improve her life and that of her husband. I try to visit as often as I can.

Downstairs in the cottage, there is a small, cosy living room with an inglenook fireplace. By the window overlooking the garden gate is a table. The table is covered by a pretty embroidered tablecloth and there are usually some wild flowers that Sophie and Emily have picked and arranged in an old jam jar.
The walls are painted white and decorated with various amateur artistic attempts by all three of us. On the wall opposite the fireplace stands a pine dresser housing a motley collection of china and cooking utensils.

A latched door leads to a small kitchen where there is a quarry tiled floor, a blackened range, a butler sink and a small pine table and some cupboards. Then, to the side of this room is the scullery where we keep all those large or messy items that would take up too much space elsewhere – things like buckets and mops, an old zinc bath, boots, logs, and all manner of paraphernalia.

Some days, we take a picnic and our painting things and sit by the river - which is very enjoyable. I like to make the picnic – usually sandwiches and cake and bottled fruits that have been grown in our kitchen garden.

There are all manner of soft fruits, together with rhubarb, herbs and runner beans. Also, the flowers make a lovely splash of colour at this time of the year. I love to work in the garden, but unfortunately, as we are not here all the time, things have a habit of either dying, or the weeds run rampant. I must speak to Mr Jenkins, the farmer just down the lane. Perhaps his sons would like to earn a few extra shillings a week and keep an eye on things here when we are up at the Park. They could also eat anything that is ripe, so that nothing will go to waste.

I hope that Henry will be good to Emily. I think that he is a good man. Sebastian and I have had no problems with him. He seems to be hardworking, loyal and honest. I think that it will not be long before Emily and Henry become betrothed. I wonder what she will do. Will they stay with us or want to move away. Oh I hope that they do not, for I should miss her so much and I know that Sophie would be broken-hearted. But I must not stand in her way. She needs to live her life.

Sebastian told me when he proposed to me, that I could have discreet affairs. I have been admired and complimented, and there have been those who have made it plain that they would like to take advantage of me, but none has attracted me. I have also had suggestions made to me by men who are married and there is no way that I would even consider such a thing. I shall never forget what it did to my poor mama. I have no desire to be the cause of unhappiness for some other woman. I must try and keep my spirits high, for I am so much more fortunate than most people and enjoy a comfortable and privileged life. But it is so empty and lonely at its core.

I hear my darling girl as she enters the garden. She is so excited and chattering ninety to the dozen - and Emily is laughing at her and pretending to chide her. I must leave this now and go and check the cake that is in the oven for our tea. Sophie is always so hungry after these expeditions. I expect that we will have to suffer a strange assortment of things that she has collected – leaves, feathers, stones and possibly some rather unattractive specimens from the river bed that she has insisted on bringing home – as if we don't already have enough! I think that she must get this love of fauna and flora from my mother.

Claude has promised to drop in today for tea, so we shall be a jolly party and I must step up to the task and appear happy.

***

I sit here writing by the light of the little oil-lamp that I have brought up to my room. It is late and the house is quiet. Sophie went to bed exhausted, but still insisted that both Emily and I read her stories.

Emily is in her room and I expect that she is reading yet another tome in her room.

The shadows dance on the wallpaper and the whole effect is quite different from that produced by daylight. I have also lit a few candles on the mantelpiece and together with the oil lamp, they give the room a warm glow.

It has been a very pleasant evening – at least, it was to begin with. Claude arrived bearing gifts for a certain excited little girl. He had hardly got through the door, when she threw herself at him in a most unladylike manner. I know that I shall have to try harder at teaching her how to behave in polite society, but at the moment I just want her to be herself – be a little girl. I noticed that she was still very grubby from her afternoon by the river.

"Emily, I think that she had better wash her face and hands before we sit down to tea" I suggested, although Emily was about to do so anyway. The two of them went into the kitchen and I poured out tea and cut some cake for Claude.

"What have you spoilt her with this time, Claude?" I pretended to be piqued.

"Oh, I went into Wells and couldn't pass the sweetshop without purchasing a few of her favourite treats. You are not cross with me, are you ma Cherie?"

"Of course not," I replied. "But we shall have to be careful that she does not become a little madam. She is getting to expect that you will always come bearing gifts."

"The odd little cadeau can do no harm." He pretended to look down at the mouth.

"Oh well." I gave in to his pleading. "But once she is older, we must be careful that she is guided correctly."

"And morally!" He said laughing and giving me a big hug and kissing me on the forehead. "You are such a worrier, ma Cherie."

At this moment, Emily and Sophie entered the room and I noticed, as I have done a number of time, that she gave me a strange look – almost of disapproval.

"Come ladies," said Claude. "Please join us before I eat all this delicious fare."

Sophie rushed to sidle up to him, as he proffered the expected gift. As she looked into the paper bag, her eyes widened. "Ooh, my favourites. Merci beaucoup Uncle Claude. I love you very much." And with this declaration, she flung her arms around him.

"You must eat your tea first," Emily said - rather too tartly. I looked at her wondering why she had spoken in such a way, but could not fathom her reasoning.

Later, after Claude had left and we were clearing away the dishes, I asked her if there was something troubling her. She was quiet for a few moments and then said.
"Do you not think that perhaps Monsieur Claude is a bit too familiar with you?"

I was shocked. "Whatever makes you say such a thing Emily? He's my friend – a brother almost."

"It's just that recently – well, no not just recently, but over the last few years, I have heard gossip about you and Monsieur that is not – how shall I say – very nice. You do know that there are many who are saying that Monsieur is Sophie's father?"

"What!" I cried. "Where has that come from?"

"I don't know – possibly from the gorgon herself, but sometimes, you do both behave in a manner that could be misunderstood. I know there's nothing in these stories, but you do need to be careful – especially in front of other people. I know it isn't my place to say anything, but I worry about you. When I was at Warrington Grange, I did once overhear a conversation between the mistress and Miss Salathial. I can't remember exactly what was said, but they seemed to be under the impression that you had been carrying on with Monsieur Claude."

"Well, I appreciate your concerns, Emily, but you needn't worry. There's nothing inappropriate about our affection and there never has been. In fact, Emily, if you *knew just how wrong you are, you would be most surprised."*

"Well, as long as the Earl doesn't go getting suspicious and upset."

"He won't Emily. I assure you."

***

The following week, they were back at the house and life resumed its routine. Aphra kept her mind occupied and drove out melancholy thoughts. However, she was noticing lately that her attention was wandering and she would find herself lost in melancholic thoughts about her situation and periods of time would lapse without her realising it.

Recently, Miss Phyllis Kincaid began working as Sophie's governess. She was a stout, middle-aged, no nonsense woman – strict but fair. Sebastian and Aphra had chosen her from a number of very eligible candidates. Her references had been excellent, and she had had much experience teaching a variety of children from different backgrounds. Both parents felt that perhaps a disciplined regime might be a good idea, as Sophie had been rather indulged by all of them. To begin with, lessons were only in the mornings and not too demanding.

After an initial feeling of sadness at this news, Emily admitted that it was time for Sophie to begin her schooling and admitted to herself that she was limited in what she could teach the little girl. Aphra reminded her that she had been most successful in her care of Sophie.

"You've done a wonderful job, but Sophie needs to have a more disciplined routine now, and besides, it will leave you more time to have your own life and you'll still be spending time with her at the beginning of the day and after lunch," said Aphra.

At first, Sophie was none too pleased about these changes in her life, and there was quite a bit of pouting and foot stamping, but after a few weeks, she settled down and began to work hard at her studies. Her favourite subject was nature study and she began to look forward to these lessons. Miss Kincaid being a wise, as well as experienced teacher, took advantage of Sophie's enthusiasm in this subject to help her improve in other areas. Sophie had already been able to read and write a little before Miss Kincaid began instructing her. However, as the months passed, she became very accomplished in both areas.

Sophie liked nothing better than to go out in the parkland with her teacher, especially by the lake and in the woods, looking for specimens to put in jars to take back to the classroom to study. Miss Kincaid encouraged the little girl to experiment and write about her collections and in this way, Sophie became a very able student – just like her mother.

Other areas that she excelled in were singing and to a lesser degree, playing the piano. Also, the time that she had spent with Claude had stood her in good stead and before long, she could converse quite well in basic French.

She liked painting and drawing, but so far, had shown little aptitude for it other than getting her clothes and the area around her covered in paint.

"Goodness, you're a messy child. Could you not restrict the paint to the paper?" Scolded Miss Kincaid – although Sophie could see that her teacher had a twinkle in her eye.

Miss Kincaid sometimes felt that the child had been a bit too indulged. However, she reported to the Countess that Sophie was generally making good progress, but, like so many teachers before her, suggested that Sophie needed to try harder.

A week before Christmas, Miss Kincaid left to spend the holidays with her elderly mother in Swindon. Aphra had been so delighted with Sophie's progress, that she gave the governess three weeks' holiday. Miss Kincaid had grown fond of the little girl and gave her a small book on flowers, which Sophie got quite excited about. She even gave the governess a kiss on the cheek as she climbed into the carriage taking her to the station.

"Now you be a good girl and don't forget to practise your reading and writing and your scales," she said. "Have a good Christmas and when I come back, we'll start on some new things to learn."

"Yes, Miss Kincaid. I promise," Sophie said, with her fingers crossed behind her back.

On Christmas Eve, the family celebrated Emily and Henry's engagement. Sebastian made a generous gift of some money and said that they could live in a small cottage on the estate. It was only a short distance from the house and would not affect their duties. Emily had been busy making things that would be useful when she was married. Aphra had helped her with the sewing and embroidery, so she had a bottom drawer that was becoming very full of tablecloths, cushion covers, antimacassars and all sorts of items too numerous to mention.

Both Henry and Emily were pleasantly surprised at the gifts they received from the family as well as from members of the household staff. Claude gave them a small French clock and the dowager presented Emily with a beautiful watercolour that she had done herself. The staff had all contributed to the purchase of a very pretty tea-set. Later, when Aphra and Emily were alone, Aphra said. "I want to make your dress for you. It will be my present to you." She knew that it would be good for her to fill her mind with a new project.

Even though it was a time of festivity with the Christmas celebrations and the engagement, Aphra was feeling sad again. Once into the New Year, she threw herself into being even busier than before. Having the dress to make, sitting on committees and assisting Sebastian at various functions, left her little time to brood about her loneliness.

Emily and Henry's wedding took place on a bright, cold afternoon at the end of March. It was a cheerful congregation that stood up as Emily entered the little church, looking resplendent in a white satin bridal gown, a diamond tiara (on loan from Aphra) and a veil made of French lace – another gift from Claude. Sophie was a bridesmaid and looked charming.

Emily's father walked her proudly down the aisle, and her family and friends looked on smiling. Afterwards, a small reception was held back at Methuen Park. As the light began to fade, the newlyweds drove the short distance to their cottage. Just before Emily climbed up into the little trap, Aphra embraced her and kissed her on the cheek. "You looked so beautiful today. I wish you a long and truly, happy life with Henry," she said.

"I hope to be as happy as you are in your marriage" Emily said. As they disappeared among the trees and Aphra had stopped waving, she turned and walked slowly back up the steps into the house. Sebastian and Claude had already gone in. She had heard Sebastian say to Claude as he put his arm across the other's shoulder "let's go and have a brandy?" Claude had assented, and Aphra knew that they wished to be alone. Now she would not have Emily to keep her company and the sadness seemed to engulf her.

When she returned indoors, she found Sophie playing draughts with her grandmother. She sat with them for a while and then took Sophie up to get ready for bed. After reading the little girl her story, she went to her room. She knew that Rose would have retired for the night, so there was little point in returning downstairs. She noticed that the old lady was going to bed earlier and earlier and often had to rest during the day. She had thought how pale and tired she had looked today, although she had put on a brave face for Emily's sake. Aphra had become very fond of her mother in law and it worried her that she was beginning to fail. She would speak to Sebastian in the morning. Perhaps they needed to call the doctor again.

But in the morning, she discovered that it was too late. Rose had died in her sleep. It was Claude who broke the news to her. He was very kind and comforting to her as she cried on his shoulder. He told her that Sebastian was very shocked.

"Shall I go to him?" She asked.

"Best not. He's with her at the moment and wants to say goodbye on his own. At least it seems that she went peacefully in her sleep. Dorothy found her when she took her morning tea in to her."

"I feel so bad. I thought that she looked very tired and pale yesterday. It was all too much for her. I should have gone and said goodnight, but I saw to Sophie and …. Oh my goodness, we have to tell her. She's going to be so upset."

***

Sophie was indeed very upset at first, but, like most children, she was very resilient and after a few weeks accepted that her grandmother was happy in heaven. As the time passed, so life returned to a routine pattern and Aphra, Sebastian and Claude were busy again. Sebastian was, as usual, often away, and Aphra and Claude spent much of their free time together, sitting reading or walking in the parkland. Sometimes, she would sit and paint or sew and he would play the piano for her. If Sophie was not at her studies, then she would join them too.

Towards the end of the year, Emily informed Aphra that she was going to have a baby.

"That's wonderful news. I'm so happy for you, When is it due?"

"I think about April. I hope that it will be alright with you and the Earl. I mean – what about looking after Sophie?"

"Don't worry about that. I did expect that you would have a child sooner or later. That was only to be expected. I could hardly expect you to get married and not have children. I'm delighted for you both. I just want you to look after yourself and have a healthy child. Besides, you can still spend time with Sophie and I'm sure that she will be thrilled at the news. Just think it will be like having a new doll."

"I hope that she doesn't get jealous," Emily replied. "You know, it's about time that you had another one. Sophie is now nearly seven. It seems odd that you fell for a child so easily, but have not had another one after all these years."

"Well, it sometimes happens that way. Who knows what the future will bring," said Aphra. "Now, we need to make some plans for Christmas," she added, trying to draw the conversation away from her own situation.

But later that night when she was in bed, she lay thinking about what Emily had said. Throughout the day, she managed to keep herself occupied, but in the quiet and solitude of her bed-chamber, the dark thoughts crept in. Perhaps if she'd had another child it would have satisfied this gnawing longing that she felt, but it did not seem likely that it was ever to happen – it was impossible. She had to put the idea out of her mind. She must keep counting her blessings. When she had these dark thoughts, she had to remember the workhouse. After all, where would Sophie and she be now if it was not for Sebastian's generosity? She missed Rose so much, and now Emily would be occupied with her baby. She felt envious of her and then she pushed that thought away. She must overcome these melancholy thoughts. Tomorrow, she would strive to keep constantly occupied.

She had noticed some time ago that there was a little walled garden in the woods. It had been neglected for decades. She had been thinking for some while that it would make an interesting project for her and would help to take her mind off her troubles. It would be nice to work in there and perhaps Sophie and Emily could join her. She would need to speak to Sebastian about it, as the garden was inside the forbidden area.

When she asked him about it, he thought that it was an excellent idea, and provided she checked with him when she took the others there, he saw no problem with the scheme. She threw herself into the work when she had spare time and it kept her absorbed. Occasionally, Claude would accompany her to the garden to check on her progress and sometimes to offer a little help.

But as Emily's pregnancy advanced and Sophie became busier with her school work, so Aphra's loneliness grew. Fortunately, she had Claude to talk to, but she did not want to bother him with her problems. Besides, he was often very busy. Although, she saw Sebastian most days, it was often for a brief meeting to make arrangements or discuss some matter regarding the running of the estate or the house.

Life continued with busy days full of committee meetings, correspondence, discussing menus with the cook, sorting out minor disputes with the staff, overseeing the gardeners and discussing the re-planting of the parterre and so on. There were often many social engagements that Aphra had to attend with Sebastian. Both found the public pretence tedious at times.

Everywhere they went, people commented on what a perfect handsome couple they made, but behind their backs, there was often rumour and gossip about the Countess and the Frenchman. Sebastian was completely unaware of this, and even though Emily had warned Aphra, she had taken little notice of it and continued to spend time with Claude. It often seemed that after one of these functions, she felt even more dispirited.

Her guilt at these times was also worse, for she had just been to a lavish a banquet, consumed the best food and wine, had been beautifully attired, often in a new gown and returned home to a palace, where servants were on hand to attend to her every need. And then she would mount the stairs with Sebastian and he would make pleasant, complimentary remarks to her. He would kiss her forehead and would go to his room, where she knew Claude would be waiting for him. She would enter her beautiful, lavish chamber, shut the door and the silence would oppress her once more. Many was the night, when she had told Dorothy to go to bed early, that she would sit at her dressing table unpinning and brushing her hair. She would remove her jewellery and her gown – as well as her public persona, and then as the tears fell, she would put her head in her hands and the bleak, all-consuming, suffocating misery would engulf her.

As Emily's confinement date neared. Aphra asked her if she would like to stay at the house until after the baby was born. Aphra wanted to assist, just as Emily had done with Sophie's birth, and in the early hours of a warm spring morning, baby Paul came into the world. Aphra found that her mood lifted considerably and she delighted in helping Emily with the baby for the first couple of weeks after he was born.

However, when he was nearly a month old, Emily went back to the cottage. It was still wonderful when she came to the house with the baby, which was almost daily. If Sophie was not at her studies, she loved to cuddle the baby and sing to him. However, before Paul was four months old, Emily was expecting again. Aphra was pleased for Emily. However, it just reminded her of what she was missing. A number of people, including Hortense, mentioned more than once, that it was about time Aphra had another child. She thought that she would scream if another person mentioned this to her. If only they knew the impossibility of this.

***

Well, last night was an educational experience that I shall never forget. I don't know which of us feels more embarrassed or humiliated.

Just recently, Sebastian, Claude and I have been discussing the matter of an heir and decided that Sebastian and I should attempt to consummate our marriage and try for a baby. Claude does not mind. What generosity of spirit!

I was very excited at the prospect of a baby. I know how fortunate I am to have Sophie and she is my life, but every day she grows up and a little bit away from me, but the thought of having another little one to cuddle and nurture again filled my heart with joy. I pictured its dear little face with its bright eyes and little rosebud lips gradually learning to smile and that wonderful sound of a heart-warming chuckle that only a little child can make. I was certain that if I had a baby, I would feel more fulfilled and it might keep the bouts of melancholia at bay.

I was unsure of my feelings about marital relations with Sebastian. I have a great deal of love and respect for him, but certainly no passion – and of course, I know that his feelings mirror my own. I realise now how naïve and innocent I have been about the facts of life. It is all so much more complicated.

Sebastian had said beforehand that he was unsure of whether he would be able to father a child. I did not know what he meant. I know now! In spite of my experience in Minehead, my knowledge of the male anatomy and the act of lovemaking is actually very limited.

We decided that we would try last night, Sebastian came to my room. He was very sweet, and in many ways, a much better lover than Thomas had been. Beforehand, he had been extremely attentive to me. He had ordered some beautiful flowers – really lovely colours and in such a cleverly arranged bouquet. (He often buys me flowers, but these were exceptional.) He had asked Travis to bring a bottle of champagne.

I had lit some extra candles, to make the atmosphere of the room more conducive to romance. The fire crackled and shadows danced around the room as we undressed. Gently, he removed my nightgown and then his own attire.

He was very complimentary to me as he admired my body. "You look like a beautiful Greek statue. You are perfection itself," he said.

I was also impressed at his physique. I had been right all those years earlier, when I had thought that he would look better with his clothes off. This brought a smile to my face and I laughed a little. When I told him about this, he laughed also. It helped us both to relax a little.

He was very tender as he slowly caressed my skin and then softly kissed my lips. As we lay on the bed, we began to explore each other's bodies. I felt a little stirring of those feelings I had experienced before, but after a short while, Sebastian sighed and said "I'm so sorry Aphra. It isn't going to work."

"I don't understand."

"It isn't that there's anything wrong with you. You are very lovely and any man would be fortunate to have you as a lover. I just cannot do this with a woman."

"What's wrong?" I said – still the innocent.

He indicated that part of his body between his legs. "My friend here just isn't going to rise to the occasion."

Then I realised. "Oh, I see."

"I had thought that I would be able to do it. I have known a number of chaps of my persuasion who are also attracted to women and for them there is not this difficulty. Besides, I care for you deeply, so thought it might happen."

Poor Sebastian – his hopes of producing an heir had been dashed. He was so sad.

"Sometimes I wonder why I am different from other men. It is not my choice to be like this. It makes life very difficult."

"I know dearest," I replied, putting my arms around him. I got up and began to replace my nightgown. "When I was at school, I was frequently criticised by some of the teachers for using my left hand. I think that if I had not been such a good student, they would have been more severe with me than they were."

"What's that got to do with this situation?" He asked despondently.

"Well, most of the pupils found it easy to use their right hands for writing. I found it very difficult. I once challenged a couple of the girls who were being quite beastly to me, suggesting that we all write a paragraph in the hand with which we were unfamiliar. All of us found it very hard to do and made a terrible mess of it. I then pointed out to them that my writing done with the left hand was neater than their writing done with the right hand. They reluctantly had to agree with me and after that they left me alone. They obviously realised that I wasn't a witch!

So maybe it's just that in this particular respect, you and Claude are left-handed and I'm right-handed, like the majority of people. We need to be doing what is correct for us and not what other people impose upon us. This isn't right for you Seb."

"Thank you Aphra," he said kissing me on the forehead. "I had never thought of it in that way."

"You know, a few centuries ago, I might have been burnt at the stake. Perhaps at some time in the distant future, society will accept you and your persuasion – perhaps you'll even be able to marry."

"Now that is a completely crazy idea, but it has lifted my spirits to think of it. You're a treasure." Putting on his robe, he walked towards the door. "I shall leave you in peace now my dear. Good night."

After he left the room, I felt anything but at peace. My hopes of having a little baby to love and cuddle had gone for good...

It seems that my old unwelcome companion is back again. I know now that as well as the lost hope of a lover, the hope for another child is gone also. It will not happen and somehow, I have to learn to accept this, but I now understand Sebastian and Claude and the complexities of life a little better.

I miss Rose so much and her kindness and quiet helpful advice. I wish that I could have confided in her, but that could never have happened. And now Emily is so preoccupied with her family. Stella, her little girl is a really bonny baby, and Paul is such a handful and into everything. I often walk down to her cottage and share a cup of tea with her and we chat and laugh, but I feel such a fraud, for there is no mirth in me. I sometimes wonder if she can tell that I am being false in my laughter – which to me sounds shrill and hollow. Every time, I leave her warm and cosy cottage and return to the house, it's as though a cloud of suffocating doom descends and envelops me and I feel as though I am entering a prison.

I glance around at my comfortable, luxurious prison – Oh, I know that I should not complain – such good fortune is mine I keep telling myself, for I am blessed with all of the comforts that money can buy and I know that I have much to be thankful for – and yet this pain gnaws at my spirit. Such secret loneliness is mine that I despair of ever knowing the warmth and tenderness and true intimacy of a lover's touch.

Are a few moments of youthful folly all that I am to experience of passion?

Sometimes, when I see Seb and Claude together – such love and tenderness for each other – a tormented jealousy grips my soul. It is as though I hate anyone who is fortunate enough to know love and warmth. How could I project these feelings at them when they have both given me so much? Where would I be if it was not for Seb? I feel guilty at this dark secret vice of mine, but tonight I feel as though I am in hell. What a nasty, ungrateful, and selfish woman I must be.

***

"You look lovely, Milady," said Dorothy, stepping backwards with an admiring expression on her face.

"Thank you Dorothy. You have done my hair so nicely. I'm really pleased with it."

"Well, it's a pleasure to dress your hair. It's such a lovely colour."

"Thank you."

"So what is the luncheon in aid of today?" Asked Dorothy.

"Today, the Earl is entertaining a number of business men and their wives. He wants to discuss some new plans that should bring prosperity and more jobs to the region."

"He's a good man. Always thinking of others, as you are ma'am."

"He certainly is, but it will probably be rather tedious. I have no head for commerce. I'll let you into a little secret. I get no pleasure from attending these events, but I have to do so. There are many other things that I would prefer to be doing, like weeding in my little garden."

"Well, I hope that today proves to be the exception to the rule and that you find something to interest you."

Aphra gave her a peck on the cheek. "You run along now and put your feet up for a while. You've worked very hard this morning." Dorothy was looking forward to a relaxing afternoon. She liked working for the Countess, for she never had to do much after events other than undo the hooks on the back of gowns. Aphra preferred to unpin her hair and undress herself. "I'm not a helpless baby," she often said.

As Aphra made her way down the stairs on Sebastian's arm, she smiled at him. "Did you manage to get that speech finished? I expect that you were up late last night working on it."

"Yes, thank you my dear. Claude and I were up until the small hours, but I'm quite happy with it. I expect that it will be of little interest to you," he said. "I recognise the glazed expression that comes into your eyes at these functions. Hopefully, today won't be too tedious for you."

As they walked out on to the terrace, Sebastian and Aphra became the perfectly happy married couple. The liveried footmen carried trays of aperitifs. There was plenty of noise as everyone seemed to be talking at once. Aphra was introduced to various people that she had not met previously. She knew a few others and made polite conversation and enquired about their families, for she always noted information about each and every one.

The gong was struck and the whole party slowly filed into the dining room to eat lunch.

**

It is almost dawn and I have been awake and pacing the house and grounds for hours. I cannot slumber – such excitement – I feel so alive. I seem to hear and smell everything – to notice everything.

Wisdom tells me that I should try and get some sleep. I have much to do in a few hours. But I cannot sleep. I don't want this night to end. I have to write down my thoughts and feelings. I have not felt like this since Thomas... Oh what naïve foolishness that was. But this will be different. I am a mature woman and so much wiser, am I not?

Perhaps putting pen to paper, I shall be able to settle my mind and get some rest.

Today, Sebastian held his annual luncheon for some business colleagues. To begin with, it was all rather tedious. I sometimes find that these events present me with a challenge. It can be such a bore making small talk and attempting to appear interested in people that I don't know and with whom I have nothing in common. One seems to pass from person to person and the conversations are repetitious. It must be just as dreadful for them. They must find me a terribly dull woman, as I struggle to find some relevant comment to make. Sebastian is always so kind and tells me that I carry out my duties perfectly, but in truth, I feel such a fraud.

We went into lunch and took our places. Mrs Pearson had prepared an excellent repast as usual. There were a number of courses – although I now struggle to remember everything we ate, which is strange when I consider the amount of time that we spent planning the menu. I recall that there were some delicious mutton cutlets with reform sauce, and a good choice of seasonal vegetables from the kitchen garden. However, it was while I was eating the lemon sorbet that ennui caused my concentration to lapse and I found myself gazing down the long table in an absent-minded fashion. My eyes passed from one guest to the next and I really was not absorbing much about anyone – other than how similar they all seemed – grey-haired, whiskered gentlemen with moustaches and their plump, middle-aged wives – all busy with their respective conversations and enjoying their food.

No one appeared to notice my intrusive study of them, so absorbed were they in their own affairs. It was a comfortable, mindless occupation that I often indulge in when I'm bored. Suddenly, I was startled out of my torpid state. There, near the far end of the table sat a striking young man whom I had never seen before. Yes, he was definitely much younger than the other guests. He was not speaking to anyone – neither was he eating. He was staring at me! I could feel myself colouring at this unexpected attention – and, I have to add – if I'm being honest, that it surprised me how much I welcomed it.

I found that I could not touch the dessert. It may have been Apple Frost with Cream - although I'm not exactly certain. This was in no way a reflection on cook, but more down to the state of my emotions. When the meal was finished, coffee was served and speeches were made. I felt restless and wanted to leave the table as soon as possible. In fact, I wanted an opportunity of meeting and speaking to the person who had produced this reaction in me, for the look he gave me and the occasional smile left me in no doubt of his interest and admiration.

Sebastian stood up and thanked his guests for their attendance and invited them to relax and feel free to roam the grounds. After I had made yet more small talk, I gratefully watched people disperse. This left me free to make my escape and venture towards a part of the grounds that I knew would not be accessible to older and more corpulent, arthritic bodies. I made my way in the direction that I had seen him walking.

"I knew you'd come."

The comment irritated me. Was I that obvious?

He was leaning casually against the gnarled trunk of a tree, staring into the water of a small pond, and smoking a cigar.

He resumed his intense staring at me. This scrutiny was both unnerving and welcome.

"These functions must be very boring for a young and beautiful woman such as yourself. How do you manage to maintain this air of the perfect hostess?"

"It's one of the duties demanded by my position. I like to be helpful and support my husband in his work and many activities, I replied – somewhat too primly.

"Ah yes, your husband," he smirked. "He seems to be devoted to you. You're a fortunate woman. You appear to have everything – beauty, wealth, position and a doting husband. Is there anything lacking in this perfect life? Perhaps excitement – intrigue?"

"You forget yourself Sir – and my position. You insult me and my husband. I bid you good day." I turned to walk back down the hill. As I passed him, he grabbed my arm.

"You'll come to me again." His sardonic smile annoyed me greatly. Such arrogance. Shaking myself free of his grip, I almost ran down the hill - my emotions in turmoil. I felt as though I could hardly breathe. I noticed nothing, yet my senses were aware of everything.

The melancholia had gone!

***

In the days that followed the luncheon party, Claude noticed a distinct change in Aphra's demeanour. He was sensitive and observant and had been aware of her low mood these last few years. He suspected that Sebastian could be oblivious to the depth of her pain and loneliness, but he could see it in her eyes and even in the way that she walked. He had some years ago decided that it was best not to discuss this with Sebastian. He was by no means a cold man – quite the reverse – but he had enough matters on his mind and did not need the worry of Aphra's sadness. Besides, Claude was by far better equipped emotionally to be a stalwart support for her. They were more alike and he saw it as his role to be a comfort to her – as though she were his little sister.

However, recently, there had definitely been a lightness in her whole being – a spring in her step even. As he sat in the shade of a weeping willow tree, he watched her at play on the lawn with Sophie. The smile now reached her eyes. He wondered what could be the cause of this change. Could it be anything to do with the young man who had attended the luncheon party? Claude was probably the only person in the room who observed the furtive glances travelling the length of the table between the young man and the Countess. He also noted the absence of both of them afterwards.

However, there was something about the young man that made him uneasy. He had thought that a discreet word or two of advice might be wise – after all, she had lived a very sheltered life and had already been very hurt. However, he decided not to say anything for the time being and to keep his own counsel. Perhaps he would find a way to approach the subject and to let her know that she could confide in him if and when she required.

***

Immediately after the encounter with the handsome young man, Aphra had taken the route around the back of the house to her own rooms. This was so that she could avoid contact with both Sebastian and Claude, or any of the remaining guests who were now departing. She knew that she should be at Seb's side to bid their guests farewell, but she was embarrassed that her face was flushed and she felt so distracted by the whole incident that she was in no mind to resume the polite small talk.
Once more in the privacy of her own room, she lay on the bed and closed her eyes and allowed herself to contemplate the day's events. As her anger subsided, so the feeling of excitement increased.

In the early hours of the following morning she did manage to fall asleep briefly before Sophie awoke. She went about her daily routine with her mind far away.

The following week, Sebastian and Claude went away on business and Aphra was left to her own devices. One morning at breakfast, Travis brought the post in to her. There was the usual large pile of correspondence for Sebastian. In his and Claude's absence, Aphra would peruse through it to see if there was anything requiring an urgent reply. Sebastian had mentioned one or two items to look out for, but she could see nothing pertaining to these matters and put everything to one side.

She usually had a few items in connection with her charity work and the occasional missive from Hortense. She went through the pile in a routine manner, placing each envelope in different groups according to priority. Suddenly, she noticed a hand that she did not recognise. Without opening the letter, she knew immediately whose hand it was. She placed the letter in her pocket and continued with the remaining items of post – hardly taking in anything that she was reading.

Sophie entered the dining room. After greeting her briefly, Aphra made an excuse to leave, which surprised Sophie, for Aphra would usually spend a great deal of time with her. "I have some matters to attend to. You'd better go up to the schoolroom. I expect that Miss Kincaid will be ready to start," she said as she kissed the child on her forehead.

Sophie reluctantly walked off as Aphra made her way straight to her room – the delay in time increasing her impatience to open the letter. When she finally opened it, she did not know whether or not she was pleased with what she read. In fact, she experienced a return of the mixed emotions that she had felt the afternoon of the luncheon.

The letter was written on headed paper from a hotel in Bath. There was neither greeting nor salutation.

He had written three words – When and Where? And his name, Preston Nash.

Under her breath, she uttered the words "Insolent bounder!" But just as she was saying this, she was seating herself at her bureau and eagerly grabbing a sheet of paper. She dipped her pen into the ink and began to write the name of a venue and a suggested date and time of meeting. As discretion was of prime importance, she went to the stables, harnessed her horse and rode into the local village and posted the letter herself.

When Seb and Claude returned, Aphra spoke to Claude and asked him to accompany her to Wells. Claude took this opportunity to gently voice his concerns about Preston. Aphra replied that she was already aware of his nature and so Claude dropped the subject for the time being.
Claude had a few errands to run – including one or two for Sebastian. He drove her to a small wood just outside Wells that was part of the Tawford estate and she stepped down onto the path.

Claude was very uncomfortable about this assignation that she was conducting with this young man. Obviously, he was delighted to see her happy again, but at this precise moment could not decide which concerned him the most – her terrible bouts of melancholia, or the risks she would probably incur in an attachment with this scoundrel.

As he drove off to Wells to carry out his errands, he was not happy about leaving her there, but she had insisted that he do so. They arranged that he would return with the carriage at three o clock.

She felt guilty at wanting him to leave, but she just could not wait to be alone with Preston. She felt a mixture of elation and apprehension. Part of her knew that what she was doing was very unwise. She walked through the woods to where there was a small clearing. Preston had laid out a blanket and beside this was a wicker hamper. It reminded Aphra of that picnic years ago with Claude. But with Claude, she was very relaxed. She was not relaxed now – quite the reverse, but she felt alive – more alive than she had felt in a long time.

As she walked towards him, he looked up at her and smiled. He said nothing, but just patted the blanket beside him. His presumption irritated her, but she knew that she wanted to sit there, so she did. God, she was being so foolish - but what harm could there be in it? He took both her hands in his and kissed them both. She showed no outward sign of reaction.

"Well, are we the haughty Countess today?" He mocked.

"Perhaps," she smiled coolly.

"Would you like some champagne?" He asked. "It will help you to relax."

"Who says that I'm not relaxed?" she asked, trying to sound confident and like a woman of the world. She refused the wine. She did not want to blunt her feelings

"You're scared stiff." He looked closely into her eyes. "But what and whom are you scared of? Is it me? Or is it yourself and the fear of losing that buttoned up self-control?"

She felt really annoyed now. How dare he question her in this way? She was about to get up and walk away, when he leaned forward and touched her hand gently. "I'm sorry. I was just teasing you. I can't resist it. You look so serious. Am I forgiven?" The look in his eyes was so earnest and he seemed so full of remorse, that she patted his hand and said "of course. You're right. I am nervous. This is all very strange to me. I don't make a habit of clandestine meetings with strange young men."

"Not even with Monsieur Tanquerel? Rumour has it that you're always with him."

"Oh, he's part of the family – he's like a brother to me."

Preston said nothing and looked down at the ground and unseen by her, raised his eyebrows.

He placed a cushion behind her head as she lay back on the blanket and closed her eyes. She expected him to kiss her immediately, but he surprised, pleased and disappointed her all in the same moment. He stood up and walked a light distance and sat on the stump of a felled tree and lit a cigar.

She watched him out of the corner of her eye. He was probably the most handsome man that she had ever seen. He turned and smiled at her. The effect on her was overwhelming. Physically, he was absolute perfection. She looked away and turned her attention to the scurrying clouds above – just visible through the canopy of shimmering leaves. Well, this was certainly not how she had expected things to go. In fact, he was being most restrained – which surprised her. He walked about, looking at the woodland flora.

"Would you like to take a stroll?" He asked. She assented and for more than an hour they walked amongst the trees and just chatted about generalities. He made no move to touch her, which she found both reassuring and frustrating.

"What's the time?" She asked him.

"It's almost a quarter past two," he said.

"It'll soon be time for me to leave,"

"But we've not eaten anything."

"We didn't come here to eat, did we?" She said provocatively.

"And what did you come here to do Countess?" He asked feigning naiveté.

She could feel her anger mount as did her desire for him and her face coloured. They had come here for one reason alone and he was not going to comply – damn the man.

Then she surprised herself as she took the lead and reached over and holding the back of his head, drew him closer to her and began to kiss him passionately. It shocked her that she had done so and it surprised him too. He in return began to unpin her hair as he responded to her kisses.

"Well, Milady. I didn't expect that today," he said mockingly as they drew apart.

"I must go. Monsieur Tanquerel will be back with the carriage at any time."

"Then let us arrange to meet again soon – tomorrow?"

"I'm not sure. I have my daughter to think about – and of course I have my duties."

"Surely, there are others who can attend to such things. You have servants to see to your daughter, do you not?"

"Yes, but I want to be with her. I have spent the whole of today away from her. I will not do the same tomorrow. This will have to wait."

Preston realised that this was a woman who knew her own mind and that he may not find it quite as easy to manipulate her as he had done others. He would have to work harder.

He looked tenderly into her eyes and when he smiled, it was like a little boy lost.

"But I need you too," he implored.

She caressed his cheek. "I will see you again, but I can't tell you when."

He knew that underneath this perceived veneer of the respectable aristocratic lady, dwelt a very passionate woman. He was determined that he should enjoy this passion and soon, but he would have to be very subtle how he handled her.

She kissed him once more and he responded passionately. Then she drew away from him and stood up.

He watched her slender, departing figure with her flowing titan hair as she walked back through the woods. The Earl was a fortunate man to have such a wife, but what about the other chap? Was she involved with him? They were obviously very close and there was all this gossip about them. She turned and smiled. She was certainly a beautiful woman. Standing there like that in the long grass, with her elegant dark blue velvet gown twisted slightly around her feet, she reminded him of a pre-Raphealite painting. He desired her beyond anything else in the world and was determined that she would soon be his. He would do anything to achieve his aim.

Over the next few weeks, they met at out of the way restaurants and teashops, as Aphra knew that she had to be very discreet. At first, Claude would accompany her in the carriage, but there were also occasions when she would take one of the small traps and drive herself. At each meeting, her feelings for Preston grew stronger and she knew that it was only a matter of time before she gave herself to him.

"We must find a way of being alone," he said. "I need to go to Devon on business for a few days. Do you think that you would be able to join me?"

She thought about it for a few minutes. "Yes, I could get away for a few days. When will you be going?"

"I have to go to Exeter next week, so we could meet in Dartmouth," he continued.

They made their plans and then Aphra said. "I must get back. Sophie will be needing me and I have neglected my duties as well. "

He leant forward, his face very close to hers. "Such a dutiful mother, but I notice that you do not seem to worry about your husband so much. I wonder what he would say if he could see you now."

"Please do not speak of my husband in that way," Aphra said, showing a trace of anger. "I prefer not to think about that."

"My apologies Countess." He kissed her hand and then he kissed her passionately on the lips and she did not want to leave him. Eventually, she managed to tear herself away from him and they made their farewells.

"Until we meet again in Dartmouth, I shall be inconsolable."

***

I am not comfortable with this situation. My mind is not quiet – so why do I continue? It is not like me – usually so sensible and level-headed and yet I seem to be prepared to behave in a way that I know is very foolish.

Perhaps it is the knowledge that without these heady moments of ecstasy, all that awaits me is the greyness which precedes the black rolling mist.

The heights are wonderful, but the yawning black pit beneath terrifies me – the fall will be terrific and I fear that it is coming. I cannot face swirling around in that darkness grasping for a foot hold or something to grab onto. Next time, when it comes, will I sink further into the blackness and will I ever find my way out? Perhaps I will be completely lost and my mind will go.

I should end it now before my addiction to him grows stronger – but I can't. I don't want to give up the dream of paradise. I seem to have days and nights of anguish and turmoil and then there is the ecstasy that may come from a short note from him or a brief meeting. I know that it will not be very long before I give myself to him completely. I long for it, but my head is telling me it will be unwise.

***

Aphra explained to Sophie that she had to go away for a few days with Uncle Claude. Emily had promised to take her back to the cottage each day after her lessons to play with her own children. Sebastian had also set aside some extra time to give Sophie one or two treats.

Aphra gave instructions to Mrs Drake regarding various matters pertaining to the running of the house in her absence. The housekeeper thought that it was odd that the Countess and the French secretary were taking this trip together. She wondered what his Lordship thought about it. Did he even know? Still, it was none of her business. She was here to do a job of work and not contemplate such matters.

Emily was also concerned about this forthcoming trip and it worried her, but she decided to mind her own business. Besides, she had enough to do these days.

Claude had agreed to accompany Aphra as far as Exeter where she would meet the coach. He felt very uneasy about this tryst of hers and said so. Aphra wondered whether or not he was perhaps a little jealous – although that seemed somewhat ridiculous under the circumstances.

"I don't trust that man," he said. "I'm afraid that he'll hurt you."

"Don't be silly, Claude," she laughed. "What possible harm could he do me?"

"There's something amoral – even dangerous about him."

"What do you mean?"

"I don't know. It's something – it's the way he looks at you. It bothers me."

"He's in love with me and you know how that feels, don't you?"

"No he's not. He's playing a game with you and your feelings. I look upon you as my own little sister and I want to protect you."

"I appreciate your concern, but I'm a big girl now Claude and can protect myself. I'm not that gauche sixteen year old girl who went to Minehead." She stroked his arm. "You and Sebastian have had each other for many years. I'm tired of being alone and have so longed for this. Please don't deny me this pleasure or spoil it for me. Can't you just be happy in the knowledge that I feel so wonderful?"

"Of course I want you to be happy, just be careful – please."

She kissed him on the cheek and he held her close to him.

"I'll be waiting for you when you return – ready to pick up the pieces if necessary."

"It won't be – but thank you all the same," she replied.

The weather was not too good on the day that they set off for Devon. The journey to Exeter took two days. Claude watched the coach for Dartmouth leave. His heart was heavy for he was deeply worried about Aphra.

Once there, Aphra checked into a small hotel in a quiet back street.

Obviously, it would not do for her to be staying at the most select hotel in the town. She just hoped that she would not meet anyone that she knew. Whilst in Exeter, she had purchased a few items of clothing - more in keeping with a person of a lower social station than herself. Her room was quite modest and overlooking the back of the building. It had been some time since she had stayed in accommodation like this. She smiled to herself. At one time, she would have been impressed and very grateful. Now, it seemed quite lacking in the facilities that she had come to expect as standard. She had become spoilt and soft!

She had intended to see him the following day, but she felt so restless that she could not just sit around aimlessly in her room, so she decided that she would go for a short walk and explore the town.

Although the hotel was situated towards the back of the town away from the main streets and the quay, in less than ten minutes, she was down by the water. She noticed a park and decided to take a stroll around it, admiring the plants and trees, many of which she recognised, for they were the same as those at Methuen Park. She found a bench in a quiet, sheltered corner. It was slightly chilly and the wind was getting up. Quietly, she observed people passing by – a single, elderly gent, a large boisterous family, two young female servants enjoying their afternoon off and a nanny pushing a pram. She felt alive and expectant, but strangely drowsy. She leant her head back and closed her eyes.

She almost drifted off to sleep when her senses brought her back to full consciousness. Without opening her eyes, she knew that he was there beside her.

Gently, his hand touched hers – the effect was instant, and overpowering. She felt as though she couldn't breathe, but loved feeling like it. It was craziness, but she wanted to remain crazy with him for all time. Still, she did not open her eyes. He leant over and kissed her ear.

"Not here!" She protested as she sat bolt upright. "People will see."

"You're just an ordinary person now. No-one will notice," he teased and repeated the action. This time, she did not stop him and started to giggle just as a matronly woman walked by and glared with pursed lips in a most disapproving manner.

"You're turning me into a wicked woman." She pushed him away from her and stood up.

He stood up and gestured for her to slip her arm through his. It felt natural and comfortable to do this and she warmed at the closeness and warmth of his touch. They walked out of the gardens and towards the river. There were a number of benches along the quayside. They walked towards the one that was furthest from the town, where there was no-one around. The sky was now overcast, but it did not worry Aphra. It could have been raining hailstones and she would have been just as deliriously happy. She did not want this to end. She felt so comfortable and alive with him. As they chatted about generalities, she looked across the water and the bobbing boats to the hills beyond. A mist was beginning to descend. However, the fields that were still visible, looked as though they were covered in lush, green velvet and the buildings on the hills surrounding the Dart looked like coloured dolls' houses.

"Please look at me," he said.

She turned her head towards him and smiled. She looked back to the river and made a comment about one of the boats.

He put his hand to her chin and turned it towards him. "I want you to look at me. Don't turn away when you talk."
She laughed nervously. "Why?" It puzzled her – why was he so insistent that she look at him and at his eyes? It seemed strange, but she dismissed the doubt as soon as it entered her head.

"I don't know," he answered casually. "I like you looking at me."

The weather worsened and the sky darkened, but it did not matter to her, for where they would be soon, the weather would be irrelevant. It had been so long since that afternoon in Minehead – she felt overwhelmed and when she looked at him again, she felt lost – as though she was drowning, but wanting to drown.

"I've rented a house just up the river. I'll take you there by boat tomorrow," he said. She wished that it was now and suggested this, but he was insistent that it be the following day.

It irritated her slightly that he was making all the decisions. It crossed her mind that he was controlling her and she felt a bit uneasy.

"We'll meet here at ten," he said. "I'll moor the boat there by that wall. Make sure that you wear something warm. It can get chilly on the water."

"Of course," she replied. It started to rain and they stood up. He offered to walk her back to the hotel, but she shook her head. "I'll go alone. I don't want the staff to gossip."

"You're so conventional my beautiful Countess," he teased.

"Perhaps not as much as you think," she replied.

"What do you mean?" He was curious now.

She shook her head. "I can't tell you – just believe me."

He was now intrigued and pressed her up against an adjacent tree letting her know in no uncertain terms that he wanted her there and then. When he kissed her, she responded passionately. However, it was important to her to be the one in control and eventually she pulled away from him.

"We need to go now. We're going to get very wet. I shall cut back through the gardens."

"Will you be all right?"

"Yes, of course. I'll see you tomorrow."

He kissed her hand and watched her disappear among the trees.

"Till tomorrow," he said to himself. "Then I will discover how unconventional you are my beautiful, enigmatic Countess."

***

I am in such turmoil. I have just spent the most wonderful afternoon with Preston and yet I feel disturbed. Claude is correct when he says that something is not right about him.

I am realising that I am not the sort of woman who can just do this for fun. Sebastian said that I was free to do as I please, on condition that I was discreet. I don't think that I want a brief, hole in the corner affair. I want a life-long love – the whole thing – the emotions, the dreams, the intimacy of sharing one's deepest spiritual thoughts and feelings – and I'm not going to have it with this man.

Tomorrow is the day that I have longed for - for so many years. At last, I shall lie in his arms and give myself to him and sink down in to that ecstasy that I shared with Thomas. Till then, I hope that I will sleep tonight and perhaps have happy dreams that will take away this unease that I feel.

***

At the agreed time, on the following morning, Aphra stood on the quayside. There was no sign of Preston. She walked up and down for some minutes trying to hide her agitation. Was he not going to show up? Was he playing games? She scanned the boats going up and down the river. Suddenly, she saw him as his small boat approached the quay.

"My apologies for my tardiness, my lady, but I overslept," he confessed in a mock pretence of contriteness. She pretended that it did not matter, but in her heart, she was aware that he was not as eager to see her as she was to see him. He threw a rope to her and she helped him to moor the craft. Then he held out his hand as she stepped into the small, rocking boat. The day was much brighter than the preceding one and the wind had dropped. The boats dotted about the river were bathed in sunshine.

The journey up the Dart took about an hour. Preston brought the boat alongside a small jetty. He jumped ashore and tied the mooring rope to a wooden pole and then lent down and helped her out of the small craft.

Aphra looked around at the river and the view across to the other side. "Oh Preston. It's lovely. You've found such a beautiful spot."

"Come," he said, holding out his hand. "Let me show you the house."

They walked the few yards up a path through the trees. Aphra felt as though she was in a dream. Preston unlocked the door and they went in. He briefly showed her around the downstairs. He began to kiss her neck and she responded to his ardour passionately.

"Shall we go upstairs?" He threw his coat onto a chair in the hallway. He began to lead her up the stairs. "I cannot wait to have you lie in my arms," he continued. "I have been going crazy for you ever since I saw you at that bloody boring lunch.

Aphra said nothing, but smiled and willingly followed him. He began to run, and they both laughed like boisterous children as they entered the bedroom and he began to kiss her again. He started to undress her with an impatience that was quite startling to Aphra. She thought that if he went any faster, he would rip her dress in two.

"Please," she protested. "This is all much too fast for me. I am not used to this. Have a heart, Preston. Please slow down"

He stopped and looked at her. "What do you mean; you're not used to this? You're a married woman. Isn't the aristocratic Sebastian just as eager?"

"I have asked you not to mention my husband. Please respect my wishes on that matter," she said.

As he kissed her neck, he ran his hands over her shoulders and beneath the fabric of her gown towards her breasts. "I'm sorry. Don't be so touchy. I meant nothing by it." As he resumed undoing the hooks on her dress, he said softly in her ear "Isn't this fun my darling? But I can't help wondering what he would say if he knew what his naughty little wife was up to behind his back?" His lips travelled to the area of flesh that he had just exposed. "He's a bit smug – so bloody high and mighty. It would wipe the smile off his face, if he knew what you'd been up to in Dartmouth." He began to slip his hands inside the bodice of her undergarment. "But if he knew and approved of this, it wouldn't be half as much fun, would it?" As he continued to caress her, Aphra froze.

"Stop," she said, but he ignored her plea and pressed her down onto the bed. "I said stop!" She raised her voice. He ignored her and began to raise her skirt and petticoats. Suddenly her voice changed. "I asked you to stop. Now I'm telling you to stop!" He was so shocked at the change in the tone of her voice, that he reluctantly did as she demanded.

"What's wrong?" He asked, kissing her neck and caressing her cheek, trying to coax her back into the mood that she had previously been in.

"This. It's all wrong. I need to leave," she said wriggling away from under him. "I've made a terrible mistake and I've only just come to my senses."

"You can't do this." He was angry now and jumped up from the bed and grabbed her arm. "No-one treats me like this. You can't lead me on and then just stop." He tried to force her down on the bed.

"Take your hands off me at once!" She demanded and freed herself from his grip. "Don't try and force me. If you do, you'll regret it. I want to leave. Now take me back to the town."

She began to refasten her dress, and reluctantly he started to dress as well.

"I don't understand you. One minute, you're all passionate and the next you go frigid on me. What's wrong with you? What did I do - or say? Surely, it wasn't what I said about the Earl. I was just joking. Let's face it, this is all just a bit of fun. It's cheating on one's spouse that gives it such a frisson. My god, you're a disappointment. I thought you said you were unconventional. You're nothing of the kind. I'll take you back and I hope that I never set eyes on you again."

As they travelled back on the water, they sat in silence. Aphra looked as though she were made of stone, but inside a dam was about to burst. She knew that she had to control herself until she was alone.

When they reached the town, she climbed up onto the quay without his help.

After he had moored the boat, he said. "Do you want me to accompany to your hotel?"

When she declined, he turned his back on her. She took one last look at him. It struck her that it was a strange irony that he was looking down at the water. He had been doing the same thing that first day at Methuen Park. As she walked away from him, it crossed her mind that he had been admiring his own reflection.

***

It is some hours since I returned to my hotel room. I have just looked in the mirror and my eyes are red and swollen. I have sobbed and sobbed till there seem to be no more tears left.

I have thought over the events of today and I feel such despair. The melancholia is back with a vengeance. Preston had no idea of what was happening to me – which is precisely why I had to draw a halt when I did. Oh, how difficult it was for me to do so. I wanted him so much, but I had to end it with him – as I knew all along that I would.

This is the paradox of my situation. I so long for a loving man with whom I can spend my life. But the kind of man that I want would not be a cheat. The right man would not be conducting this sordid liaison. He would be a man of honour and integrity.

Preston revelled in the idea that he was cuckolding Sebastian and when he said those nasty things, it brought me to my senses.

The reality of my situation is now laid out before me in all its ironic brutality. Now, as these thoughts flood my brain, I suddenly realize how trapped and alone I am. The cell door is closing as I am forced back into my lonely, emotional prison.

***

The following morning, Aphra left the hotel. She had telephoned Claude's hotel in Exeter telling him that she was returning. When he saw her, he knew from her countenance that something was wrong.

"What has happened ma Cherie?"

"I don't want to talk about. Suffice to say - you were right."
He put his arms around her and she broke down and sobbed on his shoulder.

"I should have listened to you, but I was so in love with him. I feel so foolish."

"You are anything but foolish, dearest girl. I understand the affairs of the heart. I have had mine broken once or twice in the past." He handed her a handkerchief.

She looked at him with surprise as she wiped her eyes. "I had no idea that you had been hurt. I assumed that you had always been with Sebastian."

"Mais non. I made some very unwise decisions when I was a very young man. Fortunately, I met Sebastian and we have been very happy together since that time."

They took a stroll around the shops for a short while as Aphra wanted to make a few small purchases for Sophie. The journey back to Methuen Park was unbearable for Aphra. She rested her head on his shoulder and tried to sleep, but she was too upset.

When they arrived home, she managed to put on a brave face and appear cheerful for Sophie, who was very excited to have her mama home again. When she saw that she had surprises, she jumped up and down and clapped her hands in delight. As they entered the house, Sophie chattered excitedly, telling her mama all her news of the last few days. Somehow, Aphra managed to give the impression that she had had a wonderful few days holiday near the sea and mentioned having a ride on a boat, walking, shopping and a few other experiences that she intimated had been great fun.

However, in the days that followed, she took to her bed and told Dorothy that she was unwell and unable to eat. A few times, the maid called in to see if her mistress needed anything, but Aphra did not answer and feigned sleep. Once or twice, Sebastian looked in, but she said very little, other than that she felt unwell. After a week had passed, Claude paid her a visit. He knew that he needed to be careful in case anyone saw him, as his presence in her bedchamber would be considered very inappropriate.

"You need to get up and get some fresh air, ma Cherie. Lying here is not good for you," he said. He walked over and sat on the bed and ran his hand over her hair. "You must not give in to this melancholy. It will make you very ill. Please Aphra, try." But she just turned her head away.

"I shall come back later and every day if necessary, until you do." He kissed her head and left the room.

Eventually, after a few days' coaxing, she gradually began to make a bit of an effort, and a few weeks after her return from Devon, she came downstairs one morning and ate some breakfast. Everyone was shocked to see how thin she had become. Even Sophie noticed that her mama was not herself. However, as the months passed, she did seem to improve and started taking an interest in things again and began to get involved in her charity work and her duties as Sebastian's consort.

***

It is some time since I have written in my journal. I have been very unwell since my return home. I am trying to pick up the threads of my life again, but I am finding it very hard.

The stillness of my heart bothers me. It is quiet in the house and quiet within me – or so it seems. If I allow myself, the pounding comes back and I long for the feelings to return – the madness, the expectation of the next feeling of soaring up into the sky when I am with him.

It is some while since I finished it with him, but the longing – not necessarily for him, but for the passion and the excitement – will not leave me. I fear that I may spend the rest of my life with this insatiable longing – and yet it isn't just the physical longing that haunts me. It is something more than that.

In fact, when I think of Preston, I knew all along that he could not satisfy my needs. I remember those beautiful blue eyes looking into my own with such passion and desire, but if the truth be known, there was little behind them. I see now that what he probably saw in my eyes was his own reflection, which I should imagine was what he was looking at all the time. If one's eyes are the windows of the soul, what sort of soul did he have – did he have a soul at all?

I now realise that what I really long for is the joining of my soul with a compatible other, and that all the physical attraction, desire and climactic passion are merely steps on the journey to reaching that total oneness with a kindred spirit - perhaps one that I shall be joined with to explore eternity.

Twice I have fallen for unsuitable men – firstly, with Thomas in my youth. I was so naïve and unworldly and gave myself to him without thought of the consequences – although I have no regrets about Sophie.

But with Preston, I pulled back in time – although it has left me feeling like this. I feel that I extricated myself from him and retained my integrity and my dignity – perhaps a lucky escape.

No, I will not make the same mistake a third time. I will close my heart and accept that I must live my life alone.

***

Dr Lucas Thornton-Ellis felt very uncomfortable and out of place as he sat at the long table amongst the large number of guests attending the dinner at Clarkes Hotel. He looked down at his place setting with its vast array of silver implements for the many courses. He was far more at home with surgical implements. The middle-aged woman on his left simpered and he had no idea what she was talking about. It was a real effort to try and show some interest – let alone enthusiasm. In his opinion, she was an overdressed, over indulged, vacuous, useless sponge. The unkind thought crossed his mind that he would like to use a surgical implement on her tongue! However, he smiled politely, if coolly, and nodded his head – hoping that he was not required to give some kind of answer.

Why had he let that blasted Grenville woman persuade him to attend this nightmare of a social occasion? He detested these functions and most of the people who attended them. However, a new hospital was urgently needed and if this project was to succeed, then he must be seen to attend and support the fundraising events and to get to know the influential people in the region. Reluctantly, he had agreed to come. He tolerated her, but found it difficult to hide his dislike and contempt of her and her kind. He considered them all to be parasites that thrived on the exploitation of the poor and weak and then salved their consciences by giving a little to charity in the most public and ostentatious manner possible.

He gazed around the room and his attention stopped at the Earl and Countess of Tawford. They were the guests of honour tonight – as they often were at these lavish functions - and were seated in the centre just across the table from him. Lucas thought that the Earl, for all his wealth and privilege, to be a very good man and admired him greatly. He knew that the Earl did much to help those less fortunate than himself and was actively involved in many worthwhile schemes. Lucas had heard numerous tales related by his patients of the kindness and generosity of the Earl – many of them either tenants or employees whose medical expenses were often paid by him. Lucas tried not to stare at his wife, but hard as he might try to drag his eyes away from her, they seemed to find themselves looking at her again of their own volition. She was the focal point of the room as surely as a glowing fire is in the middle of winter. There was not a woman in the room to touch her – not even the ice-maiden herself. It vexed him greatly that he had to struggle to resist the urge to keep returning his gaze to her.

He knew that it was wrong to dislike people without knowing them, but he had disliked the Countess from the first moment Miss Grenville had mentioned her. Apparently, she had been romantically involved with both the Earl and his French secretary whilst still in her employment. It did not bother him that the Countess had been a servant at the time. Generally, he had little time for the aristocracy and admired anyone who earned a living by hard work. No, it was the deceitful way in which she had tricked the Earl into marriage and then continued to cheat on him that he found so despicable. Caroline (he found it hard to think of her as this. He much preferred to keep their relationship on a formal footing, but she insisted that he call her by her Christian name) told him that the Countess had really wanted to marry the Frenchman, but as neither of them had any money she had been forced to marry the Earl when she discovered that she was expecting a child.

"How can you be sure of this?" Lucas asked her.

Caroline told him that she had seen proof of the Countess's infidelity, openly admitting that her housekeeper had steamed open correspondence between her maid and the Frenchman, and that the incriminating letter was still in her possession. She added that the Earl was a fool who would not listen to reason when she had told him that she had evidence which proved that the Frenchman was the father of the child. Initially, he had just laughed at her. Lucas suspected that much of Caroline's behaviour could be attributed to jealousy, for he had heard, that some years earlier, Caroline had gone to Methuen Park expecting a proposal and had left bitterly disappointed.

Caroline shared the information regarding the letter with Lucas, completely unaware of the bad light in which she showed herself. For her, this was very unfortunate, because something had happened to Caroline that no one would have believed possible. She had fallen in love with the handsome young doctor who had recently settled in nearby Westbridge where he had a small practice as well as devoting much of his time to the infirmary there. He was far too serious for her and lacked many of the social graces she deemed necessary to fit in with her social circle.

However, Caroline hoped that she would one day mould him into behaving as she wanted. To gain access to him, she had made a great deal of effort recently becoming involved in as much charity work as possible - even becoming a hospital visitor. Most of it was an absolute bind and she found the working class patients dirty, and conversation with them tedious, and their sores and injuries disgusted her. In fact, sick people irritated her - they were weak and also careless. If she could remain strong and healthy, she could not understand why others could not do the same. She tolerated all of this to impress him and get his attention, but she was unaware that he saw straight through this ruse and it had completely the opposite effect on him.

Lucas had also heard a great deal of gossip about the Countess, the Frenchman and the child from other sources. By all accounts, the girl had none of the physical appearance of the Earl or any of the Raemond line. It was said that she resembled her mother in some ways, but she also had the colouring of the Frenchman. Lucas decided that he would make up his own mind when he eventually saw the child, which he was sure to do before too long. All he knew was that he hated beautiful women who cheated and hurt men, and if what Caroline said was true, then the Countess was the worst of this kind.

He tried to stop his thoughts straying to Lavinia, but they always seemed to rush headlong down the same steep road to that moment when he found out. The emotional pain was excruciating and he tried to blot it out, but it refused to go away. First of all, he remembered the shock at the discovery and then the feeling that he was going to be sick. Then came the pain - the pain that would not go away - even after all these years.

"Doctor, are you all right?" It was one of the other guests.

"Oh. It's nothing - just a mild headache," he replied rubbing his brow.

"You looked miles away. Must be all this hospital business on your mind, the man continued. "I should think that would give you a big headache!"

Lucas smiled and said, "yes, something like that."

As he worked his way through the numerous courses, Lucas turned his attention to the young Frenchman who was engrossed in conversation with a very frail, elderly female seated to his right. He was charming and attentive to the old lady who was having difficulty cutting the meat into smaller pieces. Lucas admired the kind and discreet manner in which the Frenchman assisted her. He seemed like a decent and caring person and Lucas found it hard to believe that he was capable of doing something so underhand as cuckolding his employer and friend.
But just as the final course was being served, something happened that made Lucas wonder whether or not Caroline was telling the truth – for there certainly seemed to be some basis for her allegations. He noticed something that he was sure no one else witnessed – except of course Caroline, for nothing connected with the Countess ever went unobserved by her. The Earl and his wife both had their hands on the table, and as they accidentally touched, Lucas saw the Earl lean his head towards his wife and say something inaudible to anyone else, but obviously of an affectionate nature, for she turned to him and smiled warmly, and as he placed his hand on her wrist in a loving gesture, she then placed hers on his and caressed his hand. Lucas was just thinking how touching this little scenario had been, when he saw her look across the table to the secretary. As her husband turned to speak to someone else, Lucas was in no doubt that as she made eye to eye contact with the Frenchman, there seemed to be a secret and enigmatic signal that passed between them. The Frenchman raised his eyebrows to her and her nod of the head accompanied by a slight smile seemed to confirm all the gossip. He felt very angry and was finding it increasingly difficult to be civil to his fellow guests.

At long last, the meal came to an end and the ladies began to leave the room to take coffee in the lounge, while the men were served port and cigars. Lucas noticed that the Frenchman helped the elderly lady from the room. As he was returning to the dining room, he walked towards the Countess, who was chatting and laughing with a group of the ladies as they exited the room. She stopped and said something to him. He nodded and then put his hands up in a gesture of shaking them as though to negate something that she had said. Then he looked around furtively at the other women and leaned over and whispered in her ear. At this, she nodded and placed her hand on his arm and continued towards the door. They both turned and looked at each other and smiled.

It was at least another hour before Lucas could finally leave. In the carriage home, Caroline immediately remarked, as he knew she would, on the incident between the Countess and the Frenchman.

"You saw it, didn't you?" She said. "I've seen that sort of thing happen a number of times in the past. It makes me sick," she continued in this spiteful vein for the rest of the journey.

Her carriage made a detour to drop him off first. As he got out of the carriage, he turned and said to her. "You need to try and focus your mind on something else Miss Grenville - eh Caroline. This obsession that you have with the Countess is not good for your health and is making you bitter. I hope that perhaps your hospital visits next week will help to give you a more balanced perspective about life. Witnessing the troubles of those less fortunate than yourself may help you to appreciate your own good fortune."

He tipped his hat to her. "Goodnight." He walked towards his modest house. Caroline tapped for the driver to move on. She fumed with rage at his remarks, but worse than this, she felt very sad at his obvious dislike of her. Was there nothing that she could do to make him love her? Sadness was a new and unwelcome emotion for her.

***

We attended a social gathering in Taunton this evening. We are staying at Clarkes for a few days – they always make us so comfortable. Claude has returned to Methuen Park to attend to some business matters for Seb. The whole thing was very tedious for me – although Sebastian was very kind and attentive as usual. What a dear man he is.

Claude was also very kind to Mrs Palmer. I noticed him helping her with her food. Her sight is now so very bad and her hands shake a great deal. I think that these events are really too much for her. I had said that it was not necessary for her to come, but she really wanted to help and added that it is nice to get out of the house sometimes. She told me a few weeks ago how much she wants the new hospital to be built.

Apparently, as Claude escorted her from the dining room, she told him that she needed help in a personal matter and was obviously very embarrassed to have to ask him. He quickly returned and spoke to me, being extra careful that no-one should overhear what he said to me. I tried to be of assistance to her. She'd had a little accident, but I managed to clean her up a little. She reminded me of dear Mrs Brookes. Becoming old and infirm can be so cruel.

Caroline was there. Need I say more! Actually, I have seen very little of her over the last few years. However, it is inevitable that our paths should cross from time to time. She was accompanied by a tall, dark haired man who scowled throughout the whole meal. More than once, I detected him staring at me with what seemed like real hostility. I felt most uncomfortable. When we were introduced, it was all he could do to be civil towards me. He seemed courteous enough towards Sebastian, so I made an excuse to vacate the room and left them talking together. Perhaps he doesn't like women. He certainly doesn't like me – and the feeling is mutual. I shall do my best to avoid him in future. Caroline seems to admire him and I wonder if she is hoping for a proposal of marriage. She certainly seems to hang around him and tries to monopolise his attention. As far as I'm concerned, they're welcome to each other.

***

The following day, Sebastian and Aphra were seated in the carriage on their way back to Methuen Park.

"That Doctor seems a nice chap," said Sebastian. "He has some good ideas for the new hospital. Just the sort of thing we need in this part of the world."

Aphra said nothing for a few moments trying to find an appropriate response. She felt like saying something caustic, for she was not in a good mood. She had been somewhat out of sorts since the dinner. Seeing Caroline always reminded her of her dismissal and the dreadful months following it.

"That's good," she said, trying to inject some enthusiasm into her voice.

"What sort of things has he in mind?"

"Oh, he was telling me about anaesthetics like chloroform, ether, nitrous oxide and also about the work of Lister and Pasteur. He's a clever chap and wants this new hospital to have the most up to date surgical rooms, and he's a great believer in vaccines. Oh, I can't remember all the things that we discussed. Suffice to say, he'll be a good man to have at the helm."

"Well, it sounds as though he knows his subject. He struck me as a rather taciturn man. Am I incorrect in my judgement of him?" She enquired.

"Do you know? I think that he's very shy. He doesn't enjoy these social functions one bit and seems to be very out of place. That's probably all there is to it. Also, I heard that there was some tragedy regarding his wife - don't know the exact details. Apparently, he took it very badly. Can't say I blame him. If I lost Claude, I don't think that I'd survive it. I certainly shouldn't feel very sociable."

She was quiet for a while and then added. "Perhaps it's just women he doesn't like. He seemed to get on very well with you," she said.

"Give it time, dear. You'll probably become firm friends with him. You'll need to spend quite a bit of time with him, so I hope that you two can get along."

"I'll do my best," she replied rather grudgingly.

"I'm sure you will. You always rise to the challenge. I'm glad to see that you are happier these days, Aphra, and that you have managed to put that unfortunate business behind you. You seem much more like your old self. It's nice to have you back my dear." He gently patted her hand.

She smiled at him. "It's nice to be back."

When they arrived at Methuen Park, they were met by Travis.

"Shall I send tea up to you and the Earl?"

"Oh, yes please. I think that we're both ready for it. It's been a long and tiresome journey."

Later, when she got to her room, she found Dorothy had already begun unpacking for her.

"Thank you. I'll see to the rest of it. Could you please take a look at my blue gown? I spilt something on it."

"Very well, Milady."

***

Well, so much for avoiding the doctor. We seem to be forced to attend the same functions and events. He seems to be such a boring man. He has almost nothing to say to anyone and makes little effort to converse. Fortunately, I'm usually successful in avoiding actual contact and he does not seek me out, but it isn't always the case.

Sebastian and I have just returned from a memorial service for a local dignitary. He was not someone that I had ever met and Sebastian only knew him slightly. We only attended because of Sebastian's position.

I was surprised to see the doctor there, for being new to the neighbourhood, I would not have expected him to know the deceased. I asked Sebastian why he would have been there and it seems that they had been in meetings regarding the building of the new hospital. "Old Jackson was very much in favour of the plans and would have been a great supporter. It's a shame that he's gone. However, he was nearly eighty and had been in ill-health for some time."

The choir began singing and the coffin was brought into the church and Sebastian and I ceased our conversation. The funeral was much the same as many we attended before – hymns, sermon and eulogies.

After the service, outside the church, Sebastian made a point of speaking to the widow to offer his condolences. As we were saying goodbye to her, Sebastian said "Ah, here's our friend the doctor. Let's go and say hello."

"Oh Seb, do I have to?" I knew my voice sounded like a whining child, but I just wasn't in the mood for any more gloom and doom.

"Come now, my dear. We must be kind to the man."
"Why don't you go and speak to him, and I'll just take a stroll around the churchyard. You know the man can't stand me and he makes me feel uncomfortable."

"Aphra, I can't believe that you are taking this attitude towards the man. He's quite harmless. It's not like you to behave in this way. Come now. It's our duty."

Suitably admonished, I reluctantly agreed and put my arm through Sebastian's and walked over to the doctor.

"Hello Lucas," Sebastian said holding out his hand. "A sad occasion. Jackson was a good man."

"Yes indeed," said the doctor, shaking hands with him. He looked towards me and nodded. "Countess," he said. I noticed that he had very unusual light brown eyes. They would have been considered attractive, if it wasn't for the coldness with which they beheld me.

I responded with a nod of the head too.

"A sad business," said Sebastian.

"Very sad," replied the doctor. "It will be a great loss. I had been looking forward to working with him. He had already done much to get things started."

"Then we mustn't let all that good work go to waste," said Sebastian. "My wife is eager to become more involved and I'm sure that you will find her to be a very useful asset to the cause."

The doctor turned to look at me and I returned his gaze with the briefest look. I made some trite comment and he, in turn made a similar remark back. The two men discussed generalities for a few minutes and then we made our farewells.

"Thank God that's over," I said with a childish sigh of relief as I climbed into the carriage. "It's such a strain having to deal with that man."

"I don't know what you have against him. I find him very civil. Yes, he's rather shy and perhaps a little taciturn, but I think that with a little help from you, he could find himself more at ease in company. You're usually so good with people Aphra. I don't understand this antagonism towards him."

"I'm sorry. I promise to try harder in future. I'll have to if I'm to work with him."

We spent the rest of the journey home in silence and I think that Sebastian was rather annoyed with me.

***

This evening, we attended yet another charity function to raise funds for the new hospital. Dr Lucas - as everyone seems to call him - gave a speech. What a surprise! He was quite magnificent. It was as though he had come to life. He spoke so eloquently and articulately about what was obviously his passion and managed to transmit that enthusiasm to others - including me! He even smiled a few times. Goodness – what a difference. I hadn't noticed before. He's actually very handsome!

Afterwards, Sebastian insisted that we congratulate him. I was reluctant to face the ordeal of his unfriendly nature, but Sebastian's warmth, together with his confident and outgoing personality, made it easier and I felt that I could hide behind this.

I made polite but brief comments and then after a short time, made my excuses and escaped to speak to Mrs Hillard about some church committee business that needed discussing the following week.

I think that all in all, the evening was very successful and that substantial sums will be raised for the hospital. It is a most deserving cause and I am very hopeful that it will come to fruition.

***

I'm glad that this evening is over. To begin with, it was quite an ordeal - for I was so nervous. Yet, once I got started, I felt quite fired up. In fact, if I'm honest, I almost enjoyed it. I think that the evening was a success and that the financial support is going to be there for the project. The Earl's patronage will be instrumental in getting things started. He is a good man and so devoted to his wife. It is hard to believe what Caroline has told me about her, for she appears to return his feelings. Perhaps Caroline is mistaken about the secretary.

The Countess is certainly a charming woman – although she does not try out her charms on me. In fact, I think that she is quite hostile towards me, despite trying to conceal it beneath a veneer of civility. She probably knows that her beautiful smile which lights up her perfect features would be wasted on me. I am not to be swayed by such wiles. I made that mistake when I allowed myself to be fooled by Lavinia. I try not to think about her, for the pain is still so intense, but she has a habit of creeping into my mind - even though she has been dead all these years.

When I think of that night, I feel physically sick. I must not think of it. I must try and forget. I must keep busy.

***

The fundraising for the hospital had been so successful, that work soon began on drawing up the plans. Sebastian was very keen that Aphra should be on the planning committee in place of him.

"I think that it will be good for you to be involved with this project. You'll gain much experience from it. Besides, I have so many demands on my time, that I just cannot fit it in."

"But Sebastian, I know nothing about this kind of thing. It needs expertise and experience and I have neither," she argued.

"Aphra, you have intelligence, education, common sense and a great deal of experience of all manner of things. Also, you learn things quickly. Look how well you run this house, manage the servants with tact and diplomacy and don't forget the life that you lead before you lived here. Surely, that is more experience of life than most people can lay claim to."

Reluctantly, she agreed to take on the task knowing that it would force her to have to spend even more time with Dr Lucas.

The following week, she welcomed the committee members, including Dr Lucas. He arrived a few minutes before the others and spent a short time briefing her on the matters to be discussed. These included the plans, finding an appropriate site and the date that the work was to begin on the foundations of the building. Aphra soon found that she was very interested in the whole project.

She invited everyone into the large parlour on the south side of the house. After she had introduced everyone, it was soon agreed that she would act as the chairwoman of the committee. Initially, she declined, but was eventually persuaded to accept. Time passed swiftly and soon the meeting was over. When all the others had left, Dr Lucas coldly thanked her for her part in it.

"You're most accomplished at this sort of thing Countess," he said. "You appear very experienced in this field."

"No, Doctor." Her response was equally cool. "But I intend to do my best. My husband is very keen for me to become involved with this project. As I'm sure Miss Grenville has told you, I have had experience of a life different from that of a Countess. The Earl believes that it will prove useful in what I can bring to establishing a good hospital in this area."

"Yes, she did touch briefly on your previous acquaintance with her," he said, and then added, "I'm sure that your vast and varied experience of life will bring a different dimension to our discussions."

"I'm sure that she did more than touch briefly on our relationship. I am very aware of her feelings towards me. She has made no secret of them. However, I thank you for your confidence in my ability to carry out my duties in this respect. I have no doubt that working long hours, being awoken in the middle of the night to deal with trivial tasks, carrying and fetching, lugging buckets of water to fill and empty a hip bath when a modern bathroom with hot and cold running water was available down the corridor, lighting fires in midsummer, composing responses to correspondence, running up and down stairs with trays, biting my tongue when being verbally abused, repairing and cleaning gowns that have been treated carelessly, listening to someone complaining at the difficulties of her life when she has every luxury at hand, being constantly criticised no matter how hard I worked, will bring a different dimension to our discussions. Yes, Doctor, I agree with you. It will prove very useful. I hope that I shall be able to empathise with the hospital staff and patients alike." As she was saying this, she gathered up her papers. "Well, I mustn't keep you Doctor. No doubt you have much to do - as have I. I wish you a safe journey home."

He looked chastened as he walked towards the door and held it open for her. She walked through briskly with her papers clasped in her arms. "I bid you good day." She gave him a brief cold smile that did not reach her eyes, and then walked up the stairs. He bowed and turned away.

Travis was hovering in the hallway. He handed the doctor his hat and cane and opened the main door.

"Good afternoon sir," said the butler with a slight bow.

"Thank you," came the brusque response.

The doctor placed his hat on his head and walked through the door and down the steps to his waiting carriage.

From the top of the stairs, Aphra watched as Travis closed the door and disappeared into the servants' quarters.

"Irksome and infuriating man!" She thought and strutted off to her room.

***

By the time the foundation stone was laid at the end of April, Aphra and Lucas had at least formed a reasonably civil working relationship. Aphra discovered that he had a quiet, dry sense of humour and he observed her natural humanity. She had become a frequent visitor at the old infirmary, and unlike Caroline, took a genuine interest in the patients - often annoying Matron by sitting on the patients' beds, holding their hands and chatting with them. This was strictly forbidden and no-one else would have been allowed to get away with it. Matron said nothing to the Countess, although inwardly she fumed. However, she did once complain about it to the Doctor and when he mentioned it to Aphra, she just did it all the more, which rather amused him. She would often bring small gifts –things that could not embarrass them - like ointment for dry skin, some lavender for their pillows, or something seasonal from the kitchen garden or orchard. Matron was affronted at the flowers that Aphra arranged and placed in a prominent position in the ward.

"They're most unhygienic Milady," she once said, trying to control her rage at her authority being undermined.

"Nonsense! These beautiful blooms will help to lift our patients' spirits. A little colour in this drab room can surely do no harm." At this, she turned to seek their opinions. Naturally, they all agreed with her, much to the chagrin of the Matron. Aphra had experienced enough of overbearing, spiteful shrews using their positions of power over others. She wasn't going to allow this harridan to beat her.

"Now Matron. I don't want to hear that these flowers have been removed during the day. Obviously, they can be taken out at night, but I trust that they will be returned the following morning. Please ensure that all members of your staff are aware of my request. Besides, I hope that you too will derive joy from them as well. I believe that having a joyful spirit can have much benefit for the body too

Lucas was attending to one of the patients further along the ward and the elderly lady, whose pulse he was taking, was surprised to see a furtive smile appear at the corners of his mouth upon listening to this exchange. She had always thought of him as being much too serious and buttoned up.

Later, when the patients were on their own, she said, "Dr Lucas thought that very funny."

A large, red-faced woman in the bed opposite replied. "Really! 'e always seem to 'ave such a long face."

"Well it weren't that long. E' were killin 'imself laffin, I can tell 'ee." She sat up and forward to add emphasis. E' don't like ol' frostyknickers."

They all started to chuckle. One laughed so much that it precipitated a coughing fit.

"Well no-one like 'er, do 'e."

"Now Milady's a bonny lass and our doc 'as a soft spot for 'er," said a toothless elderly woman.

"No, 'E ain't interested in women. 'E just thinks about 'is work."

"Oh yeah. Then why do 'e blush every-time 'e see 'er? I's telling yer, that's a man in love!"

"I 'ear there's been a few a them. It be said that she carryin on with the froggy fella."

"No. She too much a lady an' a real goodun. She wouldn'a' cheat on 'is Lordship."

"Well, I 'ears from Sally - 'er youngest works up at "the Park", that there are all kinda goins on with that fella. They're as thick as thieves - specially when master ain't at 'ome. Why, only the other day, she told me that ...."

At this moment, the Matron entered the ward and the conversation came to a close. She muttered something about the unpleasant and overpowering scent of the flowers. The patients waited until she went out and started laughing, but eventually became quiet again as they exhausted themselves.

***

As the walls of the new hospital were erected, Aphra became very interested in all aspects connected with it. One day, Lucas and she were walking around the site. He pointed out where the different rooms would be.

"That part there will be the operating theatre and next to it is the anaesthesia room," he said.

"And what is that section over there?" She asked pointing to an area that was slightly separate from the rest of the building. "Is that the isolation ward?"

"Yes. I'm just hoping that it will be big enough. If we have an outbreak of one of the infectious diseases like there was last year, then we could be overwhelmed."

As they walked around the site, they discussed the various problems to be addressed and agreed that further consultations with the committee and the planners were necessary.

Aphra found the subject of medicine most absorbing and wanted to know all about the latest discoveries and treatments. Lucas welcomed and encouraged this interest by lending her some of his text books and teaching her all manner of things about his chosen subject. He was impressed by her enthusiasm and the fact that she did not flinch if the details became too descriptive and gory. He thought that she would make an excellent Doctor. She had the intelligence and the strength of character that would stand a medic in good stead.

However, no sooner had the word character come into his mind, so his thoughts returned to that old doubt about the paternity of her daughter. He found that he had this internal wrestling regarding the Countess. On the one hand, she seemed to be a woman of great strength of character - albeit, a rather feisty one. However, on the other hand, there was this question about her fidelity to her husband. Lucas tried not to think about it, but his thoughts continually strayed to her and he had to fight off the growing feelings of affection and admiration that he had towards her. After all, what good would falling in love with her do? He would never indulge in a clandestine affair with a married woman.

***

Sebastian often invited Lucas to stay at Methuen Park, and Aphra noticed that he rarely refused an invitation these days. Sometimes, there were parties, or smaller, social gathering and although he did not really like crowds of people, he still attended. However, it was often just the family – and Emily, Henry and their children. These were the times that Aphra loved best.

A stroll around the lake had become a regular activity. Sometimes, all of them would take the walk after lunch, but more often than not, Aphra and Lucas would do so on their own. Aphra was beginning to find his company very enjoyable. The park was lovely in all the seasons, but particularly so in the autumn. There had been one afternoon in early October that she looked back on with particular fondness. Lucas and she had begun the walk discussing the hospital which was nearing completion. For some reason, the conversation had turned to their respective childhoods and formative years.

Aphra began to talk about her father and the day that she and her mother had discovered him with Agnes. "It was such a shock. Of course, at the time, I didn't understand the full significance, but I did understand that my mother was suffering terribly. She just cried and cried. Sometimes she did not come out of her room for days. She was never the same after that. She just seemed to fade away. She tried her best to get over it and I know that she was pretending to be jolly around me, but she could not hide the deadness that seemed to be taking her over. Two years later, she was dead from a tumour. I lay on the bed next to her and held her in my arms as she passed away.

Before she died, she emphasised to me the importance of fidelity, and also choosing one's life partner wisely. She said that someone who would cheat in their private life, would be dishonest elsewhere. I have tried my best to follow her advice. As I have got older, I have understood the significance of her words."

Lucas thought that she had a very faraway look about her as she quietly said. "Looking back over my life, I see that I have made foolish choices which I now regret, but there is nothing that I can do about it. I must live with the consequences of those decisions."

They were both silent for a few minutes. Then Lucas said. "I can appreciate your mother's pain. I too have experienced the deep hurt of betrayal. My wife, Lavinia, died some years ago. A few weeks after the funeral, when I began to go through her possessions, I discovered letters from another man. There was no doubt in my mind that they were involved in a love affair. Like your mother, I was deeply shocked. Also, she was dead, so I could not even talk to her. I became very depressed and I have to admit that I became a very angry man. I am now trying to separate my feelings of anger towards her from those towards other people. I know that I cannot blame everyone for her weakness and cruelty, but it does seem to have tainted the way I feel about everyone and everything."

"I am so sorry, Lucas. It must have been terrible for you - such suffering. I wish that there was something that I could do or say that would be a comfort to you, but I realise that nothing I can say can heal your pain."

They stopped walking and sat on a bench overlooking the lake. After a few minutes, Aphra's faraway look had returned as she said, "sometimes marriages have secrets and people on the outside of that inner sanctum cannot begin to understand. Triangles are difficult, but sometimes triangles can be inverted and everything is different."
"I don't understand what you mean," he said confused.

Suddenly, it was as though she had woken up from a trance. "Sorry, what did you say?"

"What are you talking about? I don't quite ..."

"Oh, just ignore me. I'm talking nonsense. Let's get back indoors. The light is beginning to fade and there is a distinct chill in the air."

She got up and slowly started to walk back along the path. Lucas followed her, wondering to himself what on earth she had been talking about. Was she confessing to having cuckolded her husband? It sounded like it - and yet he was not sure.

Their journey back to the house took twenty minutes and they spent the remainder of the walk in the comfortable silence of those truly at ease with one another. However, just before they reached the house, she put her hand on his arm and said. "I do believe that people who betray their spouses are guilty of a terrible act. The damage that they do can be as harmful as an assault - even murder. I am so sorry that you have had all this pain to bear and I hope that one day your heart will be free of this cruel legacy that your wife left you. I pray that you will be free to love and be happy, which is what you deserve, for you are a truly good man."

After this, it felt as though they had crossed a line in their friendship and many of their future walks were conducted in the same peaceful, quiet manner with many confidences shared.

As time passed, Aphra realised that her feelings for him had changed. Although they never once indicated this to each other, both felt instinctively that their own feelings were reciprocated.

***

Lucas joined the family at Christmas. He had no close family, so the Earl invited him for the holiday. At first, Lucas had been reluctant to accept the invitation. He felt very uncomfortable about his growing affection for the Countess, which he knew to be inappropriate. However, when danger loomed in the form of an invitation from Caroline, he made up his mind quickly and agreed to spend the festive season at Methuen Park. As a Doctor, he was always on duty to some extent, but he found that he was actually looking forward to a few days' break from the constant hard work and interrupted sleep. Another Doctor, a friend from medical school wanting to escape London over the holiday for some mysterious reason, had agreed to cover for him over the Christmas period. So Lucas was hoping that if no major emergency arose, then he could relax for at least two or three days.

He arrived at Methuen Park late on Christmas Eve. It was just beginning to snow and as the carriage made its way up the drive, he thought how pretty the snow was as it settled on the leaves of the trees and the rhododendron bushes. Approaching the house, it surprised him that he was suddenly filled with a sense of joy. Light shone out from every window and reflected on the snow and it made him feel very welcome. It was as though he had been transported into a fairy-tale world.

As he stepped from the carriage, he stood still and listened to the silence. It was as though a vast comforting blanket covered and sheltered him from the trials and tribulations of life. A footman descended the steps and took his luggage. "Good evening Doctor. It looks as though we are going to have a white Christmas. Please take care, sir. We have not yet salted these steps."

"Thank you. I'll be careful."

As Lucas entered the vestibule, Sebastian greeted him warmly. "What a night! Come on into the drawing room. We have a good fire going in here."

Claude rose from his chair by the fireside. "Good evening Lucas. Please - take this seat." He indicated the chair. Lucas gratefully accepted and sat opposite Aphra and Sophie. As he had entered the room, he had noticed that they were both engrossed in a picture book. Aphra closed the book and greeted Lucas.

"Sophie," she said. "Go and say hello to Dr Lucas." The little girl stood up and walked over to him.

"Good evening sir. It's very nice to see you again," she said very politely and curtsied. Then held out her hand to him. Lucas was not sure whether he was supposed to shake it or kiss it. He decided to give it a rather limp shake and said "it's very nice to see you again Lady Sophie."

"I think young lady that it's well past your bedtime now. Come on. I'll finish reading this to you upstairs. Say goodnight to papa and Uncle Claude," said her mother.

The little girl embraced both Sebastian and Claude in such a way as to leave no doubt of her deep affection for them both. Then she turned and said "goodnight Dr Lucas. Will you be here for Christmas?"

"I certainly will Lady Sophie and I'm really looking forward to it as I expect you are too," he replied.

"I'm looking forward to it very much. I have some big parcels under the tree, but I'm not allowed to open them until mama and papa give me permission, which isn't fair because Paul and Stella are allow.."
"That's enough, you little madam. Off to bed with you," chided the Earl, feigning to clip her on the ear. As Aphra and Sophie left the room, Sebastian fetched Lucas a whisky. "Can we get you something to eat?"

Lucas told him that he had eaten supper at *The Swan*. "I thought it best to stop and eat on the way as I would be arriving so late. To be honest, I'm very tired. I had a very early start this morning. Would you think me impolite if I retired for the night?"

"Not at all," said Sebastian. "I'm pretty tired myself. The last few days have been quite hectic with preparations for the festivities – and Sophie wears us all out with her chatter and excitement," he added as he rang the bell for a servant to take Lucas to his room.

"She's a pretty child," said Lucas as he stood up. "Who does she take after?"

"Oh, she's much more like her mother than me," said the Earl. "She doesn't look anything like me or my family. She must be a throwback to some earlier generation," he laughed heartily as there was a light tap at the door and Henry, recently promoted to under butler, entered the room. "Could you please take the Doctor up to his room?" Henry stood patiently holding the door open.

"Goodnight Lucas," said Sebastian. "If there's anything that you need, Henry here will arrange it for you. I hope that you get a restful night. It'll be an early start – Sophie will see to that!" Then turning to Henry, he added. "I don't expect that you and Emily will get much sleep either. The little ones will have you both awake at the crack of dawn."

"Indeed Sir. They have been so excited, that I'm not sure they'll sleep at all tonight. Emily is worn out with their non-stop chatter and constant pleading to open the parcels."

"Well, after you have seen the Doctor upstairs, get off home yourself. I'll see you tomorrow."

Everyone exchanged wishes for a good night and then Sebastian and Claude were alone.

"Ah, the best time of the day – when we can be alone and ourselves at last," he said as he sat down next to Claude.

***

As Lucas settled down for the night, he thought about Sophie. She was a delightful little girl and there was definitely a similarity between her and her mother, but as the Earl had stated, she looked nothing like him. Then Lucas turned his attention to the secretary. There was a definite resemblance between him and the girl, although it was nothing marked – just a similarity of fair hair and of course, the eye colour, which was an exceptional, brilliant blue in both cases. He pondered on these matters before drifting off to sleep.

***

Dear Mildred,

I am writing this just before I go to bed. I want to be up early in the morning, to see that all the arrangements are carried out as planned.

Well, the feast of Our Lord's birth has come around again I can tell you that it has been all go here for the last few weeks. Not that I'm complaining. I really enjoy the festivities and the Master and Mistress are very thoughtful about how the servants enjoy themselves.

Of course, I've had to chivvy up one or two of the girls. We have a new one, who is a bit lazy, but I think that I am winning with her and she is improving.

We have a lovely big tree in the hall as one comes into the house. There is also another one in the drawing room. There is a huge pile of presents under the tree and I expect that the majority of them are for a special little lady. The little darling has been so excited for over a week now and is driving everyone up the wall with her questions and requests to open parcels.

Dr Lucas arrived a short while ago in a terrible snowstorm. At first, I thought him to be a rather surly man, but he has grown on me during the last few months. He has become more relaxed and easy going - well he certainly is when he's here.

He does seem to spend a great deal of time in the company of the Countess. The other week, he came for a few days. After Sunday lunch, the two of them took a walk down by the lake as seems to be their habit. I can see that part of the estate from the window of my sitting room. I saw them leave, and when I looked out an hour later, they were sitting together on one of the stone benches near the woods. Then, when I looked out about another hour later, they were nowhere to be seen. I know that they had not come back to the house, for I had kept an eye on the path. Also, I can hear if someone walks that way. I had my window open, for the day was close. When they did return, they seemed to be very deep in conversation. I know that they work together on the hospital project, but I feel that it is something more than that. Of course, I know that I should not say such things. After all, she is my employer, but I know that I can count on you not to let this go any further.

She still spends a lot of time with Monsieur - although when the doctor is around, he seems to keep his distance. It is all very perplexing. Still, it is not my place to question the ways of the aristocracy.

Well, I shall close as I am quite fatigued and there is much to organise in the morning. I wish you the compliments of the season and trust that the coming year will favour you with good health.

Your friend

Hetty

***

As predicted, Sophie was awake very early in spite of finding it difficult to get to sleep. She got up and switched on the electric light. She liked these switches. It was so nice being able to do it herself. She was not allowed to touch candles or oil lamps. She looked at the clock on the mantelpiece. It was just past six o clock. Mama said that she was not to go into her room until after seven thirty. She shivered and put on her dressing gown and slippers. She looked around at her toys. The shelves were full of books. She took down one or two, but could not concentrate. There was a jigsaw puzzle that she had been working on, but she had done it many times and it was boring. In the corner, was a small table laid for tea. Around the table sat three dollies and Mr Punch, who had one eye missing and was slumped in his chair.

"It's time for breakfast," she said. "Who's going to pour the tea? What about you Mr Punch. You've been very lazy of late." She pretended that he was carrying out this activity, but again her interest waned. Her heart was not in it. The idea of food and drink was now in her mind. She decided that she would go down to the kitchen in search of refreshment.

On her way down the stairs, she met Dr Lucas. "Merry Christmas doctor," she said, trying to sound grown up and dignified.

"And a very Merry Christmas to you too."

"You're up very early. Are you excited?" Asked Sophie.

"Do you know, I think that I am?"

"Me too. I can't sleep. I want to open my presents."

As they descended the stairs, a footman walked towards them. "May I be of assistance?" He enquired.

Lucas went to speak, but before he could do so, Sophie said in an effort to sound imperious.

"We'll take some hot milk in the drawing room. Oh and some toast too and chocolate cake – and if there are any gingerbread men, we'll take them too."

The footman walked over to the drawing room door and held it open. The fire was already burning brightly and they went in.

"Would you like me to bring you some tea Sir?" Asked the footman.

At this, Sophie realised that she had made a mistake in not including the Doctor's needs when giving her orders. "Oh yes, and some tea for the Doctor." She then remembered how mama and papa were always stressing good manners. "Thank you."

A few minutes later, Lucas sat by the fire sipping his hot tea. He watched Sophie with amusement as she lifted one parcel after another from under the tree and then replaced them with a rather sulky expression on her face. "It's not fair that I have to wait so long to open my presents. Emily's children will have opened theirs by now. Why do I have to wait? It's gone seven and mama should be up."

"What time does she normally get up?"

Sophie thought about this and bit her lip. "I don't really know. She usually comes and awakens me."

Suddenly, the door opened and Aphra walked in. "Mama!" Squealed the little girl with delight as she ran towards her mother. "May I open my presents?"

"Merry Christmas Sophie," said Aphra with a mock admonishing look. As she said this, she discreetly wiped chocolate cake from the little girl's face with a lace handkerchief.

Looking suitably chastised, Sophie replied, "Merry Christmas mama. Shall I pour you some tea?"

"Yes please. That will be most welcome." Turning to Lucas, Aphra wished him the complements of the season. "I see that my daughter is playing hostess. I hope that she is looking after you well."

"Very well, thank you Countess," he replied.

"Do you think that we could dispense with the titles? I think that we know each other well enough. You are now a friend of the family – almost one of us now – so please call me Aphra."

His response was to agree with her and she held out her hand to him. "Thank you. Merry Christmas Lucas."

Sophie handed her a cup of very strong, sweet, luke-warm tea and hovered expectantly.

Aphra thanked her and sipped slowly. "Ah lovely," she exclaimed. "I suppose you've earned one small present – only one, mind you, until later." As Sophie ran over to the tree, Aphra placed the cup and saucer on the table next to her and grimaced. She leant across to Lucas and whispered. "It's a bit early in the day for cold stew!" They exchanged conspiratorial smiles.

***

Christmas lunch was a very happy and informal occasion, with the servants placing the dishes on the table and leaving the family to serve themselves. As Sebastian carved the goose, he explained to Lucas that the servants would now be enjoying their own festivities downstairs.

"I expect that quite a few of them will be the worse for wear afterwards and little use for anything. It's a good thing that Travis and a few of the others are tee-total, otherwise we'd be washing the dishes ourselves," he chuckled.

Claude then said. "Yes, but Aphra likes to roll up her sleeves and wash the dishes. Is that not so, Emily?"

Lucas thought this a strange comment. Aphra noticed the puzzled expression on his face.

"We have a little cottage on the estate, a few miles from here, where we like to escape to sometimes with the children, don't we Emily. It's great fun. They like to run in the woods and fish in the river and I just enjoy getting away from being Countess for a few days - and yes, I don't mind getting my hands dirty," she smiled at him and he noticed the genuine warmth in the smile that now reached her eyes. "Perhaps next time we stay there, you'll come and visit us."

"Oh yes Dr Lucas. You can come with me to catch tiddlers and tadpoles," said Sophie. "And Paul knows all the best trees to climb."

"I shall be delighted – although I'm not too sure about the tree climbing," Lucas replied.

He found this manner of dining much more to his liking and he suspected that everyone else felt the same, even Sebastian. Sophie was impatient to have the meal over, so that she could open more presents. Earlier, when they had all gathered in the drawing room at about ten thirty, a few gifts had been exchanged, but the majority of them were to be distributed after lunch. Lucas found himself warming to Aphra as the day wore on. Gone was the public persona of the Countess. Today, she was being herself – mother, wife and friend. Lucas could not remember being this happy for a long time.

***

At Warrington Grange, Caroline sat eating in the dining room. Each time she placed her knife or fork on the bone china plate, it echoed loudly. She took a sip of her Madeira. Isaacs stood to attention by the door.

"Oh leave me in peace," she snapped, waving her hand in a dismissive gesture. "I'll ring for you if I need anything else."

"Yes, Ma'am." He bowed slightly and closed the door behind him. His departure seemed to make the echoing even louder.

He, in his turn, was glad to escape from her bad temper. Besides, he was quite hungry and none of the servants had eaten lunch. She had been so difficult today, that everything was behind. He walked into the servants' hall. Everyone was present, with the exception of the housekeeper, who was visiting her sister.

"Can I dish up now?" Asked Gracie.
"Please do, Mrs Flowers," he said opening a bottle of elderberry wine. "I think we all need a glass of this. It's been a very difficult morning."

"I should say so," said Gracie. "I've just about had enough of all this chopping and changing.

As they sat down and began to tuck into their tasty meals, he couldn't help but think about that Christmas a few years ago, when Aphra and Emily had been here. It had been such a happy occasion – well, except for that nasty business at the end.

"To absent friends," he toasted.

***

Caroline listened as the footsteps disappeared down the corridor. She had never felt so unhappy in her life. In fact, she had never before even suspected that one could feel such sadness. When her invitation for Lucas to come and stay had been refused, she was at first disappointed, but when she discovered that he would be spending the holiday at Methuen Park, she seethed with rage. Politely, he had written that he could not refuse the Earl's invitation. She knew that Lucas and Sebastian had become firm friends, but it was not only this reason that had persuaded the hardworking and dedicated Doctor to take a few days off. At first, Caroline had merely had suspicions, but now she was certain of the real reason for his enthusiasm. She had seen him looking at Aphra and she knew the cause. Why was it that she was able to entice every man to be infatuated with her? It all seemed so unfair.

She remembered back to the first time that she had met her at that interview so many years earlier. How could Caroline have thought that she was unattractive and no threat to her? The blasted girl had been a thorn in her side ever since.

She tried to eat her food, but she had no appetite. After a few more minutes of picking at it, she got up and left the room. There was nothing for it, but to go to her room, where she could let the mask of indifference slip. After turning the key, she walked over to the bed and flung herself upon the damask cover and did something very rare for her, she wept.

***

During the winter months, when he visited Methuen Park, Aphra and Lucas still continued their walks. If it was not too cold or damp, they would sit for a while on the little seat below a pergola which supported some magnificent roses in the summer.

However, if the pathways were either too wet or slippery, they would often sit in the drawing room by the fire. He would read and she would sew – often in companionable silence. Claude had observed their closeness and he and Seb would deliberately find an excuse to vacate the room, leaving them alone.

She had also discovered that he played the pianoforte, and had a fine tenor voice. Many were the times when the sound of their duets could be heard around the house.

Once, during the following summer, when she and Emily were at the cottage, he joined them for Sunday lunch, and afterwards sat with her in the garden watching the children playing. He had arrived a bit early, and was surprised to find both women picking fruit and vegetables for the meal. Emily was up a ladder collecting cooking apples and Aphra, wearing a pinafore over her rather plain dress and a pair of old boots, was digging up potatoes. The children were helping. There was much laughter as they helped fill baskets and carry them to the cottage door.

"There is so much here that we will never eat it all ourselves," said Emily, handing an apple to Paul. "I'll get Henry to organise a cart to collect it."

"That sounds like an excellent idea," said Aphra, wiping the sweat from her brow. "Phew, I'm hot. I need a cool drink. Sophie what's the time?"

Her daughter told her that it was almost noon.

"Goodness! I must go and tidy myself up. Our guest will be here soon. Look at the state of me?"

"You do look a bit of a sight," laughed Emily. "Like something the cat dragged in." The children all thought that this was very funny and they all began to repeat Emily's remark.

"Well, I'd better go and tidy myself and check that meat as well. We don't want to be serving charred remnants."

"No, we don't want a repeat of the other night," teased Emily, as she descended the ladder.

"Well thank you very much for your vote of confidence," laughed Aphra as she disappeared into the cottage.

Lucas watched all of this from a distance where he was hidden by some bushes. Realising that his early arrival would cause Aphra some embarrassment, he quietly retraced his steps and walked back up the lane. He thought about the scene that he had just observed and knew for certain at this moment, that he loved her very much. She had commented on her dishevelled appearance, being concerned that it would give him the wrong impression of her. But she was so wrong. In fact, he loved her all the more for it.

He felt a stab of despair as he realised that all he wanted was to live in a little cottage with her and for them to be in the garden together like this. He imagined them living there with a brood of children playing and laughing in the sunshine. Perhaps, he would be working in the garden and she would be cooking the lunch. She would call to say that it was ready, and they would all troop in, dirty and famished and she would chide them for leaving marks on the newly washed flagstone floor. But this was never going to happen. She could never be his.

After a few minutes, he turned back towards the cottage and began to whistle a tune so as to announce his arrival.
Paul heard him and ran into the cottage, where everyone had already gone in. "Dr Lucas is here," he shouted.

Lucas quietly opened the gate and strolled around the garden looking at the pretty flowers.

"Good day, Lucas." Aphra stood in the doorway, wiping her floury hands on her apron. "Excuse me. I'm just finishing off the pastry. Please come in or would you like to sit out here. It's such a beautiful day, isn't it?"

"I would like to join you all. Perhaps I could be of assistance."

"Well, you can lay the table, if you don't mind."

"Not at all. It would be a pleasure." He followed her inside. It took a minute or so for his eyes to adjust to the change in light. What he saw delighted him. "This is absolutely charming, Aphra. It's so cosy."

"Isn't it? I just love being here. It's much more like home than Methuen Park, but that is where I have to live. Besides, I am very lucky to have two homes."

"Four actually," shouted Emily from the kitchen. "Don't forget the London House and the estate in Ireland!"

"Alright, four, if you are going to be pedantic, Emily,"

"I'll have to look that up in the dictionary."

Lunch consisted of a leg of lamb, new potatoes, carrots and peas. Aphra had made some mint sauce and Emily had made the gravy. "Emily's gravy is the best I've ever tasted. But don't let Mrs Pearson know that I just said that," she laughed. Emily thanked her for the compliment and returned it by saying that Aphra made lovely light pastry. "You'll be able to judge for yourself as we have apple pie, and cream from our neighbour just along the lane."

Lucas felt really at home and raised his glass of cider. "Let me make a toast to the cooks. This is an excellent repast." They all tucked in and the children made a lot of noise and were constantly being told not to talk with their mouths full, which they continued to do. Lucas was thoroughly enjoying it all. Sophie insisted on sitting next to him, considering him to be her special friend, and tended to monopolise his attention.

A glass of lemonade was knocked over and by the end of the meal, in the vicinity of each child's place, were stains of gravy and mint sauce, and all of them seemed to have half of their food down their fronts. Aphra was surprised and delighted to hear a hearty laugh come from Lucas on several occasions. He was wonderful with the children and she could not help wishing that they could be together with a family of their own.

"Look at the state of you all," said Emily. "I've never seen such a mess." Which wasn't exactly true, for they got into a similar mess at every meal.

As they got up from the table, Lucas insisted on helping with the clearing up. Emily saw to the smaller children and then went with them into the garden. Aphra and Lucas watched them through the small kitchen window as she washed and he wiped the dishes.

"You're a most unusual aristocrat to be doing this," he said.

"I'm not an aristocrat by choice."

He raised his eyebrows.

"What I mean is that my background was not one of privilege. Yes, I am related by birth to Viscount Westbridge and of course I am the wife of an

Earl, but I was brought up as the grand-daughter of a clergyman and that is the life that I knew as a child. I was very loved – at least by my mother and my grand-father, and I had a very comfortable and happy life with them until they died, but it was not a privileged one."

"Do you ever wish for a life other than what you have at present?" He asked.

She was quiet for a few moments, trying to think of a way to answer this difficult question truthfully.

"Do you know Lucas, there are times when I feel decidedly ill at ease with things in my life. I have spells of such melancholy – you can have no idea, but then I remind myself of my good fortune. Yet, there is a part of me that longs to be here in the cottage away from the world. It is my secret dream. I know that it's a dream that can never come true, but it doesn't stop me having it." She was staring out of the window as though miles away in her thoughts.

"Listen to me. What am I going on about? I shall just put this meat pan in to soak and then I'll make some tea and we can take it out to the garden." She began busying herself again and tried to laugh off the candid revelation that she had just made.

Later, as they sat in the shade under a tree in the corner of the garden and watched Emily playing with the children, he reflected on what she had said. He thought of her face as she had looked. Before her gaze had become far away, she had turned and looked at him. What he saw had shocked him. In her eyes, he saw real misery. It was only briefly, but its intensity could not be denied. As he looked at her now, she seemed to be back to normal – quietly embroidering a small handkerchief, probably for Sophie. He took another sip of his tea.

"What a lovely day," he said as he lay back on a large reclining chair. "The sun is so warm, but not too much. I feel quite drowsy and could fall asleep."

She got up and walked into the cottage. A couple of minutes later, she had returned with a cushion. "Please feel free to relax and sleep if you wish. I would consider it a compliment if you felt able to do so." Gently, she lifted his head and placed the cushion beneath it. It was the first time that she had actually touched him. She returned to her seat and resumed her sewing, unaware that his world had just turned upside down.

***

It was some months after this, that plans began for the annual ball. For the first time in a number of years, Aphra found that she was really excited about it. A new gown had been made and she had been walking around her bedroom for days, trying to wear in the beautiful matching satin shoes.

On the evening of the ball, both Emily and Dorothy assisted her with her toilet. Aphra always asked Emily to attend, but as usual, she declined the invitation. She had to admit to herself that she had never seen Aphra looking lovelier. As they put the finishing touches to her hair, they could hear the wheels of the carriages on the gravel. As the orchestra began to play, Aphra collected her fan and kissed both Emily and Dorothy. "Thank you both for everything." Her eyes sparkled and her skin had a slight flush.

Lucas arrived on his own, a few minutes before eight. He had managed to avoid travelling with Caroline. He felt uncomfortable in top hat and formal dress. Sebastian, who was standing in the hall, greeted him warmly.

"So glad you could join us Lucas," he said as he shook hands. "I hope the evening won't be too much of a bore for you. I know that these things aren't really your cup of tea, but we are very pleased to have you here."

Outside, more carriages stopped as a throng of people continued to arrive. The sounds of footsteps and chatter, together with the rustle of silk, began to fill the vestibule. Liveried footmen took hats, cloaks and capes to a small side-room which was being used as a cloakroom. Sebastian greeted everyone individually as they arrived, and although the guest list included aristocrats, politicians and celebrities, he treated Lucas as though he were the guest of honour.

"Aphra has been slightly delayed this evening. There was a little upset with one of the staff earlier. One of the maids has had a broken romance or some such thing and was in floods of tears. Aphra is very good with these situations," he said walking towards the foot of the staircase. "Ah, here she is now."

Lucas observed Sebastian as he looked up at his wife who was slowly and elegantly descending the stairs. What Lucas saw, left him in no doubt as to the Earl's deep affection for his wife as he smiled with pride. She was wearing a simple oyster satin gown trimmed with a small amount of pale green lace and a small gold brooch with seed pearls pinned to the dress at her décolletage. A small emerald tiara sat amidst her titian hair which was dressed high on her head, small ringlets tumbled about her face and the nape of her neck, and the matching stones in her ears and about her throat brought out the soft green in her eyes.

As she took Sebastian's proffered hand, she smiled warmly at him and kissed him on the cheek. Lucas, who had followed Sebastian to the foot of the stairs, overheard him whisper to her "my dear, you look lovelier than ever. None of our guests here tonight can fully appreciate how fortunate I am to have you as my wife."

To this, she replied something in his ear and he roared with laughter. "Only you could say something like that," he joked. "You naughty girl!" At this remark of his, she began to laugh too and Lucas thought how happy they seemed and felt an overwhelming pang of envy and loss mixed with confusion.

After welcoming and greeting their guests for what seemed like an eternity, Sebastian led Aphra onto the dance floor. The orchestra began to play a Strauss waltz and soon many couples followed their hosts and began to dance too.

Lucas reluctantly went into the ballroom where he was soon accosted by Caroline, whom he'd been trying to avoid. He took one of the glasses of champagne being carried on trays by one of the many liveried flunkies.

"Lucas. I've been looking for you everywhere. Are you going to ask me to dance?"

"You know that I only attend these events out of duty Caroline. I'm not really one for dancing."

"Nonsense." She was not going to be put off that easily. "I've danced with you more than once and you're a first rate dancer – in spite of being so disagreeable and disapproving of having fun," she teased.

"Very well," he replied, without trying to hide the note of despondent resignation in his voice. "Perhaps later on."

Suddenly, there was a flurry of excitement. A voice, struggling to compete with the orchestra, announced "Mr Oscar Wilde and Lord Alfred Douglas."

For a few seconds, there was a slight hush in the level of chatter about the room as the famous playwright and his "close friend" - both sporting green carnation buttonholes, entered the room. Within minutes, a crowd had surrounded him and the room was full of laughter, as he entertained them with his witty epigrams.

Lucas drank the remainder of his champagne. "Shall I get you another?" He asked.

"Yes. I was just about to ask you," replied Caroline. "Why is there always such a fuss about that man? I can't see the attraction and why is that ghastly son of Queensbury always hanging around. It seems decidedly odd to me."

"Well, he must have something going for him. He's quite the toast in London."

At that moment, Lucas spied someone that he knew. "Good evening, George. How're you keeping? Have you met Miss Grenville?" Swiftly, he made the necessary introductions. Whilst he was doing this, another tray of champagne was to hand, and he took one for Caroline, one for George and another for himself. After making a few polite comments, he made his excuses and disappeared into the crush of people. He wanted to be free to watch Aphra dancing and perhaps get an opportunity to speak to her - even if it was just for a few minutes.
He suspected that Caroline knew he was trying to get away from her, but he didn't care. Surely, she realised by now that he couldn't stand her and yet it didn't stop her forcing her blasted company on him. "Damn the woman," he muttered under his breath. "Why can't she leave me alone?"

He found a spot by a pillar, where hopefully, he could watch unobserved by others. But he was wrong in thinking that he could not be seen. "This won't do my dear fellow." said Sebastian as he led Aphra from the dance floor. "We can't have you standing here all alone. Aphra, I insist that you take this poor lonely chap for a turnabout the room."

"I'd be delighted," she said quietly and with some obvious discomfort. "But maybe the doctor prefers not to dance."

"Not at all. It would be my pleasure." He held out his hand. She took it nervously and he was surprised to discover that she was shaking.

The music resumed and they began to dance. For both of them, the experience was exhilarating. Nothing was said and their demeanour towards one another was absolutely correct and formal – and yet each one sensed that the other was feeling something special - something neither had experienced before and neither wanted to end. But end it must. Lucas bowed correctly and led her back to Sebastian, who was engaged in deep conversation with Claude. Lucas kissed her hand. "Thank you Countess."

"Thank you doctor. You dance very well." She smiled at him. He made some general comment about a recent function that they had both attended, and she made polite enquiries about the hospital. He was so nervous that he found it hard to think straight and answer her.

"Wilde!" Sebastian called out to his friend. "Thought you weren't coming man."

"Sorry, got a bit held up before we left yesterday." He walked over and slapped Sebastian on the back. "Anyway we're here now. Looks like a most successful bash as usual." He sipped his champagne.

"I see that you look lovelier than ever my dear." He kissed Aphra's hand. "Now, if I were a different kind of man, I'd be tempted to run off with you and would be in serious trouble – no doubt your husband would be challenging me to a duel. However, I shall just have to make do with claiming a dance later on."

Everyone laughed, except Lucas, who neither understood nor liked this remark. Sebastian noticed that Lucas was looking uncomfortable.

"Oscar let me introduce you to our wonderful pioneering doctor here." The introductions were made and Lucas felt slightly more at ease.

Shortly after this, food was served and everyone made their way towards the dining room where tables were piled high with plates bearing all manner of delicacies. The chatter seemed to subside for a few minutes, while people were eating, but soon the din resumed.

The musicians had been taking a short break, but soon the orchestra began playing again and Sebastian took to the floor with an elderly lady, who was obviously delighted to be dancing with the Earl.

As the dancers swirled about the room, Lucas saw that Aphra was now dancing with Claude. Again, she seemed to be fully at ease with Claude as she was with Sebastian. They danced well together – in fact, they looked better together, for the Earl was so very tall. Claude was only a few inches taller than Aphra and they seemed physically to be a perfect match. Lucas stood there transfixed for some minutes. He was so absorbed that he didn't realise that Caroline was beside him until she spoke.

"Are you trying to wriggle out of that dance with me?" She made a vain attempt at being coquettish. He found it really annoying and had to try even harder to conceal it.

"Don't be so foolish." He held out his hand and they joined the other dancers.

He saw that Aphra was dancing with the Earl again, and he just wanted to concentrate on looking at her. Both Caroline and Lucas were extremely adept and needed to pay little attention to their steps. As she chatted maliciously about several of the guests, he nodded and made what he hoped were appropriate responses at the required moments. However, all his attention was focused on the hosts of the ball as they glided around the room. At one point, he thought he was going to lose control and shout at Caroline to shut up. It was strange how, in spite of her undeniable beauty, there was something so very repellent about her.

He watched as Sebastian, with his arm casually supporting Aphra's back with the ease of familiarity, guided her around the room. They appeared so happy and comfortable together chatting and their eyes full of warmth and laughter. Occasionally, she would let go of his hand and touch his face and once brushed a stray lock of hair from his forehead.

Sometimes, she would glance across at Claude, who was propped against a pillar with a glass of cognac in one hand and a cigar in the other. They exchanged a couple of smiles and nods with one another. When this happened, it made Lucas feel uneasy. Sebastian didn't seem to notice and if he did, he didn't seem bothered by the familiarity of his friend towards the Countess. It would appear that he was totally assured of her loyalty. At one point, as the Earl swung her around, the trailing hem of her gown swept across the feet of the Count and he stepped backwards so that the ash that fell from his cigar would not burn the back of her gown. Sebastian laughed and made some comment to him as they whirled around in front of him. Claude smiled and for a moment, Lucas could have sworn that he winked.

Lucas watched with a sense of despair, his longing for Aphra unbearable. He didn't think that he would get through the entire evening feeling this way. As his thoughts ran freely along these lines, he'd completely stopped listening to Caroline. His attention was brought back to her with a jolt.

"Did you see that?" Demanded Caroline self-righteously. "I tell you, there's something going on there. That Frenchie chap just winked at her as she passed him and all under her husband's nose. It's a disgrace!"

Lucas made no comment. The music ended. He bowed to Caroline and walked away towards The Earl.

"You're not leaving already?" Asked Sebastian, as Lucas held out his hand to him. "The night is still young."

"I've an early start tomorrow," said Lucas. "Please make my apologies to the Countess."

Sebastian leant forward as he said, "Actually, you've done very well to stick it out as long as this. Well done, ol' chap. We'll be seeing you again soon. Please feel free to visit anytime."

Caroline stood and watched as he left the ballroom.

***

Ten minutes, later, he was in his carriage on his way home. He shut his eyes and thought about what had just happened. Was Caroline right? Was there something going on between Aphra and Claude? He couldn't believe it of her. She seemed to genuinely care for her husband. And what did it say about him? Admittedly, it made him jealous – he was overwhelmed with envy about everything to do with her. But what was he most jealous about - the happy marriage or the supposed affair with Claude? However, the thing that bothered him most was the thought that she was capable of being so duplicitous and disloyal. Yes, he was in love with her external beauty, but he also loved her deeply because he believed – sincerely hoped - that she was intrinsically full of genuine goodness.

As the carriage rocked, he stared out into the darkness. Something was gnawing away at him. Something was wrong, but he couldn't work out what it was. It was something that Caroline had said. He'd seen the wink, but surely it was quite innocent and meant nothing.

When he was in bed later, he closed his eyes again and just remembered her in his arms. He had waited a lifetime to feel like that – bittersweet ecstasy and agony mixed up together. He allowed himself to savour each moment and recall it over and over again.

But as he drifted off to sleep, the gnawing feeling of something being wrong with that remark Caroline had made, stayed with him.

***

It is wonderful up here floating in the clouds. The view of the world is so much altered and everything is so clear.

I know that this is a kind of insanity. It is so frustrating not being able to say anything to him. Obviously, I could tell Claude – and yet I don't want to for some reason. I am so confused. It is as though I want to tell the world about this feeling, but at the same time it is my precious secret.

It was wonderful tonight when I danced with him. It was as though we were completely separated from everyone else in the room. It is strange, but he did and said nothing that indicated that he had any feelings for me and yet I am convinced that he reciprocates the intensity of my own. I don't know why this is, but I feel it.

I know that sometime soon, I shall have to land and return to normality and the minutiae of everyday life, but I don't want to – not yet.

I feel a mixture of strange paradoxical emotions – excited contentment and a calm passion (goodness, I sound like Oscar!) – feelings of wanting to do millions of things – feeling that I have the fire and energy to attend to every detail of everyday life and yet I want to lie still and mull over every action and event, every intense look and smile – how foolish, but so joyous.

Months of wondering, questioning myself as to whether or not I was misreading the signs – perhaps a hopeless dream of joy and bliss even. The waiting is over. I now know that I was right – he does reciprocate. Gone is the gnawing dread of rejection. In its place is a smile in my heart at our secret.

***

"You know, Lucas, I must be the luckiest man in the world. Who else has a wife like mine? Just look at her. Isn't she beautiful? But you know, that beauty is not just visual, but in every facet of her nature. She is truly a good woman."

"It sounds as though you are very blessed in your fortunes," said Lucas.

"Oh I am – I am," he said. "Outsiders cannot know what she means to me, and how very important she is in my life – how necessary to the core of my happiness. Sometimes lovers need to be sheltered and protected from the dangers of the world."

Lucas thought that Sebastian seemed to be far away in his thoughts as he said this.

"She provides that shelter and protection for me in a way that no one outside our inner sanctum could ever really understand."

It was a warm day in late summer and they were seated by a round table bearing a jug of lemonade and numerous glasses under a large oak tree.

"At the ball, when I watched you two dancing together, I thought that you seemed such a devoted couple," said Lucas.

"Oh, we are. I cannot ever remember us having a cross word – well certainly nothing of any moment."

"Many of the guests remarked on what a perfect couple you made."

"Yes. People have said that for many years – and they can have no idea how perfect I find our situation. Being married to me cannot always be easy for her, but she bears it with good grace and humour." He leant towards Lucas in a mock confidential manner. "She has been known, when I am in a particularly difficult mood, to call me Mr Grumpygrowl!"

He laughed at this, but then his mood seemed to change and he became rather quiet and pensive. Lucas noticed that his eyes were moistening. "She's just right as no other wife could be. I care for her as I could never ever care for another woman. What we share will live beyond the grave."

"And she shares this special love for you too?"

"Oh yes. I know that she does. I'm absolutely certain that nothing will ever break the bond that we forged at our nuptials. I'm convinced that she would never do anything to harm me and that she would always put me first. She is beyond reproach and incapable of betrayal. It is not in her character."

Their attention turned to the noisy activity taking place on the lawn. Aphra, Emily, Claude and Sophie were throwing a ball back and forth with Emily's children. There was a lot of shouting and running about. Away from the prying eyes of outsiders, Aphra was running and shouting as much as the children.

"Look at that," said Sebastian. "Ha Ha! Completely unladylike! I love it when she is able to let her hair down and really enjoy herself. She was somewhat down in spirits some while back. If she has one weakness, it is a propensity for repeated bouts of melancholia. So it is good to see her laughing and having such fun. We always enjoy these times with Claude, Emily and the children. I love to hear them all playing and to see the happiness on their faces. I'm not one for this kind of activity myself, but it gives me joy to observe it."

Suddenly, the ball was thrown some distance and Aphra began to run after it, with Claude in hot pursuit. As she stooped to grab it, Claude encircled her waist with his arms and lifted her off her feet and swung her around. Their laughter was almost hysterical and they had slipped into speaking French. Lucas understood a little of what they were saying and it seemed to consist of Aphra beseeching him to put her down and insulting him in the mock annoyed manner of the familiar and intimate. Sebastian watched this and laughed out loud. "Put her down Claude." When Claude ignored him, Sebastian shouted. "I order you to release my wife." Claude let go of her and bowed and saluted to Sebastian. "Pardon, Milord." Then he turned and snatched the ball from Aphra and ran back to the children with it. She began to run after him and pretended to sulk. "It isn't fair," she cried and stamped her foot. At this, the children laughed even more.

"What do you think children? Is Uncle Claude being beastly to me?"
Seeing as he had returned their ball, they all replied loudly and in unison "No!"

"And there is my good friend, Claude," said Sebastian.

"You have a very happy little community here, but do you not think that he is just a little bit too familiar with your wife for a servant?" Asked Lucas.

"Yes, my blessings are many. Of course, Claude is my private secretary. However, we have been great pals for years, since we met when I was on holiday in the Loire valley. His family's estate is there. They have a beautiful, but crumbling chateau on the Loire itself. They are an old and respected family, but their financial situation is not good. Claude is the younger son, so does not carry the burden in the sense that he will one day be the owner, but of course, he does worry about what will become of his family and their home in the future. I know that it is a relief for him to be employed by me, and I have tried to help his family where I can – but he is also a great help to me in so many ways. Aphra understands how much I need his comfort and support – and you can see that they have become great friends."

"They certainly seem very close indeed. It must be a comfort to him too, to have you to rely upon financially."

"I'm glad to be of help, but I certainly don't want him to feel obligated to me – our friendship is above that."

"Do you think that he is really appreciative of your generosity?"

Sebastian looked at him with a questioning look on his face. "What d'you mean?"

"Well, you seem to trust him completely. Is that always wise?"

"What an odd thing to say, Lucas. What's your point?"

"Well. Don't you ever feel uncomfortable at the amount of time they spend together?"

"Good Lord no! They're the best of friends – like brother and sister, and he's like a second father to Sophie. I'm often so busy with all the affairs of this place – for I need to be involved with the tenants and the farmers. I know that I'm guilty of neglecting my family sometimes. My business affairs also take me away from home a lot. There always seems to be some committee or other to attend." He was quiet for a moment. "And of course, I have to be in the House from time to time. I know that a lot of the chaps can't be bothered, but I feel that it's important that I do my bit if I can."

Their conversation was interrupted by the boisterous clan joining them briefly to quench their thirsts. There was a lot of jostling and arguing.

"I'm not surprised you're all so thirsty with all that shouting. You must all be hoarse," chided Sebastian gently.

"That's enough pushing and shoving," said Aphra. "There's plenty to go around, so just take your turn." She slumped into the chair next to

Sebastian. "I'm exhausted," she panted, before slaking her own thirst with the cool refreshing drink. Claude took the last vacant seat, next to Lucas. When he too had finished his lemonade, he turned to Lucas and said. "You must think us a horde of barbarians, Lucas, but it is good sometimes to – how do you English put it? – Ah, let off steam. I do not have a wife and young family of my own, but at moments like these, it feels as though I do."

"It could certainly give that impression to an onlooker," replied Lucas in a manner that made Aphra look up. She wondered whether or not there was some kind of implication in the remark. She was tempted to question his meaning, but thought better of it.

No sooner had the children finished their drinks, then they were off running about the lawn again. Sophie, being the eldest, suggested playing with their hoops.

After a while, Aphra suggested a walk down to the lake. Both Sebastian and Lucas, who wanted to continue their conversation, declined the offer, so Aphra and Claude strolled off down the hill.

Lucas took a sip of his drink as he watched the free and easy manner that Aphra had with Claude as they walked down towards the water. "Do you think that you're fully aware of all the affairs that go on here?" He hesitated for a moment, and then continued. "I've noticed that Claude accompanies your wife to some social functions when you are away, and I've occasionally overheard people comment upon this." He did not tell him, that it was, in fact, not an occasional comment, but something that was often said.

"Really! How amusing! I wonder what sort of people would discuss other people's private affairs – especially something so innocent."

"Do you not think that perhaps you're the innocent one here? Don't you think that maybe they spend too much time together and that this is unwise?"

"Not at all. If people wish to gossip, then let them do so. I'm not my wife's keeper and she's free to spend her time how and with whom she likes."

"Well, all I can say is that you must be a most unusual husband."

"Oh I am. I am." He smiled enigmatically in what Lucas thought was a smug and foolish way.

***

When your heart is in the country, it is so difficult having to spend time away from it. Normally, I do not enjoy my visits to London – the long tiresome journey, especially if the weather is inclement – and of course some of the roads are dreadful. There are times, when I have felt quite nauseous with all the bumping and swaying of the carriage as we make our way through the country lanes to Bristol Station.

Admittedly, some of the views are spectacular and I do love to watch the changing landscape and seasons, for we make the journey a number of times annually - but then I am still in the country.

The train journey itself is not too bad – and again, I love to watch the passing scenery, and the carriage is quite comfortable.

As the train draws into Paddington, I feel quite overwhelmed as the hustle and bustle of London life seems to engulf us. The station itself is so noisy with the hissing and chugging of the trains, whistles blowing and porters shouting. It seems extremely dirty too, with all the soot and smoke and I am always eager to wash my hands as soon as possible.

The traffic and sheer number of people thronging and rushing everywhere, makes me yearn for the silence and tranquillity of Somerset. Of course, it is not silent – quite the reverse, the countryside has its own sounds but they do not jar on one's nerves and assault the ears as London noises often do.

Yet the city does have its own charm and I should not be so harsh in my criticism of it. Obviously, there are the usual sites and attractions of any major capital city and I do appreciate these. The architecture and history are both very interesting to me and I do enjoy taking a carriage ride in one or other of the parks, and of course there is the theatre - which is the reason for this coming trip.

The London house, which is situated in Mayfair, is very grand - though much smaller than Methuen Park. Even though I miss the countryside, I do prefer being in a smaller house. Each room is more compact, but still decorated in a very opulent way. My own chamber is very comfortable and I do prefer the bed here, for it is not a four poster, neither does it have a tester above it.

As I sit here writing, a glowing fire burns in the grate. Like Methuen Park, the house now has electricity - very modern - so I don't need to worry about candles or oil lamps. I suppose that what I really like about the house is that in some ways, it reminds me of my childhood home. Of course, my home in Bishop's Langley was nowhere near as grand, but there are things that bring it to mind - it is nothing of great moment, but there are times when I seem to experience a sense of déjà vu. It could be the sound of the chiming clock in the drawing room, or the glass cabinet in the dining room, or just the way the drapes hang at the window in my bedchamber.

We always stay here when in London. Sebastian makes regular visits up to town, so it is always open for him. Obviously, being a much smaller establishment, the household consists of a butler, housekeeper, two maids, a cook, scullery maid and footman. When I am in town, Maisie, the senior housemaid, assists me with my toilet and dressing. She does not have the experience and flair that Dorothy has, but I am trying to help her learn. She needs to pay more attention to detail, but she is making good progress. I suspect that she would like to become a lady's maid and I am keen to help her fulfil her ambition. She is still young and there is plenty of time for her to do so.

I'm sure that Dorothy noticed my eagerness at packing and the indecision over which gowns and jewels to take. I must have driven her to distraction with the constant changes of my mind.

I am now about to retire for the night. Dorothy, as always, has worked so hard at preparing my clothes. The dear heart is such a blessing. What a comfort to know that she will keep an eye on Sophie in my absence. Nowadays, Emily is rather preoccupied with her own children – although she still spends a lot of time with Sophie. Of course, Miss Kincaid will be responsible for her supervision during the day, but she can be a bit severe at times, and although Sophie is a child who needs a firm hand, she also needs kindness and cuddles too. I know that Dorothy will spoil her a little bit and I don't mind her doing so on special occasions.

Sebastian is very enthusiastic about the play. Oscar is becoming such a celebrity. I don't really approve of the uninhibited and dangerous way that he flaunts this relationship with Bosie. Neither do I think that Bosie treats him well. Oscar indulges him far too much and his good nature is abused. I think that Bosie is far too reckless. It worries me where it will all end. I just wish that they would be more discreet. I know that it makes Sebastian quite nervous - understandably so.

The whole thing must be dreadful for Constance. I wish that I could comfort her, but to raise the subject would not be seemly – and probably so painful for her – and perhaps like us, they have their own secret arrangements! But then, secrets can be terribly wearing. It is ironic that the play is called An Ideal Husband. Oscar is certainly not that!

Oh, how the hours drag. I really must try and sleep or I shall feel so tired tomorrow and will then be out of sorts all day. I shall switch off the lamp and lay my head on my cool pillow and dream – although I shall still be wide awake.

A hundred times, I have pictured the scene. Seb, Claude and I enter the foyer of the theatre. It will be crowded. Seb will catch Oscar's eye and he will beckon us over to him and Bosie. They will be surrounded by a group of cronies and hangers' on. We will fight our way through the jostling mass of satin and silk, starched shirt fronts, white ties and top hats. Seb will slap Oscar on the back and congratulate him on his success – although no one has yet seen the play. However, I am sure that it will be brilliant as usual. I hear that another one is about to be staged. Seb says that it will be Oscar's masterpiece. It is all about the confusion surrounding someone's name.

I expect to feel Caroline's ice cold eyes burning with hatred into my back. No matter. I am used to that. I will turn around and near to her yet somehow very distant, he will be standing there – twisting his champagne glass around and around - looking uncomfortable and out of place. He would normally not want to be here. There is only one reason for his attendance tonight. His gaze will move in my direction and he will nod and smile slightly, but he will say nothing and outwardly show nothing, yet I know that he has been waiting – waiting and longing - as have I.

PART SIX - INTO THE DEPTHS

Some weeks after they had returned to Somerset, Lucas came to stay for the weekend. On the Saturday afternoon, he was sitting in the study with Sebastian and Claude. They were discussing some legal matters to do with the new hospital over a rather good malt. It was March, and Lucas was looking out of the window and thinking that soon there would be daffodils opening. He was hoping that perhaps he and Aphra would be able to go for a walk by their favourite spot around the lake after the meeting.

She was sitting at her desk in her bedroom dealing with some correspondence and her mind was running along the same lines. She found it very hard to keep her mind on the tedium of the job in hand and not let it continually wander to thoughts of Lucas. If only she could tell him the truth about her situation, she was sure that he would understand and they would be able to spend time alone together without this shadow in the way.

Suddenly, there was an almighty explosion which seemed to rock the house. She ran out of the room and looked over the balustrade down to the main entrance hall.

What's happened?" She called down.

Sebastian had rushed out of the study with Lucas and Claude behind him.

"I don't know," he called up to her. "It came from the kitchen area. I hope no one's been hurt."

At that moment, Henry rushed through the baize door from the servants' quarters. "Milord, the kitchen boiler has exploded and brought down a lot of masonry. We're going to need a lot of help to shift it and there are people trapped under it."

"Get as many men as you can. There are quite a few groundsmen nearby," said Sebastian.

Lucas rushed upstairs to his room to collect his medical bag and ran down again towards the kitchen. The sight that met him was absolute chaos. Through the smoke and dust, he could see that a complete corner of the room and the chimney breast had been completely blown out. Overhead, more masonry and timbers balanced precariously.

Sebastian, Claude and three of the footmen were trying to shore up the ceiling before it collapsed. One of the young kitchen maids was sitting crying at the table. She was obviously badly shaken and covered in cuts and bruises which could hardly be seen for the brick dust that covered her. Her normally brown hair looked grey.

Lucas turned his attention to two figures lying next to the hearth. One of them was an elderly man, who was screaming in agony. "For God's sake someone help me. I think my leg's broken." Lucas noticed that the man also had a nasty gash across his forehead.

Lucas shifted a large, heavy timber lying across the leg which had a bone sticking out of it and moved the man slightly away from the danger area. "I think that you may be right. It does look broken. I'll have a look at it in a minute, but first, I need to see to this other person."

He took a look at the silent figure. It was difficult to see if it was a man or a woman, for it was lying under a large mound of rubble and timbers.

"Hello, can you hear me?" He said firmly but gently. There was no answer. He checked the pulse. It was very faint. He noticed that the figure was wearing a dress. "Does anyone know who this is?" He called out.

"It's Mrs Pearson, the cook," said the tearful kitchen maid. "She was just about to make a roux sauce when the whole place blew up. Is she dead?"

"No," said Lucas. "But she's losing a lot of blood. I need to staunch the flow or else she'll die. Can someone put some pressure on that man's leg where it is bleeding? Be careful - it's badly broken and he's in a lot of pain. I'll see to it when I've dealt with things here."

Mrs Drake went over to the man and did just as Lucas had ordered.

"Lucas be careful," demanded Sebastian. "That lot isn't safe. We've not secured it yet."

"I've got to get to her right arm. That seems to be where the blood is coming from. I think that I can squeeze through here."

He managed to wriggle beneath a large slab of masonry and placed a tourniquet on the upper part of her arm. For some minutes, he managed to examine her in spite of the limited space.

"She's taken a nasty bang on the head, but I can't find any other injuries. If we can get her out, I can stitch this arm."

"Her Ladyship has telephoned for Dr Osborne from the village. He's on his way," said Mrs Drake. "And the estate fire-crew are just arriving."

Lucas stayed next to Mrs Pearson and kept loosening and then tightening the tourniquet so as not to restrict the blood flow to the lower part of the limb. She started to come around. "What's 'appened?" She asked very faintly. "I can't bloody move!"

"It's alright," said Lucas kindly. "There's been an accident and you've cut your arm, but you're going to be alright, so don't worry." Just as he was saying this, there was a terrific rumbling sound and the remainder of the damaged part of the ceiling collapsed on him and Mrs Pearson.

At that precise moment, Aphra rushed into the kitchen. The noise of the masonry falling, together with the screams and shouts of everyone in the room created an atmosphere of confusion and terror.

As the dust began to clear, it became apparent that both the cook and the doctor were trapped even further.

"Oh God!" Aphra screamed out. "Lucas!"

Claude immediately rushed to her side. "I'm sure they'll be alright," he said taking her hand and squeezing it. "Try not to worry."

"Of course," Aphra said, taking his hint to be discreet. "Now what can I do to help?"

At that moment, both Dr Osborne and the fire-crew entered the scene. Sebastian suggested that anyone not needed should leave the kitchen, as it was getting very overcrowded. The fire-crew set to work to make the rest of the ceiling safe and to release the two people trapped under the rubble. Dr Osborne attended to the man with the broken leg, and Aphra took the young maid up to her own rooms to clean her up and dress her wounds. She gave her a glass of brandy and let her talk about what had happened. After a while, the girl seemed much calmer and had stopped crying.

"Now," said Aphra. "I want you to go to your room and go to bed. You've had a bad shock. You need to rest for a while."

"But milady, what about Mrs Pearson and the doctor? Shouldn't I go back down there?"

"There's nothing that you can do to help them. They're in good hands. You'll be helping by resting and getting yourself well again. Now off you go. When things have calmed down someone will come and see you."

"Yes, milady," she said and left the room.

After she had gone, Aphra sat and pondered on what she should do. She wanted to rush back down there to be near Lucas, but she would probably be getting in the way herself. She poured herself a large brandy and tried to sit quietly for a few minutes. However, once the brandy was finished, she decided that she couldn't stand it any longer and ran down the stairs. She saw one of the footmen standing there.

"What's happening?" She asked. "Is there any news?"

"They've got them out, Milady. Mrs Pearson isn't as bad as we first thought. She's awake and talking," he replied. "And old Barney's leg will have to be set."

"And Doctor Lucas?" She asked anxiously.

"I'm afraid he's not too good, milady. He's taken a very bad knock to the head and Dr Osborne thinks he has a number of broken bones."

"Oh my God!" Aphra cried out as she put her hand up to her moth. "I must go and see if I can help in any way."

"May I suggest milady that his room is made ready, for I think that they'll be bringing him out in a few moments."

"Of course," she said. "I'll see to it myself." She ran back up the stairs. Once in his room, she turned back the bed covers and cleared the side tables in readiness.

As she was hastily moving various items, she knocked what looked like a journal on to the floor. She stooped to pick up some loose sheets of paper that had fallen out of it. When she heard the sound of voices and footsteps coming up the stairs, she threw the papers on to the dressing table and rushed to the door. Sebastian, Claude and two of the footmen were carrying a stretcher. Upon it lay an inert, bloodstained Lucas, covered in grey dust.

Following on behind came Doctor Osborne. He was issuing orders to be careful not to move him too much. "I haven't been able to tell how extensive his injuries are as yet. That's it. Lay him gently on the bed, so that I can examine him."

Everyone discreetly left the room, while the doctor examined Lucas. Claude put his hand around Aphra's shoulders. "I am so sorry, ma Cherie. I know how much you care about him. We must pray for his full recovery."

Sebastian said. "He's in the best hands. Try not to worry too much my dear. He's a strong, healthy young man. I'm sure he'll pull through."

"Yes, hopefully," said Aphra with little conviction in her voice.

They needed to try and return to some semblance of normality and so Aphra set about organising a cleaning up operation. The fire-crew had made the kitchen safe and she made arrangements with a local building and plumbing firm for the replacement of the boiler, and the rebuilding and redecoration of the damaged part of the kitchen. Once this had been attended to, Aphra went in search of Emily and Sophie to let them know what was happening.

In the meantime, the kitchen staff had to manage as best they could by working in the scullery and servants' dining room. The pantry had not been touched so there was no shortage of food. It was just that preparing it was very difficult, and cold meals would have to suffice for a short while. However, they managed it very well and with good humour.

Mrs Pearson made a rapid recovery and in less than a week, was ordering everyone about as usual in spite of a huge lump the size of an orange on her head. It transpired that Dr Lucas had thrown himself over her to protect her, and had taken the full force of the collapse. She never stopped telling people how the poor man had risked his life to save her.

"I wouldn't be 'ere now if it weren't for 'im."

Once everything had been taken care of, Aphra returned to Lucas' room. The doctor was just finishing up and washing his hands in a basin.

"How is he?"

"There's nothing more that I can do for him tonight. I've set his arm. It's broken in two places and he has a couple of broken ribs, but it's the head injury that I'm most concerned about. The next few hours will be crucial. I'm afraid, the prognosis is not good. He's in a deep coma and I don't think that he will awake from it. He was a brave man to do what he did. He could have got out of there and saved himself."

"Yes," said Aphra. "He's a very brave and good man. He just cannot die. Too many of us need him," she said this with such anguish in her voice that Dr Osborne looked up in surprise.

"I think that someone should stay with him through the night," he said. "Can you arrange that?"

"Yes, of course Doctor," she replied in her best matter of fact voice. She realised that she had already displayed too much emotion.

After the doctor left, Aphra requested that a jug of water be brought up to her. She dipped a cloth in it and moistened Lucas' lips. The hours ticked by and she sat quietly by his side. Gently, she spoke to him – although she knew that he could not hear her. It grew dark and the night's vigil began.

All that night, she sat by his bedside. When there was no-one around, she caressed his hand. It was then that she finally broke down and cried.

The days passed and still he did not wake up. A second doctor, a specialist in head injuries, who had been sent for from Bath, told her that he thought Lucas would live, but had no idea how much damage had been done to his brain.

Mrs Drake usually checked whether there was anything that she could get or do before she went to bed. She placed a cup of tea on the bedside cabinet.

"This is very good of you Milady to sit by him night after night, but you must be exhausted and you've eaten nothing for days." Aphra assured her that it was no trouble and that she would eat when she knew that Dr Lucas was alright. "Then I shall say goodnight, Milady."

"Goodnight Mrs Drake – and thank you for everything."

***

Dear Mildred,

I had to write to tell you of the goings on here just recently. As you know, the young doctor has become a great favourite with the Earl and Countess, and stays regularly.

Well, there's been a terrible accident. The gas boiler in the kitchen exploded and part of the outside wall collapsed. The windows blew out and there was masonry, glass, china and goodness knows what everywhere. It's amazing that no-one was killed. Mrs Pearson, the cook and Barney, the old odd job man, were both pinned under the rubble. Everyone rushed to help. His Lordship was wonderful and didn't mind getting his hands dirty trying to prop up the wall and ceiling.

But, it was the young doctor who was the hero of the hour. He risked his own life to save Mrs Pearson. There was a second collapse while they were both underneath the rubble, he threw himself on top of her and has been so badly injured himself. It is not known whether or not he will ever recover. He is still unconscious. The Countess has hardly left his side. It is not my place to pass judgement, but it does strike me as rather unseemly of her to spend every waking hour at his side. The other night, I popped in before I retired for the night and found her sitting sobbing and holding his hand. As you know, I am not one to jump to conclusions, but I do wonder whether or not there is something between them. I've noticed that when the doctor is around, Monsieur seems to keep his distance. Can it be that she is carrying on with both of them?

Fortunately, both Barney and Mrs Pearson are making an excellent recovery. Needless to say, that the latter was up and bossing the kitchen maids within no time! Barney will have his leg in plaster for some months.

Well, that is all my news for the present. I'll write again, if there are any further developments.

Best wishes, Hetty

***

Aphra changed the dressings to Lucas' wounds and applied the antiseptic spray that the doctor had left on the bedside cabinet. She was relieved to see that they were healing without infection. Also, the swelling on his head had reduced a little bit.

The days were now turning into weeks. She knew that she was neglecting her other duties and she felt very guilty about giving Sophie so little attention, but she feared so much that Lucas would die or that he would never return to his old self, that she could not bear to be away from his bedside.

She had hardly slept for weeks. Sitting by the bed, she'd had the odd short nap - usually for no more than an hour or so. One night, as she paced about the room, she noticed the diary on the dressing table. She remembered knocking it over on the day of the accident. She saw that the loose sheets of paper were untidy, so she tried to put them in some kind of order. Without meaning to, she could not stop her eyes being drawn to what was written. She knew that she should not read it, but she just could not resist.

***

How can I bear this pain – this longing and loving her so much, that my spirit yearns to reach out and clasp hers, and to know that this I can never do?

Today, I watched her and Sebastian together. They have such a deep and genuine affection for each other. Rarely have I seen a couple who seem so harmonious. There never appears to be any discord as there is so often with many married couples. They are also such wonderful caring parents and Sophie is much loved and happy.

It is Aphra's intrinsic goodness and honesty that I love most of all. Surely, she would never cheat or betray Sebastian – and what if I betrayed or hurt him – my friend – could she truly love or respect me? I think not! I torture myself about the triangle that is constantly rumoured to exist between the three of them, but I cannot really believe such a thing. Both she and Claude are honourable and care for him deeply. It cannot be - surely.

I have known moments of exquisite pain and bliss just being in her company. Sometimes the gentleness and warmth – the stillness of togetherness, the oneness and harmony has been so comfortable, rippling over me like a warm breeze on a June afternoon.

Oh my precious girl, I can never tell you how I feel, and if I did, how would you respond and would I want you to reciprocate? I long to hold you – and yet if you acted in the way that my heart desires, then you would not be my soul-mate.

I know that I must leave you for I cannot bear the pain any longer – and yet how will I bear the pain of parting from you? How will I endure every second for the rest of my life, knowing that there will never be anyone who will be so welcome in my heart?

***

When she had read this, she covered her face with her hands and began to weep. She went and sat by the bed and looked at the inert figure lying there.

"Oh my dearest Lucas, please don't leave me. If only I could tell you that there is a triangle - but not as you think. I am completely free to love you and to be loved by you, but I am not free to tell you this, nor the reason why. If only you knew the secret pain that I carry around with me - but I cannot tell you. I cannot break my word.

It brings me some comfort that I am speaking these words to you, for if you were conscious, I would have to remain silent." As she said these words, she felt that the engulfing pain would suffocate her. Gradually, the sobbing subsided and she became calm again. For some minutes, she sat in silence holding his hand and rubbing the back of it. Then, very slowly, he turned his head towards her and opened his eyes. Never before in her life had she been so pleased to see a pair of eyes looking at her.

"Well, hello. Welcome back hero," she said with a voice full of relief and emotion.

He tried to smile and speak, but was unsuccessful at both.

"Don't try to speak yet. Would you like some water?"
He nodded his head slightly and she fetched a glass and held his head while he sipped at it.

"He looked at her with a questioning expression on his face. She guessed what he wanted to ask.

"Everyone is safe. In fact, you're the only serious casualty. You've had a very bad bang on the head, your left arm and some ribs are broken, and you're covered in cuts and bruises. You resemble a patchwork quilt!"

At this last remark, he managed a tiny smile. She sat with him until he fell asleep again, and when the sun began to peep through the edges of the curtains, she felt that she could leave him for a short while.

She decided that she would go downstairs for breakfast and tell Sebastian and Claude of Lucas' improvement. As she swiftly descended the stairs, she decided to ask Seb if he would allow her to explain their situation to Lucas. She was sure that he would understand her desperate need, in view of the terrible bouts of melancholia she had suffered over the years. This gave her hope for the future and the feeling of despair began to dissipate.

It felt strange to share breakfast with Sebastian and Claude. It had been some weeks since she had done so. Apart from them looking in to enquire of Lucas' progress, she had not seen them. She had been so engrossed in caring for him, that she had been aware of little except his recovery. She thought that it would be nice to catch up with their news and to hear what they had been doing. She was excited to tell them of the improvement in Lucas's condition.

Sebastian was seated at the table engrossed in *The Times*. In front of him, his breakfast plate remained untouched. Although the newspaper hid his face, Aphra could tell that he was very tense and agitated. He was holding the paper in a tight grip. He always did that when he was anxious. Claude was at the sideboard serving himself with scrambled eggs and kidneys. Normally chatty or whistling, he was quiet and obviously trying not to exacerbate the situation. He turned around, about to greet Aphra and enquire about Lucas, when Seb suddenly flung the paper down. His chair fell over as he pushed it back and stood up. Under his breath, she heard him mutter something about him and Claude needing to leave the country. It was so faint, that she almost missed it. He swiftly left the room and rushed along the corridor to his study. Both Aphra and Claude looked at his departing figure and then at each other. Quietly, Claude replaced his dish on the sideboard.

"Excuse me, Aphra," he said as he briskly followed Seb. Just before he left the room, he turned and said to her. "Thank God that we can rely on your discretion – although I think he's getting things out of proportion. He's been a bundle of nerves for days now."

Aphra was puzzled. What did he mean by that? She returned the chair to its proper position and poured herself some coffee. She sat in her usual seat and picked up the paper from where Seb had thrown it, she laid it beside her cup. She was about to reach for some toast, then changed her mind.
Snatching the paper, she scanned through it trying to see what it was that had upset Sebastian. Her eyes glanced across various items that were generally of little interest to her. There were the usual reports of events in both Houses, and which Minister had said what. She could see nothing in

the business section that should worry him. She perused the columns covering military matters - nothing there. She had a brief look at the obituaries - perhaps a friend of his had died, but she could see nothing. She moved on to the court reports. She had completely forgotten about the libel trial. Coming to the end of the rather long report about it, she found what she was looking for. There it was on page 10 in the fourth column. Oscar had been arrested. This was Sebastian's greatest fear. He was terrified of his secret being discovered and being arrested himself. He could not face the shame and the discredit that this would bring to his family name.

In despair, she laid the paper down again. She could not ask Sebastian now. She had no way out. She sat for some time staring straight ahead of her. There was no hope for her. She finally had to accept that she was trapped.

***

In the following two weeks, Aphra spent every day with Lucas. Their closeness intensified - although neither acknowledged this. In some ways, it was the happiest time of their lives.

Visitors began to arrive and Sophie came in at least once a day and helped his recuperation with her childish chatter. To everyone's surprise, he made a full recovery and within a month, he was back at work. His arm was still in a sling, and although, he could not carry out any surgery, he managed to attend to most of his patients and did not complain.

Sebastian was calmer about Oscar's arrest, although he still became agitated if there was anything in the newspapers about it. It took all of Claude and Aphra's best efforts to convince him that they would be safe and not the victims of a witch-hunt.

***

At the end of May, Lucas paid Aphra and Sebastian a visit. They were sitting in the drawing room, when he announced that he had accepted a post in Bath. Aphra found it hard to conceal her shock and sadness at this news.

"But why should you want to leave, when you are doing such good work here and everyone knows you?" She said, trying to keep the emotion out of her voice.

"I expect it's a better position, my dear," said Sebastian. "Is that not the case?" He asked Lucas. "Better prospects and salary."

Lucas said. "Something of the kind."

"Yes, of course," she said. "We wish you all the best Lucas. Please keep in touch. When do you go?"
"They have asked me to begin next week, I have a buyer for my practice and my house. I shall be moving within the week.

They sat chatting for some while as they drank coffee, and Sophie and Claude joined them. Sophie was very upset that the doctor was going away and threw her arms about his neck and hugged him. Aphra thought that it was so easy for her daughter to show her feelings in such an open way and wished that she did not have to hide hers.

When it was time for him to go, she accompanied him outside to say goodbye. The sun was setting. There were no footmen about and they were quite alone.

"Take good care of yourself," she said. "We shall miss you a great deal. In fact, you have no idea how very much."

"Yes, life will be different from now on."

"I fear ..." she stopped. He said nothing for a moment, then asked, "what is it that you fear Aphra?"

She hesitated. "I've never told you this, but I have a secret – a weakness."

"A weakness?"

"Yes, it is something that could be harmful for my family, and I am very afraid that I am going to succumb to it once again very shortly. I feel ashamed to admit it."

He went to say something, but changed his mind.

"Yes?" She said with hope in her heart as he stepped towards her.

"Thank you for everything. For my life." Taking both her hands in his, he lifted each and pressed them to his lips. "Goodbye my dearest, most precious friend." He could say no more. He let go of her hands, turned and walked down the steps.

As he mounted his horse, he looked back and gave a brief wave and then rode down the drive.

For a couple of minutes she stood there alone trying to keep her emotions in check. She could not bear this. He was leaving and she would never see him again. Her heart was breaking and there was nothing that she could do. As the tears began to fall, Claude, who had anticipated her sorrow, joined her.

When Lucas turned to take one final look at the woman he loved, he saw that she was in the arms of the Frenchman with her head on his chest.

***

I know that my heart will never mend.

What unjust and cruel twist of fate brought this soul-mate to me and yet made it impossible for me to tell him that I am free to love him?

Tonight as he rode away and I stood watching him from the steps, I felt as though I was dying inside.

Thank God for Claude, my dear brother who anticipated my anguish and was there to comfort me.

I know that he'll be here when the blackness returns - as it surely will. I sit here tonight waiting for it to descend again, sliding down the walls and engulfing me once again in it's cold, heartless embrace.

***

"You need to get up ma Cherie," said Claude. "This cannot go on. You have been lying here for weeks. We have been here before, Aphra. I know it's worse this time, but you need to try – for Sophie's sake."

For six weeks, Aphra had stayed in her room and had hardly eaten a thing. Emily was very worried about her and the effect it was having on Sophie.

"What is wrong with mama?" She asked Emily.

"She isn't well. Sometimes she gets an illness which makes her sad."

Emily told her kindly. "We have to be patient. She has been like this before. She will get better, we just have to try and be kind and help her."

Emily, Claude and Sebastian had tried everything to get Aphra to respond, but without success.

However, this time she seemed to take notice. "I have been such a bad mother," she said crying. "I have been so sad and have not given any thought to Sophie's needs. I'll try and get up."

Emily helped Aphra get out of bed. Later that day, Sophie came into her mother's room. She looked very happy. "Mama, you are out of bed," she cried as she rushed towards her and gave her a cuddle. "I am so pleased to see that you are up. Does this mean that you're better?" She asked hopefully.

"Not yet," came the faint reply. "But perhaps it is a beginning. I shall try to do something every day."

"You need to start eating," said Emily. "I shall go and get you something from the kitchen."

A few minutes later, she returned carrying a bowl of broth. At first, Aphra was reluctant to eat it, but after a while she managed to eat a little.
As the days passed, so she began to eat more and her strength improved. After a week, she took a bath and washed her hair. Dorothy helped her to dress and she began to look a little better. She was very thin and her clothes hung on her. "Oh, my lady, you have been so poorly. You have lost so much weight. We must get you better - fatten you up," she said.

It was another two weeks before she came downstairs and yet another two before she ventured outdoors. Slowly, she began to pick up the threads of her life and do things. Firstly, she spent a lot of time with Sophie and after a time, she found that she was laughing and playing with the little girl again.

The household staff had been most concerned, and Mrs Drake had done extra work while Aphra had been ill. It was almost autumn before she was more or less back to her old self and busy again. She still felt very sad, but was learning to manage the pain of her loss.

Christmas came and went. Aphra did not feel as though her heart was in it, but she made a big effort for Sophie's sake. But on New Year's Day, she resolved that she must put her troubles behind her. So she determined that she would keep busy and try to enjoy life as best she could. It took the best part of a year before Aphra really felt as though she could function normally again. As spring approached, she threw herself into her work, and appeared to be her old self again. She constantly reminded herself of life in the workhouse.

***

The years passed and a new century arrived. Life continued very much as normal. One afternoon in June, the children were playing on the lawn and making quite a lot of noise. The two women were reclining on comfy chairs under an oak tree. Aphra was reading and Emily had her eyes shut. Aphra looked up at the children and smiled. "They're certainly a boisterous crew. They seem to have been even worse since Philip's recent arrival. I shouldn't like to have the responsibility of looking after him all the time. It can be quite wearing."

There was no response from Emily. She had obviously fallen asleep again. Aphra thought that she was doing that quite a bit lately. As she sat there and looked at her friend, it occurred to her that for some time she had not been looking too well. She looked pale and seemed to have lost weight. Perhaps she was overdoing it or she needed a tonic of some kind. Perhaps a short spell at the cottage would be beneficial and Aphra would look after her. So, less than a week later, they let themselves into their little holiday retreat.

"Ooh, it smells funny in here mama," said Sophie, wrinkling her nose.

"Well, let's get the windows open and some fresh air blowing through. It will soon seem better. It's just that it's been shut up for a long time."

Within no time at all, the children were running up and down the stairs and in and out of the back door discovering forgotten toys, and places to have adventures. It seemed so long ago that it was just Aphra, Emily and Sophie. Nowadays there were five children including Philip. And if there was to be any mischief, nine year old Philip was sure to be at the helm. To accommodate the extra children in the cottage, Emily now shared the bedroom with Aphra and the boys had one room, and the girls the other one. It was rather a tight squeeze, especially now that Philip had joined them.

He was a distant cousin of Sebastian and his heir. His father had died recently and his mother was unwell. She was a rather ineffectual parent and had asked Sebastian if he could have the boy to stay with them for a while. She thought that having an adult male to discipline him might help to curb his unruly behaviour. However, it would seem that most of the care and discipline of the boy had fallen to Aphra. She was a bit peeved at Sebastian for this, but said nothing.

"Keep that noise down," Aphra called out. "Emily is very tired and is going to have a rest. I don't want you disturbing her."

Emily flopped down in an armchair by the fireplace.

"You put your feet up. I'll make some tea," Aphra said, as she went into the kitchen. "I'm going to look after you for a few days – and I'll brook no arguments about it," she added bossily.

Emily felt too tired to argue. A few minutes later, Aphra returned and placed a cup of tea on the table beside Emily, who was asleep again. She opened her eyes and Aphra noticed that there were dark shadows around them.

"Emily, I want you to see a doctor."

"I'm alright – just a bit tired these days. Don't make a fuss."

"No, you're not, and I will make a fuss. Something's wrong and I want to find out what it is and get you treated. You're tired all the time and have been for some while now."

The night before they went back to Methuen Park, Aphra lay on the couch downstairs, which she had decided to do after the first night that they had been there. She listened to Emily coughing. This was not the first time that she had heard her, but it was getting worse. She was now very worried and suspicious about the symptoms.

When they returned home, Aphra insisted that Emily be taken to one of the bedrooms in the house and telephoned for the doctor. She was very concerned that what she had, could be spread to the children.

At first, Emily refused, but Aphra over-ruled her. "I am not only your friend, but your employer too. I have the right to insist on a diagnosis and also to see that you do not infect other members of the household." She knew that she was sounding harsh, and didn't like pulling rank on Emily, but felt that it was necessary.

After the doctor had finished his examination, Aphra saw him to the door and they stepped out into the corridor.

His words confirmed her worst fear. "She has consumption, Milady. She will need to be moved to a sanatorium today."

"I suspected as much. Do you think that she will be alright? Can you help her? I could not bear to lose her. She is so precious – like a sister to me."

"The illness is quite advanced. She admitted to me that she has been coughing up blood for some time now. That is not a good sign."

"Oh my God! When and where could she have been infected? I know of no cases in this area."

"She told me that she went back to visit her relatives in Watheford some while back."

"That's right, she did."

"Well, a few cases in the vicinity have been reported and it seems that she probably contracted it there."

"Why on earth has she been trying to hide it?"

"She said that she didn't want to be sent away. She's worried about her children."

"Foolish girl – did she not see that she was putting them at risk as well?"

"I think, Milady that we need to remember that she does not possess the knowledge that you and I have."

"Yes, of course. I'm being too harsh, but I'm so afraid of losing her. Could you please make the arrangements to have her taken to the sanatorium? She is to have the best of everything. I will take care of any expense."

"I will see to it immediately, Milady."

She indicated to him where the telephone was and left him to make the arrangements. He bowed and went down the stairs. Aphra returned to

Emily and explained what was going to happen. At first, Emily protested, but Aphra would brook no refusal. "You have to go Emily. You will die if you do not get treated. Besides, you are infectious and could risk the children becoming ill too - not to mention everyone else in the household."

At the mention of her children, Emily capitulated and also had to accept that she would not be able to kiss them goodbye. Shortly afterwards, Aphra and Henry stood and watched as the carriage disappeared down the drive. Aphra placed her hand on Henry's arm. "I know how difficult this is for you, but hopefully she is going to the best place where they will make her better."

"I hope so," he said. He turned and looked at her. "What am I going to do about the children?"

"We'll sort something out. For the time being, they can stay here at the house and Tilly can keep an eye on them until we decide what to do. She's a very sensible girl and good with them."

As soon as Aphra had made temporary arrangements for the children, which included Philip having to return to his mother, she sat and wrote a letter to Emily. She thought that it was important for her friend's morale to get regular correspondence. She also decided that she would get the children to write to their mama and draw her little pictures.

The following evening, Sebastian reminded her about the lunch invitation that they had received from Donald and Hortense for the following Saturday at Clarkes Hotel.

"I really don't feel like it at the moment, Seb," she replied. "I'm much too worried about Emily."

"I know, my dear. But it's one of those occasions where we are obliged to attend. They'll be so disappointed if we don't go. Besides, it might help to take your mind off your worries – for an hour or two at least."

"Very well - I'll do my best to rise to the occasion," she agreed reluctantly.

"They want us to bring Sophie with us. I'm sure that she will enjoy it and it's about time that she started to learn how to behave in formal company. What do you think?"

"I think it's a good idea. It's about time that she began to behave like a lady."

"If she doesn't behave like a lady, you have no-one to blame but yourself – allowing her to act like a savage at the cottage, climbing trees and building camps, amassing armies and waging wars etc. Her arms and legs are covered in scabs and bruises," he said smiling.

"I know, but I'm glad that she's had the chance to be a child and just have fun. I'd better make sure that she keeps the adventures to a minimum this week, or just choose a dress that covers everything up."

"Either that, or try her out in that armour in the hall!"

Aphra tried to smile at his joke, but felt too anxious.

It was agreed that they would attend the following Saturday.

Aphra continued to write to Emily daily, keeping her informed of the children's activities. The children also wrote regularly. These missives were usually accompanied by little treats, such as items from the kitchen and little gifts of all kinds, and books too. At first, Emily wrote back, but after a while Aphra realised that Emily was not well enough to do so. She tried to visit her, but was told that she was too sick and besides, it was not safe for Aphra.

***

C'mon man. Put some effort into it. If you can't work faster, I'll soon find someone who can," said George Lambert.

Sweating profusely, Thomas Weedon picked up a tray of Venison in a port wine sauce and carried it through the swing doors to the dining room. He muttered an expletive under his breath, as the sauce dribbled onto the tray.

Seated near the top of the table next to her father, Lady Sophie was nervously copying him and making sure that she used the correct item of cutlery for each course. He, in turn, was discreetly guiding her. Anyone watching would be in no doubt of their closeness and his deep affection for this pretty girl. Although she was used to numerous courses and some degree of formality at home, this was the first time that she had attended such a large and important function. Her mother was seated opposite, next to Lord Albert Proctor, who was an undersecretary to someone in the treasury, and she was trying to look interested in what he had to say.

As the waiter bringing the venison was about to serve Sophie, he glanced across the table at the Countess. He had heard accounts of her beauty. They had not been exaggerated. She was definitely a striking woman. Strangely, she seemed familiar, but that was ridiculous. Where would he be rubbing shoulders with the likes of her kind? This distraction caused him to knock against the shoulder of the Earl's daughter. He had bumped against her twice before. On the second occasion, she had given him a look that made her displeasure quite clear. Now at this, the third time, he spilled a small amount of the hot contents on to her sleeve.

The Earl, who was sitting to her left, saw her flinch, and in an outburst quite at variance with his usual good humour, he snapped at the man. Watch what you're doing! You've hurt my daughter." The strong voice with its Irish lilt carried throughout the room and the chatter was replaced with a deathly hush which seemed to last an age, but was in reality only a second or two. "This will not do. You've already soiled my jacket with the soup. Do be careful man."

Thomas mopped at Sophie's shoulder and apologised to them both. He served the Earl without further spillage and then moved on to the next diner. When he returned to the kitchen, he slammed down the tray and started cursing the aristocracy and upper classes and the way that they spoke to hard working folk. George had to chivvy him up yet again. "Stop moaning and get moving. These dishes are getting cold."

As he served the diners on the opposite side of the table, he looked across at the Earl and his daughter and was suddenly so shocked that he almost dropped the tray. For a few seconds, he stood there staring, and the diner whom he was attending to, had to speak quite harshly to snap him out of his reverie. "Pay attention to what you're doing, for goodness sake, you nearly did it again you clumsy oaf." The diner turned to the guest on his right and made some derogatory comments about the dreadful service and the drop in standards lately.

Back in the kitchen, George warned him. "Just one more mistake and you're out mate!"

"Alright. Alright," retorted Thomas. "I'm doing my best."
He returned with another tray. Again, his attention wandered. He looked again at the Countess. He definitely knew her from somewhere. There had been so many women over the years, that it was difficult to place her. Then it came to him - The virgin at Minehead! It must have been about

fifteen years ago, but she was quite unforgettable. She was nothing at all like his usual type. He remembered now – yes, what a challenge she'd been - bloody hard work, as he remembered, but it had been worth it. She might have looked all coy and demure, but she had been quite a firecracker when he'd got her into bed – very, very passionate.

"Blimey," he thought, fancy having bedded a Countess. But, she'd said she was a servant of some kind – a lady's maid - that was it. Well, she'd gone up in the world. Not like him, having to stoop to taking on casual waiting jobs like this. Life had been so unfair to him and he was definitely heading in the opposite direction and not only in the money department. He knew that his looks had gone. He had aged prematurely, and the drink and tobacco hadn't helped. His bespectacled eyes now lacked the bright lustre of former years and the thinning grey hair struggled to cover his balding, pink pate.

He laughed to himself, when he thought how naïve she'd been to believe him when he'd spoken of marriage and undying love. She must've been stupid to believe that ol' chestnut. Still, she'd done all right for herself since then and he had to admit, she was even more beautiful than she'd been as that innocent young chit of a girl. As he returned to the kitchen, he felt as though something was niggling him, but he pushed it to the back of his mind.

"Com'n Tom, get your mind back on the job. You don't want to lose another one."

He returned the empty tray and picked up another one.

Leaning across sideways, Sophie pleaded with her father to let her have a sip of his wine. At first, he said no, but then, as with everything else in her life, he indulged her

"Alright," he whispered under his breath. "Don't let your mother see or I'll be in trouble. You're far too young."

Aphra saw from across the table and smiled inwardly. Goodness, how that girl twisted daddy around her little finger, she thought. Sophie surreptitiously lifted the claret to her lips unaware that she was being watched by the waiter.

When his boss handed him his money at the end of the day, he informed him that he would not be employing him again and neither would he recommend him to anyone else.

Thomas stomped out of the building and down the road – but not before helping himself to three silver teaspoons and two damask napkins. He was seething. He chewed at his lip. How on earth was he going to manage? Money was really short and his wife never let up about the bills. As he made his way home, his temper began to abate and he went over the incident in his mind. He kept thinking about the girl. He couldn't get her out of his mind

Then his attention turned to her father. There was something familiar about him as well. The Bloody Earl of Tawford. Stuck up git! He'd liked to have punched him on the nose. Hadn't he heard some odd rumour about him – and wasn't he chummy with that queer playwright, Oscar somebody or other – the one that went to jail a few years back for being a poof? Now wasn't that interesting?

As he turned the key in the lock, the boisterous sounds of a large family met his ears. His youngest daughter, Daphne, skipped down the stairs.

"Hello daddy. You're home early," she said. "Haven't lost your job again have you?"

"Don't be so bloody cheeky or I'll clip your ear. Where are you off to?" he demanded in a gruff voice.

"I'm off to see Elsie," she replied as she adjusted her hat. Looking in the hall mirror, she primped and preened herself. Thomas was about to tell her not to stay out too late. He stared at her reflection and then at her again. The hair colour was all wrong and the build was slightly different, but he was in no doubt that he was staring at the face of the daughter of the Earl of Tawford.

He opened the door for Daphne and stepped out of her way as she flounced past him.

"I shan't be long Mama," she called. He watched her as she lightly stepped off the pavement and crossed the road. Closing the door, he smiled secretly to himself. He had very little paternal tenderness, but his mind was fathering a scheme that would satisfy his avaricious nature.

He felt sure that his money worries would soon be over!

***

Sebastian read the letter and thought that he was going to be sick.

Your highness

We have a business deal to put to you, concerning you and your French friend. We know you're not the father of the girl. £10 would do nicely for the time being. Make sure it's in coins. We'll be waiting for you tomorrow night at 7 of the clock outside the parish church in Westbridge. Don't tell anyone about this or the story goes to the papers – and you don't want to end up in Reading Gaol do you?

A well wisher

"What's the matter?" Said Claude. "You've gone as white as a sheet."

"It's nothing," he said, stuffing the letter into his inside pocket. "A personal matter that one of the tenants wants to talk to me about. He's asked that I keep it confidential. Sorry – can't share it with you. Excuse me." He got up and went to his study.

Claude looked at Aphra. "He's hiding something."

"Give him time. He'll tell you when he's ready," she said.

***

The following evening, Sebastian dismounted his horse and tied it up to the lych-gate. He was not a violent man and unused to carrying weapons, but in his hand, he clutched a small knife. He felt that he needed to protect himself from these brigands as he walked warily through the churchyard.

"I'm glad to see that you've made the sensible choice and decided to attend our little gathering." A hooded man stepped from the shadows. He gestured to a figure moving around a short distance from them.

"What's all this about?" Sebastian tried to use his most imperious tone of voice. "What do you mean by writing to me in such an offensive manner?"

"Oh I think that we both know the answer to that question – otherwise you wouldn't be here, would you, your highness?" He sneered. "Now, 'ave you got the money?"

"I'm not paying you anything until you tell me what this is about!"

"Well, let's begin with your daughter. I know things about you and I know that you're not her real father, so don't deny it."

Sebastian was sweating now. God this was a nightmare. How did he find this out? What else did this man know? He was now really scared, but needed to keep his mind clear. "What utter nonsense!" His voice shook.

"No it isn't nonsense. It's a fact. Now tell me about your French friend. I'm very interested to hear about him."

"There's nothing to tell. Look, take this money and I don't want to hear from you again. You're nothing but a bloodsucking thief."

Thomas snatched the purse from the shaking outstretched hand. "I hope it's all there. We don't want to have to come all the way up to the grand house to collect the remainder."

"How dare you – just stay away from my family, you bastard."

"I don't really want to go to the trouble of coming up to the house, so let's say that we'll meet again in four weeks' time – same time, same place." He tossed the purse from one hand to the other flippantly. "And don't try any funny business. Remember I've got proof which is being kept in a safe place – with friends." He began to walk off and then turned around. "Oh, I nearly forgot – make it twenty next time." As he walked towards the other figure, he began to whistle to himself.

Sebastian staggered to a bench by the church wall. He put his head in his hands and couldn't stop shaking. He kept going over and over the same questions in his mind. How did these people know about him and Claude? How did they know the truth about Sophie? What was the evidence that they had? Claude and he had always been so careful. He knew that he could completely trust Aphra. She would never say anything, so where had the information come from? God, what was he going to do?"

***

Thomas could not believe his luck. Ten quid for a few minutes work and there would be more where that came from. He had been very clever – very clever indeed. It was funny when he thought about it now. What a stroke of luck to have had those two jobs.

Firstly, the one where he was serving drinks in that posh place in London a few years back. That was where that queer writer and his boyfriend held court. What was it called now – Ah yes, the Café Royale. He hadn't realised it at first, but now he remembered that the Earl of Tawford had been present and so had that French chap – more than once. He recognised the Earl at that luncheon a couple of weeks back along. Since then, he had been asking a lot of questions and listening to a lot of gossip. Word had it that the Countess, his own dear little virgin, was carrying on with the French chap and that he had fathered the girl. Well, he knew for a fact that the latter was not the case. He only had to look at her to know that she was his own daughter.

So was there any truth behind all these rumours about the grand lady and the frog? He suspected not – or at least, not in the way that everyone else thought there was. One of the few things he remembered about the Countess - now that he recalled it, because it had really annoyed him at the time - was her telling him about her father – he sounded a bit like himself – liked the ladies and a good time and didn't much like being tied down to some goody goody. He remembered thinking how silly she was to get so upset because her father had a mistress. She believed that her mother had pined away because of it. If that was the case, she must have been a very stupid woman – but then most women were stupid – only good for one thing. Anyway, from that recollection, he did not think that she would be the kind of woman to cheat on her husband. So, what was going on?

Then it had come to him in a blinding flash. It was the other way around. The Earl was carrying on with the Frenchman!

The other thing that he thought he had been very clever to think of, was to bring his sixteen year old son, Jimmy with him. He was ideal for jobs like this. He was very tall and with a stocky build, but not very bright. Thomas had promised to give him sixpence if he hung about in the churchyard while he had a business meeting. It worked out very well. The stupid toff got the impression that there was a gang.

He would use Jimmy again next month. He would tell him to keep his mouth shut and promise him a shilling, if he said nothing to his mother.

Pushing open the door of the *Dog and Duck*, he said, "Come on son, we've earned ourselves a tankard of ale each. I've made over ten shillings tonight. I'll be in your mother's good books when I give her five of them. As the ale quenched his thirst, he also thought that it was inspired of him to mention having proof. That clinched it. The Earl definitely had something to hide.

***

As summer moved into autumn, so Emily's condition seemed to deteriorate. Aphra did what she could to comfort Henry and the children, but it was becoming increasingly apparent that Emily was very ill. As the nights drew in, so Aphra struggled with her feelings of sadness about the inevitable loss that was approaching.

Also, she had noticed recently that Sebastian had seemed different. Claude had noticed it too.

"What do you think is wrong with him?" She asked.

"I don't know. I've asked him, but he says there's nothing wrong and to leave him alone. I can't help him, if he won't confide in me."

"Perhaps he has some business worries."

"It's not that. He always talks to me about any problems of that kind. No this is something more serious. I can trace it back to when he received that letter. Do you remember?"

"Yes. His reaction was very strange."

"I've tried asking him again and again about it, but he just gets more annoyed."

"I do hope that he isn't ill. I couldn't stand anyone else being ill. I can't seem to think of anything but Emily lately."

***

The news that we have all been dreading has come. My darling Emily is dead, and I am inconsolable. I have cried so much. I cannot believe how many tears a body can hold. I am trying to be strong for her dear little children and Henry.

It has been so difficult, these last few weeks. The superintendent of the sanatorium has repeatedly refused to allow us to visit her – except on one occasion a couple of weeks ago – and then it was only from a distance. They had wheeled her bed out onto the terrace, as they did daily with all of the patients – no matter what the temperature. Henry and the children and I stood a few yards away on the lawn by the trees. It was as much as we could do to stop the little ones from running to her.

She looked so thin and pale. It was as though she had shrunk away to nothing. It broke my heart. I could see that she was very weak and as she waved to us, it was apparent that even that was too much effort for her. She could not speak to us, but we called out to her, and the children sang a song that they had been practising. I told her how well the children were doing and not to worry about them.

"I'll write to you," I said.

When we turned and walked away, I knew in my heart that we would not see her again, and sadly, I have been proved right.

Henry and I are making the arrangements for her funeral. She wishes to be buried in the churchyard at Watheford. It is going to be so hard on her family there. Her father recently died and her mother is now elderly and not at all well.

There is also the problem of what to do about the children. Since Emily became ill, Miss Kincaid has kindly been teaching them. However, we need to make some permanent arrangements for them. Perhaps Emily's sister, Peggy, might look after them and bring them up with her own children. This would mean that Henry could visit them regularly and they could come and stay here during the school holidays. Naturally, I will put aside some funds to make things easier for the family.

Today, we made the journey to Watheford for Emily's funeral. Sebastian had intended to come, but he was so drunk last night, that he was in no fit state to attend. I made apologies for his absence to Mrs Frances – explaining that he was not well enough to travel and saying that he sent his condolences. This was not strictly an untruth – for I know that had he been in his right mind, he would have been very sad and sympathetic about the loss of Emily. However, he seems so preoccupied with whatever it is that is troubling him, that he seems to show no concern or interest in anyone or anything else. Thank goodness for Claude, he has been a rock for me.

The little church was full of Emily's family and many friends from the village. Some of the staff from Warrington Grange were there too. I was very surprised to see Caroline standing at the back of the church. I could not understand why she had come – especially when one thinks about how she and Emily parted company. Perhaps, she thinks that as her previous employer, it would be bad form for her not to attend.

When they brought Emily's coffin in, I thought that my heart would break. The sobbing and wailing in the church was so loud, that at first it was difficult to hear the vicar.

As we sang hymns and prayed, my mind went back to that Christmas that we had shared at Warrington Grange and the service that we had attended at the church. I remembered us trying not to giggle as some pompous gentlemen read from the bible, and the joy that we shared together when we celebrated back at the Grange and the gifts that we exchanged.

I recalled that first day, when I arrived at Warrington Grange, almost close to death myself and how caring she had been to me.

Then I remembered her radiant as a beautiful young bride on the arm of her proud father.
Oh my dear friend, I miss you so much. I hope that there is a life beyond this, where we will meet again one day and laugh and play together in the sunshine.

As we stood by the grave and they lowered the coffin into the ground, I thought that poor Henry was going to pass out, as he fell to his knees. I felt as though I could not stand to see that wooden box containing the ravished body of my best friend being lowered into that dark pit. Dear Claude put his arms around me and I turned my head and cried on his shoulder as he rubbed my arm.

After a few minutes, I pulled myself together and as I wiped my eyes, I looked straight ahead and into the cold, judgemental eyes of Caroline. Even here on this tragic occasion, she could not hide the hatred that she felt for me.

***

Claude and I are becoming increasingly concerned about Sebastian. He is drinking so much and he keeps going out alone at night. He will not tell us where he is going. We hear him riding off and he is gone for hours. When he returns, he just goes to his study and won't speak to us. I'm convinced that it has something to do with that letter he received a few months ago, for the change in him began around that time. I wish that I could comfort him, but until he accepts our offers *of help, there is nothing that Claude or I can do.*

It is now some weeks since we lost our dear Emily. I feel as though I cannot stand it. Both Sophie and I are devastated by this tragedy. Fortunately for her, her youth enables her to have periods of freedom from the grief. I suppose that this is the resilience of children. We try to keep ourselves occupied by walking in the grounds and playing the piano together and reading stories. This helps a little - and Miss Kincaid has been wonderful– doing her best to come up with interesting diversions for her, but I know that Sophie's school work is suffering a great deal. I am grateful that Miss Kincaid is not being too harsh with her at present.

I am trying to keep on top of things as far as running the household and answering correspondence is concerned, but my concentration is not good. Mrs Drake has been wonderful. I don't know what I would do without her.

Claude has done his best to console us, but he is now so worried about Sebastian, that I know it is very hard for him to have the time and energy to devote to us. I think that it is making him depressed as well. I am also very concerned. It has occurred to me that Sebastian is becoming insane, for his behaviour is very odd. I have been wondering if I should send for the doctor, but then I would be exposing Sebastian to goodness knows what. He is not dealing with any of his affairs and Claude and I are at our wits ends trying to cover up his lapses.

I have had to cancel a number of engagements and have also had to telephone to apologise on Sebastian's behalf for his absence at certain functions, or the delay in dealing with urgent matters. Fortunately, because he has done so much good work in the past, people have been very understanding about his present indisposition. I have told them that he is suffering from exhaustion due to overwork and this seems to be the best explanation at the moment.

As for myself, I am, once again, fighting my unwanted companion which seems to return to me time and again. The black clouds swirl around outside the windows and it feels as though they are trying to find a way in. The dark, cold, early hours in the morning are the worst time. This is when the longing for Lucas returns so strongly and I ache for him to lie here beside me and hold me, telling me that it is alright – and that one day, I will see Emily again. But this is sheer foolishness. I will not see him again, and my faith is at such a low ebb, that I doubt that I will ever see Emily again either – or my mother and grandparents or Rose, or Mrs Brookes. Perhaps all the suffering in this life is for nothing – no purpose at all.

But I must not dwell on these gloomy thoughts. I must be strong for my family – especially Sebastian, who needs me now so much. I think that I must make a firm decision to speak to him tomorrow – insisting that he tells me what is wrong. If I knew what the problem was, then I'm sure that I could be of help to him.

***

My mood is even lower. The melancholy is so overwhelming, but I am trying to overcome it. I must not let it get the better of me. I must win this battle, but the worry over Sebastian is becoming very wearying.

Today, he seemed very agitated and went off alone in the woods. He could hardly bring himself to speak to us. Yesterday, he spoke quite harshly to Sophie – a thing that he never does. She ran to her room and I found her weeping there. It took me some time to pacify her. However, he has apologised to her and she seems much consoled. They are the best of friends again – much to my relief.

I am also very concerned about the drinking. It seems to be getting worse. Also, the trips that he takes out at night are becoming more frequent. Where can he be going?

Tonight, after dinner, he said that he was going down to the gunroom. I don't understand. He doesn't like guns. He certainly never shoots them. All this is putting a tremendous strain on Claude. When he offered to accompany Sebastian, he put his hand up and said that he preferred to be alone.

He was still downstairs when we retired for the night. This is becoming a frequent practice and I have wondered whether or not something is wrong between them, but Claude says not and I don't like to pry. It is now past midnight and I have a terrible sense of foreboding.

Tomorrow, I will insist that he tells us what is wrong, for we cannot go on like this.

***

5th December 1900

I have not written in my journal for a number of days – terrible, terrible days – the worst yet. I cannot stand this pain - this sadness, this dreadful shock.

It was past midnight in the early hours of the 30th when I finally went to bed. It took me a long time to get to sleep, but I finally drifted off. It could only have been a few minutes later, when a loud noise awoke me. At first, I thought that it had been in my dream, but shortly afterwards, I heard the sound of someone running down the stairs. I switched on the light and went and opened my door to see what was happening. All was silent and I was about to return to my bed when I heard a high pitched wailing - like the sound of an animal in pain.

I knew where the sound was coming from – the gun room - and in my heart, I knew what I would find. However, this did not prepare me for the carnage that I beheld when I entered the room. On the floor, cradled in Claude's arms, lay the inert body of our dear Sebastian. The blood was everywhere. Claude looked at me with agony in his eyes. He turned to his dead lover and kissed him repeatedly, as if it would restore life. I knelt down beside them both. I felt Sebastian's wrist for a pulse, although I knew that this was futile, for most of his head was splattered across the walls and ceiling of the gun room.

I put my arms around Claude. It was the living that needed caring for now. "Come away from here Claude," I said. "There is nothing more that we can do for him."

"I don't want to leave him. I want to die with him," he sobbed.

I wiped his blood soaked face with a rag that I had found. By this time, we were both covered in blood as we were kneeling in it. I held Claude's head on my shoulder and tried to comfort him – goodness knows what I said.

Then I heard footsteps. "Claude, you must pull yourself together," I said a little more sharply. "We must not let the servants see you so distraught." I had to prise his fingers away from Seb's body. As Travis and Mrs Drake entered the room, I had my arms around Claude, helping him to his feet and was whispering that he must compose himself until I could get him back to his room.

"Oh my God!" Screamed Mrs Drake. "What's happened?"

"There's been a dreadful accident. His Lordship must have knocked the trigger whilst cleaning the gun." I tried to sound convincing. "It's given Monsieur a bad shock. It was he who found him. I shall take him upstairs. I'm sorry to leave you with this Travis. I don't know what to do." I was struggling to hold on to Claude as I was shaking so much myself that I thought I was going to faint.

"I shall telephone for the doctor, Milady."

"But there's nothing that can be done for him," I said.

"I realise that Ma'am, but a doctor will be needed to complete the death certificate."

"Of course – I'm not thinking straight. Thank you. Can you please keep the other servants away from here? We don't want anyone else to witness this dreadful scene."

"Are you alright Milady? Is there anything that we can get you?"

"Perhaps some brandy for us. Thank you." I made my way to the door and kept a tight grip on Claude's arm. "Please, have some yourselves too. This must be a terrible shock for you both as well."

I managed to get Claude up to his bathroom and ran a bath for him. While he got into it, I went to my room and dressed. Mrs Drake had left a tray with the brandy on it. I drank some quickly and poured a glass for Claude.

I was going to have to attend to a number of difficult tasks. The worst of these was telling Sophie. I waited until she awoke at seven thirty, by which time, the doctor and the police had been and gone. The body had been taken away and the servants had begun to clean the gun room. I told her that daddy had had a nasty accident with a gun and had gone to join Emily in heaven.

She is so shocked and I have never seen her sob so much. This is a terrible burden for a child to have to bear - especially on top of her recent loss. I think that when the funeral is over, I shall take her on a holiday – perhaps we will go with Claude to his family. Some sunshine will help all of us to come to terms with this tragedy.

I keep going to see to Claude in his room. Most of the time, he is in a drunken stupor. Although I know that this amount of alcohol is not good for him, I have decided that perhaps it is for the best for the time being. At least if he is asleep, he is not running screaming around the house.

Thank God that the doctor and the police both think that it was a terrible accident. If they'd had any suspicion that it was suicide, then there would no doubt be all manner of problems – one of them being that Sebastian would not be able to be buried in consecrated ground.

Travis and Mrs Drake have been stalwarts in helping me make the arrangements for the funeral in a week's time. It is going to be a huge affair and I am dreading it. Goodness knows how Claude is going to cope. Perhaps it would be better if he did not attend, but I cannot see him agreeing to that.

Somehow, I must just take each day as it comes and deal with each problem as it occurs.

***

Dear Mildred,

Well there's has been a real carry on here I can tell you. No doubt, you'll have heard the dreadful news. Oh my God – it was the worst thing I've ever seen in my life. Mr Travis and I were awoken in the early hours by a loud noise (which we now know was the gunshot) and then this dreadful screaming - like a banshee. It must have been the mistress. We rushed downstairs to where the noise was coming from. When we walked into the gun room (that was where it happened), both the mistress and Monsieur were covered in blood.

Oh Mildred, the poor man's brains were plastered all over the walls. Fortunately, his face was not touched. I don't understand how it could have happened. The mistress said that the gun must have gone off while he was cleaning it, but I don't see how it could have removed the whole of the back of his head and not touched his face.

When we got there, the two of them seemed to be huddled together. As you know, I don't like to fan the flames, but they do seem very close. Also, he seems to spend a lot of time in his room and she keeps going in there. It's all very odd. I feel bad about saying such harsh things about the Countess, for I do really like her and she does have some wonderful qualities, but this conduct is most unseemly.

Well, I must close, as there are so many arrangements to be made before the funeral.

Your friend,

Hetty

***

The vast, gothic cathedral was at full capacity. As Lucas sat waiting for the solemn service to commence, he wondered to himself how many people were actually present. Could they be numbered in the hundreds or thousands, and how many people were there outside on the green facing the west front – let alone the multitude lining the cobbled, rain-soaked streets? He'd had no idea how popular Sebastian had been, and had been moved by the numbers that he had seen sobbing – even grown men. In the days following the Earl's mysterious accident, he had heard countless tales of his goodness and generosity to so many people.

The usual chilled atmosphere of the cathedral had been replaced by a stuffy, damp – almost steamy ambiance, and its musty smell filled his nostrils. Next to him, resplendent in black lace and taffeta, sat Caroline. He looked at her and attempted a wan smile. Looking into her eyes, he saw no sign of grief or sorrow. Earlier, when they had been discussing the terrible accident, he had been shocked at a remark that she had made.

"Yes, it's very unfortunate, but not surprising. I wonder which it was – suicide or murder."

He had not known how to reply. "Caroline, that's a dreadful thing to say. Surely, you don't really think that."

"Well, I heard that both the secretary fellow and the grieving widow were covered in blood – all over them apparently."

Lucas was so troubled by the idea, that he asked her not to persist in this vein. She shrugged her shoulders and looked away sulkily. Now, as his eyes roamed around the medieval building, his mind went over and over the conversation. It made him feel nauseous.

His reverie was interrupted by the sound of the huge wooden doors being pushed back and scraping on the flagstones beneath. At the same moment, the music began. The choir started to sing out the sombre and moving notes of Mozart's Requiem. He shuddered. It needed eight pallbearers to carry Sebastian's coffin. He had been a big man. They swayed slightly as they stepped in time to the dramatic music. As they passed Lucas, he subconsciously noted that a spray of green and white flowers lay upon the lid of the coffin. They reminded him of something, but he could not remember what it was.

Slowly, the procession of family and close friends made its way up the aisle towards the quire. At the head, was the Bishop, closely followed by Sebastian's widow and his best friend. Behind them, walked Sophie – frightened, pale faced and trying to be brave and grown up as she walked through this nightmare.

As they passed the row of seats where Lucas and Caroline were sitting, he noticed that Aphra and Claude had linked arms, as though he was supporting the grieving widow – and yet somehow it looked all wrong. Caroline leaned towards him and whispered "See – what did I tell you? She has no shame. She's even caressing him in public – in church, in front of the Bishop, the congregation and the child."

Lucas thought that perhaps that was it. That was what was wrong.

Caroline continued her malicious diatribe against Aphra. Would she never tire of her hatred of Aphra? It was a well-fed emotion.

By the time the music had ended and the coffin had been laid on the bier, the entire congregation was seated and the Bishop began the service, which took the traditional form. Prayers were said and hymns sung and the Bishop spoke at length about the Earl's full life and good works which were numerous. But it was after this that the service took an unexpected turn. Lucas noticed that the Bishop looked non-too pleased as he sat down on his throne. Quietly, Aphra stood up and walked towards the lectern. Placing a piece of paper on it, she coughed slightly and stood still for some moments. Lucas, like everyone else in the congregation, was surprised – shocked even that a woman in her position should do such a thing.

At first, her voice was very quiet – almost inaudible. Then, as her confidence grew, it resonated around the cathedral. Her words were moving and carefully chosen.

"I am sure that many of you will be surprised at my giving this eulogy for my husband. I know that this is unusual – perhaps unprecedented, but I have my own private reasons for doing this.

I knew my husband, the Earl, like no one else did. No man could have been a kinder spouse or honourable friend. He was known to all of you as a benevolent man – a good and fair master and landlord. Yes, he was privileged to have been born into the aristocracy, but he never abused his position of wealth and status. In fact, he used both of these to improve the lives of those whom he considered to be his responsibility. He cared very much for those people and for the land that he had inherited. Outwardly, he always appeared to be extremely confident and self-assured, but privately, he was a different man and it was the role of a spouse to share his private fears and secrets, his weaknesses as well as his strengths together with his personal suffering. Naturally, I could not mention them and I intend to take them to my grave, but life is not always what one expects it to be and one can often make the mistake of misinterpreting situations.

I felt that I wanted to tell you how great and kind the private man was - what a kind, gentle and loving father. It is not a public thing for people to know those little moments of tenderness and even one's idiosyncrasies, but for the person to whom he was closest, there are a million treasured memories that are secure in their secrecy from the outside world. I ask you all to pray for the soul of Sebastian Raemond, whom I believe is now with his maker, and for the two people who will morn his loss the most – his daughter and his spouse."

There was a two minute silence, while the whole congregation, with heads bowed, prayed for the spirit of the dead Earl. It was a strange eulogy, and even though it only failed to reach the heart of one person there, Lucas did feel that there was something detached about the way it was delivered – almost spoken in the third person. He heard Caroline snort and tut to herself a number of times.

As Aphra spoke, he felt guilty that his thoughts had turned to his feelings for her. Now that she was widowed, he could perhaps let these feelings for her be known. He made the decision that he would call on her after a respectable period of three or four weeks. He had already sent his condolences by letter, but felt that it would be in order to call in person. This would give him the opportunity to become reacquainted with her and renew their friendship.

As the service came to an end, Aphra, Sophie and Claude approached the coffin. Firstly, Aphra put her left hand out and touched the lid. Sophie was holding her right hand, but laid her other hand on the lid as her mother was doing. Together they silently prayed and then stepped back and Claude moved closer. He knelt down and put his hands over his face and leaned towards the coffin. For some seconds, he was silent, but then he made a strange noise as though he was choking.

"Looks as though he's losing his nerve. That's guilt talking," Caroline muttered under her breath. At the same moment, Aphra moved forward and grabbed Claude by the shoulders, leaning over him and saying something to him in private. She seemed to touch his shoulders in a rather familiar way.

"You can see who's in control there," said Caroline. "That one won't lose her nerve."

"Shut up Caroline," Lucas whispered, hardly moving his lips or turning his head.

Soon after this, the main exodus from the cathedral began. Lucas waited to see Aphra and the rest of funeral cortege pass his pew. Caroline drew his attention to the familiarity between Aphra and Claude. Although she held Sophie's hand, her head was leaning very close towards Claude, so that their faces were obscured from view and her other hand appeared to be caressing his arm. Lucas had to accept that Caroline's accusations were now confirmed. He could not deny it. At first, Aphra did not see him, for she only seemed to have eyes for Claude. But then, she looked to the side and saw Lucas. What was it that he saw in her expression? Sorrow, guilt, surprise, pleasure? It was as though a multitude of emotions crossed her face. Whatever it was, it was irrelevant now. Within twenty-four hours he would be on his way back to Bath.

***

Now I have quite a headache. I should not have had as much brandy as I did, but I felt that I needed something to help me relax. I'm not sure that it has been successful. I suppose people who drink a lot must feel like this much of the time – how unpleasant!

Thank God today is over.

When everyone had left, I did something I never do. When I asked Travis to bring me a brandy, he raised his eyebrows as I added "Leave the bottle as well please."

Claude has gone straight to his room. Sophie has done the same. Poor lamb. She is quite exhausted. I keep looking in on her and fortunately, she is fast asleep. That is one of the advantages of youth. One can sleep and get a few hours release from the tribulations of life. I just hope that she does not have nightmares like she did after Emily died.

At least we managed to get through this ordeal without anything too disastrous happening. It was most daunting, getting up to give the eulogy and I suspect that many were surprised – even shocked at my doing so – but it was something that I wanted – needed to do for Sebastian and Claude.

Towards the end of the service, Sophie and I stepped towards the coffin. She was sobbing. I felt strangely numb, as though I was in a dream.

She put her hand on the lid of the coffin. "Goodbye daddy. I'll see you in heaven."

She turned towards me and I put my arm around her.

"You're being a very brave girl. Daddy will still love you very much now that he is in heaven and he will be happy."

Yet I felt so angry with him for what he had done, guilty that I had been unable to help him and desolate that my dear friend had gone. I was giving Sophie my assurance about his being happy in the afterlife, but did I believe that his maker would forgive him for taking his own life? Would he be burning in the fires of hell for eternity? Was there anything after this?

Suddenly, Claude approached the coffin. He dropped to his knees, placing both hands on the lid.

"Don't leave me, my love," he whispered as he leant his head close to the wood.

"Claude, you must stand up," I pleaded under my breath. "Don't do this – please."

His choked weeping was audible to me and would soon be so to others if it got any louder.

"I can't survive without you – please come back," he sobbed in French– hopefully no-one else could hear or understand what he said. As he began to slump forward onto the coffin, I leant over him.

"Get up Claude – now!" I demanded in a hushed but forceful tone. I gripped his shoulders with both hands and with my lips next to his right ear, I repeated my words. He seemed not to hear me. Any moment now, he would prostrate himself on the flagstones.

"Claude, you're drawing attention to yourself. Stop it at once!" I commanded him and he seemed to hear me at last.

"I don't care. I want to die."

"I know, but not here. Think of the harm that you'll do to Seb's memory. You must pull yourself together – now!"

I put a hand beneath his elbow and pulled. He responded at last and got to his knees. I tried to guide him back to his seat. Thinking that he was going to collapse, I put my arm around his waist. Goodness knows what impression this must have made upon the congregation. I looked at him and it shocked me to see how red and swollen his eyes were in contrast to his pale, drawn complexion.

"God," I prayed silently. "Please don't let anyone see this. It will be his undoing."

I managed to get him seated and as I sat down too, I tried to compose myself.

After this, much of what happened seems to be a blur to me now. I remember that we were walking back down the aisle. I was trying to steady him when we passed the seat where Lucas was sitting. I turned and looked at him for a second. He returned my gaze. For a few seconds, my spirits soared as I realised that I was now free and that perhaps we could be together at last.

However, I must not be selfish and must attend to Claude's and Sophie's needs.

Now, as I sit here once again in the lonely, bleak hours of the night, my thoughts drift to him and hope and longing return.

***

Dear Mildred,

My apologies for the delay in replying to your last letter, but as you can imagine, things have been at sixes and sevens here.

The service was very moving with beautiful music – but the behaviour of the Countess and the French chap was quite peculiar - shocking even. She seemed to keep holding on to him. I understand that a widow needs support, but it was rather undignified and the eulogy that she gave – most odd I call it. Still, it isn't my place to pass judgement on the behaviour of others.

I expect that they will marry soon.

I wonder what will happen next. The new Earl, Master Philip, is far too young to take over the running of things. We shall just have to wait and see. The Countess has mentioned going to France for the winter to Monsieur's family. Of course, Mr Travis and I shall look after things here.

Well, it won't do to sit here. I have the accounts to attend to.

I'll let you know if there are any further developments.

Yours truly,

Hetty

***

Another day begins as I sit here waiting and hoping that he will come. It is now some weeks and there has been no word since his kind letter of condolence. Surely he must be coming - soon. Perhaps he is waiting for a decent period of time to elapse. Yet I felt sure that after everything that he had written in his journal, he would not be able to wait to be with me.

I need to keep busy to make time pass and hope that this pain will lessen in time – but I do not want time to pass without him – for that would be to waste time. I want time to stop. I am in such turmoil. I don't understand. I shall never forget the way that he looked at me in the cathedral. There was such love in his eyes, but there was something else too. What was it? Perhaps I'm wrong. Perhaps his love for me has died. Perhaps it was a transitory thing and it's just me doing the feeling, and wanting to keep it alive.

I'm being so selfish and self-absorbed and sorry for myself. People have worse things than this to deal with, and manage to get on with their lives and cope. But I feel so burnt out trying to be strong for Sophie and Claude.

God, it was a terrible Christmas - my poor child trying to enjoy her presents and none of us being able to eat the food. Even the servants were depressed and sombre. The tree seemed like a tasteless joke stuck there in the hall. The decorations looked so garish, but we had to try and make an effort for Sophie. What burden will she carry through life? I am so angry with Sebastian. How could he do this to us? I know that Claude will never recover. In fact, I fear that he may also take his own life. I am exhausted trying to keep constant watch over him. His drinking worries me greatly. He needs to have the attention of a doctor, but of course, I cannot let the doctor near him, for he would not understand the depth of Claude's grief and I cannot trust Claude's ability to be discreet. I must just hope that his pain will lessen in time.

I must dress and plan my day. Perhaps if the weather is not too inclement, I could take Sophie out for a walk in the parkland. The fresh air and exercise will be good for us. But I don't know if I have the energy. I just want to crawl back into bed and sleep. Oh how I wish I could sleep. Perhaps Dr Osborne could prescribe me some laudanum. Then I could drift off and get away from all this, but maybe that would not be such a good idea, for it may become a habit, or perhaps I might be tempted to take too much!

But it is not Dr Osborne or his remedies that I need – it is the other doctor – the one who lives in my soul. If only he would come, my soul would soar in spite of all the death and mourning around me. But somehow I sense that he is not coming and when I know this for sure, how will I live with that knowledge day after day for the rest of my life?

***

Today, I had to attend a meeting in Westbridge. I didn't feel like going - I didn't have to, but I thought that I really must try and get back to some semblance of normality. Everyone was very kind to me - offering their condolences and asking if there was anything that they could do. I say that everyone was very kind - there was one exception. Caroline was there.

"Aphra," she said. "I must tell you. I received a lovely letter from Lucas yesterday. He tells me that he has now settled back into the routine of hospital life. The man is an absolute saint. We saw quite a bit of each other while he was here. It was so enjoyable."

I didn't know what to say, other than "Oh!"

She continued with relish! "Such a detailed letter and so thoughtful. I really think that he's missing me."

It was as though she knew how much it would hurt me, but surely she can have no knowledge of my feelings for him - but she had that "cat's got the cream" look in her eyes.

Of course, they were together in the cathedral – but there's nothing in that, is there? Surely he is not interested in her. In fact, I've always sensed that he positively disliked her. Naturally, he has never said anything derogatory about her – it would not be in his nature. Besides, he keeps his own counsel and yet I'm sure that he finds her quite repellent (as I think most people do!). There I'm being spiteful now – but she does bring out the worst in me.
I sometimes get the feeling that she says malicious things about me behind my back. I have no actual knowledge of this other than a vague suspicion. What she says to my face is hardly complimentary, so why should I expect anything better said in my absence? But I do wonder whether she says things to Lucas to poison his mind against me, for looking back in the past, there were times when his attitude towards me was changeable and inexplicable.

Why, why has he gone?

***

When Caroline returned home after the meeting, she was in a strange mood. Firstly, she felt a smug sense of satisfaction as she remembered the hurt look on Aphra's face. It had been a long time since she'd had the opportunity to attack her in person. Usually, it was done behind her back. She crowed to herself as she thought of the crestfallen expression that was so apparent on Aphra's face. It had made an exceedingly tedious meeting tolerable.

The maid brought in her tea and placed it on the table beside her. Will there be anything else ma'am?" She enquired nervously.

"No. You may go," she suddenly found herself snapping. In a less harsh tone, she added. "I'll ring for you, if I need anything else. Thank you."

"Blimey!" Thought the girl, as she closed the door behind her. "She actually thanked me."

As Caroline poured out the tea, she reminded herself that she needed to be careful that she did not lose another servant. Over the years, so many had come and gone. The only original ones that were left were Isaacs, Mildred, Grace Flowers and that dimwit of a scullery maid - she couldn't remember the girl's name. As she brooded on these matters, her thoughts once again turned to Aphra. She had to admit that no personal maid ever even remotely attained her high standards. She had been so smart, so quick-thinking and efficient. She had used her initiative, and even though Caroline had tried to undermine her at every turn, Aphra somehow, seemed to rise above it. God! How she hated her. Even that blasted girl Emily had been a very good servant, and she hadn't been able to match her either. She hated her as well. Damn the pair of them!

She thought again about the conversation that afternoon. She had always suspected that Aphra had feelings for Lucas. She could never quite understand it, for there was always the question of the Frenchman. Perhaps she would marry him now.

Soon the satisfaction that she had felt began to evaporate. She went to her bureau and re-read the letter for the umpteenth time. No matter how much she wished it, she could not make the words say what she wanted to hear from him.

***

Dear Miss Grenville,

Thank you for your invitation to dinner next month. I am very busy at the hospital and will be unable to attend.

It was a strange coincidence how we bumped into each other at the County Hotel whilst I was staying there.

I trust that the coming year will continue to be prosperous for you.

Yours sincerely,

Dr L Thornton-Ellis

***

She may have been able to insinuate to Aphra that there was some bond between Lucas and herself, but she knew the truth. He could not abide her. Nothing had ever been said by anyone to indicate Aphra and Lucas' feelings for one another, but Caroline had been only too aware of it - especially after that night at the ball years before. Since Aphra had married Sebastian, Caroline had made it her business to know everything about her and when they were in each other's company she watched her continually. She also watched Lucas, and he could not take his eyes off her.

As she remembered all this, the terrible feeling of sadness was soon superseded by rage and envy that she found almost impossible to control. She could never win Lucas' love, but somehow, she must do something to exact revenge on Aphra. If it took her the rest of her life, she would make her pay.

***

As Aphra walked into the small teashop, she heard the bells of the parish church across the road chime. She was wearing a veil which covered her face. She didn't want people to recognise her. She took a rear facing seat in a corner of the room and a lady wearing a floral dress and a white apron approached her.

"Good day modom," she said in an attempt to sound what she considered to be "posh". "What can I get you?"

"Just a pot of Earl Grey for two, please," replied Aphra. "Oh, and some lemon if you have it."

At that moment, the door to the café opened and a pale, drawn-looking woman with wisps of grey hair escaping numerous pins and an old battered hat walked towards the back of the room with a look about her that told Aphra this was the person that she was expecting.

"Mrs Raemond?" Said the woman discreetly.

"Yes. Please, do sit down, Mrs Weedon. I've just ordered some tea. Would you like anything to eat?"

"No." She shook her head. "Thank you," she added.

The shop was quite warm, so the woman removed a shabby brown coat, revealing an equally shabby nondescript skirt and blouse. She placed the coat on the coat-stand at the back of the room and sat down.

The door from the kitchen opened and the waitress bustled in with a tray bearing a teapot, milk jug and two cups and saucers."

"There we are," she said as she placed the items on the table. "Oh dear, I've forgotten the lemon." She rushed off again.

Mrs Weedon spoke softly as she furtively looked around the room. "It is very good of you to see me, Milady."

"I could hardly ignore your letter Mrs Weedon. Naturally anything that concerned my husband concerns me," she said as she began to pour out the tea. The waitress returned with the lemon. "Will there be anything else."

"No, thank you. That will be all," Aphra replied as she handed a cup of steaming tea to the nervous woman sitting opposite her.

"There is certainly a chill in the air today. This should help to warm us a little - although it's nice and cosy in here," she said kindly, trying to put the woman at her ease. "Now, what was it that you wanted to tell me?" She had been curious and even somewhat anxious to solve the mystery ever since she had received this woman's letter a few days earlier.

"I don't really know where to begin." She was obviously very agitated.

"Just take your time," Aphra said. There's no need to rush.

"Well, Tom - that's my husband - he isn't a very nice man. I do sometimes wonder why I married him. Of course, he was very handsome when he was young and I was very foolish. My parents and other people warned me against it, but I wouldn't listen. Goodness knows I've paid for my mistake. Sorry, you don't want to hear all this."

"That's alright. You carry on. I'm in no hurry." Aphra sipped her tea.

"He had a good job at the time. He worked for Turner's as a salesman and earned good money - not that I saw much of it. Anyway, as the years passed, his drinking, poor time-keeping - and other things - pilfering, I should imagine, got him into trouble and he lost job after job.

Life with him has been dreadful for me and my children - to say nothing of the other women he carried on with. I've even had them calling at my door. One of them was holding a baby in her arms. I felt very sorry for her.
Anyway, last week, he came home from the pub - drunk as usual. I dread his returning home - never knowing if he will lash out at one of us. He staggered upstairs. Just lately, the drinking has been worse than ever. Until the other day, I had no idea where the money was coming from. He hasn't worked for months.

Daphne, my youngest, was passing the bedroom and saw him on his knees taking something out from under the floorboards. When he realised that she had seen him, he went mad and started cussing and shouting at her. She was so scared that she ran down the stairs to me in the kitchen.

Suddenly, there was an enormous crash. We went out into the hall and there he was lying unconscious at the foot of the stairs. We called the doctor. He told us to move him to the sofa.

Since then, he has opened his eyes but is unable to speak or walk. The doctor has told us that he will not survive. I know this sounds wicked, but I'm glad. Our lives have been hell with him."

"I quite understand Mrs Weedon. You have been through a terrible ordeal. Hopefully, when he has passed on, you and your family can begin a new life"

Mrs Weedon nodded her head and then took another sip of her tea. "You must be wondering what all this has to do with you."

Aphra smiled patiently.

"Well, as I said, Daphne had caught him taking something from under the floor boards. Well, we went up there and had a look. We were very shocked to discover a number of purses containing lots of coins. Daphne handed them to me and I counted the money. There was almost fifty pounds.

He's been going out even more than usual lately, and not just to the pub I reckon. Well, my son Jimmy came into the room and he had that sheepish look that he gets when he's something to hide. He isn't a very bright lad and is easily led by his father. Anyway, I won't bore you with that.

Well, to cut a long story short, it turns out that Tom and him had been meeting a gentleman regularly and he'd been giving my husband money. The lad doesn't know who the gentleman is or why he was paying the money, for he was always kept some distance away - sort of hovering in the shadows. I think that the idea was to make the gentleman think that there was a gang of them."

"I see," said Aphra pouring out more tea. "But how ..."

"Forgive me interrupting you Milady, but you see I found something in one of those purses." She opened her bag and handed Aphra a piece of paper.

It was a scruffy, wrinkled scrap, but on it was some writing. The writer had obviously been trying out some ideas, but the tone and intent could not be misunderstood. Also, the addressee was named – the Earl of Tawford.
"I realised then where all the money had been coming from. Tom was blackmailing your husband. I don't know why and don't want to know. It's none of my business. I just wanted to tell you how sorry I am and to return his Lordship's money."

She went to open her bag to take out the money, but suddenly Aphra's hand was on her arm. "Please keep the money and give yourself and your family a good life. There is nothing that can be done for my husband now. He was a kind and generous man and would wish that some good came out of this sad business."

"When I realised what Tom had done and how the Earl had died, I was so concerned that he had been driven to take his own life.

"Mrs Weedon, please do not add to your burden by speculating on such things. Please take comfort from the knowledge that the doctor who came at the time of my husband's death wrote on the certificate that it was death by accident, so you need not worry about that anymore."

Mrs Weedon gave a sigh of relief. "Oh thank the Lord for that. I've been so worried. I should hate to think that my children's father could do such a wicked thing as to drive a good man like the Earl to his death."

The bell on the door tinkled announcing that someone had entered the café. A very pretty, frivolously dressed girl aged about sixteen walked over to Mrs Weedon. "Mama, are you going to be much longer? I want to get home soon," she whined peevishly.

"This is my daughter Daphne," said Mrs Weedon collecting her things together as she prepared to depart.

The girl turned and looked at Aphra with a sulky pout on her lips. Aphra recognised that pout. She had seen it a thousand times before.

***

It is almost daylight and I have been sitting here for some time. All is now clear. As I think back upon the meeting yesterday with Thomas' wife, I wonder that I did not put two and two together more quickly – the names Weedon and Tom. As the poor lady was talking about Seb being blackmailed, I soon guessed at why he had been so agitated. I now realise that he was scared – absolutely terrified of exposure of his secret. But what did Thomas know about Seb? Had he discovered something about his relationship with Claude?

Obviously, he must have seen Sophie and noticed the incredible likeness to his own daughter. I wonder where he saw her. Strange to think that Sophie has siblings. If only it were possible to introduce her to them. What foolishness - that connection must never be revealed. One day, I will have to destroy all these books, but for now they are my solace. Where else – other than my journals can I share my intimate thoughts and secrets and offload this burden that I carry with me?

I have been sitting here thinking about that other foolish, naive, young girl - the one that I used to be – so in love and credulous. Thomas was so handsome and charming - she was just one of many. I feel such a mixture of emotions as I remember those few wonderful days that I spent with him. I felt such joy and when we made love, it was ecstasy. But now, as I sit here, I feel such rage against him and his kind. How dare they use women like that!

Yet I realise that I have been more fortunate than most of his victims. At least I have had no physical or monetary hardships since I married Seb – and in a different kind of way, I have known love – the real and genuine love and affection that I have received from him and Claude. My child has not wanted for anything and has been brought up in a home of warmth and security. She is getting a good education and in this new century, I believe that there will be opportunities for women of education to be independent and have fulfilling lives.

I know that I must put these thoughts of anger and regret behind me. I need to focus my thoughts and energies on helping Sophie and Claude come to terms with this terrible loss.

In the next few days, I will speak to Claude about going to France. Dorothy, Travis and Mrs Drake will help me to make the arrangements. Hopefully, a few weeks away from this miserable winter weather will lift our spirits a little - and perhaps for Claude, being back with his relatives will help him to mourn his dead love. I know that his mother is aware of the relationship with Seb, and is a kind woman and so will console him.

Oh how I wish Lucas was here – but even if he was, I could not share with him this burden, nor the pain that hangs heavy in my heart. I have been so foolish as to believe that recent events would enable me to be with the man I love. For some reason, he either does not love me, or something else has made him abandon me. What could have stopped him from coming to me? It is as if some dark shadow is always there between us. I believe that this shadow will hang over me for the rest of my life and that I will never know the true happiness and intimacy of real love.

***

It is now almost three weeks since I last wrote in here. They have been difficult – very busy weeks and I have not had the opportunity to do so until now.

We are here at the Chateau of Claude's family and I think that I have made the correct decision to come here. Seeing his mother again has been something of a comfort to him.

She, however, was very shocked to see the sorry state that he was in. He has hardly eaten anything since Seb's death and has lost much weight and is very gaunt. He has dark circles around those lovely blue eyes which are usually so bright and sparkling, but now seem so lacklustre. His drinking has been excessive - in fact, he drank throughout the journey and was hardly coherent when we arrived.

The journey itself was difficult – the crossing quite rough and both Sophie and Dorothy were sea-sick. We have now been here for a few days and they have recovered from their ordeal and we are trying to keep ourselves occupied with various things.

I have seen very little of Claude since we got here, for he is spending much of his time in his room.

I think that I must try and cajole him - much as he has done so many times with me each time I have succumbed to the melancholia. Although of course, this is far more serious. Sebastian was the love of his life and he is dead by his own hand. I think that I need to tell him about my meeting with Mrs Weedon. Perhaps knowing what led to Sebastian's death may help him come to terms with it.

I have managed to keep the black rolling mist at bay so far - perhaps because I have had to look after Sophie and Claude and have not had him to rely upon this time.

***

It is now late March and Sophie, Dorothy and I are in Nice. The weather is mild and we have plenty of sunshine and blue skies to help cheer our spirits.

Today, it was warm enough to walk on the beach. It did my heart good to see Sophie running and even laughing again for a little while. It is a good sign. Hopefully, she will continue to be happy and soon return to her old self.

Our hotel is very comfortable and every need is catered for. Dorothy has been a great comfort and support to us both. I don't know what I would have done without her all these months.

***

We have been back in England for two weeks now.

We called and spent a few days with Claude on our return from Nice. He is still very depressed, but less distraught and seems calmer. His mother's affection and the warmer, sunnier climate must help a bit. He says that when he feels better, he will visit us. This is definitely an improvement. Before, he said that he would *never feel better. He has promised to write soon and I think that his mother will encourage him to do so.*

Sophie is now fifteen and I have been wondering whether or not it would be a good idea to send her to school. She is very intelligent and could do well. I also think that being with other girls will be good for her. She needs to have friends of her own age, for she spends too much time with adults. Also, she tends to be indulged by everybody and this is not good for her. Of course, we have all made allowances just lately, but she needs some discipline - even though she gets this from Miss Kincaid – although even she has been won over and is twisted around the proverbial little finger! I shall speak to Miss Kincaid about this and be guided by her advice.

***

The two women agreed that going to school would be good for Sophie. It was decided that she would commence the following term. The school chosen was St Monica's convent in Bristol. It had a reputation for excellent pastoral care, discipline and education.

At first, Sophie was unsure about going and there was a bit of sulking and door slamming as a result. However, when Aphra pointed out the advantages of making friends, she became more enthusiastic.

As the day approached, Aphra dreaded it, and when her carriage finally departed, having left Sophie at the school, she broke down and cried.

The weeks leading up to Sophie starting school had been busy ones. They had gone and stayed at a hotel in Bristol for a few days while they purchased uniform and various items that she would need.

On the morning when they had set off in the carriage, Sophie had been very excited and proud in her new clothes. When they had arrived at the convent, Henry, who had accompanied them, supervised the men carrying her trunk to her dormitory.

Aphra hugged Sophie. Kissing her affectionately, she whispered in her ear, "if you aren't happy at the end of this term, you can leave." But by the end of the term, Sophie was settled happily and when the holiday arrived, she couldn't wait to return to school.

On Aphra's return to Methuen Park, she had, once again to struggle with the melancholia that seeped into the empty space that Sophie, Sebastian and Claude had left.

Aphra would have liked to move out of the great house, but she had promised to remain and run the household until Phillip was able to take over.

There were still a number of affairs of Sebastian's estate to be settled and this entailed a number of meetings with lawyers.

Although she rarely attended any social engagements unless strictly necessary, she kept herself busy with her charity work. One of the advantages of this was that she saw very little of Caroline.

She wrote to Sophie and Claude regularly and tried to occupy the long lonely hours with drawing, painting, sewing, music – and working on her little garden - often with Dorothy, who was a great help and comfort. From time to time, she heard news of Lucas, but on the whole, she had little contact with the outside world.

She often felt as though she lived in a beautiful, rambling prison, and fighting the melancholia was a daily battle that she did not always win. She received the occasional visits and invitations from Hortense and Donald, which were very welcome and enjoyable, but she had few real friends as such and found the isolation at times unbearable. Sometimes, to escape the loneliness, she would go down into the kitchens and help prepare the meals. This was something that the servants thought very eccentric of her. She knew this, but did not mind. She had not been to the cottage since Emily's death, and working with the servants in the kitchens was the nearest that she could get to pretending that she was not a Countess.

***

Today, Donald and Hortense came for lunch. They have been so good to me. They either visit regularly, or insist on my visiting them. Both have been towers of strength. If it was not for them, I think that I would shut myself away from the world altogether. Their company has even been known to make me laugh at times. I do so little of that these days.

After lunch, Hortense and I took a short stroll down by the lake. Donald did not join us. He is getting quite elderly and likes to doze in the armchair. Hortense is worried about him. "He seems to sleep nearly all the time," she told me. "I suppose that we're both getting on. Even I don't seem to have the energy that I used to have."

We walked on a bit and into the woods. No need now to worry about the rules. There would be no more secret trysts between Seb and Claude. As we walked through the trees, I thought back to that day so many years before, when I had stepped on a twig and Seb had been furious with me, and then full of contrition and remorse for his behaviour. It had changed my life completely.

"I expect that you can't wait for that girl of yours to come home at the end of term," Hortense said.

"Yes," I replied. "I live for the holidays when she is here. It is as though the house comes alive with her arrival."

"Do you hear much from Monsieur Tanquerel these days?"

I replied that I got the odd letter. "He seems to have settled back into his old routine at the chateau," I said. "We hope to visit during the summer."

"I did not think that he looked too well on his last visit here," Hortense said. "He looked like an old man. I hardly recognised him."

"Yes, he seems to have things on his mind."

"Probably worry over the finances of the family. I understand that things are difficult in that respect."

"Yes, these things can take their toll. Sophie said the same thing about his appearance when she saw him on his last visit. I think it was a great shock to her. He has always been like an Uncle to her. It is as though she has lost him as well as her father."

His first couple of visits were while Sophie was away at school. I thought it best – as he was still so depressed. The first visit lasted for three weeks and he spent almost all the time in the chapel where Seb was buried.
If I could not find him in the house, I knew where he would be. Eventually, I told him that it was not healthy for him to spend so much time there and tried to encourage him to walk in the grounds around by the lake and in the woods. More than once, he broke down and cried. It was on one of these occasions that I decided to tell him about Thomas. At first, I was unsure if I was doing the right thing, but then I decided it was the correct thing to do, for it was a logical explanation of Sebastian's behaviour in the weeks leading up to his suicide.

Claude's initial reaction after the shock was anger, and he vowed to kill Thomas. Fortunately, I was able to inform him that he was too late as I had recently heard that Thomas had died.

I'm glad that he's dead. The thought of Claude being a murderer is too much to bear.

Sophie has made two friends – Elizabeth and Virginia. They have visited a few times. They are nice girls and I like them very much. Hopefully, they will be joining us on Sophie's next trip home. It will be so good to hear their chatter and laughter in the house.

***

Dear Mildred,

I felt that I had to write to you immediately. Something has happened that has disturbed me.

Yesterday, I had to speak to the mistress about some matters to do with the laundry. I went into the morning room, only to find that she was not there. I thought that I would wait for a few minutes, for she is usually in there at that time of the day. Also, I could see that there were papers and her journal, which was open, on the desk, together with her pen, which she had laid down on the book - so thought that she would be returning shortly.

I know that I should not have gone over to the desk, but something made me do so. Perhaps it was the thought that the pen would leak onto the page. For, as you know, I am not one to pry or snoop.

However, I saw that she had placed a pile of papers over whatever it was she was writing in her journal. I have seen her writing journals many times over the years, and I'm convinced that they would make interesting, perhaps even shocking reading. I was just about to move away from the desk, when my eye caught a few words that had erroneously been left uncovered. Those words were - (I couldn't make it all out due to her handwriting being very small) and I only glanced at it for a second, but it looked like "I'm glad he's dead. The thought of Claude being a murderer is too much to bear."

I heard her footsteps outside the room, so moved away from the desk. When she came in, she looked at me and then towards the desk. I was sure that she was worried that I had read her journal.
I quickly brought up the subject of the laundry - which we discussed and then left the room.

I know that I can rely on you not to discuss this with anyone, for I do not wish to get involved in any scandal - neither do I want to lose my position. There could of course, be an entirely innocent explanation and we don't want to go making accusations on such slim evidence.

I had better get this in the post now, for I have much work to do today. The young lady will be returning from school tomorrow, with two of her friends and it always makes extra work for us all - although she is such a delight to have around.

With all good wishes.

Hetty

***

Mildred closed the door behind her as she left the room. Once her footsteps had faded away, Caroline looked again at the letter from her housekeeper's crony at Methuen Park. As she did so, she thought about the conversation that they had just had.

The whole thing sounded pretty damning. Mildred was very keen to get the police involved and had suggested calling the local magistrate. However, Caroline was not quite so sure that this would be the best course of action. If what this blasted woman had written turned out to be untrue, then Caroline would look a fool - and a malicious one at that. It was well known in the county, that Caroline and Aphra were adversaries. She certainly didn't want it to appear that she was being in any way spiteful.

She decided that she would put the letter in her dresser with the other one - the one that she had kept all these years. It might come in useful one day. She was determined that she would get her revenge on Aphra, but it would take a different form. One that would wound her deeply. It is said that revenge is a dish served cold. This one would be ice cold and it would be a sliver of ice that would pierce Aphra's heart.

***

When Sophie was about sixteen, she made a new friend called Pamela Levenson and dropped the other two girls. "They don't like Pamela and they're so boring – not fun like Pam. Besides, she doesn't like them."

"I thought that they were very pleasant," said Aphra. "They were very friendly and most polite. Perhaps it would be a good idea to stay friendly with them. Why not be friends with all of them. We could have all three girls to stay."

"I told you they're boring. I'm not interested in them anymore," Sophie snapped.

"Very well," Aphra said. "I'm sorry I spoke. There's no need to bite my head off."
"Well, you say such stupid things and anyway, it's none of your business who I'm friends with. So can we change the subject now?"

"I'd be delighted. I just don't understand why you're behaving this way."

"Perhaps you need to consider your own behaviour before you start judging mine."

What is that supposed to mean?"

"Forget it. Just leave me alone!" She screamed as she stormed out of the room slamming the door.

Since Sophie had made friends with Pamela, who was a strong, but bad influence, she had become increasingly difficult and hostile towards Aphra, which upset and mystified her greatly. Pamela's mother, Gertrude, was a wealthy widow. What Aphra didn't know was that Gertrude was a friend of Caroline.

One of the things that drew Caroline to Gertrude was some information that the other woman had imparted to her. Some years earlier, she had been visiting a friend in Dartmouth and had spotted Aphra and Preston together in the park. She recognised Aphra immediately from the many photographs of her in society magazines. Her good looks, together with her titian hair, made her stand out from the crowd. Gertrude had been scandalised at the behaviour of the Countess and could not wait to tell Caroline when she discovered her intense dislike of Aphra. Both women had assumed that the man was Claude.

The two women were influencing the girls against Aphra. Caroline pretended to really like Sophie, and she, in her naiveté, reciprocated. Caroline arranged for Sophie to see the letter that Aphra wrote many years before to Claude. She removed it from her writing bureau and "accidently" left it lying on a table, and once the girl had read enough, she then pretended to hide it from her. "Oh, you shouldn't have seen that," she said. "Please forget all about it." But the damage had been done, just as she had intended. Naturally, misunderstanding the meaning of the letter, Sophie jumped to the wrong conclusion.

Caroline was continually making comments that aroused Sophie's suspicions about her mother, saying things that were left open to misinterpretation and then retracting the comments, telling Sophie to forget that she had said anything at all.

Caroline encouraged Gertrude to tell Sophie about the incident in Dartmouth. She suggested that Gertrude adopt her method of imparting this information - supposedly by accident - and so between them, the drip, drip of poison against Aphra had begun to work.

Caroline eventually showed Sophie the letter from Hetty. This was the final triumph for Caroline. Sophie was now convinced that Claude was her father, and that he had murdered the man she thought was her darling papa. She began to hate her mother and Uncle Claude.

During this time, Sophie began to spend her school holidays at Gertrude's house. This was partly because she was becoming alienated from Aphra, but also because she was becoming increasingly attracted to Pamela's older brother, Lionel, who was at university during term time, but came home during the holidays.

When Sophie did come home to Methuen Park, she made Aphra's life so miserable, that Aphra often retreated to her own rooms to escape the verbal attacks. She tried very hard to fight against the melancholia, but it was made even worse by Sophie's intolerance of her illness.

At the age of eighteen, both girls finished their education and became debutantes. Sophie reluctantly allowed Aphra to organise her coming out Ball and her presentation at court. Aphra thought that the whole thing was rather ridiculous, but agreed to Sophie's requests and gave her everything that she demanded. For Aphra, every moment was an ordeal, but she tolerated it because of her love for her child.

Time passed and Aphra saw less and less of Sophie, who now spent all of her time with Pamela and her family. Aphra kept writing to her and asking her to come home, but rarely got a reply, and when she did it was usually to ask for something - often money.

***

As the years passed, Aphra saw little of Claude, although they corresponded much. Gradually, he came to terms with his loss and started to make a new life for himself. At first, he travelled a lot, but eventually, he returned to the chateau and started to take an interest in the wine production. It was this interest and the effort that he put in, that resulted in the saving of the family estate, for the new wine that he produced, proved to be a great commercial success and the profits were high. His time with Sebastian had taught him much about the business side of things.

Claude wrote to say that his elder brother had died without issue, and that he had inherited the title of Le Comte de La Morciere. He, like Sebastian, took his responsibilities seriously, and was a good and caring master to his servants and tenant farmers. Throwing himself into his work and duties helped him to deal with his grief.

So life went on, seasons came and went and Aphra kept herself busy, running the household and attending to her charity work. She was still invited to many social events throughout the county, where she was still admired for her beauty and elegance, but she rarely accepted any. She had more or less turned her back on the world and had learnt to live with her loneliness. Never a day passed, when she did not think of Lucas and wonder how he was, and if he still cared for her. She occasionally heard news about him and it seemed that he was still alone.

She sat at her desk in the office, where a pile of correspondence awaited her. There were times when she wished that she could relinquish the duties attached to the estate. However, Philip, the young Earl, was up at Oxford. When he completed his studies – he was expected to get a first in Classics – he would be taking over the reins at Methuen Park. Aphra had remained living in the house, but when he came down from university, she intended to make other plans and hand over everything to him. There were times when it seemed an overwhelming burden – although she often reminded herself why she was doing it and what she had received in exchange over the years. This was the price that she had to pay for her release from the workhouse. But hadn't she paid enough dues. Would her debt never be settled?

***

In the years following Sophie's disconnection with Aphra, her only consolations were the get-togethers with her aunt and uncle. They made frequent visits to each other's homes – usually for the weekend or Sunday lunch and sometimes at Christmas, Easter or birthdays. She said very little to them about the problems with Sophie, but Hortense knew what was going on. In fact, she had written to Sophie to try and intervene, but had just received a very curt reply.

It was on one of these Sundays in early July that Aphra, Donald and Hortense were relaxing in the drawing room. Her aunt and uncle had arrived mid-morning for lunch which they had taken out on the terrace. It had got a bit hot out in the sun and so they had retired to the drawing room. Donald had fallen asleep as usual and Hortense had been telling Aphra that she was worried about his gout. "It's getting worse and it doesn't help with all the port he drinks. He won't listen to the doctor. No, he knows best."

For a while, the two women sat in silence and did some embroidery. Aphra showed her aunt some water colours that she had been working on and was much praised. A maid knocked and entered carrying a tray bearing the tea things. "Just put the tray on the table there, Milly and I'll serve it. Thank you."

"Very well, Milady." She curtsied and left the room. The noise had awoken Donald, who made a spluttering noise and Hortense enquired. "Did you have a nice little nap dear?"

Donald spluttered again and said something completely incomprehensible and it took him some minutes to fully come to. He seemed pensive for a few minutes. When he did speak, he surprised the two women.

"There's going to be a war, you know."

Aphra and Hortense both stared at him with the same look of anxiety mixed with resignation.

"Do you really think so?" Aphra poured out the tea and handed a cup to him.

"No doubt about it. This assassination'll do it. You mark my words." He sipped at his tea and limped over to the French windows and gazed out at the grounds. "I was lunching at the club with ol' Smithy the other day. He's in the know."

He tapped the side of his nose. "All a bit hush-hush – but he was telling me that he'd heard it from Willy Williams."

The two women were quiet for a while as the Viscount held court and droned on a bit. Aphra guessed that he was actually quite enjoying the feeling of superiority that having contacts "in the know" gave him – although the topic certainly brought no-one any pleasure. He mentioned a number of the chiefs of staff and one or two prominent politicians who'd said this or that. None of this posturing was new to either woman.

After a polite pause, when he'd run out of steam, Aphra said. "I've had a letter from Claude and he says very much the same thing." She turned to her aunt. "Can I tempt you to another scone?" She handed her the plate. Her aunt went to refuse, but Aphra insisted. "I'll not take no for an answer. Made them myself yesterday. I think that I was getting in the way of the staff, but I do enjoy cooking so much."

"We sound a bit like Marie-Antoinette – eating cake while all around is falling apart," said Hortense, as she wiped her lips with a napkin.

"Should be a short lived thing though – give the Hun a bit of a thrashing and get it over and done with, I say," Donald added.

Later as they were leaving, Aphra told them. "Claude says that he'll join up if there's a war."

"What! At his age?" Donald blustered. "He must be mad."

"Yes, ridiculous isn't it. I've written to him and pleaded with him not to do so, but you know how stubborn he can be."

"It must be something to do with being French," mumbled Donald.

"You're not French," said Hortense and Aphra smiled. Donald didn't get the point that his wife was making and she raised her eyes to the ceiling. "C'mon dear, let's be on our way," she said in a motherly tone. "We've taken up enough of Aphra's time. I'm sure that she has plenty to do."

As she waved goodbye to their departing carriage, Aphra turned and walked back up the steps. It had been a very pleasant day, but it was a shame that it had to end on such a worrying note. She hoped that there would not be a war. She did not think that she could stand any more death, and the thought of Claude enlisting filled her with dread.

***

Today, I received a rather worrying missive from Hortense - she is very concerned about Donald. His health is not good. I suppose that this is to be expected at his age. The doctor has told her it is his heart. If this is the case, then we must accept that nothing can be done and must expect the worst.

I thought when I saw him two weeks ago that he had an unhealthy pallor. He has always seemed so flushed - especially after a few brandies. Hortense says that he does not seem to want to drink brandy or port now and is very breathless.

In recent years, I have noticed that he seems less inclined to take part in any physical activity. Ever since I have known him, he has been a rather sedentary person, but of late, this has become more pronounced.

He is such a dear and I am very fond of him. I know that he cares for me and has always been so pleased to have blood relatives. Sophie and I are the only ones he has, and her behaviour over recent years has hurt him greatly, I know. I wish I knew why she has become so hostile towards me. I cannot think of anything that I've done to deserve such treatment.

Poor Hortense. When he goes, how will she cope? I don't mean that she needs his support - quite the reverse. She is the one who is his rock. But they have lived for one another for so long.

It is three days later and I am returning to my journal. My writing was interrupted by the telephone. It was Hortense calling to say that our dear Donald has passed away. I am so sad. Yet another death of someone that I care for. Is there no end to it?

What is to happen to Hortense now? She will be bereft. I am now about to leave to help her with the funeral arrangements.

***

Shortly after Donald's death, war was declared. At first, Aphra and Hortense were only just about aware of what was going on outside their own sphere of grief. Both were also upset that Sophie did not bother to attend the funeral. It seemed that she wanted nothing to do with anyone connected with her mother.

A few days after the funeral, Donald's will was read. Aphra was shocked to discover that, apart from financial provisions made for Hortense, she was the sole heir to his entire estate, including Westbridge Hall.

"This cannot be!" She exclaimed. "This is your home, Hortense."

"My dear. You are his blood relation. Of course it must go to you."

"Well, you can go on living here as if it belonged to you. I won't have you turned out."

"Actually, I don't want to be rattling around here on my own. Donald has left me enough money, so that I shall be able to rent a small, comfortable place to live out my final days."

"No, you must come and live with me. We would be good for each other. We are both alone."

Hortense gladly accepted the invitation. "Thank you my dear. I really would appreciate your company. I'm finding widowhood hard to adjust to."

As the months passed, so life at Methuen Park settled into a new routine. Aphra gave Hortense the suite of rooms that had once belonged to Rose and they each found the company of the other a great comfort. Aphra felt as though she had a mother and Hortense felt like she had a daughter. They enjoyed doing many things together like sewing and painting. They even managed a reasonable duet on the pianoforte.

Claude visited at the end of November - in time for Sebastian's anniversary and stayed until the New Year. The three of them enjoyed Christmas, although it was a very quiet affair. Just before he left, he told Aphra that he would be enlisting on his return to France. She begged him not to. "You're too old," she said. "You don't have to do this."

"Yes, I do and nothing you can say will make me change my mind. I am not afraid of dying. If I get killed, then I will be with Sebastian. When I die, I want to be buried next to him. Will you see to it Aphra?"

She had no option but to agree to his request. "Perhaps they'll give you a desk job and you'll be nowhere near the front."

"Maybe. We'll see."

But she knew that he would not settle for a desk job and as she said goodbye to him, she feared that she would not see him again.

***

It was in February, that Aphra noticed that Hortense had become rather withdrawn and often remained in her room. It was soon very apparent that she was unwell. She was eating very little and losing weight. Aphra felt as though a cold hand clutched at her heart. She was very afraid that she was going to lose her. By the beginning of April, Hortense was very ill indeed. The doctor was unsure what was wrong, but suspected a tumour of some kind. As the old lady began to fade away, Aphra remained at her bedside. While she sat through the long hours of the night, Aphra's mind turned to thoughts of Mrs Brookes and the vigil that she had kept at her bedside until the end.

On a warm, sunny day in May, Hortense lay in bed struggling to breathe. Aphra sat holding her hand. With great difficulty, Hortense managed to speak a few words.

"Aphra, tell me, is there any truth in the gossip about you and Claude?"

Aphra was shocked at the bluntness of this question.

"Tell me that he is not Sophie's father and that you have never done anything inappropriate with him

Absolutely not!" She replied. "Is that what people think of me?"

Hortense gently squeezed her hand. "I'm sorry, my dear," she mouthed. "I should've known better than to ask you such a thing, but over the years, there have been all kinds of rumours, and Sophie does look so much like him."

"Oh Hortense, if only I could tell you the truth about my life. There is no-one in the world with whom I can share a terrible, burdensome secret. If only you knew how foolishly people have jumped to a completely erroneous conclusion. I give you my word that there has never been anything improper about my friendship with Claude, I have never betrayed Sebastian, and Sophie is most definitely not Claude's child."

At this, Hortense looked very relieved and gently squeezed Aphra's hand and smiled. "I never believed the rumours my dear. I just wanted you to tell me so. It would be beneath you to do anything wrong or devious. I can go to my maker and my dear Donald, a happy woman." Aphra looked into the eyes of her dear aunt and friend as they closed and the hand went limp.

***

It is now two months since I lost Hortense. I feel as though I am overwhelmed with death. I am struggling to keep my shameful weakness at bay. I have opened both houses as hospitals. It will keep my mind occupied and hopefully keep the blackness from engulfing me again.

The news from the front is not good and the numbers of casualties are mounting up. They said that it would be all over by Christmas. That was what we all believed. All those brave, but foolish young men enlisting and marching off proudly to the sound of bugles and drums, and cheering crowds waving flags. Did they not think that it may not be glory, but terrible suffering, mutilation and death?

I have discussed matters with some of the ladies that I know through some of the charities to which I belong, and they have agreed to take over the running of Westbridge Hall. I know that I can rely fully of them to oversee all the arrangements. The patients should be arriving there in a day or two.

I have been extremely busy getting things organised here. At present, we have twenty four men recuperating, but we have room for a few more. I am so impressed at the positive response to my request for volunteers. The villagers have been wonderful, as have the members of the household staff. The plight of some of these poor men is heart-breaking. Some of the injuries are so bad - burns, blindness, amputations and horrendous disfigurements of their faces. What will their lives be like? How will they earn a living? - and what a terrible shock for their families when they see how maimed and disabled they are.

I have also heard from Claude that he has joined up. Oh how I wish that he had not. I'm surprised that he was accepted at his age, but I suppose that they need as many men as they can get. I do hope that they give him a desk job or something else behind the lines. I don't think that I can cope with losing anyone else. He said very little about what he was doing, or where he was being posted. I don't even know if he has a commission or has joined the ranks. Hopefully, I will hear from him soon and it will not be bad news.
There is still no communication from Sophie. I have tried using the telephone yet again, but to no avail. Apparently, she was busy.

I shall finish now, as it is almost midnight and I am exhausted. I shall be up again before five to do what I can to assist the qualified nurses. I have much to learn, although I hope that the time that I spent working with Lucas will have given me a good grounding in medical matters. I have been reading some medical books in the few spare moments that I manage to get.

***

I have just heard the most hurtful news and it has come from my old adversary. I have had to come to my room as I do not want others to see my anguish.

Caroline paid a visit this morning. Ostensibly, this was to appear to take an interest in the hospital and the poor men that are patients here. It did not fool me. It was apparent as soon as she entered the first ward, that the sight of the horrific injuries and disfigurements sickened her. She did little to hide her revulsion from the men, and I was very concerned about the effect that this would have on their morale.

"Perhaps you would like some tea," I suggested to get her away from the ward.

"Yes, that would be very nice," she said and I led her to a small room that I had been using as an office.

"I'll leave you here for a few minutes and fetch the tea. Please make yourself comfortable," I said.

I went down to the kitchen and made a pot of tea, which I placed on a tray with all the necessary accoutrements for the drinking of such a beverage. When I returned to my office, I saw that old smile of smugness on her face and knew that I was about to find out the real reason for her visit.

I poured the tea, and we made small talk for a few minutes. Then she said.

"The wedding was so nice - simple, but very romantic - lovely flowers."

"Wedding?" I uttered, quite confused. "Whose wedding?"

"Why Sophie and Lionel's. Did you not know? I wondered why you weren't there. I assumed it was because you were so busy with your war work."

"Sophie's married?" I gasped. "No, I didn't know. Things have not been very good between us of late."

"It was such a lovely ceremony and all the close family and friends were there. It's a shame that you were unable to attend. She looked so beautiful. I'm sure that you would have been proud of her. It was a simple but exquisite gown and I believe that the veil was a family heirloom - very fitting." She sipped her tea and then rose to leave. The expression on her face said it all. It was a look of complete triumph!
As she swept out of the room, I thought that I was going to be sick. How could Sophie do this to me? I love her so much and have never done her any wrong, so why is she being so cruel? Caroline has to have a hand in this somewhere.

I feel so broken. There is nothing left for me - except Claude and he is in France. I cannot even confide in him - other than by letter, and he does not need to hear bad news.

I must try and take this in my stride. I must not succumb to my weakness again. I must remain strong for the patients.

***

Tomorrow will be Christmas day. Everyone has worked so hard to try and bring some comfort to these poor men. We have decorated a tree and the children of the village made paper chains which we have hung in the main hall. This evening, they gave a carol concert. It was very moving, as the soldiers tried to join in. We all tried very hard to make it as merry as possible.

The villagers and the staff have done their best to ensure that every man has a present of one kind or another and the school-children have made some very pretty cards for them. It seems that for the last few weeks, everyone has been sewing, knitting, making sweets and biscuits, painting, cutting and gluing. A few of the shopkeepers have donated presents and this has helped enormously to swell the pile of gifts.

In spite of the shortages caused by the war, we will be able to put on a reasonably good spread. We will have goose, pork and beef. We have plenty of fruit and vegetables that are grown on the estate. The kitchen staff have been beavering away making plum puddings and fruit cakes. Travis tells me that there is still a good selection of wines in the cellar, and quite a large batch of beer has been brewed. So hopefully, we shall be able to have a feast that will do the men proud.

A few of the men who are not so seriously injured, and who should be returning home in the New Year, have been working on the idea of a show for Boxing Day.
A couple of them are quite musical. Ted plays the piano and Jimmy has a harmonica. I have heard them practising together and they are very good. There is also a chap called Bertie, who, in spite of his terrible injuries, always manages to

make everyone laugh. We have managed to rustle up some dressing up clothes and some of the male members of the household staff have sorted out some props and scenery. The show should be a success. I do hope so, for it will be good for morale.

I shall try not to be sad - although my thoughts of all those that I have lost are not far from my mind. I wonder how Sophie will spend the day. There has been no card and I did not expect one.

Claude wrote and told me that he would be unable to visit this year. His rank is Sous Lieutenant. I do not understand the French military ranking system, but I believe he was in the army as a young man, so I should imagine, he will be in charge of troops. Obviously, he cannot tell me where he has been posted. I just pray that it is not at the front. I know that he is indifferent as to whether or not he gets killed. Although, he has made something of his life over the last few years, I know that he is bereft without Sebastian. He puts on a brave front, but inside he is a broken man.

Perhaps he will be able to get some leave next year. It is so long since we were together - although he does write often. Maybe the war will be over soon and we can all begin to rebuild our lives. I don't think I shall be able to stand it if he gets killed.

***

Well, a new year has dawned. Let's hope that it is better than the one that has just ended. We all thought it would be over in a few months and that it was going to be a glorious victory.

However, Christmas turned out to be a great success, in spite of the situation. Everything went off like clockwork and I know that everyone enjoyed the fruits of their labours. The house felt alive again and some of the soldiers were able to dance a little bit with the maids. It took me back to the night of that ball, when I was briefly in Lucas' arms. I remembered the feeling of ecstasy that I felt and I know that he felt it too. I must try not to dwell on that and must keep looking forward.

"Would you care to dance Milady?" Suddenly I was shaken out of my reverie. It was Reggie, one of the badly burned patients.

"Of course," I replied. "I should be delighted young man. It is a long while since I danced with a young man." He took my hand and we took a turn around the ballroom. Obviously, it was not the same, but I was glad to help this poor creature have a little happiness, if only for a few minutes.

I can see that the snow is falling again. I feel quite cold. Although we do try to keep the house as warm as possible for the men, it is still draughty, and as we are trying to ration out the logs and coal, I have decided not to have a fire in my room. Besides, the girls have enough to do these days without having to see to my fire and clean it all out.

Anyway, I shall soon be tucked up in my bed. I have two hot water bottles, a warm pair of bed-socks and I shall keep my dressing gown on.

***

As the year progressed, so more and more men were admitted to both hospitals. It didn't seem to matter how many times she saw these terrible injuries, Aphra never failed to feel shock and horror - although she never let it show on her face. Every few weeks, two or three would be discharged - usually to their families or perhaps to a specialised centre where they could be rehabilitated. As soon as a bed was emptied, so it was filled immediately and there was always a waiting list of other poor souls.

Claude continued to write when he could, and although he was restricted regarding any details, she was able to read between the lines to understand that it was absolute hell. When she replied, she tried to write something uplifting and comforting to him. It was not easy, for she did not want to write about the terrible injuries that she witnessed daily, but neither did she want to make things harder for him by giving the impression that life was easy back in England. It was a narrow path to tread.

***

The sound of the pounding guns in the distance filled the air. The big push had begun this morning. It was the 1st of July and the Battle of the Somme was now underway. Lucas felt as though his head was pounding in time to the firing. He was very tired. He had been working for hours without a break. The constant flow of patients in such a wretched state was never ending. He was frustrated at the limitations of what he could do for these men - some of them little more than boys. "How on earth were they allowed to enlist?" He thought.

He had little time or mental energy for such reflection. He moved from man to man, trying to assess which ones needed his help most urgently. It was a hopeless balance of filling these needs, and giving assistance to those that were considered to have the best chance of survival.

He stood by the bed of a young soldier who was obviously very badly injured. His experienced eyes and hands examined the man as he quietly spoke to him.

"What's your name lad?" He asked kindly.

The ashen-faced soldier, who had looked almost as though he was dead, opened his pale blue eyes. Lucas saw the suffering and the fear in them.

"Private John Turner, Tyneside Irish. Please, please help me – Stop the pain! I'm in agony."

Lucas smiled at him as he recognised the Geordie accent. He continued the examination. He knew that this one was not going to make it. The injuries to his head and chest were far too severe.

"If I'm going to die, I need a priest," said John.

"We'll do what we can. I'll see about the priest for you, but I can't make any promises. I haven't seen him for a while, but if I do see him, I'll tell him to come to you," he replied.

Lucas beckoned a young nurse and gave her some instructions regarding medication – to which she nodded and then walked away briskly to fetch the drugs that would alleviate some of the pain. He resumed his conversation with the young man and patted his arm.

"You're a brave lad. Keep your chin up. I'll come back and see you in a short while."

He moved on to the next bed in which lay a middle-aged man dressed in a filthy, blood-soaked French uniform.

The nurse attending him said to Lucas. "This one's delirious. I can't make any sense of what he's saying. Sometimes it's in French and sometimes it's in English."

She washed the blood and dirt from his face. As she did so, Lucas recognised him. "Claude! Can you hear me?"

"You know him?" Asked the nurse.

"Yes. He's an old friend of mine."

"Claude, open your eyes. Look at me," he said firmly.

Claude slowly opened his eyes. It took some moments before he focused them on Lucas. At first, there was no recognition, but then slowly, he realised who it was. Suddenly, he seemed mentally alert.

"Lucas – can it be you? I'm in a bad way."

"I know, Claude. I'll do all I can for you. We'll get some pain relief."

He knew that his voice could not hide his pessimism regarding the prognosis. Claude obviously had very bad internal injuries and both legs were smashed beyond any hope of repair.

Claude looked directly at Lucas. "Do not worry about my dying. I know that I am done for. That is your British expression, is it not? Death does not frighten me. I welcome it."

"Come on now. Let's have no more of that kind of talk," interrupted the nurse as she continued to administer to her patient. Claude turned to Lucas.

"Please make sure that I am returned to England – to Aphra. She knows my wishes."

Lucas was surprised at this odd request. "I have to move on now, but I'll be back in a little while and we can talk."

"Yes, please don't be long," said the dying man. "There is something that I need to tell you about Aphra. It's very, very important." Suddenly he reached out and clutched at Lucas' hand. Lucas felt great compassion for this man and kindly patted him on the shoulder.

"Later. I'll be as quick as I can." He laid the bloodstained hand back on the sheet and continued on his rounds.

Claude watched the doctor as he approached the next bed and then turned his head the other way. The cots that they were lying on were so closely packed together that he could have reached out and touched the man's arm. He saw how young he was and noticed a tear running from his eye to his ear.

Claude spoke and John turned his head and looked at him.
"I'm scared of dying and I need a priest," John whispered.

"Ah. You are a Catholic? Me, also. Shall we pray together?"

For a few minutes they prayed together – one *Our Father* and two *Hail Mary's* and then the Frenchman seemed to drift off again. John watched as he starting muttering again. Although some of it was in French, which John did not understand, he could make out certain things.

"That one seems to be going off his head. Still it was nice to have said the prayers together," John thought and felt comforted by this.

The medicine had helped a little bit and he drifted in and out of sleep. During his conscious moments, he caught snatches of words. It was very strange what the Frenchman was saying. He understood everything that was said in English, but none of it made sense. He slept again and then opened his eyes. The doctor was standing by his bed.

"I've spoken to the priest and he will be with you shortly," Lucas said quietly.

"Thank you. It's very important to me. By the way, the French chap might need him too. He's a Catholic. He's in a bad way – keeps ranting on about all sorts of things. You should hear him."

Lucas turned to attend to Claude. He put his hand to his forehead. It was damp and very hot. His colour was not good. As he took his pulse, the young Geordie chattered on.

"He said the oddest things. He mentioned something about an inverted triangle. It seemed to amuse him and he laughed - a bit hysterically if you ask me. Then he started talking about flowers – green ones. Now what were they? Roses? No. Tulips? No. Perhaps, it was daffodils. Oh, I can't remember. Anyway, it was as though he was talking to someone at the foot of the bed. He said, 'I'll be with you soon. I'm coming to you.' - must have been talking about his wife or his sweetheart."

This jarred slightly on Lucas. He called a nurse over and gave her instructions. Until now, he had only been partly listening to what the soldier was saying. He felt a bit rude, so turned back to him. Also, his attention had been aroused.

"I'm sorry. What did you say about flowers?" He enquired. "I wasn't paying attention."

"Oh. That's all right. I'm just wittering on. It takes my mind off my own troubles you know.

Suddenly, Claude made a slight gurgling sound. Lucas looked at him. The eyes were focused straight ahead of him and his arms were outstretched as though he was about to embrace someone. It was strange, for although he was dying, his eyes were bright and shining and the intensity of the blue seemed to have returned. He smiled as though at someone in front of him.
"You know, she never said anything. She kept her word." And with that, he was gone.

Although Lucas felt a mixture of intense emotions, he needed to be professional. He beckoned the nurse. "This man has just died," he said, trying to choke back the tears of grief.

"Carnations! That was it," John said. Pleased with himself that he had remembered.

"He's a French nobleman," continued Lucas. "However, he has requested that his body is to be returned to England. We will need to make the necessary arrangements for transport to Methuen Park in Somerset. Notification and letters of condolence are to go to the Countess of Tawford and to his family here in France. I will let you have the details later."

He closed Claude's eyes and pulled the sheet over his head.

The young Geordie was asleep again. Lucas was called away to attend to another patient. Hours passed and he had no chance to think about Claude or what he had said.

Later, before he went off duty, he decided to go and speak to Private Turner and ask him to repeat to him what he had overheard. Standing by the cot, he saw that the young soldier had also died.

***

Lucas soon discovered that it was going to be a logistical nightmare to have Claude's body returned to England. He had a number of meetings with senior officers, who all refused, saying that a ban had been implemented in 1915. The only way around it, was to have his body sent to his family in France. It took a lot of arguments and persuading. In the end, it was agreed that it could be done if Lucas himself accompanied the body to the Chateau in the Loire valley.

At first, he said that he could not possibly desert his post. However, his senior officer ordered him to go and so he had to obey. He was to make the journey in an ambulance driven by a Corporal, who was delighted to have a few days away from the front. The journey took almost a week to get there. At first, the roads were almost impassable, but as they travelled further south, things got easier. Also, the weather seemed better and it was a relief to get away from the mud of the trenches and the noise of the gunfire.

As they approached the Chateau, they were full of admiration for the beautiful white building, glittering in the summer sunshine. However, their mood lowered, as they reached the steps where Claude's mother awaited the return of her dead son.

As Lucas stepped down from the ambulance, he shook her hand and offered her his condolences.

Claude's body was to lie in the family chapel overnight. The following morning, a mass was said and afterwards, his remains were cremated. This was the only way that Claude could be returned to England. His younger brother, now the new Comte, told Lucas that he would take the ashes back to England.

Lucas asked Claude's mother why he should wish his remains to be returned to Methuen Park. "Would it not be more fitting for him to be buried here with his family and ancestors?"

Her reply to this question surprised him. "It might appear that his remains should be interred here, but I know where his heart lay and that is where he needs to be. He requested this of me many years ago and I promised him that I would accede to this request. I cannot say more. Thank you for bringing him home, but he needs to be in the chapel at Methuen Park."

After being made comfortable for a couple of days, Lucas and his companion took their leave of the family and returned to northern France and the Somme.

As they travelled north towards the war zone, the comparative peace allowed him to think about the past. Since coming to France, he had been so busy and preoccupied with his work, that it had not allowed him to dwell on the emotional pain that he felt about Aphra. He had long ago stopped feeling any sadness about Lavinia. In fact, any hurt that he had felt about her, had been eclipsed by the depth of his feelings for Aphra. He knew that he would never love another woman as he loved Aphra. In fact, he knew that he would never love again and he did not want to.

It was almost a relief to be back at the casualty clearing station with the vast numbers of men awaiting his help. Now, once again, he could forget for a while.

***

I can't seem to feel anymore. What is wrong with me? I cannot weep. I should be weeping, shouldn't I? A few minutes ago, I came back from the chapel in the woods. I have just Interred Claude's ashes with Sebastian's remains. I thought that I was going to pass out when I saw that brass urn. To think that my dear friend, my brother, was reduced to a few ashes in a pot. Those beautiful blue eyes no longer see, and that radiant smile is no more, and the soft lilt of his Gallic tones I shall never hear again. I cannot bear it. If only Sophie was here to mourn with me, I would be able to cope. I have written to tell her what has happened, but I do not expect a reply.

It was a very simple service and the chaplain spoke some very kind words about him. I placed some simple white flowers there for him. I will see to the green carnations, as soon as I can. I usually place them beneath the plaque with Sebastian's inscription on it.

I must arrange for another one - for Claude - to go next to it.

I feel completely dead, and cold in my heart. Why can't I cry? I fear that if and when I start, I shan't stop. I think that my body and my brain just can't absorb any more pain. The dark black mist is not rolling down the walls as I expected, but I feel as though I have disappeared down a long tunnel and everyone seems far away.

I must get back to work. There is much to be done and in that way, I can keep my mind off this strange feeling inside me.

***

The battle had now been raging for months and there seemed to be no let up from the noise of the guns and the numbers of wounded men arriving all the time. Outside the casualty clearing station there were dead bodies to be seen lying on stretchers everywhere. However, many of the dead were lying in no man's land - blown to bits, with no means of identification possible.

The medical orderlies were constantly bringing more casualties from the front in tired-looking ambulances or horse drawn wagons.

The medical officer in charge looked exhausted. His apron was covered in blood. He had just carried out yet another limb amputation. He had worked all night without sleep. This was the third night in a row.

One of the orderlies came up to him. "Dr Lucas. We need you at the front. There are a couple of chaps that we daren't move. They're pretty bad Sir."

Lucas thought to himself that he was going to fall asleep whilst standing. He didn't know how much longer he could go on. "Very well. I'll just get my bag. Fetch some more dressings to take with us," He said, as he went to his supply of medicines and removed a few ampoules of morphine and some syringes.

They climbed into the waiting ambulance and the driver headed back to the front lines. As they got near, the guns got louder. "God," thought Lucas. "How much more of this can we stand? What a bloody mess and what a ridiculous loss of young lives. Damn the idiots that are responsible for this carnage!"

The journey was precarious as the driver avoided potholes and stray shells as they got nearer. It took less than fifteen minutes and they were soon at the front amidst the chaos and further bloodshed. Lucas followed the orderlies into the trench and began to work on the two men who were seriously injured. First, he administered pain relief and then did a temporary job of patching them up so that they could be transported back to the clearing station.

Just as they were about to leave, they heard a shot and then a terrible blood-curdling scream coming from no man's land.

"Ignore it," shouted one of the orderlies. "There's nothing that we can do for him."

Lucas turned back and said. "We can't leave him. He's in agony."

"We have to," said the other orderly. "It's too dangerous to go up there."

"I can't leave someone screaming in such terrible pain. I have to try," said Lucas.

"Don't be a bloody fool, man," said an officer in the trench, as Lucas climbed up the ladder and out of the trench. "You'll get killed."

Lucas continued to climb and as he reached the top, he began to crawl towards the screaming man. "Alright lad. It's nearly over. Just hang on." Quickly he filled a syringe with morphine and injected it into the young man's arm. Instantly, the screaming stopped and the man became drowsy. Lucas saw that his tibia was shattered and that an artery had been severed. He did his best to immobilise the limb and tied a tourniquet above the knee. He managed to drag the man to the edge of the trench, where the men waiting below were able to pull him down and move him to a stretcher. Just as Lucas was about to climb down, another man called out for help. He was not as badly injured, but still was unable to walk unaided. Lucas ran back the few yards to help him, when a sniper shot him in the calf muscle. At first, he fell to the ground, screaming in pain. After the initial shock, he got up and managed to hobble to the man, and together they made it back to the trench. Just as they slid down the ladder, another bullet whistled past them. "You, bastard!" Lucas shouted back at the German lines.

"You crazy bloody idiot," said the officer. "You're lucky to be alive." Then he patted him on the back. "Well done!"

When they got back to the casualty clearing station, Lucas hobbled in behind the orderlies carrying the men on the stretchers. Word soon got around about Lucas' bravery and people started cheering him.

"Good ol' doc," they chanted. "You'll be getting a medal for this."

It turned out that the injury was not life threatening, but serious enough for him to be suspended from duties until further notice. As he had not taken any leave since the beginning of the war, he was given a blighty ticket.

After being patched up, he found himself making the difficult trek across northern France to the coast for the boat trip back to England.

After a few weeks in a London hospital, followed by some convalescence, he was discharged. He still had a limp and quite a bit of pain. He had been told that he would no longer be required to go back to the front, but would be more use back in London.

***

I have not written in my Journal for three months. I seem to have been somewhere else losing great chunks of time. Dorothy has been very good and seems to have been here with me whenever I became conscious. Apparently, I have been in bed for much of the time. I was worried about the soldiers, but she told me that everything was in order and that I was to rest.

I don't know what has happened to me. Dorothy tells me that the doctor says I've had some kind of breakdown. She says that Claude's death was the last straw and I collapsed on the floor and she could not awaken me, and had to fetch the doctor.

I feel very ashamed that I gave into this. It must be some flaw in my character to give up like that. I must get better, so that I can get back to work.

***

It is the early hours and I cannot sleep for I am so afraid. Outside, the wind is howling, but I am howling within my head. It is the 21st of November - my birthday - and I feel as though I am getting old.

I do not feel well, but I cannot tell anyone about my fears. Who would there be to tell? Am I to follow mama soon – to take the same journey? Perhaps Dr Osborne will be able to put my mind at rest.

It is nearly five months since Claude died, and almost sixteen years since Sebastian took his own life.

Recently, as I have lain each night in my bed, I have wondered if my body will soon be lying next to Sebastian and Claude, and yet, it does not seem right. For although, the three of us all loved one another, and I love them still, I feel that I should be intruding if I was with them in the woods there. How strange that is where I first saw them together and now that is where they both lie. Although I did my best to enable them to be together in life, it was so difficult for them. At least, I have been able to grant them that in death.

Maybe I could request that I be buried in the churchyard at St Lawrence's next to mama and grandfather and of course, my grandmother, whom I never knew. That is where I belong. I shall speak to Philip about this. I am sure that he will accede to my request, for he has grown into a very kind and thoughtful young man.

Dorothy has told me that I have a grand-daughter. Her name is Harriette. She was born on 28th April this year. Dorothy did not tell me earlier for fear of my having a relapse. I do wish that I could see Harriette and give her a cuddle, but that will not happen. Sophie wants nothing to do with me and does not want me to see her little girl, so I must accept this, for there is nothing to be done, but my heart is broken once again.

PART SEVEN - OUT OF THE DEPTHS

Lucas was convalescing with some friends in Westbridge. He had decided to drive into town. He limped into the teashop. As soon as he saw her, he groaned inwardly. It was Caroline. There was nothing for it, but to acknowledge her. With one hand holding his cap and the other putting his weight against his stick, he made his way towards her table.

"Caroline, how are you?"

She stood up to greet him.

"Lucas, what a wonderful surprise. How good to see you. How are you?" She indicated a chair with a sweep of her arm.

She noticed that his limp was quite pronounced, and could not fail to observe the wince as he lowered himself into the seat.

A waitress hovered a polite distance from their table.

"Girl, bring some tea," Caroline ordered. "And some of those cakes," she added haughtily.

"Still the imperial tone," thought Lucas.

Caroline continued to enquire after his health. For a few moments, he actually wondered if she had changed, but closer inspection of those beautiful, cold grey eyes told him otherwise. While they waited for the tea to arrive, he began to tell her about the events leading up to his being injured. He tried to keep it brief and not go into too much detail.

The waitress returned bearing a tray with the teapot and crockery. "I'll just fetch the cakes madam."

As Caroline poured the tea, Lucas continued his account of his experiences in France.

He sipped the hot tea as he began talking about his stay in hospital. He noticed, however, that her attention was beginning to wander and that she was becoming fidgety. Boredom was setting in. He quickly wound up his narrative and changed the subject, encouraging her to talk. She began by bemoaning her lot – how boring things had become since the war and how it was spoiling her life. Lucas asked her if she was doing any war work, but her blank stare told him that she considered the question out of order and ridiculous.

She was still very beautiful. The years had been very kind to her and although her hair was now peppered with streaks of grey, they matched her eyes perfectly. However, he noticed that there were a few rather unattractive tight lines forming around her mouth probably the result of decades of pursed lips.

It was not long before she had turned the conversation to her favourite subject – Aphra! He hated the weak way in which, time and time again, he allowed her to vent her spleen. After a while, his attention wandered and he found himself thinking of other things so that most of her words hardly touched his consciousness. Phrases such as "pretends to be such a goody-goody" and "playing the Lady Bountiful" were repeated a number of times in various guises.

"More tea?" She enquired. "Have a cake. I know they're basic, but not too bad. We all have to make sacrifices."

"No thanks. I'm not hungry. The tea will suffice." He seemed to have no appetite these days. He was tired and depressed. He had thought that in recent years he had come to terms with the situation. His work had kept his mind occupied and had stopped him from brooding – at least while he was busy. However, Claude's death had helped to re-open old wounds and raised all those old questions again. Then, when he heard that Claude had been buried next to Sebastian, he had assumed that perhaps Caroline had been right all along. His stay in hospital and the enforced inactivity had created time for introspection.

"What am I doing here?" He thought. "Why am I once again listening to the vindictive diatribe of this nasty woman?" He knew that the answer to this question was that Caroline, in spite of everything, was a connection with Aphra and he wanted – needed to know about her – what she was doing and what was happening in her life.

"Was she happy?" He wondered. "Was she mourning over Claude?"

He had heard that Claude had often spent long periods of time away – either in France at his family home, or travelling around Europe. This had surprised him, as he had expected Claude to remain with Aphra after Sebastian had died. Sometimes he had felt that something did not quite fit – was somehow slightly wrong, but he could not put his finger on it.

Caroline was droning on – same subject, but with an additional episode.

"- and she has no shame whatsoever – always up at that chapel putting flowers on their tombs. Apparently, she collapsed after the interment of the Frenchman's ashes - had a complete breakdown, they say."

Would she never tire of this?" Lucas thought. He tried to change the subject, but to no avail. He sighed and resigned himself to being subjected to more of the same. He wondered if Aphra was still unwell. He wished that he could go to her and alleviate her suffering.

"Doesn't it strike you as shameless to bury one's spouse and lover side by side?" The question was rhetorical, so he made no attempt to answer. "And what is it with these strange flowers? Apparently, she's there praying and arranging these flowers which are specially dyed green at a London florist and then transported to Methuen Park every couple of weeks. She's had this done ever since Sebastian's so called accident. As you know, I have often wondered whether or not it was an accident and I have obtained evidence that it was not. Perhaps she knows more than she's letting on about it - and yet if Frenchie and her did have any involvement with his death, it's strange that he didn't marry her. I have always been puzzled by that. I wonder why he never stayed afterwards. Probably guilt!

So what's the significance? There's never anything bright – no red or pink roses or spring flowers. No, just green carnations. Very odd, if you ask me."

Green carnations! Where had he heard that before?

"What did you say?" He snapped. The aggressive force of his tone temporarily put her off her stride.

"I – I said that she puts carnations on their graves – Sebastian's and his friend or Secretary or whatever he was," she stammered.

What was it that was troubling him? What was wrong? For some time, something had been causing him disquiet.

"I have to leave." He stood up. "Thank you for the tea, but I need some air."

Caroline was dumbfounded by the change in his demeanour. "What is it? What's wrong? Did I say something that upset you? Ah, it's Aphra as always. Why can't you accept that it was always Frenchie that she was in love with?"

"Oh, shut up! I'm sick to death of hearing all this spite and venom. Let it go, can't you." He had got up far too quickly and the pain was excruciating. He threw some coins on to the tablecloth.

"Please don't go. We can talk about this. Perhaps I was being a bit harsh. Please don't leave me alone. You have no idea how dreadful my life is and how difficult it is for me to endure this war."

"Caroline. I should have said this many years ago. Maybe I've just grown a backbone – perhaps the time spent at the front has facilitated it. I don't enjoy your company. Goodness knows why I have continued our association. It certainly brings me no pleasure. You're a vindictive and spiteful old maid. You have never done anything worthwhile in your life. You seem to think that the world owes you a favour. You don't have one redeeming quality – even your looks are fading. I know that I'm not behaving like a gentleman, but it's time that you knew the truth. Good bye Caroline."

With that, he turned and walked out of the cafe. His car was parked outside and he drove away in a turmoil of emotions. He felt so drained and tired, that after a few minutes driving, he pulled off the rod and switched off the engine.

He felt extremely agitated – not just at his anger towards Caroline, but something was gnawing away at him. What was it? What had she said, and what was the memory that it was stirring?

He shut his eyes and tried to relax, but the pain in his leg continually bothered him. It was when she had mentioned the flowers. That was what had triggered this feeling. He had not been paying much attention to her up till that point. Carnations. Green carnations. Why was Aphra going up to the chapel and placing them there? Why was she having them dyed?

If he could just sleep and put these thoughts out of his mind, then perhaps he could relax. He reached in his pocket for the small bottle that he carried everywhere these days. He took a couple of swigs of the medicine and pushed the cork back in and replaced it in his pocket. Closing his eyes again, he concentrated on his breathing and a few minutes later, he began to feel drowsy. The pain eased a bit and he drifted off to sleep. For a while, the oblivion was ecstasy.

But then, he began to dream. He was at the theatre. He was standing in the foyer watching all the theatregoers arriving dressed in their finery. Everyone was laughing and chatting. Some were drinking champagne and all the men were sporting buttonholes. However, instead of them being the conventional buttonholes comprising of flowers, they were all bloodstained rags and the blood was running down the clothes onto the floor. Looking around, he saw that all the women's satin gowns were blood spattered. He went to sip his champagne and it tasted disgusting. It was warm and sticky. Looking down, he saw that the glass was full of blood. In horror, he threw it down and as it smashed against the floor, Caroline lifted her blood filled glass to toast him and started to laugh through blood stained lips.

Standing alone in the shadows stood a V.A.D. in a spotless uniform. She was speaking to him. Suddenly, he was lying in hospital and she was sitting at his bedside holding his hand and sobbing. "It is as well that you cannot hear me, for I would not be telling you this if you could. I am free to love you my darling, but I am not free to tell you this. There is a triangle, but it is not the way everyone thinks." As she said this, she began to disappear.

He woke up sweating and shaking. Something was still bothering him. The young Geordie had said something about flowers, repeating Claude's words. If only he had paid more attention to what he had been saying or had had a chance to speak with him again before he'd died.

For a while, his thoughts returned to France and the terrible sights that he had witnessed. So many dreadful and unnecessary deaths. He was back in the casualty clearing station. What had he overheard Claude say just before he died? He remembered the look on his face – a look almost of bliss – of the expectation of the sublime as though he was talking to someone at the foot of the bed. He had supposed that he was talking as though to Aphra, but when he thought about it now, Claude wasn't talking to her, he was talking about her! Earlier, he'd said that he knew he was dying and welcomed it – hence the look upon his face.

"I need some air," he thought. He stepped out of the car and leaning on his stick, he limped over towards an opening in the hedgerow. He passed into the field beyond and over to a clump of trees. Fortunately there was a convenient stump for him to sit on. His leg was hurting quite a bit. He sat there for some minutes looking out across the fallow field. A few crows were flying low over the hard soil and swooped down looking for morsels to eat. He watched, but took in very little of what he saw – his mind was going over and over what Caroline had said and trying to put the jigsaw of his thoughts and memories into some kind of order.

He thought back to the very first time that he had met Caroline. Almost immediately, she had begun to malign Aphra, and he had to admit to having prejudged her even before they had met. When he did meet her, he had been struck by three things – her great beauty, the tender way that her husband and she were with each other, and the familiar exchange of looks between her and the secretary, culminating in his giving her a furtive wink at the ball. At first, he thought that he had imagined it – but he had not. Caroline had seen it too. It was shortly after this that she showed him the letter that she had intercepted. He had to admit that it was pretty damning – and yet it was quite ambiguous.

He spent quite a lot of time in Aphra and Sebastian's company. There was no doubt that they cared for one another deeply – in fact, he had to admit that they seemed the happiest and most affectionate couple that he knew. But then, Claude was always around – rather too much for a secretary. Aphra and he spent a lot of time together when Sebastian was away. Lucas recalled various conversations that he had had with each of the three parties. Each one always caring and complimentary – Sebastian about Aphra and vice versa – Aphra about Claude – Claude about Aphra. Yet, he could not recall Sebastian or Claude ever speaking in any depth about each other, although they also got along very well. In fact, it seemed a very harmonious threesome. It was as though the two men avoided any discussion about each other.

But it was this business with the flowers that bothered him. He faintly recalled a distant memory that he could not quite reach. He thought about Aphra arranging bunches of flowers in the chapel, but it was not a bunch of flowers that came into his mind, it was a single bloom – a carnation. Why was that? What did it mean? If only he could remember. He thought about his disturbing dream and a faint, distant memory came to him. It was the opening night of one of Wilde's plays. What was it now? Not *The Importance of being Ernest*. That was the last one before Wilde's arrest and besides, he seemed to remember that he had been very ill about that time, so he would not have been at the theatre. It was the other one. Yes, he had it. *An Ideal Husband*. Why should he remember that now? It was all so long ago and seemed so irrelevant. Sebastian and Claude were standing very close and were locked in conversation with each other. He had not taken a lot of notice of them, for his attention was fixed on Aphra. He remembered thinking at the time that something seemed out of place, although he could not have said what it was and had dismissed the idea. It was funny. He had completely forgotten that. Why should he think about it now? Wilde, and Bosie joined Sebastian and Claude. Aphra was a slight distance away, although near enough to be included in the conversation. However, she gave the impression of being something of an onlooker. Wilde went to a cardboard box on a side table and produced four green carnation buttonholes. He handed one to Bosie and one each to Sebastian and Claude and retained one himself. Lucas had watched as the four men fixed the buttonholes for each other. Aphra had gone to assist Sebastian, but he had waived her aside and Claude had helped him. Lucas overheard part of a witty remark made by Wilde about ideal husbands and Sebastian had replied something about him being a dreadful husband – to which Wilde had said something that had made the four of them laugh. Lucas remembered Aphra looking on fondly and the musical sound of her laugh and had wished that he could be close to her and join in.

At the time, he had not realised the meaning of the green carnations. It was only later, after Wilde had been arrested with all the ensuing publicity, that he fully understood the significance of wearing these particular buttonholes. But why were the Earl and his secretary wearing them? Was it a tasteless joke? Aphra seemed to find it highly amusing. Why?

He recalled the night of the ball and how she had come down the stairs and taken hold of Sebastian's outstretched hand. He had led her to the dance floor and everyone had commented what a handsome couple they made, but there was a sense of unreality about it all. Lucas had felt it at the time but had dismissed these thoughts thinking that they were just the result of his own wishful thinking about her being free and with him. As Sebastian had whirled her around the dance floor, Claude had appeared to catch her eye and she had smiled at him. He had winked, which Lucas had assumed was at her, but perhaps that was not the case.

It was as though a mist was lifting and he began to see things differently. Caroline once told him that Aphra had said to her that no woman would ever take Sebastian away from her. She had been quite taken aback at the confidence with which she had said this. How could she tell the future? How could anyone know if a spouse would remain faithful? Suddenly, he realised what she had meant by that statement. She was so confident, because he was not interested in women. He was in love with Claude –

and Claude with him. How could he have been so blind? Aphra was somehow on the edge of this and he remembered her saying to Lucas that things were not always as they seemed. He recalled those remarks of Sebastian when he was talking to him about Aphra – saying that she had a lot to put up with and how she was perfect for him. He had told Lucas how much he loved her and how good she was to him.

He saw Aphra and Claude walking down the aisle in the Cathedral together. Poor little Sophie – pale and distressed at losing her father and holding on to her mother's right hand. Aphra's left hand was touching Claude's arm. Caroline had tutted and whispered to Lucas how Aphra had no shame at caressing him in the house of God in front of the child and all the mourners. Earlier, she had intimated how suspicious and convenient Sebastian's death was. He had tried to put that vile suggestion out of his mind.

He remembered the strange behaviour of the two of them by the coffin. Claude looked terrible as though he was going to pass out, and he now recalled the fleeting emotions crossing Aphra's face as she caught sight of Lucas. Surprise? Hope? Pleasure? Grief? And then possibly confusion. He did not know what at that time. Had she been pleased to see him there? Was she mourning her husband's sudden death and caressing her lover? No, no, no! She was not caressing him. She was consoling him! He had got it all wrong.

Now it was clear why Claude had returned to France soon after the funeral and had not married Aphra. Yes, there was a triangle, but – what did the young soldier say that Claude had muttered in those last few moments? "The triangle was inverted." Then just before he had died, he had been happy in the belief of being re-united with Sebastian. Lucas remembered him saying "She never said anything. She kept her word."

So that was it. This woman, who was the subject of malicious rumours started by Caroline, was in fact all alone for years, and he, in listening to Caroline, contributed to her loneliness when he walked away after the funeral. What a bloody fool he'd been. He had also been very lonely. They could have been happy together for years. He felt so angry with himself for his own stupidity.

He stood up and limped back to the car, although there was now a slight spring in his step that had not been there before. Now he had hope, but could she forgive him?

***

Aphra made her way down towards the scullery.

"Good afternoon Milady," one of the maids said.

"Good afternoon Elsie – and how are you today?"

"Very well, Ma'am. Thanking you kindly."

"Have the flowers been delivered?"

"Yes Ma'am. I put them on the draining board."

"Thank you."

Aphra took a step and then stopped and turned. "Oh, by the way Elsie. I wanted to thank you for the excellent job you did in the dining room. The table looks beautiful – such a lovely shine. It must have taken a lot of work."

Elsie smiled to herself as she continued her duties. The mistress was always so kind and appreciated everything that the staff did.

Aphra went into the scullery and picked up the large cardboard box having slipped a small pair of scissors into her pocket first. She found it slightly awkward trying to manoeuvre the side door out onto the gravel path whilst holding the box. She had noticed now heavy the boxes seemed of late.

The afternoon was crisp, but the sky was blue and cloudless. As she walked through the woods, she marvelled at the magnificence of the colours of the Autumnal foliage. She thought about the changes of seasons that had passed over the last sixteen years. She had made this same journey many times.

Oh how difficult it seemed carrying the box. After a while, she wondered whether or not she was going to make it. At one point, she had to sit on the stump of a tree and rest for a few minutes. Perhaps she should reduce the visits to once a month, or maybe just special dates and anniversaries.
It was lovely here, and there was a sense of peace – although there was never peace in her spirit. Strangely, for some reason today, he felt close to her. She didn't know why she should feel this. It was utter nonsense and

she shrugged it off.

"You're getting fanciful in your old age," she said under her breath. She picked up the box again and continued her journey. Only a few more minutes and she would be there.

EPILOGUE

30ᵀᴴ NOVEMBER 1916

Night has fallen. Under the cloak of darkness, the figure has covered a lot of ground. As he approaches the chapel, he can now make out a flickering light shining out through the stained glass windows.

Inside, the woman continues to pray as her tears fall. She hears something stir outside and looks up for a second, but is not afraid. Perhaps it is the wind disturbing the fallen leaves or some nocturnal creature foraging for food. An owl hoots and she crosses herself. The numbness in her legs necessitates her holding on to the prie-dieu for a few moments as she tries to stand up.

She has noticed that one of the carnations has fallen to the floor. She is very tired and her body hurts as she slowly stoops down to retrieve the fallen bloom.

She has not heard the soft footfall in the doorway, so is startled to find that another hand reaches the flower at the same time as her own.

"Why didn't you tell me?" He asks her.

She tries to choke back the tears. "I gave him my word. I couldn't betray them."

Both their hands join around the flower and her final tear falls onto its tightly packed petals.

She places it where it belongs – with the other flowers.

He takes her hand and leads her back to the land of the living.

She turns around and takes one last glance at the plaques.

"Goodbye my dears - rest in peace."

***

Printed in Great Britain
by Amazon.co.uk, Ltd.,
Marston Gate.